MY SOUL TO KEEP

LYNETTE M. BURROWS

Rocket Dog Publishing

ISBN: 978-1-7325822-0-0 (pbk.)

ISBN: 978-1-7325822-1-7 (ePub)

ISBN: 978-1-7325822-2-4 (.mobi)

Edited by Julie Glover

Cover Designed by Elizabeth Leggett

Formatting by Sidekick Jenn

Published by Rocket Dog Publishing

Mission, KS 66202

Acknowledgments

I owe a huge debt of gratitude to Robert Chilson and the writers group he hosts. Their critiques and comments helped shape both the story and me as a writer. A special word of thanks to Jan S. Gephardt and to Terry Matz, each for their unique ways of offering support and encouragement for weeks and weeks and weeks.

To William F. Wu, thank you for all the discussions, the encouragement, and the gentle direction. Without your instruction and mentorship this book would not exist.

*For Bob, whose love and enthusiasm
momentarily scared me off.
Thank you for giving me all the room I needed
to learn to love again.
Without your love, your unfailing support and encouragement, this book and
my life would be very different.*

Chapter One

The giant bronze angel of death loomed over Miranda Clarke's shoulder. The statue, *Shield of Mercy, Hand of Justice*, stood at the grand entrance of the Fellowship Center as it had for all of Miranda's life. With Uncle Sam sheltered in her great black wings, the angel hovered over the fallen body of President-elect Franklin Delano Roosevelt and pointed to the pile of ash where the assassin had stood. Was it the statue or was it the tiny flare of rebellion inside her that made Miranda hesitate?

Tom, her bodyguard, closed the space between them, stood too close. "Is something wrong?"

Nothing. And everything. She hid her fears behind an angelic daughter-of-the-councilor smile. "I need to powder my nose."

"They'll be seating your family in five minutes. Tell me what you need, I'll have someone fetch it."

I need to not be the councilor's daughter. Gazing across the foyer, Miranda's pulse cranked up a notch.

Hundreds of men in sharkskin suits and women in taffeta dresses filled the foyer, waiting for the auditorium doors to open. Clusters of them here and there held onto their hats, an assortment of felt, feathers, netting, and ruffles, and peered up at the

1

mural-painted dome five stories above. They reeked of aftershave lotions, cheap colognes, and forbidden cigarette smoke.

"There are some things a girl must do on her own." Miranda dove into a sea of elbows and padded shoulders, big purses, and voluminous skirts. Her bodyguard followed.

Miranda avoided the knot of people clustered around Senator Joseph P. Kennedy, Jr. People who noticed her moved out of her way. She wished they wouldn't notice. She longed for a regular life, a job, and her own apartment. It was 1961, for goodness' sake. You'd think it would be acceptable for a girl to be on her own. But Mama said the Fellowship rules were there for a reason. Mama had survived the horrors of the Great Depression. She'd often spoken of how suicides and murders during that time made the waters of the Potomac outside run red. Mama said that the Fellowship had saved the country. And that top Fellowship members had a duty to be consummate examples and ambassadors.

But Miranda didn't want to be an exemplary Fellowship member. She didn't want an arranged marriage. And she didn't want all the public duties and appearances. She wanted to help people, not ask them to donate to the charity of the hour. Somehow she had to convince her parents she should be a guardian. She could be a good example, serving the poor and underprivileged—in private.

A pimple-faced young man materialized before her.

"Sister Clarke, what an honor." His soft, plump hand gripped hers and pumped their hands up and down with youthful exuberance.

"My pleasure." She tried to extract her hand.

He reinforced his grip with his other hand.

She took in a sharp breath. He couldn't be one of Mama's "potential matches." Mama had said she'd talk to Daddy about Miranda's guardianship training.

"Say cheese."

Miranda turned toward the voice.

A flashbulb popped.

Black dots swam in her vision.

An arm pushed into the space between her and Pimple-Face and broke the young man's grip. Tom stiff-armed her behind his back and pushed Pimple-Face away. He jerked the camera out of the photographer's hands, flipped the back of the camera open, and shoved it back into the photographer's chest.

The photographer grabbed his camera, and Tom yanked out the film.

"You can't do that." The photographer glared at Tom.

Tom folded his arms across his chest and quirked an eyebrow at the young man.

The photographer's gaze wavered. He swallowed hard and exchanged looks with Pimple-Face. They backed away into the crowd.

Miranda glanced around. The curious and judgmental circled them like the Romans had surrounded the Christians in the arena. *Probably giving me a thumbs-down too.* "It's nothing. A misunderstanding." Her daughter-of-the-councilor voice sounded reassuring, at least on the outside.

Amid murmurs and shuffling feet, the people around them returned to interrupted conversations.

Tom seized her elbow and guided her to the nearest wall.

"I'm fine, Tom." Her words sounded sharper than she'd intended.

He had been her bodyguard since she was a little girl. From his crew cut to his expensive tailored suit, and his ever-on-alert attitude, he was unmistakable and inescapable.

She tugged against his grip. "All he wanted was a picture."

Something dark and predatory flashed across Tom's face. "You don't know what he wanted."

"Neither do you." Miranda pried his fingers from her elbow and stalked away, ignoring the urge to scrub his touch off. She'd tried to tell Mama that Tom took small liberties. Mama had frowned and said, "Pray that the words of a harlot be scoured from your mind and tongue."

Miranda hurried through the pink marble colonnade supporting the balconies above and slipped through a door, relieved for the chance to be rid of him, even if just for a moment.

Accustomed to long waits outside the ladies' room, Tom planted himself outside the door.

Inside, women and children jammed the space, jostled for empty stalls and sinks. Voices, clattering heels, and the whoosh of flushing echoed off the granite walls.

Miranda pulled off her gloves, tucked them into her pocket, and waited for an empty stall.

"You're late, Miranda." Her sister's loud alto rose across the room.

Irene stood at the end of the counter. She peered into the mirror and stabbed a hatpin into her tiny, platter-shaped hat. The hat matched her mint green dress and complemented her copper-colored hair.

"Don't wait for me." Miranda waved Irene away. But Irene always waited. It was as if she were Miranda's personal do-right angel.

"Hurry. Mama will be annoyed if we enter after the lights go down."

The next stall opened up.

Miranda locked the door and braced her hands and forehead against the cool metal. She couldn't bear one more family procession to their front row seats. *Maybe, if I wait long enough, Irene will leave without me.* A long time ago, she would fantasize about escaping out of the window above the fainting couch. *But fantasy isn't reality.* Miranda sighed. Life as a guardian wouldn't be easy, but it would be out of the public eye.

She waited and listened. The noisy voices of excited women and children grew less and less.

"Miranda? What is taking so long?"

"I'm constipated." It sounded more like a question than a statement.

"Then it won't hurt to hold it a few more hours."

Miranda bowed her head, and her shoulders sagged. *One more time won't kill me.* She flushed the toilet and exited the stall with her head high and shoulders squared.

Irene stood with her back against the mirror, her arms crossed, and wore an impatient frown.

Miranda crossed to the sink and washed her hands.

The ladies' room attendant handed her a towel.

Miranda dried her hands and dropped the towel into the attendant's waiting hand. She stole a glance at her younger sister's reflection.

Two years Miranda's junior, Irene had a plump matron's demeanor and confidence. She had embraced marriage and motherhood, making her a success in their mother's eyes. By comparison, Miranda was an about-to-be-an-undesirable, twenty-five-year-old spinster. Miranda becoming a guardian would allow Mama to save face.

"We're going to the beach house this weekend," Irene said. "You should come too."

"I have other plans." Miranda fluffed her bangs, shielding her face, hiding the lie.

"Plans can change." Irene sounded pleased with herself. "That baby blue dotted Swiss is lovely on you."

"Thank you." Miranda smoothed the nubby fabric of her skirt and studied Irene through her lashes, suspicious of the compliment. Mama had insisted Miranda wear her best dress.

"We mustn't be late." Irene latched onto Miranda's wrist, dragged her out of the bathroom and into the hall. There, Irene's husband and four-year-old daughter waited, as did their bodyguards.

Irene snapped her fingers at Felix. "Fix Sandra's collar." She swept past them, pulling Miranda toward the auditorium.

Miranda cast a sympathetic glance at her brother-in-law.

Felix had a receding hairline, big ears, and an I'm-drowning-in-love expression fixed on Irene. He looked dumber than he was. He smoothed Sandra's collar and fell in behind Irene, towing their daughter behind him.

Their bodyguards trailed after.

Hunched over like a fat gargoyle, the director of the Fellowship Center sat on a stool by the auditorium door. "Mr. and Mrs. Earnshaw. Miss Clarke." He rocked the stool in his rush to greet them. "The Fellowship Center welcomes you, our honored guests. May I escort you to your seats?" He threw the auditorium doors open in a make-room, make-room way, took Irene's arm, and strutted down the aisle.

Felix picked up Sandra and hurried to follow.

Miranda stopped in the doorway, turned back toward the ladies' room.

Her bodyguard stepped in, cutting her off.

"I need to powder my nose."

"You just did."

She glanced around with pretended furtiveness and then whispered, "It's my time of the month."

Tom scoffed. "That was last week. If you're having problems, you need to talk to your mother." He gestured toward the door.

She raised her chin and walked into the auditorium.

Irene, Felix, and Sandra reached the first row before her. They slipped past Uncle Weldon and Mama and sat at the far end, next to David, Miranda's younger brother.

Miranda held her skirt close and squeezed past Uncle Weldon, who sat in the aisle seat. Weldon, Mama's younger brother, had the same hawkish nose as Mama and had deep-set eyes and a thin upper lip that drooped downward in a forever frown.

Next to him sat Mama. Small and thin, Mama was made of sharp angles.

Miranda had no choice but to take the last seat available, the one next to Mama.

Mama rested her cool, dry hand on Miranda's, a holdover

from her childhood. The pressure of Mama's hand had increased whenever a child squirmed or whispered.

At seven o'clock sharp, the crimson velvet curtains rose. In center stage sat a raised podium that bore the symbol of the Fellowship: a blood-red shield sectioned by a white cross.

The audience shushed and settled in their seats.

A moment later Miranda's father, Councilor Donald Clarke, strode onto the stage, his burgundy robes sweeping the floor behind him. He took his place at the podium.

At home, he was grumpy and gloomy. On stage, he transformed into a super-charged beacon of love for his fellow man. The spotlight lightened his swarthy skin, made his dark pompadour gleam, and added angles to the softness of his long face.

Daddy read from the First Book of Josiah in a quiet, conversational voice. "It came to pass after the Great War, the days of darkness, the Great Depression, fell upon us…"

His rich baritone and soft Southern accent rose without strain. "Thugs, thieves, and murderers ruled our land.

"After the assassination of President-elect Roosevelt, Prophet Josiah gathered the Fellowship and prayed for deliverance. And the Lord sent the Angels of Death, the Azrael, to cleanse the wicked from our land.

"The people's prayers were answered. The thugs and thieves and murderers were scoured from our lives. And America was saved from the strife across the sea. Out of the ashes of the old, divided world of Great Britain and Europe and the Third Reich, the United Federation of Germany arose. Peace and prosperity returned."

Miranda tuned out the sermon and imagined what her life as a guardian would be. A life free from public scrutiny and criticism. No more charity and political dinners. Sadly, she would also give up cruising the bay, skeet shooting, and island picnics. But she deserved—no, she needed—the quiet guardian's life.

"—Miranda."

She started. *Why did Daddy say my name?* Everyone was staring at her. Mama wore her public smile, but her eyes shot fierce, unspoken commands at Miranda.

Mama nudged her foot.

"Miranda? Won't you come up on stage?"

Her stomach plunged like an anchor. *He knows I hate getting up in front of people.*

Mama gripped Miranda's arm in a shark-bite grasp and stood, pulling Miranda to her feet.

Her legs quivered, boneless. She teetered. Her mother's grip tightened, kept her upright.

Miranda arranged her face into her daughter-of-the-councilor mask and willed strength to her legs.

Mama steered her onto the stage.

"Ladies and gentlemen, my wife and I are pleased to include you in a special surprise for my beautiful daughter." He escorted her to center stage. "Wait right here. Your mother and I will be over there." He positioned her facing stage left, then he and Mama faded into the shadows.

The stage lights dimmed, leaving Miranda centered in a cone of light. The bright light blinded her. Blinded to the audience. Blinded to her parents. Blinded to what was coming.

Murmurs and rustlings came from the audience. Soft chords of "Moonlight Serenade" rose from the piano. Her stomach pretzeled. *This isn't how one announces a novice guardian.*

Ryan Mitchell stepped into the light. He had wavy blond hair, green eyes, and a cleft in his chin. His dark blue suit with its wide lapels broadened his shoulders.

Her thoughts scrambled. *What is he doing here?*

Her parents had bought the beach house in Nassawadox when she was six years old. She and Ryan had been summertime neighbors and dueling sandcastle architects ever since. He'd gotten sweet on her. Something she'd politely discouraged.

"Hello." The dimple in his left cheek appeared and disappeared like it always did when he was nervous.

"Hello." *I have to get off this stage.*

He put one hand in and out of his pocket, straightened his tie, and smoothed his lapel.

Back the way I came or backstage?

"Remember when we first met?"

"Yes."

"You were six, playing on the beach. I thought, why did a stupid girl have to move next door?" He gazed at her with I'm-in-love-eyes and reached into his pocket.

Her councilor's-daughter mask and councilor's-daughter smile vanished. Her heart stuttered. She'd told him friends, *only* friends.

"By the end of the summer, we were building sandcastles together. By the time you were sixteen, I knew." He knelt on one knee.

The audience gasped.

Her lungs quit. Her heart skipped a beat. She spun and darted toward backstage, breaking every councilor's-daughter rule in existence.

She didn't know where she was going. Didn't care.

Chapter Two

Miranda ran behind the curtains into the dark right wing. Hands clamped down on her shoulders, brought her to a solid stop. She twisted to see Tom, her bodyguard.

"Let me go." A wooden rack on the wall held dozens of ropes that stretched like strings on a giant harp to curtains and equipment overhead. *No door. No ladder.*

Miranda's blood pounded *run-run-run* through her brain. *To the left? Yes.* An Exit sign glowed red above a door.

"Please. I've got to get out of here." She wriggled, but couldn't break Tom's grip.

"You know I can't let you go."

"You're supposed to protect me." Her words rasped through her throat.

"Protect you? From what? A proposal?"

"From losing—" Words could not express the wrongness. *—who I am.*

He cocked his head and stared down at her like she was a twit, a lunatic.

She wasn't crazy. Accepting Ryan's proposal meant a lifetime of political and charity dinners and... No, she couldn't do it. Not now. Not ever. Miranda forced herself to relax.

Tom's hold loosened.

She lunged, freed herself, and ran.

He grabbed her arm. *Riiiiip.* He spun her around and pulled her close—full body contact close.

She raised her gaze from his Adam's apple to his face.

His eyes traveled down to her chest, his expression less and less bodyguard and more and more brute.

A chill rippled across her skin. Miranda glanced down. The right side of her bodice had ripped and folded over revealing her V-neck, lace slip. Her face flamed. She reached for the torn fabric, but his grip tightened to bone bruising. Her chest constricted. She drew quick, shallow breaths. Her vision blurred.

Footsteps approached.

He forced her backward, leaving a decency space between them.

His hungry stare at her cleavage made her want to shrivel to nothing. She lowered her head. Her tears dripped onto the floor.

The hem of Mama's royal blue dress and matching pumps appeared beside Tom's size elevens.

"Young lady, are you trying to ruin your father and me?" Mama's cool, dry fingers lifted Miranda's chin.

"I can't marry Ryan. I—" Miranda swallowed her vow that she didn't love Ryan. "I'm going to be a guardian."

"Release her," Mama said. Her command was low and brusque.

Tom released Miranda so fast she had to take a half step to keep from falling.

Mama jerked her chin toward the stage door.

Tom crossed the space. Facing them, he'd replaced his leer with an impersonal stare. He spread his feet and crossed his arms over his chest, making himself an impenetrable wall between Miranda and escape.

"What have you done to yourself?" Irritation colored Mama's whisper.

Miranda focused on her dress. Her waistline sash was off center, her bodice twisted and bunched, the nubby fabric torn and frayed. She straightened her bodice and held the loose part to her chest.

"Stop slouching." Mama scrubbed Miranda's tears away with a starched, lace handkerchief. "The idea that you have to love someone *before* you marry him is storybook nonsense." Mama folded and put away her handkerchief. "I did not love your father when we got married. We were an ordained match, like you and Ryan. We grew to love one another—over time." Mama's voice softened, offered kindness. "I was as frightened the day we married as you are today."

"I'm not you, Mama."

"*You* were born with privileges *I* never had. Believe me, you do not want the dark days to return. Famine, murder, pestilence, and disease—we lived in fear. Be grateful you don't." Mama glanced over Miranda's shoulder toward the stage.

Hesitantly Miranda looked. The choir and audience sang a happy hymn. Ryan had moved out of the spotlight, into the shadows, staring at something in his hand.

"Look at me." Mama grabbed Miranda's wrists.

Miranda whipped her head around, faced her mother.

"It's a good match." Mama wetted her lips. "Ryan is one of us, one of the Elect. He has a future. He'll be a senator or councilor one day. And you *like* him. What more do you want?" Mama's voice and grip tightened with each whispered word.

She will never understand. "I'll make a good guardian, I promise."

Mama exhaled an impatient "pfft." "You are the daughter of the future First Apostle." Mama grabbed Miranda's chin, locked a shriveling glare on her. "You will *not* invite the wrath of Azrael. You *will* marry Ryan. You will be happy. And, someday, you will fall in love."

"What if I never love Ryan?" Miranda's chin trembled.

Mama brushed Miranda's cheek with hers, made a kiss-kiss sound. "Go apologize. Accept Ryan's proposal. Poor boy thinks he's been rejected."

Miranda threw a desperate glance behind her. She'd have to run onto the stage, past the choir, past Daddy and Ryan, up the aisle and out of the auditorium, and across the foyer to the doors. No way she'd make it. She faced Mama again.

"You can't go on stage like that." Mama yanked out one of her hatpins and jabbed it at Miranda.

Miranda stepped back.

"I'm not going to stab you," Mama whispered fiercely. "Let me fix this." She knocked Miranda's hand away, folded the ripped edges together, and wove the pin through the fabric. Mama used a second hatpin to secure the side seam. She stepped back, surveyed Miranda head-to-toe. "Smile."

Miranda dredged up a mask with a dutiful daughter's smile, a mask she feared would not hold.

Mama twirled Miranda around. "Make it a good show."
• Mama shoved her.

Miranda stumbled onto the stage.

The audience gasped.

Ryan jerked his head around, rushed toward her, then froze, pinned in the spotlight.

The pianist and choir stopped in mid-chorus.

It was as if a monster had stepped onto the stage. A monster named Miranda.

Miranda could barely stand, barely breathe, barely hang onto her sanity. Her hands clenched and unclenched in a battle between the monster and the good daughter.

Mama appeared on her left, Tom on her right. They crowded her, nudging and pushing her forward.

A moment before they reached center stage, Mama swept past Miranda and took her place beside Daddy. Tom faded into the shadows.

Miranda took a shaky breath and forced her feet to move. She stepped into the spotlight.

Two bright spots on Ryan's cheeks shone in his pale face. His dimple had vanished.

Miranda opened her mouth to make the expected apology. Words congealed in her throat. No sound came out. She closed her mouth and clamped her teeth on her tongue.

Mama cleared her throat.

Miranda glanced at her parents.

Daddy waited with the expression of a long-suffering saint. Mama had her councilor's-wife smile on her lips, but her eyes held a you-dare-not-cross-me threat.

A coppery taste flooded Miranda's mouth. She faced Ryan. "I'm told that most brides get cold feet." She gave a half-hearted shrug. "I guess I get cold, *running* feet."

Ryan threw back his head and laughed a too-hearty laugh.

The audience roared as if she'd uttered the funniest thing they'd ever heard.

She nodded to the pianist. *Let's get this over with.*

"Moonlight Serenade" drifted across the stage.

Miranda offered Ryan her left hand.

He squeezed her fingers tight. His warm hands did not warm her icy one. She wished the floor would swallow her, or that lightning would strike her, or even that an Azrael would Take her. But no rescue came.

Ryan knelt. He pulled a ring out of his pocket and offered the diamond to her. "Will you marry me?" His dimple winked in his cheek. Then he whispered, "And promise to always keep me smiling?"

Her chest was hollow, empty, an eternal pit of despair.

"Yes." *Too sharp.* She softened her voice. "I will."

He slid the ring on her finger.

Miranda's vision narrowed, focused on the much-larger-than-a-carat, round solitaire. The ring was so far away she could almost imagine it was on someone else's hand. As a little girl, she'd dreamed of a fairytale romance and proposal. She'd never guessed that fairy tales could warp into nightmares.

Mama made a soft noise.

Miranda forced a bright-for-the-audience-smile. She raised her hand for the crowd. The diamond winked in the spotlight.

The audience burst into applause.

"Cold running feet." Daddy barked a stage laugh. "That's my funny girl. Come on, boy. Kiss her. It's okay. You're engaged."

Ryan stood, wrapped her in a tender embrace, and kissed her deeply.

Miranda felt as if she were drowning in a pool full of wet cement.

Chapter Three

Anna climbed through a jagged area where the barn wall had rotted. The still, musty air tickled her nose. She clamped her lips tight and held in her sneeze, making her ears pop. Uncle said operational silence was more important than momentary discomfort. She scouted the barn, like Uncle had taught her. Six empty stalls ran down one side, and near the locked barn doors stood a gleaming green tractor. Attached to the tractor were rows of shiny discs for turning the soil. A workbench loaded with tools lined the opposite wall. At the end of the workbench, a ladder led to the loft.

The loft was perfect. There were bundles of hay and lots of old junk to hide behind. A faint breeze came through the open loft door and holes in the roof. The air smelled sweet, scented with hay and growing things.

She crept to the loft door and peeked out. Papa Locke, Aunt Allyson, Uncle, and his lady-friend gathered in a knot on the hillside, talking. They couldn't see her 'cause she stayed back in the shadow. Uncle had told her that she was the very best hider. Anna believed it. Every now and then, she'd see "It" catch one of the other players trying to find a hiding place or trying to tag home.

She wasn't going to try to tag home. It would catch her, like all the others. She would wait for the "olly olly oxen free," and she'd win 'cause no one could find her.

Anna liked living on the farm. The math classes and science classes were hard, but half the day they played games: bullet-bullet, who's got the bullet; conceal-and-stalk; and capture-the-unbeliever. It was fun.

Tired of being still, she explored the loft. Hay bales were stacked around an old school desk where mice had once nested, a pile of old tractor tires, and a rusted bicycle. A mewling sound drew her around another stack of hay. The sound came from seven tiny kittens in a nest of hay. They nuzzled hungrily against one another, making little crying noises.

"Are you special-born, like me?" She gathered them into her lap. One climbed her overalls. Another suckled on one of the overall buttons. A scrabbling sound beneath her made her remember the game. She swiped the kittens off her lap and threw herself flat against the hay. The noise grew closer. A cat sprang onto the loft floor. She scrambled over the hay and checked out her kittens. Soon, she settled down and nursed her babies.

After each kitten drank its fill, it curled into a ball and slept. When the last one had finished, the mother cat washed herself and her sleeping kittens with her tongue.

"What a good mommy you are." Anna held her hand out for the mother cat to sniff. "You came back to feed your babies." She picked up the cat and put it in her lap. It stiffened, hair raised on its back. Anna petted it, crooned to it. "Nice kitty." The fur was smooth and soft and warm. The cat lay down in Anna's lap and purred.

Anna reclined against the hay bale behind her and stroked the cat. She wished It would give up. A faint sound grew louder, more recognizable. Voices. Papa Locke, Aunt Allyson, Uncle, and his lady-friend too. They stopped underneath the loft door. Anna stayed still and hoped they wouldn't come into the barn.

"Reproduction happens when a sperm and an egg combine to

create a zygote. In parthenogenesis there is no sperm, there is no meiosis; therefore, the offspring is haploid." Papa Locke always talked that way 'cause he was an important scientist doctor.

"Parth-en-o-gen-sis? Doc, you gotta come up with a better sales pitch."

Anna stifled her giggle behind her hand. Uncle sounded silly when he tried to talk like Papa Locke.

"We trick the egg into acting like there is sperm," Aunt Allyson explained. She was Teacher.

"Once we have a successful parthenote—"

"Doc, our customers need simple, one-syllable words."

"Partheno from the Greek for virgin birth." Aunt Allyson was a good teacher.

"'Virgin birth' is sacrilegious," argued Uncle's lady-friend. She always argued. "Couldn't we call it cloning?"

Papa made his irritated-at-you sound in his throat. "It's not cloning. There is no transfer of a nucleus from a donor cell to an enucleated oocyte. Rather, the oocyte is stimulated to divide." Papa and the others moved away from the barn.

Anna was glad. Adults never were as interesting as they thought they were. She stroked the momma cat sleeping in her lap and closed her eyes.

"Anna?"

She started upright. The mother cat's claws pierced Anna's overalls and raked her skin. "Ow!" She grabbed the cat around its belly.

The cat clawed wildly, scratched her arm, drew blood.

"Bad cat." Anna threw the cat as hard as she could. It soared up into the air, over the edge of the loft.

The cat corkscrewed in mid-air, twisted her front, then her back, and pointed all four feet toward the floor. She dropped. Slammed into the sharp discs below.

A piercing yowl of pain split the air.

Then silence.

Anna's nostrils flared, taking in the coppery odor of death. A lighter-than-air sensation filled her chest and made her skin tingle. For an instant, she hovered above everything. The lightness vanished, and she ached with the absence of her power.

"Anna?" A head, then Aunt Allyson's frowning face appeared at the top of the loft ladder. She glanced around. "What happened?"

"It was a bad cat." Anna glanced at the dead cat, then Aunt Allyson. "It left her babies when they were hungry. And it hurt us." Anna held out her arm for inspection. "We had to punish it."

"'And she shall execute judgment in righteousness,'" Aunt Allyson said. She stood, stepped away from the loft's edge, and inspected Anna's arm. "Let no man nor beast raise his hand to hurt you."

One of the kittens opened its eyes and mewed. Anna picked it up. "You asked and are granted life." She looked at the other orphans nested together, sleeping. "Thy will be done."

Chapter Four

M iranda sat in the living room of the beach house, sliding the ring on and off her finger. She tried to listen to Irene, Felix, and Ryan, but what-ifs ping-ponged in her thoughts. What if she persuaded Ryan to break off their engagement, then Mama found an older, less desirable suitor? Ryan was a friend. Miranda couldn't imagine him as more. On and off. On and off.

Ryan sprawled in the wicker armchair next to her, opposite Irene and Felix who sat on the chocolate-brown upholstered sofa.

"I'm going to demand a raise." Felix squeezed one of the tangerine and aqua throw pillows.

"You know best, dear." Irene sat beside Felix, knitting a Sandra-sized sweater. She smiled at Ryan. "His boss, Mr. Anderson, is a lovely man."

Ryan gave an interested nod.

"We met his mother once." Irene's knitting needles clicked a steady rhythm. "At one of the office parties. Sturdy old woman with pink hair. He dotes on her."

Miranda tried to imagine herself married, knitting in her own living room. The image was distorted, warped, like a funhouse mirror, twisted and ugly. She jumped out of the chair.

Irene stared at her, and her knitting needles stilled, mid-stitch. Felix jutted out his chin. Ryan's eyes were guarded, watchful.

"I'm sorry." Her voice was too high, tight. "I should have offered everyone a drink." She tried for a laugh. "I'll get a pitcher of iced tea."

In the safety of the kitchen, she prepared a tray of sweet tea and turned toward the living room.

Ryan stood in the doorway. He gave her a glowing groom's smile, the kind a girl dreamed of receiving. "I can't wait for the day you're fixing refreshments for our guests in our home." He took the tray from her. "I sign the papers for our house next week."

"Our house?" Miranda's insides twisted. Pushing past Ryan, she stepped into the living room. She had to put a hand on the sand-colored wall to steady herself.

"I've earned a raise." Felix pushed out his large lower lip, making his perpetual pout more pronounced. "I've filed more patent petitions than anyone."

Irene finished a row of stitches and studied her handiwork. "She lives in one of those Federal-style houses in Cherrydale."

"You mean, his boss's mother's house?" Ryan put the tray of sweating glasses of tea on the coffee table.

Irene nodded and counted stitches under her breath.

Miranda stared at her sister. How did she survive an arranged marriage? Was she real happy or pretend happy?

The patter of a child's feet crossed overhead. Sandra played upstairs, alone, ignored by her mother. Would Irene arrange a marriage for *her* daughter one day?

"I hear she likes those imported chocolates." Irene frowned at her knitting. "The ones from *Die Föderation von Deutschland*, Brussels or Zurich, I forget which." Irene eyed Miranda. "I haven't gotten your RSVP for Mama's surprise birthday party." She flashed a charming smile at Ryan. "Of course, you're both invited."

"Thank you." Ryan sounded pleased. "We accept."

We? Miranda's throat tightened. She pretended a great interest in the pictures hanging on the wall.

Felix cleared his throat. "I should visit Mrs. Anderson and invite her to the party. I should take her a box of chocolates too."

Ryan came to her side. "Remember this?" He pointed to one of the pictures hung on the sand-colored wall beside her.

The picture had captured Miranda at the awkward age of thirteen. She stood with Ryan and her brother, David, behind the best sandcastle they'd ever built, pails and shovels in hands, goofy grins on their faces. Behind them, Uncle Weldon stood next to Mama, who was holding Irene. Daddy stood on the other side of Mama, and beside him, Aunt Beryl.

It had been a rare day of family togetherness unmarred by her father's outbursts or her mother's biting judgments. It was also the last time she'd seen her beloved aunt. Beryl had died in a car accident the next day.

Miranda touched her aunt's image.

Ryan slid his hand over hers.

She didn't jerk her hand free, but couldn't force herself to speak or smile.

Irene and Felix didn't speak either. Irene's knitting needles clacked, and Felix picked *The Patent Lawyer Magazine* up off the kidney-shaped coffee table and flipped pages.

Ryan pointed at another sandcastle picture. "Our first castle."

Miranda barely glanced at the picture Ryan indicated. Another photograph showed her alone in a small sailboat, holding the tiller. Her mouth dropped open.

She wore the same swimsuit and the same mouthful of metal that she had in the big sandcastle picture. It was labeled "Miranda's first." She blinked and shook her head, then blinked again. That couldn't be right. *I was sixteen and thrilled to finally be old enough to sail solo. Thirteen?* How could her memory be so wrong? How could—Everything. Be. So. Wrong?

She faced Ryan. "We have to talk."

"You mean in private?" He dropped his voice to say "in private."

Unwilling to trust her voice, she nodded. Ryan was her friend. A friend she was going to hurt and lose forever.

They walked out together. Behind them, Irene and Felix scrambled to get upstairs and chaperone from the window.

The sand sucked at her deck shoes. Cool grains of grit slipped inside, rasped against her bare feet. She welcomed the distraction.

At the end of the dock, the gazebo glistened with this season's coat of varnish, dark against the pale sky and gray water. A cool, spring breeze stirred her hair. It didn't dry her palms or soothe her jangling nerves.

Ryan took her hand, and they stepped into the gazebo side-by-side. He pulled her toward him, took her other hand, and held her hands in his, against his chest.

Resolve and regret whirlpooled, swept away the words she needed to say. *How can I hurt him?*

He cupped his hand under her chin, lifted her face to his full-beam happiness. "My parents want you, and Irene and her family, to come to a private celebration at our house tonight."

"I need to tell you something." Her voice sounded as scratchy as the sand.

The corners of his eyes crinkled with mischief. "There's a lot we need to tell each other."

"This is serious."

"Okay." His serious face cracked into I-swallowed-all-the-canaries-in-the-pet-store happiness.

She shrugged out of his grasp, walked around him to the opposite side of the gazebo. She whirled and blurted, "You can't marry me. It's wrong. I'm wrong. For you."

He blinked at her. "Why?"

"Don't you see?"

He followed her, his face drawn as if he were trying to understand a foreign language. "What?"

"I don't love you." There. She'd said it.

"Miranda." He ran his hand down her arm. "I know that I don't understand girls, but I've always thought I understood you." His fingers wrapped around her fist.

She pulled away. "I don't want us to be miserable for the rest of our lives."

"How can you think we'd be miserable?" By his expression, he had no doubts. Not one.

"You should marry someone who loves you."

"You're my friend. You respect the flag and your country. You attend Fellowship services. You obey your parents. You're kind to everyone and to animals. You're neat and clean, polite, and courteous. You'll serve the community and your husband."

She studied his face. Was he making fun of her?

He wore an earnest and paternal expression. "You've been acting strangely, running around, being childish and irresponsible. Do you have any idea how I felt when you ran off the stage?"

She gaped at him. "Do you have any idea how *I* felt?"

He smiled like one smiles at a small, frightened child. "I took you off guard. Let's schedule a real engagement party for next Saturday."

What doesn't he understand? "I'm not ready for marriage."

"I'll be a good provider. I work hard. I'm dedicated to the Fellowship. Everyone says I have a bright future."

"I want to get a job." She hadn't meant to say that out loud.

"But—you're a girl."

She put on a sultry pout and wiggled her shoulders. "What two things gave you that idea?" Her insides shrank. *What is wrong with me?*

"Oh, Miranda." Ryan caressed her face. "Evil will always tempt you. You have to face evil with courage and reject it. Like it says in Josiah, 'Stand for what is right and ye shall prosper in the light of the Lord.'" He took her hand and led her to the bench. "I'll reserve Rosemont Manor. You'll meet the chef and discuss the menu first thing on Tuesday."

What is wrong with him? He smiled and spoke of his plans for their wedding. The wedding she didn't want. She put on her good-girl mask and knew she had to find a way out.

Chapter Five

A touch startled Miranda awake. Her heart crashed against her ribs like the waves on the shore outside. She gulped air. His spicy scent lingered, and her skin shrank from his touch.

She lay curled in a ball, wedged into the corner. With the bedspread clutched under her chin, she pretended to sleep and she listened.

No heavy breathing. No footsteps.

Opening her eyes the tiniest bit, she peered into the dark, half hoping she would see him and half terrified she would. The shadowed shapes of her bedroom furniture were familiar. Nothing was out of place. The sounds of the ocean and wind from outside and her own slowing pulse grounded her.

Miranda groped for her bedside lamp, landed on the cool metal of her flashlight, and clicked it on. Its yellow-white orb stretched into the empty doorway, then danced across the slatted, bi-fold closet doors, the maple dresser, the little vanity in the corner, and the alarm clock on her bedside table. Four o'clock in the morning.

She'd been having the same nightmare at the same time every night for months. At first, she hadn't known what had frightened her awake. Then, she'd been certain someone had entered her room. This time it had been a touch. *It was a dream, a bad dream.*

She stretched out on her back and switched off the flashlight but kept it cradled in her hand. Slowly, she unclenched the fist still knotted in her bedspread. She closed her eyes and willed her body to relax, to sleep.

The twenty-four-year-old daughter of a councilor wasn't supposed to have nightmares, not even about the Angels of Death. Angels of Death? She rolled over onto her side, facing the doorway.

What is wrong with me? I haven't been afraid of the Angels of Death since I was a little girl. She repositioned her pillow. The round, teal-colored alarm clock on her bedside table still held a little of its glow-in-the-dark magic. The minute hand jumped forward with each tick and tick-tocked away the seconds, the minutes.

She sat up and stared out the window. Beyond the boathouse and across Hog Island Bay, a pinking horizon backlit the barrier islands. Slowly the pink changed to orange streaked with gold. Silhouetted against the pale sunlight, distant low-growing oaks and stunted pines created a wavy blue-gray line. Hog Island. Her refuge.

There were no cameras on the island, no Fellowship members judging her smallest misstep, no functions the daughter of the councilor must perform, and no disapproving family members. It was the one place she could sit with herself, think for herself, *be* herself.

Miranda pulled on a navy blue turtleneck sweater, the matching box-pleat skirt, and a pair of navy blue boat shoes. After tiptoeing downstairs, she grabbed a take-and-go breakfast and her windcheater jacket, then headed for the boathouse and dock.

Tendrils of the crisp, damp air chilled her. She fastened her windcheater close around her neck and shoved off in the dinghy. The little boat's engine sputtered then caught. It chugged and burbled and battled the chop.

By the time she beached the dinghy on the island and carried her breakfast to the top of a small sand dune, the sun peeked above the horizon. Early morning light bounced from wave to wave. Seagulls wheeled in the sky.

Miranda sat on a blanket facing the sunrise and nibbled her too-sweet blueberry muffin. The last remnants of her nightmare disappeared in growing sunlight. *Obviously Daddy didn't approve of Guardian Miranda. How do I not become Mrs. Ryan Mitchell?*

Restless, she left her unfinished breakfast and strolled the shoreline. She picked up a piece of driftwood, bleached and smooth, and used it for a walking stick. It broke in half before she'd gone a dozen steps. She tossed the remainder over her shoulder.

If widows and widowers can have jobs and apartments, why can't young women? She snorted. *Mama and Daddy think single women are temptresses.* Miranda couldn't believe that all single women were evil, but she didn't know any woman who'd stayed single as long as she had.

She stooped to move seaweed off a shell glinting in the sun. *Darn, it's broken.* She shucked the damaged shell back into the ocean.

Why do I have to have approval? I have plenty of pocket money. I could take a train to a faraway city, buy new identity papers, and get a job and an apartment.

The hardest part would be losing her bodyguard. Tom was at her elbow all day long, every day. There were times and places when Tom was farther away than usual, like at the beach house. The bodyguards stayed in a house near the gated end of the private drive. The only other place he'd leave her side was when she entered a ladies' room—or—a dressing room…

Mama had her scheduled to shop at Woodward & Lothrop for an engagement party dress on Monday. But the exclusive lounge put Tom right outside her dressing room door. *So I'll go to Garfinckel's and…I won't use an exclusive lounge. Tom will have to wait outside.* And she'd be at the train station before he had tired of waiting.

Miranda sidestepped a wave that lapped the shore. Something

crunched underfoot. Thousands of knife-edged pieces of ocean-pounded shells jutted from the sand, ready to shred her boat shoes. She concentrated on her footing.

"You're trespassing."

Miranda whirled toward the speaker.

Atop a small rise stood a teenage girl wearing an olive T-shirt, khaki pants, and a too-big-for-her hunting knife holstered on her hip. A mahogany-colored braid draped over her shoulder and reached to her waist. She stared at Miranda with pale, lavender eyes.

Miranda hadn't heard any sounds of approach. The girl's gaze was as unsettling as her unexpected appearance. "Where did you come from?" She glanced up and down the shoreline. There were no other boats in sight. They were the only two people on the island.

"You're Miranda."

Miranda smiled, but it went no further than her lips. It wasn't unusual for people to recognize her, but those people didn't carry a lethal weapon. "Do I know you?"

"If Uncle finds you, it'll be bad for you."

Miranda gave a small, uncertain laugh. "Your uncle can't touch me. He doesn't own this island. No one owns a barrier island."

The girl looked up into the sky. "What be Thy will?" It sounded like a prayer.

A chill spidered up Miranda's spine. She shook it off. This *child* couldn't scare her. "I'll bet your uncle doesn't know you're here threatening people." She marched up the dune, faced the girl. "You're the one who will be in trouble if he finds out." Miranda strode past the girl and down the shoreline to the dune where she'd left her blanket. She picked up her things. *I was leaving anyway. Permanently.*

The girl followed, stopped a couple of yards away, placed her hands on her hips, and planted her feet. "It is not His will that I kill you, today."

Miranda's mouth went dry. She forced herself to turn and walk to the dinghy.

All the way across the bay, Miranda didn't dare look back. She secured the dinghy, then stood on the dock and stared at the island. Although she couldn't see the girl, she could still feel those lavender eyes on her.

Chapter Six

Beryl Clarke stood in the transgressor's box in the judgment chamber. She'd endured ten years of lies. Ten years of isolation. Ten years of torture.

She wanted to shred the white blouse and long, navy blue skirt of Redemption they forced her to wear. She wanted to break the shackles that held her hands behind her back and hobbled her legs. She wanted to kill the two guardians who flanked her.

And when she escaped, she would annihilate the soulless men who accused her of murder.

Up several empty rows, a giant Philco television glowed with black and white images of the occupants of the Fellowship Council Chamber. Ten councilors and the Prophet sat at the judgment table, looking down at her. They thought the camera added protection.

She stood silent and serene, a pose she'd perfected over the past ten years.

"We recognize this sinner's profound understanding of the tenets of faith." The Prophet Palmer Gerard's once melodic voice quavered. Regal in the black robe and crimson stole of his office, he looked different, older, this year. His white hair had receded, his face grown shriveled and sallow.

One more sign that she was running out of time.

Two things had kept her alive the past ten years: she hadn't told the Council what they wanted to know, and her cousin, the Prophet, would not order his own flesh and blood executed.

She blew out cleansing breaths, releasing tension and preparing for the lies she had to say. Lies were her last hope for getting out of isolation. And getting out of isolation was her last hope of escape, her last hope for vengeance.

"Sinner." Palmer used his condemn-you-to-hell pulpit voice, but he tugged at his ear the way he had as a kid. The way that said he lied. "Do you confess your transgressions?"

She stared through the image of the Prophet on the screen. Her empty stomach pitched and rolled, rebelling against the unconscionable confession she had to make. "I, Beryl Clarke, am guilty." She curled her toes so tight they cramped. "Guilty of murdering Anna Marie Clarke, my daughter." Anger and grief surged through her muscles like a tide, threatening to betray her. She made herself breathe slowly, blink slowly, tamp those feelings down.

"And?" Palmer leaned forward, his gaze locked on her face.

She widened her eyes and spoke with rehearsed childlike innocence. "My guardians told me I had to confess to stealing a book. And I want to, but I don't remember stealing anything."

"There it is." Lucas Matthews, Councilor to the Secretary of Treasury, slammed the table with his fist. "She disrespects this Council *again*."

She forced herself to look at Lucas. As if his fleshy, age-spotted face weren't repulsive enough, next to him sat the real murderer, Weldon Lancaster.

"Councilors, please help me." She used the earnest expression she'd practiced. "I wish I could confess, but my memory is not what it was prior to my illness."

Palmer straightened. "What illness?" His eyes flicked across the occupants of one side of the table, then the other.

She quashed the urge to smirk at her guardians, but she couldn't suppress the increase in her pulse.

"Pneumonia, Your Reverence." Thumper, the taller of Beryl's two guardians, dipped her head in a respectful bow and, with her head down, shot Beryl a fierce glare.

"When was this? Why was I not told?"

To keep silent, Beryl bit down on her tongue and tasted coppery blood. She'd guessed Palmer had not been informed. If he had, he would have figured out that Thumper's rib-cracking baton had led to Beryl's illness.

"To protect you, Your Reverence." The bucktoothed guardian's little-girl voice scraped Beryl's nerves. "Our infirmary gave her their best medical care."

"She was moved?" Lucas aimed a suspicious glare at Donald. "By whose authority?"

Hope spurred her pulse faster, electrified her muscles. She maintained her mask of innocence with a disciplined relaxation of muscles that ached to act. And she savored the signs of a crack in the wall of councilor solidarity, that councilor had turned on councilor, that one had turned on her brother.

Donald, Councilor to the Secretary of State, didn't return the glare, didn't rise to the bait, didn't act like Donald. He kept his elbows on the table, his fingers laced together and close to his chest. "I authorized the move." He tipped his head toward Palmer. "You were ill, Prophet. I made certain she received the care she needed." The smile he gave Lucas held a subtle bit of victory. "And that she was well guarded."

Lucas gave Donald a bulldog frown. "As Councilor to the Treasury, I should—

"I acted in brotherly love. Surely you cannot object?" Donald used his voice like a trombone, sliding from virtuous to autocratic in a way he'd never done in the past.

Lucas spread his hands. "Are your fellow councilors not your brothers? Did we not deserve to be advised?"

"She stands there, recovered and waiting for our judgment." Donald glanced up and down the table at his colleagues. "Shall we get back to the main question?"

Beryl's practiced stillness hid her shock. Where was his infamous temper? The Donald she knew would never have answered civilly. He had been coached. Why?

Donald faced her. "Beryl, we need to know where you hid the book you stole from the Better Baby Contest office."

I'll bet you do, little brother. Hate roared in her ears, filled her with the rushing, throbbing need to rip his heart out the way his betrayal had ripped out hers. She dug her fingernails into the palms of her hands and regained her focus. Nothing mattered more than getting out of isolation, getting a chance to escape. She scrunched up her face as if she were concentrating, confused, confounded.

"From the Better Baby Contest office? What book? I don't remember stealing or hiding anything." She reached far back into memory for the right tone and allowed a little desperation with a dose of sister-brother adoration to creep into her voice. "You know me better than anyone. Don't you believe me, brother?"

To her satisfaction, his swarthy face colored. After ten years of bitter hatred, he hadn't been prepared for her to play the sister card.

He cleared his throat. "I want to believe you, Beryl, but I have a higher duty than the one to my family." An aide leaned forward and whispered in Donald's ear. Donald nodded and said, "I move for a temporary tabling of this hearing until we can determine the extent of her memory loss."

Fire raced through Beryl's veins and refused to be stamped out.

The motion was seconded, voted, and passed.

Somehow Beryl maintained the guileless amnesiac persona she'd created.

The thump of the Council Steward's staff made it official. "We table this session pending further investigation. May the Lord shepherd us to the paths of truth."

Grimace inclined her head toward Beryl and whispered, "Maybe this time the Lord will lead them to forgiveness." Her lips stretched across her beaver teeth in a smirk that told Beryl exactly what outcome she expected.

Beryl didn't expect forgiveness. Once damned, forever damned. As long as she got out of isolation, she would find a way to escape. And one of the things she'd do when she got out of this brick house would be to retrieve and decode that Better Baby Contest book. But not before she visited the people who had turned her little girl into a monster.

Chapter Seven

M iranda dragged her sweaty palms down her pleated swing skirt and tried again. *It's just another shopping trip.* But it wasn't. It was the beginning, or end, of the rest of her life. The warm sunny afternoon made her uncomfortably damp under her two layers of clothing. Her nerves hummed with energy, and acid pooled and bubbled in her stomach. *Slow down, act normal.*

"You should have told me you planned to go to Garfinckel's instead of Woodward & Lothrop." Tom leveled a hard-eyed glare at her.

"It was a last minute decision," she said, not sounding as casual as she'd intended.

"I would have secured the location," Tom said. "You never know where these crazy apostates will pop up."

"Sure, if I were a rebel, I'd hide in a ladies' dressing room." She hid her anger and fear behind her angelic daughter-of-the-councilor smile and strode inside with all the confidence she could dredge up. Designer dresses were on the third floor. She took the elevator to annoy Tom. She paused, pretending to admire a full-skirted Christian Dior evening gown on display.

"Miss Clarke." The salesclerk's tight home perm bunched her bangs on the top of her head in a poodle pom that bobbed with a life of its own. "May I help you?" She spoke in a high-pitched drawl.

Miranda checked the woman's nametag. "Olive, right?"

She nodded. Her poodle pom wobbled.

"I need a dress suitable for an afternoon engagement party, something by Anne Klein or Vera Maxwell."

Olive gave her a smile that outshone the Washington Memorial on a sunny day in July. "Oh, we have a gor-geous Vera Maxwell over here." Olive clutched Miranda's hand and took off down an aisle.

Miranda trotted to keep up.

"The mauve will complement your complexion." Olive yanked her to a second well-dressed mannequin. "And this royal blue Anne Klein will look ab-so-lute-ly stunning on you, Miss Clarke. Or we have other designers?"

"I'll try these. And please, call me Miranda." She headed toward the curtained doorway of the dressing room.

"Both?" Olive squealed. Her pumps clacked in a quickstep to catch up. She touched Miranda's arm. "Miss Clarke, I mean, Miss Miranda, we have much nicer dressing rooms over there."

Miranda shook her head. She had no intention of using the private dressing rooms with their private lounges where bodyguards could be close. "Treat me like regular folk, Olive."

Olive hesitated. She tilted her head at Tom and whispered, "Will he want to go inside?"

"Of course not. He will stay out here."

Tom grabbed Miranda's arm. "Come out every five minutes, or I *will* come in."

His eyes traveled up and down her body. Miranda blushed.

"Fifteen minutes." Miranda mimicked her mother's commanding tone.

Olive gave quick, frightened back-and-forth glances, her pom whipping to and fro.

"Takes a girl time to put herself together." Miranda made her voice soft and throaty.

He slid his hand down her arm and released her. "Fifteen."

She pushed aside the curtain, marched through the doorway, and down the hall to the last dressing bay.

Olive fussed over the state of the dressing room, despite Miranda's assurances that she was quite comfortable.

"Fetch the dresses and stop wasting my time." Her frustration laced her words with her mother's haughtiness.

Olive blanched. She bowed over and over and backed out of the dressing room, her poodle pom bouncing up and down.

Miranda almost called out an apology. She bit her lip. She couldn't afford an apology.

A subdued Olive returned, hung the two dresses on the wall, and faced Miranda.

"I can change myself," Miranda said in a gentle tone.

"Of course, Miss Miranda." Olive backed into the doorway. "Anything else I can do for you?" A worry line creased her forehead.

Miranda pretended to study the dresses, racking her brain for an errand that would distract Olive. She couldn't let a salesclerk ruin her plan. "Yes." She whirled to face Olive. "I like the style of the Anne Klein, but I'd prefer the violet-colored one."

Olive's brows drew together. "I don't believe it comes in violet."

"Check your storeroom. I'm certain I saw a violet one at Woodies." She hadn't. "Ask for a rush delivery if you don't have one." She lowered her voice to a whisper. "You know, if you get me the violet, Garfinckel's will be my new favorite store."

"Oh." Olive's face smoothed and brightened. "I'll check right now." She rushed down the hall.

Miranda closed and locked the stall door. Her hands shook. She fumbled with the clasp of her overstuffed, over-sized purse. Dumping the purse's contents onto the changing bench, she found the rubber band, the pair of scissors, the black and white scarf, and the pair of black flats she'd hidden there.

She rubber banded her hair into a ponytail, then picked up the scissors. Before she could have second thoughts, she sawed through her ponytail. Her hair fell loose around her face. Miranda studied her reflection. Unbidden her hand went to her mouth. She shook her head. Her hair framed her face. She raised her chin. "I like it," she whispered to the frightened girl in the mirror.

Her former ponytail went into her purse. Then she peeled off her long-sleeved blouse and the ankle-length skirt. Underneath she wore a sleeveless white silk blouse and a black pencil skirt. She untucked the blouse and, holding the hem, fanned her torso with the fabric, cooling herself and quick-drying the silk at the same time. Finally, she removed her engagement ring. Holding the ring over the opening of her purse, she hesitated. *I might return it to Ryan someday.* She tucked it into her bra.

Miranda changed shoes and tied the scarf around her neck. She dug around in the contents of her purse until she found a small clutch and a veiled black pillbox hat. Plopping the hat onto her head, she adjusted the veil to hide most of her face. *Ready.* She reached for the doorknob.

"Miss Miranda?" Olive's squeaky little voice had an apologetic whine. "Are you there?"

Miranda took a steadying breath. "Yes, I'm here. What do you want, Olive?"

"I'm awful sorry, Miss Miranda, but the Anne Klein Company says they never made that suit in violet."

Miranda glanced at her wristwatch. The taxi would be waiting outside soon. She needed another errand for Olive.

"And Miss Miranda?"

"Yes, Olive?" Miranda strained to keep her voice calm, civil.

"That man out there is getting awful impatient. He says to remind you he wants to see you in them pretty outfits."

If Olive won't leave me alone, maybe she'll help me. Miranda took off her hat and scarf. She tied the scarf around her hair and stuffed everything else back into the big purse. After wild glance made certain she hadn't forgotten anything, she opened the dressing room door, dragged Olive inside, and slammed the door shut.

Olive's startled expression changed to puzzlement. "Why, Miss Miranda, that's not one of our outfits, is it?"

Miranda shook her head. "No, it's not. Olive, I need your help."

Olive opened her mouth.

Miranda put a finger to Olive's lips. "You saw how he treated me?"

Olive nodded.

"I've got to get away from him. Is there another way out of here?"

Olive shook her head. "We only have two doorways. They both open to the waiting area where your man is standing."

"You mean this dressing area loops around behind Tom?"

"Yes'm." The poodle pom bobbed up and down.

"That might be enough." Miranda grabbed Olive's shoulders. "You'll have to distract him."

Olive blinked at her. "How am I supposed to do that?"

"Go to the door we came in. Stand where he can see you and yell that you have to go to the storeroom to get me the smaller size." Miranda clasped Olive's warm hand between her cool ones. "Can you do that for me?"

Olive squared her shoulders and thrust out her chin. "It'll be my pleasure to help you, Miss Miranda."

A few moments later, Miranda stood at a curtained doorway, peering out at Tom's back.

Olive opened the curtains in front of Tom. "I'm going to the storeroom right now, Miss Miranda."

"That's it. I said fifteen minutes." Tom charged the doorway.

"You can't go in there." Olive's voice had a note of hysteria.

Miranda dashed out from the curtains to the escalator and hurried down the moving steps.

Tom shouted something.

She leaped off the escalator and raced out the door. But the taxi she'd arranged to pick her up wasn't there. She glanced back at the store. Tom sprinted toward her.

Miranda took off down the street, knowing she'd never outrun him. A yellow-checkered cab motored past. She darted between parked cars and down the street after the cab. "Taxi!" The cab kept going.

A horn honked. Across the street, a cab slowed. The light on its roof was on. Miranda yelled and waved and ran. This cab stopped and waited.

Miranda yanked open the door and slammed it shut behind her. "Seventeenth and Lamont. Hurry."

"You in trouble, ma'am?" The cabbie twisted toward her, hooked one arm over the back of his seat.

A glance out the rear window sent her pulse up another notch. Tom plunged through traffic, closing on the taxi.

"You'll get an extra ten if you get me there in ten minutes."

"Ten ain't hardly worth it." The cabbie repositioned himself behind the wheel.

Tom reached for the door.

"Twenty."

The cab leaped forward, throwing Miranda back in her seat, leaving Tom empty-handed.

MIRANDA'S FEET WERE HOT AND SWOLLEN. SHE'D TAKEN THREE different buses from Old City to Georgetown, then walked miles and miles until she'd found a secondhand clothing store. Now she wore a simple, navy blue shirtwaist dress, a pink sweater, a feathered fedora, and sensible shoes. A gently used purse and a battered brown leather and fiber suitcase with three more outfits completed her transformation. She'd dumped her "Miranda" clothes, shoes, and purse in different dumpsters across Georgetown.

She walked down the sidewalk swinging her suitcase and taking deep breaths of spring-scented air.

A man wearing a faded yellow pullover and baggy pants stepped out of a recessed doorway. Her suitcase banged into his knee.

He jumped and yelled.

"Oh." Miranda jerked and drew her purse and suitcase close to her chest. "I'm sorry. I didn't see you."

He scowled at her and hurried on down the sidewalk.

She watched him a moment then, subdued, walked the other direction.

The sidewalks were vacant. Parked cars lined the street. Shops had closed for the day. The air was growing cooler, and the sky threatened a spring storm. Miranda laughed out loud and whirled around in a circle. Soon she'd be on the train to her new, *quiet* life.

Someone jostled her right shoulder. She stumbled but regained her balance, then something slammed into her left side, sending her sprawling onto the sidewalk.

Pain jolted through her knees and elbows and stole her breath. Miranda gulped air and blinked back tears. A man in a yellow pullover ran down the sidewalk with her suitcase. She scrambled to her feet. "Stop!" She ran after him, but he disappeared around a corner.

Miranda limped back to where he'd attacked her. Both elbows and knees were bloodied, and her skirt was ripped. She reached for her purse—*Oh no.*

She spun around in a circle. *Gone.* All her money. Her clothes. Her knees went weak. She had nothing but what she wore. She gulped down breaths to keep from screaming. *How am I going to live now?*

Chapter Eight

Kara stepped up onto the viewing platform and leaned over the angled observation window of her office high above the Arlington Municipal Auditorium floor. An act of confidence. Confidence that everyone from the architect to the manufacturers to the construction workers had the knowledge and skills and materials to make the perfect perch.

Four stories below, workmen scurried across the floor, erecting rows of examination booths for the contest. Supervisor for the tenth year in a row, she'd planned this, the fiftieth National Better Baby Contest, to be an extravaganza intended to secure her family's position at the top of the Fellowship. A plan threatened by her daughter's thoughtless stunt.

Slipping away from her bodyguard had been a little girl's game, a sort of hide-and-seek, long outgrown. Except this time Miranda had succeeded. Three days. Kara didn't know whether to be concerned or outraged.

Someone rapped on her door.

"Not now, Claudia."

The door opened.

Going to have to teach that secretary of mine...

"Hey." Weldon crossed the room, wrapped his arm around her waist, lifted her off the platform, and lowered her to the floor.

"You found her?"

"Yes, but you're not going to like it." He drew her to the settee in the corner of the room and pulled her onto his lap. "She's in Anacostia."

Kara's whole body turned cold. "What do you mean 'She's in Anacostia?'"

"She works nights for a janitorial service and lives in a walk-up near Anacostia Flats."

She sucked in a breath and couldn't breathe out. *Miranda is slumming? If word of this gets out...*

Weldon's sharp features softened with concern. "Hey, sis. Are you all right?"

"No. I am not all right. My daughter is trying to ruin us."

He held her close. "It'll be okay. I'll bring her home."

Kara rested her head on his shoulder. His voice and touch held such strength, such assurance. It restored her. She straightened. "That would be nice, but no." She reached up and ran her fingers through his golden brown hair. "She'd probably run away again." Kara let her hand drift down to caress his cheek.

"What do you want me to do?"

"Find out what she's up to. Then we'll come up with a plan."

He cupped her hand in his and held it against his cheek. "I'll be your snoop."

The telephone's intercom buzzed. Kara slipped off his lap, crossed the room to her writing table, and pressed the intercom button. "Yes?"

"Superintendent Clarke?"

Kara bit back a sharp who-else-were-you-expecting? "I'm listening," she said in her most patient voice. God must have had a reason he made secretaries such idiots.

"Your two-o'clock, Mr. Arnold from the *Washington Times-Herald*, is here."

Kara gave Weldon a pretty pout. "Give me five minutes, then send him in." She switched off the intercom.

Weldon came to her side. "I should go now." His voice was husky, seductive. He cleared his throat. "Meet you for lunch?"

"Usual place and time." She stood on her tiptoes, kissed him on the cheek, and whispered, "Her bodyguard failed his duty. See that he never fails again." She closed the door after him and returned to her desk.

Kara took her hand mirror out of the top right drawer, tucked a wisp of her hair back into her chignon, pinched her cheeks pink, and dabbed on lip balm.

Returning the mirror to its drawer, she crossed her ankles and opened a file folder moments before the door opened. She waited a beat, then closed the folder and looked up. The reporter was younger than the one last year.

"Mr. Arnold," she said in a voice as warm as sun tea. She waited for him to come to her desk. *When I am the wife of the First Apostle, no one will send a green reporter to interview me. Ever.*

The young man came and shook her hand. "Thank you for taking time out of your busy schedule to speak with me."

"It's nice to meet you." Overlooking his stenographer's notebook and Kodak camera, he had a pleasing symmetry to his face and general body structure. *He could have been a runner-up in a Better Baby contest.*

Kara gestured to the seating area with the settee and two Queen Anne chairs.

He shook his head. "No, thanks. I am both reporter and photographer today. May I ask questions during the tour?"

Direct and efficient? Hmm. He might be useful one day. "Of course." She led him to the elevator. "What can I tell you about the contest?"

He flipped open his notebook. "Mary de Garmo held the first Better Baby Contest at the Louisiana State Fair in 1908. Yet you're calling this year's event the fiftieth Contest. This is 1961. Shouldn't it be the fifty-third contest?"

Does no one read the promotional materials? "We honor Mrs. de Garmo as the originator of the contest, but her contest barely rose above the County Fair livestock judging which inspired her. In 1911 Mrs. Watts transformed the contest into a drive to educate parents on how to raise sound, healthy babies in every city across the nation." And converted shoddy paperwork into the world's best eugenics records second only to the United Federation of Germany, according to Kara's German correspondents.

The elevator bell dinged.

Mr. Arnold gestured for her to enter first. He followed.

The elevator operator tipped his hat to her. "Going down?"

"Arena level." Kara appreciated the faint scent of pine and the shine of polished chrome in the elevator. She smiled her approval to the operator.

Mr. Arnold pointed his pen at Kara. "The copy of the contest application I received is extensive. What if a parent doesn't remember when their baby first rolled over or how many hours he slept as a newborn?"

"I'd think she was not an attentive parent and would hope that participation in the contest would help her improve." *But in my contests, the losers are potentially as important as the winners.*

The elevator bounced gently to a halt. The bell rang.

"Arena level." The elevator operator opened the doors.

Kara led the way down a long hall.

Mr. Arnold trailed behind her. "You've expanded the contest this year to include any child from anywhere in America."

"Not any child." *Don't print that.* "They must be ten months to five years of age, whose parents are white, natural-born citizens of the United States."

"Why not keep it exclusive to the winners and runners-up of the state contests?"

She stopped beside a door labeled Private. "How better to be a national contest than to include more of the nation's children?" *And to find the unwitting donors Dr. Locke needs.*

46

She opened the door to the largest stenographers' pool in the world.

The clicking of keys, dinging and ratcheting of carriage returns filled the room. Scores of women sat at typewriters entering names, ages, and other basic information from the applications onto the five contest scorecards. Other women searched tall card catalogs that lined the room.

"Doctors and nurses assure that every application is complete. They hand the application off to the records clerks who check for previous applications. The records clerk gives this year's form and any past records to the stenographers. And they create five scoring cards for each applicant."

Mr. Arnold pointed his camera. The flashbulb popped.

Kara touched the smooth wooden surface of the cabinet to her left. "These card catalogs hold final scorecards from past nationals." She waited for him to finish taking pictures. "After the contestant has aged out of the contest, we ship the cards to the Eugenics Records Office in Cold Harbor for storage."

They left the stenographers' room. Kara waved at the accountants' rooms. "Those rooms will be as busy as the stenographers' once the scoring of the contestants begins." She led Mr. Arnold through the main lobby, past the security guard at the front entrance, to the arena floor.

The noise of hammers and saws abused her ears. The dry smell of sawdust irritated her nose.

She took him to the first of the girls' booths, the only one completed so far.

"To avoid interference, the parents cannot enter the examination booths with the child." Kara raised her voice above a swell of hammers banging, forklifts growling, and saws ripping. "But they can observe through these one-way windows."

He interrupted his note-taking long enough to take pictures. "Looks kind of like a hospital nursery." At full volume, Mr. Arnold's voice grated against her ears almost as much as the buzz saws.

Kara pointed at the scales for weighing, the height boards for checking growth, calipers for measuring symmetry, and the dynamometers for testing muscle strength.

Mr. Arnold snapped pictures of every testing station, including those for vision, hearing, intelligence, and temperament.

"What qualities are the ones every 'better baby' must have?"

That was easy. "Intelligence, an even temperament, and a pleasing symmetry."

"In the past twenty years, there's only been one baby that scored 100% and that was your niece."

It pained her, but it was true. Her own children had each scored above 98%, but none of them had met the standards as well as Anna.

"Only one perfect baby in the whole country for twenty years. Does that mean the contest is not meeting its goal of providing better babies for America?"

Kara wished she could tell him how Dr. Locke was fine-tuning his method for creating perfect babies made-to-order, but she'd learned long ago that most people had an aversion to scientific advances. She gave him the same statement she'd given all the others. "No, sir, it does not. There are dozens of measurements for each area of health. And the examinations are more rigorous as one ascends each of the four judging levels." She closed the door and muffled the construction noises. "It takes extraordinary breeding and care to have a child who scores 100% in all those measurements, in all four passes. Scores are trending upward. We are hopeful there will be more perfect babies in our future." Kara suppressed a proud, knowing smile.

"What advice would you give parents who want to improve their child's scores?"

"Besides food for a strong body and a strong mind?" She glanced over Mr. Arnold's shoulder and gave the security guard "the look." "They need to first have their child assessed by experts so they know which areas their child can improve upon. Then they should follow the advice of the experts."

The security guard crossed the lobby to stand at Mr. Arnold's side.

"I am afraid that's all the time I have for today, Mr. Arnold." Kara nodded at the security guard. "George will show you out."

"You're a busy woman. I understand." Mr. Arnold turned to follow the guard.

Kara's heels clicked softly on the linoleum lobby floor on her way to the elevator.

"Superintendent, I have one more question."

She closed her eyes and composed herself, then faced him and smiled, not a generous smile that invited a prolonged conversation, but a polite I-will-spare-one-more-minute smile.

"Ten years ago someone broke into the contest offices. It appears that the thief was apprehended, but court records were sealed. What was stolen? Who stole it? And why keep it a secret?"

A pang of irritation shot through Kara. "Mr. Arnold, the court sealed those records for a reason. You can guess at reasons if you like, but by order of the court, I cannot discuss it." She whirled and strode down the hall into the stairwell. Her shoes clacked against the concrete steps, broadcasting her anger to the upper levels.

How had the reporter found out about the robbery? Who would have talked?

Kara's secretary held a stack of telephone messages out for her. Kara waved her off, closed the office door behind her, and sank into her chair. She propped her elbow on the desk and tapped her index finger against her lips.

That irritating little reporter obviously didn't know the thief was Donald's crazy sister, Beryl.

Only a dozen people on the planet knew about that robbery. The judge had died three years ago. No one on the Fellowship Council dared talk. Maybe it was one of those apostates, those Soldiers for the American Bill of Rights?

Kara allowed herself a slow smile. If the reporter could find this person, her brother Weldon and his Soldiers of the Second

Sphere could too. She picked up the phone and dialed her brother's private line.

"Weldon? Let's have an early lunch."

Chapter Nine

Azrael waited in the near dark with her back against the wall, behind the overstuffed chair that faced the UNIVAC multi-monitor and both the front door and the doorway to the kitchen. She had borne the weight of her jumpsuit and body armor for more than an hour and listened to the sounds of the modest house, the soft tick-tock of the clock on the living room wall and the muted purr of the Kelvinator refrigerator in the kitchen. The sounds remained as steady as her pulse.

She felt right, balanced. She'd have known whether her suppressed Mauser VP60 automatic pistol was even one round light. Unaided, her eyes could discern the deeper shadows of the furniture of the living room. Pressing a button on her wrist pad would light the visor of her helmet with the eerie green glow of night vision. She preferred to rely on her own powers. Her powers —every muscle, every nerve—hummed like a tuning fork, alive with purpose.

Her target stood five-eight, a slender one hundred thirty pounds. He wore his blue-black hair swept back and sported a pencil mustache. Every day at 5:00 p.m., he left his Fellowship Center office and walked a block and a half to the sidewalk dispenser where he bought a newspaper. Newspaper in hand, he'd cross the street to his favorite diner. His meal never varied. He ate rib eye steak, medium well, which he finished before he'd eat a bite of the mashed potatoes smothered in brown gravy, then he'd eat the green beans. For dessert, he'd have a decaf coffee laced with cream and sugar and read the paper. He'd leave a twenty-five cent tip, walk to his Studebaker in the parking lot, and drive out of the city to the winding suburban street where he lived. He'd enter his home in the dark, hang up his hat and coat, and then turn on the lights.

She didn't know what he'd done. Knowing didn't matter. His sins were against the Council and the Father.

The whistle, wheeze, and pop of his Studebaker told her that he'd parked the car at the curb out front. The latch clicked, and the door opened. He stepped in and closed the door behind him, shrugged out of his overcoat, and hung his coat and hat on the brass coat rack by the door.

"We are Azrael."

He turned toward her, his mouth open. The three-round burst of polymer darts hit him in the center of his chest. His body jerked. Bits of flesh and blood splattered his overcoat and the door behind him. A red stain blossomed on his shirt. His knees buckled. He dropped to the floor.

Azrael crossed over to his body, lifted one booted foot, and rolled him onto his back. His vacant eyes stared at the ceiling.

She squatted beside him, breathed in the odors of his death: acrid nitrates, hot sweet blood, and pungent excrement. A faint ethereal lift tingled across her skin, sped her pulse and her breath. The sensation lasted mere seconds and left her hungry.

Azrael preferred the garrote. The feel of a soul leaving the body gave her more of what she craved. She curled her gloved hand into a fist, dipped the edge of her fist into his blood, then pressed it to his forehead. "Thy will be done."

She stood and cleaned her soiled glove with a blood-specific solvent from her equipment belt. Then she stepped over the still-warm body and crossed the room. At the door, she pulled out her laser pen to burn the sign of the Fellowship in the wood. Azrael sighed and, obeying her orders, returned the cold pen to her belt. She flicked her helmet mike switch twice. Uncle would send the Cleaners. She slipped out the door and faded into the night.

Chapter Ten

Two weeks ago Miranda Clarke would never have used a service elevator. Now she used it every day. She pressed the elevator's landing door handle down. The two halves yawned open, revealing the inner, metal scissors gate.

"What's got you smilin'?" Miranda's trainer, Sarah, threw open the gate. The metal screeched and rattled. Tall and chicken-bone skinny, Sarah was dark-skinned and wore her black hair in a tight knot at the nape of her neck.

"I am loving my apartment."

Sarah bumped her cleaning cart over the threshold into the elevator. "A one-room, eighth-floor walkup makes me tired."

Miranda pushed her cart in after Sarah.

Sarah flipped switches and jabbed buttons on the brass control panel, then pulled and pushed the operator handle into position. The elevator lurched upward. "Don't you wish for a big house with fine furniture?"

"Big houses and fine furniture don't mean happiness." The elevator rumbled and clanked, drowned out Miranda's words.

After the mugging, Miranda had spent a terrified and sleepless night wandering the streets. The next morning she'd answered a

Help Wanted sign in a window. Hector, of Hector's Janitorial Services, hadn't asked many questions. No experience needed. On-the-job training.

That had been two weeks ago. Now she had a job, an apartment, a new friend, and a new life.

Sarah refolded a cleaning cloth on top of her cart. "Where'd you say you came from?"

Miranda's throat tightened. "I didn't."

"Is it a secret?"

"No, silly. Standardsville." The town listed on her fake ID papers. A town picked at random. *Please don't ask any more questions.*

"Did you know the Graham Hill family?"

How do I answer? "Heard of them. Didn't *know* them." She busied herself with straightening the cleaning items on her cart.

Sarah pulled the operator handle back to the vertical, eased the elevator level with the sixth-floor landing. She opened the gate, then the landing door. "Graham Hill was my daddy. He never stepped foot in Standardsville." Her cart bumped and thumped over the threshold and into a wide corridor with rich, mahogany paneling and a pale terrazzo floor. "I think you can handle the east side on your own tonight." Sarah pointed her cart west and trudged away.

Miranda's stomach rolled.

Sarah rounded a corner.

Mama was right. Ordinary life was hard. Miranda pushed her cart down the opposite hall.

Hector had steered her to the pawnshop. The pawnshop had given her less than what Ryan's ring was worth, but it covered a month's rent and food with enough left over to buy a change of clothes.

When anyone asked if she were *the* Miranda Clarke, she rolled her eyes and said, "Do you know how many times I'm asked that?" And the subject was dropped.

A lie of omission is still a lie.

So far, she'd only lied twice. She couldn't help it if people made false assumptions.

A false witness will not go unpunished.

Miranda pressed her lips together. *Did other people's subconscious scold them?*

Let not your mouth lead you into sin. It was as if her mother were in her head.

She stopped her cart at office number 601.

Like most of the offices in the building, this one had mahogany paneling, a massive desk, and a pair of teal club chairs for visitors. Floor-to-ceiling bookcases stuffed with law books lined one wall. On the opposite wall, a sunburst clock hung above a collection of black and white photographs. She ran her feather duster over the tops of the frames.

Miranda emptied the trash and vacuumed the floor and moved on to the next office. Soon she reached the end of the corridor. She turned the corner, expecting Sarah's cart to be outside one of the offices. But the hall was vacant. *Have I finished faster than Sarah?*

"Sarah? Do you need help?"

"No, thanks." Sarah's cart clattered, announcing her approach. She came around the corner and jerked her head back down the hall. "Someone had a party in 632. Slowed me down."

Sarah pushed her cart into the next room.

Maybe I should tell her everything.

They finished the sixth-floor offices and moved to the fifth floor. Halfway through the umpteenth fifth-floor office, Miranda yawned and stretched and kneaded her aching back muscles. *Will I ever get used to working nights like Sarah?* Working the graveyard shift had seemed the perfect solution to her nightmare-haunted nights. *Who would have thought you could have nightmares while the sun was up?*

She picked up the overstuffed trashcan. It slipped through her fingers and fell to the floor with a clang, strewing papers everywhere. "Oh, pickles."

Cursing now?

"You okay, Miranda?"

"Just being a spaz." She got down on her hands and knees to chase papers that had skittered across the cold floor and under the desk.

The last piece of paper was a flyer with large typeface over an American flag. "Reclaim Your Freedom. The First Amendment to the Constitution of the United States guarantees the separation of Religion and State. Stop the Fellowship Council." Miranda dropped the paper. It fluttered to the floor.

She scooted back against the wall. *Why was that in a G-man's trash? Was he—one of them?*

The apostates called themselves Soldiers for the American Bill of Rights, or SABR. They had been responsible for kidnappings, riots, break-ins, and robberies across the country.

She had to report what she'd found. But to whom? The Fellowship Council? *And get sent back home? Not a good idea.*

She should ask Sarah. Sarah would know what to do.

Miranda picked up the flyer with two fingers, held it out as if it were a rotten fish.

Sarah's cart stood down the hall, outside of number 516.

Miranda hurried into the room, a mirror image of the one she'd just left. "Sarah, I found this—"

Sarah started. "Miranda." She clutched a piece of used carbon paper to her chest and rocked back on her heels. An empty trashcan sat in front of her. Three piles of trash surrounded her: a pile of discards; a stack of wrinkled, type-filled papers; a stack of used carbon paper.

Something cold fluttered in Miranda's stomach. "What are you doing?" She bit her lip too late. She shouldn't have said that out loud.

Sarah face hardened. "You mean am I spying on the white folk?"

"That's not what I meant." She'd meant *are you trying to lose your job? I had to sign a confidentiality statement to work here. Didn't you?*

"You white folk are all alike." Sarah picked up the used paper and carbons. "You always think someone like me is up to no good." She stalked out into the hall.

Miranda lowered the flyer to her side. She stared at the piles of papers, at the flyer in her hand, then back again. *Is Sarah an apostate?* The metal pop and click from Sarah's cart's cabinet doors echoed in the hallway.

Sarah re-entered the room, propped her fists on her hips, and glared. "You can't imagine being poor 'nuff you gotta reuse whatever you can."

Miranda flushed. Of course, Sarah had only wanted to reuse the carbons. "I'm sorry. I didn't want you to get fired." Her voice trailed off. Sarah was right. She had a lot to learn about being poor.

"Don't need no help and don't need no pity." Sarah swept the remaining trash into her apron and strode out of the room.

Miranda squared her shoulders and followed.

Sarah whirled on Miranda, her face dark, scowling. "What do you want?"

"I came because I found this." She held the flyer out for Sarah.

Sarah barely glanced at the flyer. "So?"

"Don't you think we should report it?"

"No." She pushed her cart toward the next office.

"I don't understand." Miranda raised her voice to be heard over the clattering cart.

Sarah faced Miranda, cocked her head, and narrowed her eyes. "What these hoity-toity G-men do or do not do in their fancy offices don't mean nothing to the likes of us." She stabbed a finger at Miranda and herself. "We are the cleaning ladies. They don't even know we exist. If one of them takes a fancy to one of us, we still don't exist. And it don't take nothing but a snap of their finger for our kind to disappear, 'cause we—don't—exist. And if you really was one of us, you'd know that. But you aren't, are you?"

Miranda flushed. She remembered her mother's reaction

when Miranda had called their cleaning lady by name. Hired help was supposed to be invisible.

Sarah glared at her a moment longer. "Do what you want. Ain't no never mind to me. I got work to do." She pushed her cart to the next office.

I should apologize. But Miranda couldn't find the right words. Two weeks ago she would have reported her suspicions, and Sarah would have been arrested. But Sarah wasn't an apostate. *She's my friend.*

Miranda returned to her cart, took a deep breath, then dropped the flyer into the trash receptacle. She wiped her hands on her pinafore and pushed her cart to number 568.

Unlike the other offices, the door was closed. Burned into the door at eye level was a red shield sectioned by a white cross. The Fellowship symbol. There were stories about pranksters who burned the symbol various places, a mockery of old tales meant to frighten children who had misbehaved.

She sniffed at the childishness and caught a whiff of charred wood and something else. The symbol had been burned into the door recently.

"Didn't know G-men pulled pranks on one another." She spoke loud enough to encourage Sarah to respond. "Looks like they were trying to scare this guy with the old Angel of Death stories." No response. Miranda opened the door.

Strong putrid odors assaulted her. She gagged and retreated into the hall. "Smells like a toilet in there."

Determined not to give Sarah any more reasons to doubt her, Miranda took a deep breath and re-entered the room. Sarah yelled something, but Miranda wasn't about to take a breath to answer until she aired this place out.

She crossed the room before she saw him. Sprawled on his back on the floor, she couldn't take her eyes off his face.

Cloudy eyes stared out of a pale, waxy, no-longer-human face. His purple tongue protruded from his blue lips as if he had died in a fit of coughing or choking. He had a smear of blood on his forehead and a deep red mark on his neck.

Breathless, she couldn't look away and she couldn't run. Her legs wouldn't work. She rocked back and forth. A high-pitched keening pierced the air. Her raw throat told her that the keening came from her.

Sarah appeared in the doorway. "Are you all—" She followed Miranda's finger pointing at the body.

"It's real." Miranda sucked in a ragged breath. "The Azrael stories are *real*."

"Why'd they leave his body?" Sarah sniffed. "He ain't even cold yet, is he?"

Miranda shook her head. She sucked air in and out, in and out. Waves of dizziness hit, weakened her knees.

"Ain't nobody ever seen the Taken." Sarah spoke in a slow monotone. "Nobody's *supposed* to see the Taken. Just the sign. Oh, Lordy." She rushed forward, grabbed Miranda's arm, and pulled her to a stand. "Lordy, Lordy. Somebody's gonna come for him. We got to get out of here." Sarah pushed Miranda out the door, past her cleaning cart.

Sarah skidded to a stop, whirled on Miranda. "They see our carts, they know we been here. We got to hide them." She ran down the hall, retrieved her cart, wheeled it around, and passed Miranda at a run.

"Miranda. Hurry. They're coming." Sarah's shrill, panic-stricken voice penetrated Miranda's clouded thoughts.

"The Azrael?" Miranda jerked her cart around and dashed down the hall. The cart's chittering wheels echoed in her runaway pulse. "Will we be Taken?"

Sarah yanked open the door of the fifth-floor storage closet. "The Azrael. The Cleaners. Don't matter." She shoved buckets and other cleaning supplies out of the way. "Nobody ever seen them—and lived."

They muscled the carts inside, then raced for the elevator.

Sarah reached it first, pounded the call button.

"Stop." Miranda gasped for breath. "It's—on—the way." The rattle of the elevator cage drew near.

"On the way?" Sarah's voice was high and tight. "After I pressed the button, right?"

Miranda's eyes widened. She shook her head.

"The stairs." Sarah led the way.

Miranda raced down the stairs behind Sarah, hit the exit door's panic bar, and burst outside into the dark. She slowed, blinking, trying to force her eyes to adjust. A pair of muscular arms wrapped around her and lifted her off her feet.

Men, dressed darker than the shadows, advanced on the building. Sarah hung limply in the arms of one of the men.

Miranda called, "Sarah!" A cloth clapped over Miranda's mouth and nose. Its sickly-sweet smell robbed her of breath. She jerked and twisted, uselessly.

One gasp, and her vision clouded. Her head spun. Her legs folded. Consciousness melted.

Chapter Eleven

W inded, Beryl finished her hundredth one-armed push-up, then stood and rolled her shoulders. Her morning stiffness was getting harder to shake off. The day she'd turned forty, she'd done a hundred and fifty one-arms. On her fiftieth birthday, she had vowed not to see another birthday locked in this godforsaken place. She aimed to keep that vow.

She wiped the back of her hand against her damp forehead. Outside her cell's tiny reinforced and barred window, sunlight shone on the red brick wall three meters away. The window had given her a way to track every day and night of unspent rage.

She moved to the center of the cell and leaned forward. *Neither confinement nor age matter.* Reaching out to the rough concrete block wall with her left hand, she placed her left foot waist-high against the opposite wall. A couple of deep breaths, a swift movement of her other leg and arm, and she began the brutal work of crab walking up, then down the wall. *Being ready matters.* The Prophet was ill. The Council undecided. She had managed to keep up the amnesia facade for her guardians for months. She would not give up now.

After her shower, she stood in front of the polished metal

mirror bolted to the wall above her one-piece metal sink and crapper. She'd stood there every day. Every day she fought against her memories fading. She remembered Anna's small hand in hers, the warmth of Ethan's kiss, her outrage at what Weldon had done, and her utter horror of what Anna had become.

Familiar footsteps approached. Her guardians. *Now?* Her pulse sped up. *Beating?* She combed her drying hair until she saw their reflections. *Showtime.*

"Back so soon?" She used a meek tone and turned to face them.

Grimace held a pair of handcuffs and leg irons.

Adrenaline warmed the back of Beryl's neck. *Visitor.* She stayed in character, and she followed the rules. She put away the comb and put her hands behind her head without delay. How many years had it been since her last visitor? So soon after her hearing, the visit had to be significant. *Who could it be? Cousin Palmer or brother Donald?* Long ago, each had attempted to convince her that she could buy her freedom with a confession. They each had tried—once.

Thumper entered her cell first, her stun stick leveled at Beryl's chest.

Grimace grabbed her wrist, slapped a cuff on it, then twisted her arm behind her back.

Beryl's jaw twitched. Neither Thumper nor Grimace believed her act. They tormented her with taunts and abuse, hoping to break her. She counted the breathing of her opponent to keep from reacting.

Grimace jerked her backward toward the bed.

Bolted to the floor and ceiling, the bed stood against the far wall. The top bunk's welded wire frame was bare. The bottom bunk had a thin mattress, a coarse cotton sheet, and a rough wool blanket.

A powerful yank on the handcuffs twisted Beryl's arm around to the front. A hand on her head forced her to sit on the blanketed bottom bunk.

Beryl moved like a timid mouse. She held her free hand out on the far side of the bed's metal support post.

Grimace cuffed her other wrist, then bent and dragged the chain of the leg irons around the leg of the bed. Grimace had forgotten the leg irons once. Her rib fractures had healed, but she'd never forgotten again.

Grimace pulled a chair inside. Then Grimace and Thumper vanished into the dark hall beyond Beryl's cell.

Beryl glanced up at the caged camera that swept her cell. The red camera-on light continued its evil glare.

Waiting wasn't as hard as it used to be.

Palmer shuffled into sight.

She sucked in a breath. He was skeletal, his face more sallow and sunken than it had appeared on the television. She couldn't help herself. He *was* the Prophet. She stood. Her handcuffs scraped along the bunk's metal support bar.

He entered her cell, the door clanged shut behind him, the lock clacked into place.

Gasping for air, Palmer dropped into the chair and gestured for her to sit.

She did.

He blew air out through pursed lips. "Hello, Beryl," he said. "You look well. Better than you looked on those dreadful screens." His voice fluctuated from a whisper to a croak.

"Wish I could say the same about you. Lung cancer?"

He shook his head and cleared his throat. "Heart's worn out. Soon I'll be given my heavenly body." A body-wracking cough wiped his serene smile from his face. He pulled a handkerchief from his pocket and spit into it. "Since I was on my way to an Arizona health spa, I came to give you the news myself. The Council has decided—" A fit of coughing shook him. He covered his mouth with his soggy handkerchief.

If his poor health is a ruse, he's a better actor than I am.

He wiped his mouth. "You will be moved to Renewal."

In ten years she'd heard it all and believed none of it, but hope spurred her pulse anyway. She maintained the blank expression of her amnesiac alter.

"We believe you'll regain your health, and your memory, there."

"So it's a better place?" Playing the dumb, the compliant, made her skin crawl.

"Yes, dear." The timbre of his voice sounded more like the Prophet. "You'll take part in the activities of Renewal until your memory returns. Once every member of the Council agrees that you've recovered, you'll return to your cell."

"I understand." *They believe that only death will free me.*

The Prophet stood.

So did she.

The cell door clanged opened, then closed after him. He walked into the shadows and stopped. He didn't move for a slow hundred count, then he did a three-sixty and returned to her cell. Huffing and puffing, he grabbed the bars and wedged his face between them. "You were right, Beryl. You and Ethan." The whisper was back. "I was wrong." He sighed. "You tried to tell me the Second Sphere was corrupt. I was too proud. God had called me to lead the American people. How, then, could my hand-selected assistants be so vile?" He let out a long, slow breath, his shoulders sagged, and he bowed his head. He looked as if he were deflating.

Was this a trick? Do they think I'll reveal what I know about SABR? About Ethan? About the book I stole? She tilted her head toward the camera.

He gave her a pleased-with-myself smile. "There are benefits to being the Prophet. God forgive me for taking advantage of one or two of those today."

She stared at him, not understanding.

"The camera now shows you sitting on your bed, trussed as you are and alone. That image will play until we finish the Lord's work."

He re-entered the cell and sat back in the chair.

She stood again until he sat. She didn't dare break the persona she'd spent months creating. Not until she knew what was going on.

Palmer squared his shoulders, looked her in the eye. "I am dying, Beryl. The doctors say it will be a matter of weeks, maybe months. No, no." He waved away the condolence he apparently assumed she would offer. "I am at peace with it. But there is work to be done."

He spoke in a low tone, not the voice of the Prophet, but the voice of her cousin and playmate. "I was certain another Prophet would rise from the people. But the few who have made the claim failed the tests of faith. Now I must name a successor, a First Apostle. Polls say the Fellowship favors Lucas or your brother Donald."

This isn't about his eyes being opened. It's about who gets the throne after he dies. About rooting out a councilor gone bad. Funny. Him coming to me after all these years. Her fingernails bit into her palms. She chose her words carefully to keep her sarcasm from showing. "Which one of your councilors have you chosen?"

"Before I can choose, I must have some answers." He shifted in the chair. "A staggering number of unbelievers have been Taken in the last few years. I suspect one or more of the Council members have used the Azrael for evil."

"Why would a Council member do such a thing?" She tried to sound curious, but her cynicism showed.

He stifled a cough with a fresh handkerchief. "Twelve days ago, a trusted minister to the State Department disappeared." Tears glistened in his eyes. "He was Taken. *Unsanctioned.*"

"Why should I care? Without you at the head of the Council table, I am as good as dead."

"Not if the Council is—purified."

Her jaw muscles worked. As soon as the Council had decided they had the power of life and death over people, the Fellowship had been doomed. She'd begged the Council to listen to her, to help her, to help her daughter. *No. I will not let him get to me this way. Let them destroy themselves.*

He made a phlegmy, throat-clearing noise. "I want to make amends, Beryl. To you, and to the world through you."

"How do you propose to do that?"

"I'm going to free you."

She tensed and released her calf muscles to keep from blurting out her disbelief. When she spoke, she kept her voice flat, monotone. "For what purpose?"

"Finish what you set out to do. Find Ethan and the SABR. Destroy the Azrael."

Inner klaxons set every nerve in her body on fire. She struggled to remain calm, unmoved on the outside. "You *want* me to destroy the Azrael? You, *the Prophet*, are telling me to *murder* your Angels of Death?"

"I want you to set things right." He took a tremulous breath. "Find out who has corrupted the Azrael. Stop them *and* the Azrael."

She couldn't read him nor believe him. "You suspect it's Councilor Lucas or Donald?"

"One or both of them."

She couldn't see any duplicity in his body or his face. Still, she wouldn't trust him.

"I can see you have no faith in me." He pulled a paper from his inside coat pocket and handed it to her.

She unfolded and scanned it. It was a formal commutation of her sentence, in his handwriting, dated six months in the future.

He stood.

She didn't. She didn't trust her legs to hold her.

"You will be moved to Renewal tonight. In exactly one month, tell Sister Marie that you need a new mattress."

So if she went to Renewal, Grimace would too. "A month?"

"Less suspicious that way. Thirty days. No earlier."

He stopped at the cell door.

"When do I see you again?"

He hesitated a moment. "In the next life." The cell door banged shut. He coughed and shuffled down the dark hall.

She didn't believe it. Not until Grimace and Thumper had walked her to Renewal and freed her from the handcuffs and leg irons. She lay with her hands behind her head on a real mattress with clean, cotton sheets and stared at the ceiling. Renewal was far more comfortable than her cell, but not so comfortable that she would forget why she was here.

The Council had condoned the creation of the Azrael. Had condoned the abuse that sick son of a bitch, Weldon, had used to corrupt her daughter. They were as guilty as he.

Palmer obviously didn't believe she'd become the demure amnesiac. *How does he plan to control me on the outside? Does he plan to let me run amok until—I kill Lucas and Donald?* There had to be someone he wanted to fill their shoes, to become the First Apostle. Palmer knew she wasn't a fool. But he was counting on using her. Using her anger.

Funny thing about anger. It could grow hotter, die away, or grow very, very cold.

Chapter Twelve

K ara loved the 80-foot wooden yacht she and Donald owned. But right now she was grateful that the *Faithful Seas* plowed toward its mooring home on Hog Island Bay off the eastern shore of Virginia. She sat in the corner of the white leather, wraparound bench aft of the main deck watching the seagulls wheeling overhead. Amazing that the raucous gulls annoyed her less than the constant drone of her guest's voice.

Grace, a large-boned woman in an unflattering, nautically themed dress, was the wife of Councilor Ezekiel Nichols. Her square sailor's collar fluttered behind her dishwater-blonde, perm-frizzed hair. She'd nattered on for hours about her adult children, their families, the weather, renovating her house, and other boring matters.

An absence of Grace's voice cued Kara. "Hmm."

Grace slurped her sweet tea, set the glass on the table, and gave her a shrewd look. "You and Donald have been charming hosts, Kara, but, darling, we both know why Zeke and I are here."

"Oh?" Kara kept her tone mild, curious, and innocent. An annoying wisp of hair blew in her face until she tucked it back behind her right ear. Over Grace's left shoulder, a movement behind the dining salon's sliding glass doors caught Kara's attention. The steward tilted his head toward the interior. *The appetizers must be ready.* A casual shake of her head told him to wait.

"I have been a councilor's wife for a long, long time." Grace locked eyes with Kara. "I know how this goes. Why should Zeke vote for Donald?"

"How refreshing." Kara revised her estimation of Grace's intelligence. *This will be fun.* "Not one of the other wives acknowledged that Donald was being considered for First Apostle."

Grace folded her arms on the tabletop and leaned forward. "So give me your best pitch."

"Zeke shouldn't vote for Donald." Kara gave a dismissive wave of her hand. "Unless he believes that Donald is the righteous choice." *Which he will.*

"You aren't trying to buy Zeke's vote?"

"No." Kara lowered her rhinestone studded, cat-eye sunglasses and peered over the top of them. "I can't tell you anything you don't know about Donald, or about Lucas." *I will, but not until I'm certain you will make it common knowledge in a day or two.* "Knowing them both, knowing about that thing with Lucas last year, we trust Zeke to make the right choice." She pushed her glasses back up on her nose, reached for her tea glass.

"You mean the automobile accident last year?" Grace frowned, a wary expression on her face.

"A tragedy." Kara sipped her tea and, through her lashes, watched Grace.

"Poor Lucas. The death of his secretary hit him hard." Grace raised her glass to her lips. "He paid her hospital bills *and* her funeral costs." Her sweating glass dripped onto the tablecloth.

Kara set her glass down, kept her expression and tone neutral. "I hear he gifted the family with several years' worth of her salary too."

"Unsubstantiated rumors."

Kara dried her hands with her soft linen napkin. "It would be a crime to let rumors blemish an otherwise stellar record of service. Even if there is a small piece of truth in those rumors."

"Have you heard something?"

Kara leaned back, the leather cushions squeaked. "Nothing since they discovered that someone bribed the coroner."

"Bribed?" Grace gaped at her.

"Oh, dear." Kara covered her mouth. "I thought Zeke was on the committee." She leaned forward. "Please don't tell a soul. It's all hush-hush."

Grace crossed her heart with two fingers.

Kara glanced at the steward.

He acknowledged Kara with a nod and came to the table. "Appetizers are served in the salon."

"Are Donald and Zeke there?"

"Yes, ma'am. Your brother's there too."

"Have the others arrived yet?" Dinner was going to be a family affair, a show of Fellowship values.

"Not yet, ma'am."

"And the appetizers?" She stole a glance at Grace. Her guest had a faraway look and ran the tip of her index finger around the rim of her nearly empty tea glass.

"Fresh clams. Baked in Chef's special sauce."

"Did you hear that, Grace?"

"What?"

"Chef has prepared fresh clams in a divine sauce for our appetizers. They're in the salon." She gestured toward the glass doors.

Grace flashed a campaign smile at the steward. "Sounds wonderful." She stood. "I should freshen up."

"Please show Mrs. Nichols to the guest stateroom."

The steward led her inside.

Kara closed her eyes and lifted her face to the sun. She'd planted the seeds. Grace would ask her best friend about the bribe. The same friend who had gotten the scoop from one of Kara's earliest guests and, by now, believed she'd discovered the facts herself. By the time the Prophet croaked, the rumors would solidify into proof. Labeled an adulterer and a murder suspect, Lucas's campaign would fail.

She savored the warm, briny air. Life rewards the prepared. From the spectacular Better Baby Contest, to Donald's investiture as First Apostle, to launching the full-scale Azrael project, it was all coming together. Her naysayers and the malicious gossips who had tried to stop her would finally get what they deserved.

One problem remained unsolved—Miranda. Kara had hoped that a few days of life without luxuries would bring Miranda back home. It hadn't. Now Miranda was like a hair out of place. Well, a wild hair can either be tamed or plucked.

The glass doors slid open. Donald crossed the deck to her, his swarthy skin darkened after hours of fishing on the lower deck. Since his heavy, arch-less brows weren't bunched together in his usual scowl, she guessed that his day had been at least as successful as hers.

She stood and met him with a peck on his stubbled cheek. "How was your day, dear?"

"I didn't catch a thing worth keeping." He licked his lips, and his face lit with self-satisfaction. "On the other hand, the Lord smiled upon Zeke. He caught a twenty-pound sea bass. Dinner?" He offered her his arm.

"Excellent." Kara slipped her hand through his arm. Zeke would feel heady with his fishing prowess. When his wife tired of fish stories during their pillow talk tonight, she'd share her growing suspicion of Lucas.

"Ahoy!" A familiar voice called from the port side of the ship. "Permission to board, Captain?"

"Ryan?" Donald's glance said "I forgot about Ryan." He cupped his hands around his mouth and bellowed, "Permission granted."

Kara faced port and called, "Miranda? Are you there too?"

Donald gave Kara a puzzled look.

She blew out an impatient breath. *Remember the plan, Donald.*

"I thought she was with you." Ryan's voice betrayed his surprise.

Donald's face clouded. He spoke low and fast. "I thought Weldon was going to make certain Miranda came tonight." His frown deepened. "I need to talk to Weldon."

"Not now, Donald. We need to greet Ryan. He's family." She hoped that reminding him of the pending union would prevent one of his mood swings. But he'd already headed down below. She hurried after him.

Ryan climbed out of the ketch onto the swim platform. One of the crew secured the little boat so that it floated behind the yacht's sporty, twenty-five-foot tender.

Tanned and towheaded, Ryan climbed the three-step aft ladder. His crisp blue button-down sports shirt and khaki Saturday shorts were barely wrinkled. He stuck his hand out for Donald.

"We don't shake anymore." Donald enveloped him in a bear hug. "You're family."

Ryan freed himself and greeted Kara with a quick, citrus-scented hug. "She didn't answer at the house. I figured she'd come with you after all." He stared man-to-man with Donald.

Donald shook his head, his scowl darker and his eyes bright. "That's not like my little girl."

Kara put a restraining hand on Donald's arm. "I'm sure she's lost track of time shopping with one of the girls or with Irene. She and Irene were planning on shopping for new outfits." She beamed a smile from Donald to Ryan. And when Irene arrived without Miranda, Irene would say that Miranda got sick and went to bed.

Ryan made a comical face. "I forgot. She told me they were going shopping. I'm sorry to worry you." He clapped Donald on the shoulder. "Women and shopping." He rolled his eyes.

Kara blinked. Why was Ryan playing along? Did he know? "Miranda will be here when Irene and her family arrive."

"Good." Donald nodded, then hooked an arm around Ryan's

shoulders. "You missed it." He guided Ryan below deck. "A great fishing day. The monster that broke my rig…"

Kara lingered on deck. She couldn't cover for Miranda much longer. *Daughter, your normal life charade is over. Time for the taming to begin.*

Chapter Thirteen

Faint echoes of screams and nightmarish images writhed in Miranda's head. She struggled against her soft, warm restraints. *Wake up.* She forced her eyes open. Everything was out of focus. She blinked until her vision cleared.

She lay, unrestrained, in a twin-sized bed in an unfamiliar room. The room's ceiling and walls were an institutional beige. A writing table stood beneath a window with wire mesh embedded in the glass. A dark-haired young woman, wearing a starched white blouse and long charcoal gray skirt, sat in a straight-backed wooden chair near the head of the bed.

"Where am I?" Miranda's tongue was thick and coated. Her words were garbled. She sat up. A warm tingle crept up her neck and curled around her ears. Her vision darkened, and her stomach rolled. She leaned forward, braced her hands on the bed. She took slow, even breaths and worked the gunk out of her mouth. When she could focus again, she stared at the light blue cotton nightgown she wore. "Where are my clothes? And who are you?" She had meant to sound demanding, not hoarse and barely audible.

"I'm Susanna, guardian apprentice, first class, your guide

through Renewal." Susanna's smile showed every tooth in her head.

"Renewal?" Miranda's chest constricted. Renewal was part of the Redemption system. "Do you know who I am? I don't need re-education."

Susanna's smile softened. "Miranda, the Lord does not care whether you are the daughter of a councilor or the daughter of a pauper. Redemption is for all who have strayed." She patted Miranda's hand. "'When a man or a woman is unfaithful to the Lord, that person's sin condemns him. If, full of contrition, he confesses his sins, and he heeds correction, and he makes restitution and renews his faith, he is redeemed.' So sayeth Josiah in the first book of the Third Testament."

Sluggish, Miranda struggled to focus, to make sense of Susanna's words. "They drugged me."

"The Fellowship doesn't use drugs." Susanna's accent wasn't Piedmont or Bostonian or Deep South. "We believe in the power of the Spirit. Renewal is the final phase of Redemption. It's a community of petitioners and guardians who will lead you through correction and restitution. We'll pray and do good works until your soul's infused with the Spirit." Susanna's ever-present smile grew from big to Cheshire cat size.

Outside the room a deep bell rang.

"Oh." Susanna stood. "I'm sorry for going on so. God has given me a chatterbox tongue to teach me control, but I'm afraid it is a challenge." She nodded toward one of two doors on the far wall. "Let's get you showered and changed so you may join your fellow petitioners for lunch."

"Will Sarah be there?"

Susanna's smile vanished. "We don't seek out individuals in Redemption. We respect each petitioner's privacy. That's why we don't use names. You are petitioner number sixty-seven twelve. And you will be late if we don't hurry." She bent and put a warm, firm hand under Miranda's elbow. "Upsy daisy."

Miranda showered and dressed in a white shirt and dark blue

skirt. Then Susanna led her on a tour of the facility. She also recited a long list of rules: how one should address a guardian; what the different bells meant; and how the point system worked.

One earned points for praying, points for reading the Bible, points for cleanliness, and points for charity work. Points were taken away for tardiness or failure to fully participate in all petitioner duties. Petitioners with negative points paid penance in the Prayer Room. Susanna nodded at a petitioner who sat away from the others and started with every loud noise. She turned her back on the petitioner. Her pious pity vanished from her face, and she beamed at Miranda. "Don't worry. You'll have no trouble making your thousand points and earning a bus ride to the airport."

Miranda nodded. She would be a perfect petitioner.

~

Susanna didn't warn Miranda about the bland cafeteria food, didn't warn her that the daily Bible lessons were not-so-subtle scoldings, and didn't warn her that minutes dragged into meaningless days.

Miranda marked the number of days on the hinge-side of the closet door. She told time by the last meal she'd eaten and which bell had sounded.

Today was day four. The double chimes rang.

She hurried to the Community Room, hoping she could stay awake during the lesson. She took a seat at one of the long, folding tables. Her nights in Renewal were as nightmare-riddled as they'd been at home. She was afraid nightmares would earn demerits, afraid that talking about them would make them more real.

"Did everyone enjoy their noontime meal?" Sister Louisa, a senior-level guardian, had a round shape that could not be disguised by the pale gray robes she wore. She stood behind a lectern at the head of the Community Room. Behind her, high on the blood red wall, hung a white cross. "I can't hear you." She spoke in singsong. "Did you enjoy your meal?"

"Yes, Sister Louisa," Miranda said. *Did the other petitioners fake their enthusiasm too?*

"Today's project is for the needy in our missions in Kansas City. Please take one package from each box that's passed down the row and place it in the rattan basket in front of you."

Kansas City? This was the first mention of any city. *How did I get here?*

Miranda took a box from the woman on her right. Inside were bars of bath soaps bundled in groups of three. The soapy floral scent made her want to sneeze. She placed a bundle in her basket.

"The Bible tells us of a young man who wanted worldly things." Sister Louisa spoke like one of the traveling preachers at a tent revival, loud and full of emotion.

Miranda put a package of toothbrushes into the basket. She passed the box of toothbrushes to her left and nearly dropped the box. The woman seated two seats to her left had an uncanny resemblance to Aunt Beryl. But Aunt Beryl was dead. Forgetting where she was, Miranda gaped at the lookalike.

The petitioner on Miranda's right nudged her.

Miranda accepted the next box of goods. She transferred a ribbon-tied packet of washcloths from the box to her basket, then handed the box to the next woman. The Aunt Beryl lookalike faced the other direction. Miranda stared until the petitioner between them gave Miranda a strange look. Miranda pretended to straighten the items in her basket.

"He'd spent all his money. He couldn't pay his rent and had to beg for a place to stay."

She concentrated on filling her basket. A tube of Pepsodent toothpaste went into the basket next. Miranda passed the box left. Violet eyes locked with hers. A chill zipped down her spine. She sat back in her chair, stared straight ahead.

It can't be her. I went to Aunt Beryl's funeral.

"The young man thought, why am I in these rags, in the mud,

eating with pigs, when my father has a beautiful farm? What a sinful person I've been."

A throat-clogging spicy scent rose from the next box: Old Spice aftershave. Miranda breathed through her mouth. She reached into the box. Her hands shook. *What is wrong with me?*

Miranda swallowed and forced herself to pick up one of the red and white boxes and place it in her basket. She handed the carton of boxes to the next woman and caught violet eyes watching her again. Violet eyes winked right, left, right, and left again. *Aunt Beryl used to— How?*

Miranda focused on her basket, forced her breathing to slow, and put her hands in her lap to hide the palsy that shook her. She moved only when she had to and continued to fill her basket, never looking to her left. Silent questions without answers screamed through her.

"And the father said to the eldest son, this your brother was dead, and is alive: he was lost, and is found."

Chapter Fourteen

Beryl plucked a package of Pepsodent out of the box and dropped it into the basket in front of her. She hadn't anticipated Renewal being so crowded. The presence and the nattering of the guardians and the petitioners irritated her. After two weeks she wanted to punch someone. She'd start with the girl with the blonde hair who gawked at her. But the girl had an uncanny resemblance to Donald, an attractive, *feminine* Donald. Sigh. Punching someone wasn't worth going back to isolation. Beryl bit the inside of her cheek and made a face she'd made in another lifetime. The girl blanched, shrank away, and didn't look Beryl's direction again.

A councilor's daughter wouldn't be sent to Redemption. Perhaps a more distant relation? Her chair jerked. Every time she didn't fill her basket quickly enough or chorus "Praise God" enthusiastically enough, Thumper or Grimace kicked her chair. *They wouldn't dare beat me here, would they?*

The bell rang. Beryl rose, but a hand on each of her shoulders forced her back into her chair. Every muscle in her body tightened. It took more effort to act compliant in Renewal than it did in isolation.

She forced herself to relax one muscle group at a time. After every petitioner and the other guardians had left, Thumper and Grimace pulled her to a stand.

She took a deep breath, exhaled slowly. "Where to now?"

Grimace led the way. Thumper clamped a hand on Beryl's shoulder, pushing her more than necessary. They took her down a hall of doorways, back to her room.

At the door, Grimace blocked Beryl's view of the rotary dial on the combination lock. The rotary dial clicked eleven times, then six times, then four. They never bothered to keep her from listening, not even on the first day.

She had memorized the rhythm on the first day. And she'd memorized every step, every sound, and every face since.

"I thought this was open activities time in the recreation room." Beryl used her soft, amnesiac persona voice.

"You aren't used to crowds yet." Thumper glared a challenge at her. "You'll stay in your room during open activities."

Beryl didn't rise to the bait but stepped inside. "Thank you." She made her voice drip with gratitude.

The door sighed shut, and the lock snicked into place. Beryl did a slow three-sixty. *Too much room, too many choices.* She dropped to the floor and did one-armed push-ups. After one hundred, she was calmer, more like herself.

Sitting cross-legged on the floor, Beryl ran her fingers through the thick fibers of the carpet. Sister Louisa had said they were taking the baskets to the mission in Kansas City.

There was only one Redemption facility in Kansas: Leavenworth. *Kansas? Damn.* She not only had to escape this place but also had to cross more than a thousand miles without getting caught.

Soft pink-gold light filled the large wire mesh reinforced window in the west wall, drew her across the room. Her throat tightened, and her chest ached. Down below, slightly blurred by the wire mesh, part of a courtyard was visible: spring greens, acorn browns, and the brick wall that surrounded Redemption. Beyond the top of the wall, the sunset and horizon beckoned.

The western sky was awash with colors: gold, rose, and lavender that blended into darker hues. Unbidden, her hand went to the cool glass, straining to feel and smell the air.

Being in Kansas doesn't matter. I'll cross a million miles if I have to. She meant to keep her promise to her dying daughter.

Chapter Fifteen

M iranda pulled her needle through the fabric. The thread snarled into a huge knot. She groaned. *Another knot?* She set her hoop-stretched fabric on the side table and scanned the solarium. Quilters clustered around a quilting frame and chatted in hushed tones. Other petitioners sat on divans and upholstered armchairs scattered throughout the room. Knitting needles, crochet hooks, and stitching needles danced up and down, in and out. In the whole room, only one woman paid any attention to her.

Miranda had only seen Aunt Beryl's doppelgänger a few times in the past week and had never seen her during free activity time before. Today the woman sat in a green armchair across the room and stared. *I should talk to her. And say what? Hello, you look like my dead aunt?*

The doppelgänger crossed the room and stood in front of the blue and yellow striped drapes. In the sunshine-bright west window, she was a silhouette.

I have to find out. Miranda joined the woman. Close up, the resemblance to her dead aunt was disconcerting. "Hello, I'm

Miranda. I'm sorry for staring, but you look very much like someone I used to know."

"I almost didn't recognize you either." The woman's throaty voice gave Miranda goosebumps.

Miranda masked her unease with her daughter-of-the-councilor smile. "You recognize me from the news and have me at a disadvantage. You are?"

"I'm your Aunt Beryl."

Miranda's smile failed. "That's not possible. My aunt died in a car accident years ago."

The woman gave a forced laugh. "I guess the past ten years have been harder on me than I had hoped."

Miranda shook her head. "My father identified her at the hospital. We buried her."

The woman's face went very still. "Funny, Donald never mentioned that to me. Bet it made his life easier though, me being 'dead.'"

Miranda put a hand on the warm glass of the window to steady herself. *This must be some kind of trick or a test.*

"You're still the little skeptic, aren't you?"

A cold sweat covered her upper lip, moistened Miranda's palms. *The winks. Calling me the little skeptic. It* is *Aunt Beryl. But, how?*

"Miranda?" Susanna stood where Aunt Beryl had stood. "Are you all right?" Concern creased Susanna's face.

No, I've seen a ghost. "I'm fine." What else could she say? Aunt Beryl stood a few feet away, her back to Miranda but close enough to listen. Miranda glanced out the window. She wobbled.

Susanna put a hand on her arm, steadied her.

Miranda dredged up a smiling mask. "I guess looking down made me dizzy."

"Why don't you sit back down and finish your needlepoint?" Susanna's voice hinted she wasn't making a suggestion.

Miranda glanced at her abandoned stitchery project. There was nothing she wanted to do less. "It's tangled."

"There are other crafts to try." Susanna grasped Miranda's elbow firmly and guided her to the tables. "Mosaics, for example."

Six petitioners sat at the round table, each of them bent over boxes of tiny tiles sorting sizes, shapes, and colors. The tangy smell of Elmer's Glue hung over the table. Their mosaics depicted familiar biblical scenes.

Mosaics? When I've just learned my aunt isn't dead? "I'm not much of an artist."

"You don't have to be an artist. The scenes are stamped on the board." Susanna pulled out a chair for her.

Miranda sat.

Susanna set a box of backboards in front of her. "Fill in the shapes and colors with tiles. Glue the tiles to the board."

Miranda forced herself to give Susanna a grateful smile. "Seems easy enough." She flipped through the backboards stamped with pictures of Moses parting the Red Sea, the Prophet Josiah calming the mob at the Philadelphia Riot, and other famous scenes. She chose a backboard with the image of Daniel in the Lion's Den.

She pulled a box of yellow tiles toward her. Susanna hovered over her.

She pushed yellow tiles around on her board. She had to talk to Aunt Beryl. She couldn't wait to tell Daddy that his sister was alive. *Alive and in Redemption. How? Why?*

She reached into a box of blue tiles and bumped hands with another petitioner. Aunt Beryl. Miranda opened her mouth, but Beryl gave a tiny shake of her head and rolled her eyes. Miranda followed her look. A guardian stood very close behind Beryl and gave Miranda a big, bucktoothed smile. Miranda smiled uncertainly and pretended great interest in green tiles.

She'd assumed the bucktoothed guardian was Aunt Beryl's Susanna. Miranda pawed through red tiles and watched the guardians out of the corner of her eye. Eventually, Susanna moved away. The bucktoothed guardian never moved. A second guardian also stayed focused on Aunt Beryl. *Does she have two Susan-nas? Did they see us talking? Was that why they stood so close?*

The hour dragged on. When the lunch bell chimed, Miranda had more than half her tiles glued to her backboard, and Beryl's two guardians still hadn't moved.

Miranda carried her unfinished backboard to the storage closet. Other petitioners jostled her in the scramble to put things away and get to the lunch line in guardian-pleasing timeliness.

"Courtyard."

Miranda stole a sidelong glance at her aunt. She gave a slight nod and slid her backboard onto a shelf. After lunch, the petitioners had a two-hour exercise period. Miranda had never seen Beryl during her exercise period, but it was the one place in Renewal where they could talk in private.

Chapter Sixteen

Kara stopped at her secretary's desk and shoved her radio handset at the woman. "Booth sixty-one needs a brace for the backdrop. Get engineering down there." She paused to gather herself. "How long has Dr. Locke been waiting?"

"I radioed you immediately."

Kara breezed into her office with a smile big enough to hide her what-are-you-doing-here anxiety. "Dr. Locke, I'm sorry to have kept you waiting."

The short, slender man turned and peered at her through thick, oversized glasses. "No problem," Dr. Locke said. His dark, slicked-back hair and his large glasses gave him a big-eyed, King Solomon look. "Your secretary let me in. I've been viewing the show from up here." One didn't expect such a deep, rumbling voice from such an anemic-looking scientist. He turned back to the window. "This year's vendor additions are impressive: Beech-Nut, Heinz, Nabisco, Carter's, Frigidaire. What is going on over there?" He jabbed a finger at the window.

Oh no. Has he seen Weldon showing the Russian ambassador around? She hurried across the room and onto the platform. Locke pointed at the stage in the northeast corner. Her stomach unknotted. "That's Big Brother Bob Emery from *The Small Fry Club*."

Dr. Locke gave her a blank look.

She swallowed a smile. "He's a children's television show host. He's reading to the children."

"I see. Better babies must have their minds developed as well." Below them, thousands of families lined up at the examination booths. Others studied the displays, learned new parenting skills, and enjoyed the small entertainments. "Smokey Bear is over there, and those clowns on stilts are making balloon animals." Up here, a low, indistinct rumble was all that remained of the din of voices, children's squeals and cries, and overhead announcements below.

"You should be proud of yourself, Kara. Look at all the lives you've improved."

"It's not enough." Some of the children's health would improve because of what their parents learned at the contest. But many of the families would forget what they learned the minute they left the arena. She glanced at Dr. Locke out of the corner of her eyes. "Did you drive all the way up here to see the contest?"

"Lord, no. I don't have the fortitude to hurtle a couple of tons of metal down a narrow ribbon of asphalt." He actually shuddered. "Louis drove me here."

She guided him to the settee in the corner of the room. "That must have been stressful. Please sit." The fragrant smell of Dr. Locke's favorite ginger tea rose from her tea service. The silver tea service sat on the coffee table between the settee and the Queen Anne chairs. "I see my secretary has been useful. Let me pour tea for you, and you tell me why you've troubled yourself."

She poured tea into his cup, then sat back in the chair, crossed her ankles, folded her hands in her lap, and waited.

Dr. Locke peered at her over the rim of his teacup. "I need six hundred thousand dollars' worth of equipment."

She forced herself to smile so her voice would sound friendlier. "I thought you had all the equipment you needed."

"The refrigeration unit developed a leak last night."

Kara gripped the front edge of the silken cushion of her chair and leaned forward. "And the eggs?"

"We lost one whole unit before we plugged the leak."

Scarcely daring to breathe, she asked, "How many eggs were in the unit?"

"Three hundred."

Kara relaxed, breathed easier. *Bad news, but not bad enough that the deal Weldon was brokering downstairs would be undone.* "Quick thinking to plug the leak. The damage could have been worse."

"The damage will be worse." He set his teacup down carefully on the polished walnut coffee table. He spoke slowly, pronouncing every syllable. "You must understand. The patch is temporary. Imprecise. The temperature in those units must be precise, or ten years of harvesting will be for nothing."

Only by squeezing the life out of the soft cushion beneath her could she pleasantly remind him, "There are plenty more idiots and epileptics in the state of Virginia."

Dr. Locke stood. "Have you understood nothing of my research?" His voice dipped low like a growl. He paced to the observation windows and back. "Harvesting the eggs during the sterilization process is nothing if we lose subject one. Without subject one's cells, we will have to start all over again. Find another subject one." He planted himself in front of her. "The refrigeration units must be replaced. Immediately. If you don't have the funds, ask the J.D. Wagner Foundation for more."

"We can't ask the Wagner Foundation for more money." *Their grant people will demand answers. That would be—inconvenient.*

Weldon burst through the door. "We did—it."

"Weldon, darling." She tilted her head toward the doctor. "We have a guest."

Weldon's gaze took in Dr. Locke. "I see." His expression settled into his business face.

"I'm glad you're here." Dr. Locke crossed the room and pumped Weldon's hand. "You understand these things."

Her jaw tightened. She had researched and funded his project, yet he refused to admit that *she*, not Weldon or Donald, was his patron. "He has an equipment problem." She indicated the sitting area. "Won't you join us for a cup of tea?"

Weldon's nose wrinkled. He hated tea, but he played along and sipped from the cup she poured for him. He put his teacup down and gave Dr. Locke an appraising look. "How much do you need?"

"Six hundred thousand dollars. The refrigeration unit is failing." He explained that the failure had destroyed three hundred eggs.

"Don't worry, Doctor, we will take care of everything." Weldon stood. "Is your driver waiting for you?"

Dr. Locke stood. "Why, yes, he is."

Kara remained seated, her temples throbbing, her smile frozen in place.

Weldon shook his hand. "We won't keep you any longer then. I'm sure they need you at the facility to make certain those eggs are cool. We'll wire you the money after the banks open tomorrow." Weldon guided Dr. Locke across the room, practically shoved him out of the room, and closed and locked the door behind him.

Weldon raced back to Kara, pulled her to her feet, and danced her in circles.

"Let go of me, Weldon." She pushed him away. "How big is this deal you made? Can they deliver six *hundred thousand* dollars by tomorrow?"

His eyes glittered, and a triumphant smile lit his face. "How about a cool one-point-two *million* first thing tomorrow?"

Her mouth dropped open. "How many Azrael do they expect for that kind of money?"

"A mere one hundred."

What she could do with that money... But her stomach clenched. Dr. Locke had only produced a dozen functional Azrael thus far. *What if he can't produce a hundred?*

"Ah, come on, Kara, celebrate." Weldon grabbed her and waltzed the length of the room. "This is only the beginning."

It *was* the beginning. But Weldon couldn't see past the potential wealth. Neither could Donald. Only she knew how a few cells grown in a lab would change America.

Chapter Seventeen

Grimace pushed Beryl through the door. Beryl exaggerated her stumble out into the cool sunshine.

"Promises made to the Prophet must be kept," Grimace muttered, whether to her or to Thumper, Beryl couldn't say.

"Of course they must," Beryl answered, her amnesia persona intact. "Did you make a promise to the Prophet?"

Thumper snatched Beryl's arm and forced a quick march to the farthest corner of the courtyard. "You know the promise we speak of," Thumper whispered in her ear. She and Grimace retreated to their respective stations by the door and the gate.

The courtyard was a huge expanse of concrete divided into smaller areas by a ten-foot-tall chain-link fence.

Warm-up stretches ended in push-ups. Beryl dusted off her hands and breathed in scents of dust and sun-warmed concrete. She couldn't get enough fresh air. It wasn't free of the stench of Redemption, but that would come.

In two weeks of observing, she'd heard whispers about punishments, the Prayer Room, and, for the fortunate, a bus or plane ticket home. Escape from Renewal was possible.

She started jumping jacks, turning a quarter-turn with every fifth jumping jack. Every twenty jumping jacks she viewed the entire fenced courtyard.

Each football-field-sized, fenced area had a distinct use: basketball, softball, walking, and calisthenics. Two sections held buildings: one labeled Infirmary, the other Maximum Security.

A twelve-foot chain-link fence topped with barbed wire circled the perimeter of the yard. Six feet beyond the perimeter fence stood a thick, twenty-foot-tall, red brick wall. Every hundred feet along that wall stood a sentry tower. She could smell lilacs growing somewhere outside the walls.

Miranda milled around the door with other petitioners. "Brother dear held my funeral, did he?" Beryl had considered the possibility that they'd say she was dead. Ten years was a long time. Besides, an aspiring First Apostle couldn't have a sister serving a life sentence in Redemption.

Twenty jumping jacks later, Beryl noticed that Thumper and Grimace had moved back toward the main building. The main building was a long rectangle of white limestone with a large central dome. Renewal was the wing that jutted out from this end of the rectangle. An identical wing stood on at the far end.

Petitioners flocked together in small groups that moved aimlessly around the yard. They sounded like sheep bleating. *They do what they're told, think what they're told, and see what they're told.* She had thought Miranda was different, but the girl followed the flock.

Beryl turned again. Miranda broke away from the others. *I may have misjudged my niece.* She stopped, wiped sweat from her eyes, then bent with her hands on her thighs and caught her breath. She stayed bent over until Miranda's shadow was visible.

"Don't come any closer. Drop and do push-ups." Beryl stood and glared at Miranda.

Miranda dropped to the concrete and began awkward push-ups.

Beryl went to the chin-up bar. Perpendicular to Thumper's position and parallel to Miranda, she could watch both. "Questions?" She grunted, lifted her chin to the bar. Despite the sunshine, the bar was cool.

"My father"—Miranda's huffing and puffing revealed how out-of-shape she was—"was tricked."

A sheep after all. Beryl considered not responding, but she needed Miranda to confirm or belie the Prophet's story. "Nope."

"You can't believe that. He loved"—Miranda's voice caught —"loves you."

"Wrong again." The fire in Beryl's blood lent energy to her chin-ups.

"What if *you're* wrong?" Miranda rolled over and sat up facing Beryl.

Out of the corner of her eye, Beryl caught movement. Thumper walked toward them. "They're watching."

Miranda lay on the ground, did one sit-up.

Thumper paused, watchful.

"I came here by unanimous Council vote." Beryl's chin touched the bar. She lowered herself again.

"The Council voted?" Miranda's face clouded. She groaned during her second sit-up.

Beryl studied her niece. *How can she not know that her councilor daddy isn't a nice man?*

"I heard Donald's about to become the First Apostle." Beryl winced; she sounded so—coffee klatch.

"Daddy says it's in poor taste to talk about it before the Prophet's death. May the Prophet's health be restored."

So proper of Donald. She changed the direction of her questions. "Why are you here?"

Miranda wrapped her arms around her legs. "I found a dead man."

What? Beryl dropped from the bar into a deep knee bend.

Miranda busied herself doing more sit-ups. She didn't speak again until she'd done a set of five. "I never saw a dead man before." She stretched out on the ground, her arms over her head, breathing hard. "Sarah and I ran, but they caught us. They drugged me." Miranda rolled onto her knees and stood. "I woke up in Renewal." She flattened her hands on the ground in front of her toes. "I don't know where Sarah is."

Beryl didn't miss the trembling Miranda tried to disguise by shaking out her muscles before doing more toe-touches. "So you're saying Donald didn't send you here?"

Miranda stopped, bent over, hands on the ground. "How can you think Daddy would do that?"

Beryl changed to her cool-down routine. She wasn't sure if she knew how to have a conversation anymore, but she'd have to have several with Miranda. She needed to know whether the girl was as innocent as she acted, or if she were a Trojan gift.

Miranda raised her arms into the air and leaned to her right. "They told Daddy you died in an automobile accident. Burned beyond recognition."

"I wonder whose body was in that wreck?"

The color in Miranda's face drained away.

The bell clanged.

Miranda straightened. She wiped her cheeks with the backs of her hands, then walked past Beryl without another word.

Beryl stretched and watched Miranda pass Thumper and join the line of petitioners at the gate. *No matter what Miranda has done or what she's up to, she's a councilor's daughter. She won't stay here long. I can use that. Make certain I don't stay a minute longer than she does.*

Thumper approached, bouncing her truncheon on one hand.

Beryl settled back into her mousy, amnesiac personality. She crossed the yard and joined the line of petitioners. Grimace and Thumper fell in behind her. She could hear *the thwack-thwack* of the truncheon. Her back prickled. *Before I leave Redemption, you'll pay for every blow.*

Chapter Eighteen

K ara clenched her teeth and walked around yet another group of tourists holding their hats and tipping their heads up. Many people pilgrimaged to the seven-story, white marble Fellowship Center perched on the banks of the Potomac.

More tourists clogged the rotunda. They ooohed and ahhhed in response to the tour guide's patter about the larger-than-life-sized painting of the Prophet Josiah's visitation by Gabriel. Kara pushed through the gawking crowd. *We shouldn't have to put up with tourists. As the wife of the First Apostle, I will give the councilors' wives access to the councilors-only door.*

She made her way to the guard's desk that blocked access to the elevators.

"Good morning, Sister Clarke. I didn't see your name on your husband's guest list today."

She bristled. "You wouldn't." *The man knows me by name, but I have to be on a guest list?* Another change she'd be making. She reminded herself to relax, smile graciously, and give him a little of her Piedmont accent. "You may call me Sister Kara."

"Yes, Sister Clarke, I mean, Sister Kara."

She put her hand on the gate. "Weldon Lancaster called me

here." An inconvenience she had tried to avoid. She'd asked Weldon to attend the weekly briefings during the contest. But this morning he had insisted she had to come. *If only Miranda had appreciated her life. No other mother gives her children the advantages I've given mine.*

The guard consulted his loose-leaf notebook and shook his head. "I'm afraid your name isn't on his guest list either."

"Kara, there you are." Weldon rushed out of an elevator to stand by the guard.

The guard frowned at Weldon. "You should have put Sister Kara on the guest list."

"I called down, but your line was busy." Weldon opened the gate.

The guard pressed his lips together and pushed the visitors' register toward Kara.

"You can trust a Senior Councilor's wife with one of these." Weldon reached in front of the guard and picked up a plastic encased ID card labeled "Guest."

Kara clipped the ID to the lapel of her gray lightweight wool suit. She swept past the guard, past Weldon, and past the attendant who held the elevator door open.

Weldon followed. "Down."

The attendant pressed the button. The elevator doors whooshed shut.

Kara opened her mouth. Weldon's sidelong glance at a camera attached to ceiling stopped her. She covered a pretend yawn.

The doors opened, and the elevator bell dinged. Weldon gestured for her to exit first. He guided her down an institutional beige corridor devoid of any decoration.

He didn't speak until they'd rounded the corner. "I know you're upset, Kara." He spoke fast and low. "But when I saw what the guardian brought, there was no doubt you had to see it."

His tone made the vein in her temple throb. "What did she bring?"

He locked eyes with hers. "Classroom ten. Whatever you see or do, be Miranda's loving mother."

"Is all this secrecy necessary? Can't you just tell me what's going on?" She couldn't help but speak in a husky whisper. He was spooking her.

"Classroom ten." He kissed the top of her head and hurried back down the hall.

Room ten was a tiered lecture theater. She'd entered at the top.

The guardian waiting for her wore the pale gray robe of a Level Four. "Peace to you, Sister Clarke."

"And to you." This guardian had a significant overbite. It would have earned her a low score on lip symmetry and dentition, had she ever attended a Better Baby Contest. "My brother said you had something to show me."

The guardian blinked as if she were taken aback by Kara's directness. "Please take a seat."

"Get on with it." Kara pushed an unpadded wooden seat down and sat. The coolness of the chair sent a shiver across her shoulders. "I have to get back to the contest."

The guardian went to a film projector sitting atop a wheeled cart on the apron of the next tier down. Film snaked from a large, 8mm reel on the backside, through the machine, and back to an empty reel. The room lights darkened, and the projector hummed. The screen erupted into bright black-and-white images of a sparsely furnished bedroom. Miranda entered the room, sat, and read the Bible.

"Fast forward to what you need to show me." Kara used as civil a tone as she could manage. *Does no one understand that I have a contest to run?*

The image of Miranda double-timed through her bedtime routine. She climbed into bed and tossed and turned in her sleep. The images blurred from one night to the next.

Kara didn't know whether she should be relieved that Miranda's big problem was getting a good night's sleep or fly into a rage at the waste of time. The images slowed, continued with another fitful night. Miranda flailed her arms as if she fended off an attacker. She woke, scrambled to where the bed met the corner of the room, hugged her knees, and glanced wide-eyed around the room. The screen blurred through more nights.

Again and again, Miranda woke, sat up, and cast terrified glances around the room. Sometimes she muttered something, sometimes she was silent.

"Enough." Kara bit her lower lip. *This is precisely what Redemption was to stop.* She eyed the guardian. "What does she say?"

"Foreign-sounding words, but not in any known language."

No secrets to cover up. Kara expelled the breath she'd been holding. *But what to do? Miranda has to stop having these nightmares and come home before the Prophet dies. And she must meet the guardians' idea of a proper Redemption.* "Why did you show me this?"

"She is failing Redemption."

Kara marched down the aisle and planted herself in front of the guardian. "Miranda is the daughter of a councilor. She *cannot* fail Redemption. It's your job to see that she does not."

The guardian drew her lips up over her huge teeth in a mockery of a smile. "Redemption is a personal journey tailored to each individual's needs. We didn't know how powerful Miranda's demon is."

Kara caught her breath. *We.* "Others have seen this film?"

The guardian nodded.

Kara calmed her breathing. She remembered Weldon's advice and smiled a worried-mother smile. "Forgive me. Her father and I don't understand. We raised our children to be good citizens of the Fellowship. Why is Miranda so afflicted?" Her voice dripped with sweetness.

The guardian's expression softened. "I understand, but have faith. Like the Prodigal Son, she will return to the path of righteousness, and to you."

"So she will finish Redemption in a week, two at the most?"

"Only the Lord knows when her spirit will be moved." The guardian shook her head mournfully.

Kara put on a mother's look of desperation. "Her father and I would do anything to help her heal faster." She clasped the guardian's rough hands in hers and hoped the guardian was bright enough to take the hint.

The guardian's pious expression registered surprise, then settled into a saintly serenity. "For a tithe, there is the Prayer Room." The guardian studied Kara.

A tithe, she says. Kara suppressed a sigh of satisfaction. She released her hold on the guardian and blinked slowly, turning on her best innocent face and voice. "And this Prayer Room will redeem Miranda?"

"The first stage is prayer and fasting for two or three days."

"So long?" Kara made her voice crack.

The guardian gave her a sharp look, then clasped her hands together and bowed her head. "If the demon resists the first stage, the Seminarian may find it necessary to drive the demon out with his cane."

"And he can do that in a day?"

"The cane can be—effective, but it takes time to heal after such a vigorous exorcism."

"A week?"

"Two or three."

Kara lowered her head. *I'll have Weldon apply pressure, make certain it takes no more than two weeks.* "We praise the Lord for his healing."

The guardian gave Kara a sly look. "You would pay to have your daughter caned?"

Kara returned her look without blinking. "Spare the rod, spoil the child."

Chapter Nineteen

M iranda woke struggling for air. Her chest ached from the weight of him. His scent made her stomach roll. She took shallow breaths, trying not to vomit.

It was a dream. A nightmare.

Dreams don't make me sick. Not even nightmares. Someone was here. An intruder in Redemption?

She drew her knees to her chest. After hundreds of these episodes, she still had never seen an intruder. *Maybe it's not a here-and-now reality. Maybe it's a memory of something that happened.*

If it is a memory, why haven't you always remembered?

I don't know.

Miranda trembled. Her teeth chattered. The bed creaked with her shuddering.

The overhead light flashed on.

Oh no. She hugged herself tighter, but it only made her quaking worse.

"What are you doing, petitioner?" The disembodied voice crackled over the tinny intercom.

"Praying."

You lie to the guardian?

She laced her fingers together. *Thoughts are prayers too.* She spoke aloud. "Father of Truth, I am lost. Help me find my way." Her voice trembled.

You are lost.

"Why didn't you ask for our intercession?"

"I am unworthy." Her chattering teeth made her words indistinct. *Is intercession what happened to the other petitioners? The ones that didn't return?*

"Do you ask for intercession now?"

What else could she say? "Yes."

The door lock clicked, and the door opened.

A dark figure slipped in and shut the door behind her. The lock cycled again.

"Father of Truth, give me a sign."

You ask the Father of Truth for help? With your lies?

"Shall we kneel?" The guardian lowered herself to her knees. Her skirts swished, and her petticoats crinkled.

Miranda threw back her covers and slid to the floor. She caught a glimpse of a bucktoothed smile and had to brace herself against the bed frame to keep from falling. *Where's Susanna?*

"A demon haunts you in sleep."

Miranda tightened her grip on the cold bed frame. "It was a bad dream." Tremors added a vibrato to her voice.

"This time, the demon nearly won your soul."

No. Not a demon. "It was a nightmare."

"In sleep, your soul is honest. Your repentance isn't soul deep." The guardian sounded like she was enjoying this.

Foreboding rose like bile in her throat. Miranda tried not to sound desperate. "I have repented."

The guardian put a warm hand on the top of Miranda's head. "With our Father's aid, we, the guardians, will light your path and lead you to righteousness. Repeat after me: Holy Father, unto whom all hearts are open, all desires known, and from whom no secrets are hid…"

Miranda repeated the prayer flawlessly. She'd learned that one as a toddler.

But you don't believe, do you?

The guardian's hand moved from Miranda's head to her shoulder and squeezed. "Your soul is weak. But fear not, we will exorcise the demon from you in the Prayer Room."

Miranda swayed, blinked rapidly, and struggled against a wave of dizziness. *The Prayer Room.*

You need their prayers.

No.

You are damned.

My nightmares aren't demons. They're memories of something terrible.

You are crazy.

No. I'm not. I won't be crazy.

~

MIRANDA FOLLOWED THE GUARDIAN DOWN A LONG, BEIGE HALLWAY. The guardian's skirt billowed and swayed, making her appear to float above the floor.

The blank walls ended, and Miranda stood in front of a metal door etched with the sign of the Fellowship.

Miranda sucked in a breath and took a half step backwards.

The guardian's grip stopped her. "One of the lost needs your intercession, Brother."

Metal clanked against metal, and the door slid open.

Bright light spilled from the room. Miranda squinted and shielded her eyes with both hands.

"Here you will find your Redemption."

Miranda's pulse beat a double-time rhythm. Her chest ached with the need for more air. She stepped over the threshold into a barren white room.

The door clanked shut behind her. She couldn't swallow. She had no spit.

"Kneel at the altar." The deep voice was so close his breath brushed across her ear.

She shrank away. Her back hit the cold metal door.

In his white robe, the Seminarian's head appeared to hover in midair. In one hand, he held a bamboo staff. He banged the staff against the floor. "Prostrate yourself at the altar and beg the Lord's forgiveness."

Covered with a deep royal purple altar cloth, it stood three feet high on sturdy slab legs.

Where did that come from?

A firm thwack across the back of her thighs dropped her to her knees. She swallowed a shout of surprise and pain and scuttled to the altar. She propped her elbows on the top of the altar and laced her fingers together.

The staff rapped her knuckles.

She gasped and resisted the instinct to pull her hands apart.

"Raise your hands in supplication."

She raised her hands above her head.

A smooth, recorded tenor prayed, "Forgive me, Father, for I have sinned."

She repeated the prayers aloud. And she prayed silently for salvation from the Prayer Room, from her nightmares, from the staff that stung her shoulders whenever she moved.

The prayer went on and on. The words ran together in a humming, pulsing, almost tangible thing.

Her muscles shook and strained to keep her arms in the air. Her feet were numb. Her shoulders ached and burned. She grew hoarse.

The voice reciting the prayers grew louder and changed pitch, from tenor to baritone: "—a sinner like me." *Daddy?* She looked for him, and the staff stung her shoulders. Her father's voice prayed and shamed and scolded. Then, he touched her.

❧

His hand started at the top of her head and stroked downward, his thumb caressing her cheek. From the top of her head down her cheek to her shoulder, then her arm. The top of her head, her cheek, shoulder, arm, then her leg. His hand slid down her arm to her leg, then plucked at her panties.

She whimpered, "Daddy, don't."

"Can you hear me?"

Miranda shrank from the hand. Shrank from the voice. She was cold. Her head hurt and lay on something silky, yet hard.

"Do you hear me?"

The Seminarian. "Yes." She blinked her eyes open, raised her head. She'd slumped onto the altar. She touched the tender place on her forehead. *I'm in the Prayer Room. Not home. Not five years old.*

"Demon, who are you that possesses this woman?"

"Demon?"

"Name yourself, demon."

No. Not a demon. Daddy— Miranda's stomach heaved and twisted and heaved again. Empty, her stomach found no relief.

"Release this woman to praise the name of God."

"Not a demon." Miranda rose to her knees. Her legs cramped. She grabbed her thighs and remembered other hands grabbing her. A moan escaped her. "Noooo. Please. No." She hid her face in her hands and rocked back and forth.

"Out, I command you, in the name of the Lord, *out.*

A sharp sting whipped across her shoulders. She cried out.

The voices of the Seminarian, her father, and her own cries blended unintelligibly. She couldn't make sense of it. Sobs shook her. She had no answer to the Seminarian's questions, nor her own. Miranda shook her head. "I don't know, I don't know, I don't know."

The staff whistled through the air and cracked across her shoulders.

She screamed and fell to the floor, curled in a ball. *I won't be crazy. I won't.*

～

MIRANDA SAT IN THE NOISY CAFETERIA CHOKING DOWN COLD, pasty oatmeal. She'd awakened in Renewal this morning. Alone. In her old room. No junior guardian to greet her. No orientation tour.

She couldn't guess how many drug-fogged days she'd spent in the infirmary. Judging from the tenderness of her shoulders and back, not long enough and yet too long. She stirred her oatmeal without eating, consumed by her nightmares. She probed them and her memory trying to reconcile the irreconcilable. *If my nightmares are truth, are my memories lies?*

She vacillated. Her father had violated her. Her father hadn't violated her; a stranger had violated her. Her father had violated her…

Miranda couldn't stand the uncertainty. She had to find proof one way or the other.

Someone bumped her chair, hard. She spun out of her chair to her feet, her hands knotted into fists.

"'Scuse me," Beryl said.

Miranda struggled to bring her breathing and her pulse back to normal. *Beryl is still here!* Miranda made her voice serene. "You're excused. Next time, be more careful."

"Good advice." One of her guardians nudged Beryl forward.

Miranda took her tray with her bowl of uneaten oatmeal to the conveyor belt and followed Beryl out of the cafeteria. Questions burned inside her. She rolled a shoulder and winced at the pain that sliced across her back. Exercising in the courtyard would hurt. Beryl's answers might be more painful. Miranda put her hand on the wall for a moment, steadied herself, and then strode out of the room toward answers.

Chapter Twenty

Kara held Donald's hand and watched the Prophet's limousine pull away from the curb. The Prophet had performed the blessing of the Better Baby Contest winners but excused himself immediately after. *How much longer could he last?* The night swallowed the limo's taillights. The sun had set hours ago, taking its warmth and leaving a chill in the air. She shivered and nudged Donald, who took the hint. They re-entered the Arlington Municipal Auditorium's ballroom.

The room sparkled with light reflected from fine crystal glasses and ice sculptures. More than a thousand voices and the distinctive chime of crystal and bone china filled the air. Her only disappointment was that neither the president nor the vice president could attend.

"You've outdone yourself." Donald's chest puffed out in pride.

"All for a good cause, dear." Kara permitted herself a smile. The Prophet's appearance had all but sealed Donald's appointment as the First Apostle. She patted Donald's arm, and they descended to mingle among her guests.

Dressed in their best suits and beautiful silk, taffeta, and lace dresses, her guests included distinguished and influential people from up and down the Eastern Seaboard. She guided Donald through the room, speaking to each of their important guests. After they'd stopped at Senator Nixon's table, she and Donald split up to cover the room more efficiently.

She made certain she mentioned a Better Baby Contest crew member or patron by name at each table. She answered questions about eugenics and voiced her dream that someday every baby born would be a "better baby." She smiled for pictures, donations flowed, and her mood soared.

"Gram-ma." Sandra stood on her chair and waved.

"Sit down, Sandra." Kara hurried to her side and helped her sit. "Remember, you must be on your best behavior. You are a councilor's granddaughter."

"Mama, this has been the best contest ever." Irene rounded the table and threw her arms around Kara in an embarrassing hug.

Kara extracted herself from her youngest daughter. "Thank you, dear." She nodded at her son-in-law. "Felix."

Felix tipped his head in greeting. He was a quiet man, but he made her daughter happy and he wouldn't be a patent attorney forever.

David, the redhead and the youngest of her brood, grinned. "This is a killer shindig." Twenty-one and on his own for the first time, he wore a brown tweed suit and a crooked, bright yellow bow tie. *For heaven's sake. He's forgotten everything I taught him.*

She straightened his tie. "You look like a salesman."

David blushed. "It's new."

"Tomorrow you must give it to the needy at the mission."

He glowered at her as if he might argue. She locked eyes with him. He looked away and murmured, "Yes, Mother."

"Ladies and gentlemen. Please take your seats." The master of ceremonies had an announcer's voice. "You won't want to miss our next guests."

Kara excused herself and hurried to join Donald at the head table.

Donald held her chair. "I wish Miranda could be here. She'd have been the belle of the ball." He flashed a charming smile. "Next to you, of course, my dear."

Now he'd done it. She'd managed not to think of Miranda for the last couple of hours.

She smiled at her clueless table companions and took a sip of the sparkling fruit punch. Applause broke out, welcoming the Blackwood Brothers Quartet and their featured singer, Elvis Presley, onto the stage. They launched into their hit song, "Peace in the Valley."

Those blasted guardians and their rules of Redemption had delayed Miranda's return too long. No one had questioned Kara's cover story about a remote spa getaway for the bride-to-be. But if the Prophet died and Miranda didn't attend her father's inauguration as First Apostle, people would talk in a most unchristian way.

She concentrated on the singers. They sang a lively version of "Joshua Fought the Battle of Jericho." She clapped along with the audience.

A movement in the corner of her eye caught her attention. Weldon stood in the aisle next to the far wall. He beckoned to her. *I can't leave in the middle of a performance. I'm at the head table.*

The final strains of "Satisfied" hung in the air when the tuxedoed master of ceremonies made an unscheduled appearance on stage. Kara couldn't imagine what he thought he was doing. She glanced at Weldon, who shrugged.

"Excuse me, folks." The master of ceremonies waved his hands in a quieting motion. The applause for the song died away. "I hate to intrude on everyone's good time, but I have an important announcement to make." He cleared his throat. "I regret to inform you that our revered Prophet Palmer Gerard"—a sob escaped him—"rests in the arms of Jesus."

Kara gasped and rose to her feet. Everyone in the audience was on their feet too. She stood on her tippy toes. *Where is Weldon? Miranda has to come home. Now.*

Chapter Twenty-One

Miranda sat on the edge of the bed, stunned. *The Prophet is dead.* After the guardians had made the announcement, they'd cleared the community room. *How should I react?* He was her father's cousin once removed, but she'd never known him as family. He'd been the Prophet her whole life.

The guardians had escorted her back to her room. Pray, they'd told her. Ask God to guide the Fellowship Assembly in choosing a First Apostle. But Miranda couldn't pray. Not for the Assembly. Definitely not for them to elect her father First Apostle.

She needed to warn the Council, warn everyone. They had to know that her father was—that he had— She forced herself to finish the thought: *my father violated me. No one will believe me. Not without proof.* How could she prove it?

She had hoped to question Aunt Beryl. But she hadn't seen her aunt since breakfast her first day back. No matter what Aunt Beryl said, she couldn't prove the abuse happened. She wasn't there. *I can't even say I remember anything more than a nightmare.* Miranda's head throbbed. She went to the bathroom and splashed cold water on her face.

The door to her room opened. "Miranda?"

Miranda recognized Susanna's voice, though she hadn't seen her in weeks. "I'm here." She grabbed the towel and left the bathroom.

Susanna gave Miranda a tremulous smile and placed a medium-sized cardboard box on the bed. "There." She wiped her hands on her skirt. Her face clouded, and tears trickled down her cheeks. She swiped at her tears with the backs of her hands. "I'm sorry. I shouldn't be sad. He's gone to a much better place." She took a deep breath and gave Miranda a forced smile. "Besides, now is a time for you to rejoice."

"Me?" Miranda towel-dried her face and tossed the towel into the bathroom. "Why would I rejoice?"

"You're going home tomorrow."

Miranda's stomach tightened like she'd been punched. She couldn't move.

Susanna rushed to her side, put a supportive arm around her waist, and helped her to the bed.

"I'm sorry," Susanna said. "I should have remembered the Prophet was more than a prophet to you. He was family." She stroked Miranda's hand.

Susanna's hands were warm. Miranda's weren't.

"It's confusing, I'm sure. But it's okay to be sad and happy. You're redeemed and going home to your loved ones." Susanna opened the box. "Your mother sent fresh clothes—"

"My mother?" Miranda struggled to understand.

Susanna frowned. "You didn't expect us not to tell your mother, did you? She'd have thought you were Taken."

Miranda put her hand over her pounding heart. *Of course Mama knew.*

"She's overjoyed that you'll be home in plenty of time to finish planning your wedding."

Mama thought they would make me an obedient daughter. A daughter who would marry the man of Mama's dreams.

"What's wrong?"

Normal petitioners would be happy to go home. She scrambled for a reasonable explanation. "I'm afraid it will be awkward."

"Aw, sweetie. Relax."

If she took her hand off her chest, she would fly apart.

"Remember things are only awkward for the sinners, the unredeemed. They'll welcome you home as warmly as if you've been on vacation. In a way, you have. You've been on a *spiritual* vacation." Susanna gave Miranda's shoulders a squeeze, then reached into the box. "Let's see what we have here." She pulled out Miranda's blue polka-dot dress, gave it a practiced snap, and laid it on the bed. Next came underclothes, shoes, and a purse. "Oh, look. This will remind you of your family's love." She held a photograph out to Miranda.

Miranda stared at it. Her mother, father, sister, brother, and she sat posed in front of last year's Christmas tree and stared back at her. She held the photograph and trembled.

"I'll take you to the bus at seven o'clock sharp. I'll give you your plane ticket then. The bus driver will take you to the airport and stay with you until you board the plane. You'll land in Washington, DC at two-ten. Your family will pick you up at the airport."

She prattled on about how life after Renewal would be wonderful. Miranda stared at the picture, trying to see the truth behind the smiles.

Chapter Twenty-Two

They had locked Beryl in her room hours ago with a roughness that had set off her internal alarms. After they'd left, she had reached into her bra for the Prophet's pardon. It was gone. She didn't know how they'd gotten it without her knowing, but they did.

Now they were back. Their steps were heavy, their shoulders slumped, their expressions grim.

Something was wrong.

Grimace closed the door. Thumper aimed her stun stick at Beryl.

Beryl didn't like the way they looked. She didn't expect it to work, but she had to try. "Sister Marie, I'll take that new mattress now."

Grimace didn't respond to the code words. Thumper handed the stun stick to Grimace.

"Palmer won't like it that you've ignored his orders," Beryl said.

Thumper drove a fist into Beryl's stomach.

She doubled over, coughing and gasping. *Damn.* She'd gotten soft without the daily bouts as Thumper's punching bag. She straightened up and readied herself for the next blow.

"Dead or not, you call him the Prophet."

Palmer dead? Son of a bitch died too soon. "Ooof." The second blow robbed her of breath. *Thumper isn't using the truncheon.* "Uhn." *That means she can't leave visible injuries. There's still a chance.* Beryl fell to the floor and curled into a ball.

"She's had enough," Grimace said.

Thumper pulled her to her feet. "Clean up." Grimace gave the stun stick back to Thumper.

Beryl went into the bathroom. She tied the bath towel around her head and splashed water on her face. She limped out of the bathroom.

"Oh, I forgot." Slowly she moved as if to return to the bathroom. Thumper closed the short distance between them.

Beryl wheeled around, jabbed Thumper in the chest, hard. She slid her fist up Thumper's sternum, rammed her thumb into the woman's soft throat. Thumper dropped the stun stick. She fell to her knees, gurgling and gasping for air.

Grimace fumbled with her guardian's robe, tried to pull something from its deep pocket.

Beryl slammed her palm into Grimace's nose. Bones cracked. Grimace's hands flew to her face. Blood flowed between her fingers.

Beryl drove her fists down into Grimace's collarbones. The woman's eyes widened. She fell back against the wall, unconscious before she hit the floor.

Thumper crawled after the stun stick she'd dropped. Beryl kicked it across the room. She grabbed the guardian by her hair. Drove her face into the bathroom doorframe. Thumper fell to her knees. Beryl pulled Thumper up by her robe. Thumper slumped forward, and her limp body slid out of the robe.

Beryl tossed the robe aside, bent, hands braced on her thighs, and took three long, steadying breaths. She had no time. She crossed the room to where Grimace had fallen. Rolled Grimace over. Blood saturated the front of her robe. A quick search yielded less than five dollars, a heavy key ring, and a silver whistle. Beryl pocketed her finds. She pulled Grimace by an arm across the room, then shoved and kicked the body under the bed. Once the bedspread was in place, it looked like any other empty bed. The room reeked of blood and shit, but there was nothing Beryl could do about that.

Beryl held Thumper's robe up for inspection. Only a few small blood drops. No keys, but there was a five-dollar bill, some change, and another whistle. These, too, went into her pockets. She hung the robe on the back of the bathroom door.

She dragged Thumper into the bathroom and dumped her body in the shower.

The final "come to breakfast" bell rang. Beryl glanced at the door. Someone would miss her guardians soon.

She scooped up the towel that had fallen off her head and wet it. Mopped blood off the floor and the doorframe. A spare skirt from the closet finished the cleaning job.

Beryl tossed the soiled skirt and towel on top of Thumper, then closed the shower curtain. She scanned the room one last time. To a casual glance, it looked serene and empty. She put Thumper's robe on and adjusted the hood so it covered most of her face. It took a few seconds to find the right key to unlock her door, and then she was out.

Her footsteps echoed in the vacant hall. The other petitioners were still at breakfast. She walked too fast. Adrenaline. She forced herself to slow to a sedate pace. She made it past the first and second security booths and down the stairs. No one paid attention to her.

At the final security gate, a tinny voice came over the intercom. "What is your business outside the gate?"

Beryl took a guess. "Need to alert the bus driver that her passenger's running late. Nervous stomach." She kept her tone level, bored.

The guardian chuckled. "If I had a penny for everyone who had a nervous stomach…"

Beryl grunted. A buzzer buzzed. Metal grated against metal, and the door clanged open. All she had to do now was cross the lobby. Every inch of her skin tingled. Her stomach fluttered like a silly schoolgirl. The journey across the marble floor of the lobby seemed to take forever. She pushed open the massive wooden doors and stepped outside. The sky was bright. She breathed in sweet spring air that smelled of rain. Energy bubbled inside, and her muscles strained to run, to break free. *Not yet. Not free yet.* Chain-link fencing lined the staircase and walkway. She descended the stairs. An empty guard shack at the bottom presided over an open gate.

A short, yellow school bus sat on the west end of the circle drive. Its diesel engine chugged and belched, idling, waiting for its passenger.

Beryl scanned the grassy front lawn of Redemption. No one was in sight. She glanced up at the sentry towers. Their occupants watched the yard inside the brick walls.

The passenger and the driver's doors stood open. *Damn. Did the driver go inside for passengers? No. Otherwise, my ruse at the last gate would have failed. Time to improvise.* She climbed into the bus, hid her guardian's robe under a seat, then sat and waited.

A few minutes later, the bus driver appeared at the west corner of the building. She came toward the bus whistling "Amazing Grace." Her robe flapped in the breeze.

Beryl waited until the driver had climbed into the driver's seat. Beryl stood. "Hello."

The driver jumped. "Oh. Hello there." She twisted around and faced Beryl. "You must be Sister Clarke. You're early." She peered around. "Didn't they send someone with you to say goodbye?"

Beryl stepped closer to the driver. "She went looking for you. Should I go get her?"

The driver shook her head. "No. You can't go in there without an escort." She leaned to one side and peered around Beryl. "Did you put your luggage on board already?"

"I didn't have any."

"Don't be embarrassed. Few folks leave Redemption with a whole lot o' luggage. If you're ready, we might as well leave early. Give me a chance to eat lunch in Kansas City after I pick up supplies." She turned her back on Beryl and pulled the door control arm, closing the door.

Chapter Twenty-Three

M iranda followed Susanna down the hall, casting backward glances, hoping to say goodbye to Beryl. But the halls were empty. Her breakfast lay heavy and uneasy in her stomach. Her muscles were tense, ready to spring.

They passed through guarded gates. Then they descended a staircase, crossed a grand lobby, and exited through a pair of glass doors. The air was cool and damp and smelled of a recent spring rain. Susanna took Miranda's elbow and guided her down a fence-lined staircase. They wound around a final guard tower and exited the final gate. A wide, grassy mall separated the north-bound incoming drive from the outgoing, southbound drive. Parked vehicles lined each drive. A short school bus waited at the curb. Miranda stopped. *That bus could hold twenty people. Who else is going with me? Susanna? Other petitioners?*

"Are you all right?" Susanna searched her face.

The bus belched a cloud of pungent diesel exhaust. "I'm fine." She plunged through the cloud. Her pulse rate soared. Each step she grew less and less certain that she would find the courage to bribe the bus driver or sell her airplane ticket and more and more certain she was going home.

Susanna stopped at the open bus door and faced Miranda. Susanna's face radiated angelic joy. "This is it." She pulled a stiff blue envelope out of a pocket in her skirt and handed it to Miranda. "Your plane ticket home."

Miranda held the envelope between her thumb and first finger.

"Everything will be all right, you'll see. You're Renewed. You'll have a wonderful life. Won't she, Sister Ruth?" Susanna turned her rapturous smile on the bus driver. "Oh. You must be new." Susanna peered up at the bus driver whose face was shadowed by her hood. "Where is Sister Ruth?"

"Terrible food poisoning." The bus driver's nasal drawl sounded vaguely familiar. The driver jerked her hood-covered head toward the building.

"Oh, dear." Susanna glanced toward the building. She hugged Miranda tight and released her with a shove. "Safe travels, Miranda."

Miranda grabbed the handrail, put her foot on the first step, and hesitated. *Should I say something?* She had nothing except "don't send me home," so she climbed aboard the bus. She reached the top step and caught the driver giving her a sidelong glance.

She froze, mesmerized by the violet eyes that locked with hers. *Aunt Beryl? Oh, no. This isn't right.*

Those violet eyes narrowed the tiniest bit. Beryl adjusted the hood of her guardian's robe, breaking the spell that held Miranda.

Miranda took two steps down the aisle, the back of her neck prickling.

Report her. Who knows what kind of trouble you'll be in if you don't. They'll lock you away, and you'll never be able to leave.

Miranda glanced at the imposing facade of Redemption. Susanna stopped at the front door and waved. Miranda blew out a long breath, strode down the aisle, sat in the window seat on the driver's side, and looked straight ahead.

An impassive face and dark aviator glasses stared, reflected in the rearview mirror.

Miranda's tongue was thick and dry. Her pulse drummed in her throat.

You are condemning yourself.

She folded her hands in her lap.

Beryl reached for the door control arm.

Do something or be damned.

"God go with you, Sister Miranda." The door swung closed, muffling the last of Susanna's farewell. The engine roared, and the bus lurched forward.

Chapter Twenty-Four

M iranda half expected armed and angry guardians to burst out of Redemption's front door. The bus pulled away from the curb. She twisted in her seat and stared out the rear window. But the doors stayed closed. The white limestone building with its gleaming dome stood in stark relief against acres of brilliant green grass in the mild morning sun. It could have been a domed government building at home in DC. White limestone walls would never look the same.

Bushy woods swallowed the last glimpse of Redemption, and Miranda faced front. The bus rumbled down the narrow, two-lane street. Squeaking seats and rattling windows drowned out the droning static of the dispatch radio. Her aunt was a hooded shadow against the pale, east-facing windshield.

A chill crawled across Miranda's skin. A lot of things could happen in ten years, things that could change a person. "Aunt Beryl, where are we going?"

"The airport."

"Why?"

"You have a plane to catch. Your parents are expecting you."

She pressed against the knot growing in her stomach. "No, ma'am, I am not going home."

"Oh?" Her pacifying tone was the one used when a child said something foolish. "Where do you think you're going?"

"With you."

"Not part of the plan. You got on this bus to go home. Home is where you're going."

"I got on this bus planning to go anywhere but home." The bus bucked and bounced over the uneven pavement. Miranda raised her voice over the increased squeaks and rattles. "Go ahead. Take me to the airport. Even if you force me onto the plane, I won't go home. I escaped once. I'll escape again."

"What did you escape from?"

"My parents and my bodyguard. I found a job. I had an apartment. I was doing all right."

Beryl snorted. "Until you ended up in Redemption."

"Nothing but bad luck. I can find another job and get another apartment, but I'd rather go with you."

"A princess of the Fellowship like you wouldn't last ten minutes where I'm going."

"How do you know you'll last more than ten minutes? How do you know you don't need me?"

"You think I need you?"

"I have a lot to learn, but so do you. You haven't been outside of Redemption in ten years. A lot has changed." Miranda wrinkled her nose at a faint ammonia-like odor.

"Did they change the national language to German? Change our currency *to deutsche marks*?"

Miranda's neck and face grew warm. "Of course not." It took a moment to gather her wits. "There are new roads, new buildings, new rules. How do you expect to get identity papers? Did you know you need them?" She leaned forward and rested her arm on the sun-warmed metal seat frame. "Do you know the Azrael are real? Do you know current members of the Soldiers for the American Bill of Rights?" She cocked her head and let a little attitude come out. "I do."

A jerk of the steering wheel sent the bus onto the road's soft shoulder. The bus jolted to a stop. Miranda grabbed the seat back and narrowly avoided flying into the aisle.

Amid the squeaks and rattles of the bus, a sliding sound came from the back. A woman's legs stuck out from under the seat. The bus lurched to a stop. The body slid into the aisle. The woman's eyes and lips were closed, her skin a waxy, blue-gray.

A new sound filled Miranda's ears. Harsh breathing. Her own. She had assumed Aunt Beryl had killed to escape, but the dead body made it real. The vibrations in her chest weren't from the bus, but her own heartbeat.

The parking brake ratcheted. Beryl strode past Miranda and stuffed the body between two benches on the downward side of the bus. Then Beryl faced Miranda.

Miranda locked her gaze on her aunt's face.

Beryl sat on the bench behind her and took off her sunglasses. "Who do you know from SABR?"

"Sarah." Miranda's voice caught. She cleared her throat. "I worked with her." She quashed the memory of her last look at Sarah.

"You were a member of SABR?"

"No. We worked for a cleaning service." Her stomach dipped. "I didn't know at first. I saw her—stealing papers from a government office."

"You were a cleaning lady?" Beryl stared at her, mouth half open.

"It's good, honest labor."

"They felt compelled to hire you, the councilor's daughter."

Miranda sucked in a breath and forced her jaw to unclench. "The first place I applied hired me. And they didn't know I was a councilor's daughter. After I escaped my bodyguard, there was no way I would crawl back and ask Mama and—Daddy—for money."

"You escaped your bodyguard...but you didn't bring any money?" Beryl's expression was just short of an eye roll.

"I'm not an idiot." That came out clipped and hot. Miranda recovered herself and continued in a controlled tone. "Of course I had money. I'd planned to get new ID papers and a job, but the mugger stole my money so I had to get a job in DC."

"And you chose a janitorial service?"

"I chose it over a forced and loveless marriage. I chose it because Mama and—Daddy would never guess I'd work as a cleaning lady. I chose it because I wanted to be normal." Hector had been kind. When he'd learned she'd been robbed, he'd helped her get new identity papers. "You know what? I liked it. I liked the work, and I liked the people I worked for and with. If I hadn't found that dead body, I'd still be there."

"I see." Beryl sounded like she didn't understand at all.

The radio squawked. Miranda jumped.

"All vehicles report! This is a lockdown."

Beryl rushed to the driver's seat. The engine roared. "They're coming for me, Miranda," Beryl shouted over the noise. The bus fishtailed until its wheels gripped the pavement. "They'll kill me and anyone with me. Go home."

"If I go home, they might as well kill me."

"Next stop is Kansas City Municipal Airport. I'll hide the bus and steal a car. If you can't stomach what I do, use your plane ticket."

"Don't steal a car," Miranda said. "They'll expect that. I'll give my airplane ticket to someone and get cash from my Bank-Americard. We'll rent a car with the cash. That, they won't expect."

"What's a BankAmericard?"

"It's a card the bank issues." She was supposed to have used it to buy her wedding dress. "You use it instead of cash. It's sort of like a loan, but a whole lot easier."

Beryl grunted.

Miranda hoped it meant she approved of the plan.

The radio crackled. "Petitioner fourteen-ninety-nine unaccounted for. Consider her armed and dangerous." In the background, a siren whooped.

Chapter Twenty-Five

Kara's bodyguards cleared a path through the crowd at the Washington National Airport. Shouts, whistles, ringing phones, and clattering luggage carts echoed between the dark tile floor and the arched ceiling of the terminal.

"Many blessings, Sister," murmured some when she strode past. "Blessed day, Sister," others said. She put on an Apostle's wife smile for the people and followed her guards to the windows overlooking the planes already on the tarmac.

She shielded her eyes with a gloved hand. Mid-morning in early June, the sun's rays were warm but not yet unbearable. She watched planes arrive and leave and wished Miranda had come home yesterday. Only three and a half hours remained until Donald's interview. The courier service had delivered her gift to the last Assembly member holdout. Donald's best shirt and suit hung in his closet, cleaned and pressed. She'd refined Donald's speech, and he'd perfected every inflection. She was confident that the Assembly would confirm Donald as the First Apostle. And Miranda's wedding would be an extravaganza fit for the First Apostle's daughter.

Sunlight reflected off a silver plane that rolled to a stop outside the terminal. Its clamshell door opened, and the steps lowered to the tarmac. Four men in dark suits raced up the steps and boarded the plane.

"They're Second Sphere." The stranger's voice cracked. Silence fell. People looked away, moved from the window. Kara stood her ground.

The men dragged a struggling, young blonde woman off the plane.

A businessman appeared in the doorway. He descended the steps, trailed by a single-file procession of men and women. Finally, the air stewardess exited the plane.

Kara whirled and confronted the bodyguard on her left. "Did you see her? Where's Miranda?"

"Mrs. Clarke? Mrs. Donald Clarke?" a pleasant baritone asked from behind her.

"What?" She swiveled and faced a youngish-looking man with light brown hair. He wore a dark suit and a serious expression.

Her bodyguards moved in, one on each side.

"Ma'am, I'm with the Second Sphere." He flashed the white and red metal of a Fellowship shield in a leather wallet. "You need to come with me."

"You've made a mistake."

"No mistake." He took her elbow.

She jerked her arm free, then noticed bystanders watching. She forced a cordial smile. "I respect the Second Sphere, but I am on important business."

"Ma'am, Director Lancaster said it is imperative that he speak to you *now*."

Her back muscles tightened, and acid churned in her stomach. "Why didn't you say so?" She gestured for him to lead the way.

The young man led her to the VIP lounge. Beside the lounge's door stood another young man who wore the same haircut, the same suit, the same serious expression.

Overstuffed chairs, tufted sofas, and console television sets dotted the lemon-scented room. Weldon stood at the full-service bar that lined one wall.

"Weldon? What's wrong?"

He hurried to her side. "Shhh." He put his finger to her lips. "We've sent for Donald."

"You did what? You know he's—" A chill knifed through her. "It's Miranda, isn't it? Tell me."

Weldon guided her to a chair. "Please sit down."

She couldn't remember the last time she'd seen him so tense. She sat, removed her gloves, and braced herself. "I'm listening."

Weldon sat beside her. "There was an escape."

"Miranda escaped?" She couldn't keep the incredulity from her voice. Couldn't grasp the idea that anyone could escape Redemption. Couldn't believe that even after Redemption, Miranda had run away again.

He covered her too-warm hands with his cool ones. "One of the petitioners hijacked Miranda's bus. We found the abandoned bus at the Kansas City Airport. The driver is dead. Broken neck."

The quiet *thump-bump* of her heart grew too loud. Her mouth went dry. "And Miranda?"

"We don't know."

"How can you not know? Is she dead or kidnapped or what?"

Weldon stroked her hair. "We found no sign of a struggle. No blood. Someone, maybe Miranda, withdrew a thousand dollars from her BankAmericard at the airport. A young woman occupied Miranda's seat on the airplane."

Kara nodded. "The young woman your men arrested." *There are Assembly members who have daughters close to Miranda's age. They would be sympathetic.* "No struggle or blood? Then Miranda's alive, right?"

"The escapee probably took Miranda hostage and forced her to get cash. They flew somewhere. We're checking the other flights, the car rentals, and the bus terminal."

"Will there will be a ransom demand?" *The abduction of a coun-*

cilor's daughter would be headline news. Donald's appointment and investiture would be below the fold or, God forbid, second-page news.

He shrugged. From his expression, she could tell he did not think this would end well.

She drew a deep breath and rubbed her aching forehead. *Donald is on his way here. The Assembly won't postpone his interview.* She had to turn this disaster into an advantage. She locked onto Weldon. "What is your plan?"

"My men are bringing the young woman from the plane here. I'll question her."

"Does the Council know where Miranda was?"

"Not yet."

His answer raised her blood pressure at least ten points. "How many people know Miranda was in that place?"

Weldon looked hurt. "Only you, me, Donald, and my first lieutenant. No one else."

"Good. We must keep the kidnapping quiet."

Weldon gave her a stunned look.

Kara patted his leg. "Just until after the investiture. We stick to the original explanation. Miranda coming home from the spa, but —there was plane trouble. No, she fell ill and can't travel until she's well." She glanced at her watch. *Donald's interview will begin in two and a half hours.* His was the last one. Afterward, the Assembly would be sequestered until they were unanimous in their choice for the First Apostle.

The door banged opened. She smothered her gasp and stood a little faster than normal.

Donald appeared in the doorway, his hair wind-tossed and his white shirt haphazardly tucked into his pants. His eyes sought her.

She gave him a stiff-upper-lip smile. She sat and patted the chair next to her.

He sat, leaned toward her, and whispered, "Have they found Miranda?"

"No, but it will be all right." She finger-combed his hair. "Everything will work out." *What if Miranda is killed? Mourning for his daughter would make even staunch political opponents sympathetic. What if we don't find Miranda for days or weeks? Weldon will make it appear that Donald managed a successful rescue. Donald will be a hero. All I have to do is control what news gets out when.*

The young man returned, carrying a tray with a tiny gold-trimmed pitcher of cream, a matching sugar bowl, and two steaming cups of aromatic coffee. He bent and held the tray for Kara. She stirred sugar and cream into Donald's cup, then handed it to him. He sipped the coffee in morose silence. She took hers black. It smelled better than it tasted.

The clock ticked hundreds of seconds before the door to the room opened a second time.

A young blonde woman struggled between two of the Second Sphere members. The woman's eyes widened and her face paled when she recognized Kara and Donald.

Kara grabbed Weldon's lapels. "Find her, Weldon. Whatever it takes, bring Miranda home."

Chapter Twenty-Six

Miranda woke to the hum of tires on asphalt and the stale scents of pine air freshener, sun-warmed vinyl, and old sweat. She straightened up and rolled her shoulders. Beryl glanced her way, then stared at the empty highway lined with wide-leafed crops. Her aunt wore a "borrowed" felt fedora with a bird perched on one side. The silly hat was part of the clothing she'd stolen from the airport. "How long have I been asleep?"

"Six hours."

Miranda yawned, covering her mouth with her hand. Dried drool stretched from her mouth to her chin. Her cheeks heated. She faced the window and rubbed the drool off. She hadn't slept well since long before Redemption. "Sorry."

"What for?"

"I haven't been much of a traveling companion."

"We're not companions, Miranda."

"Then what are we?"

"Fugitives."

Miranda's insides hummed in an echo of the tires on the pavement. She wished she'd thought before she'd spoken. "I guess we are. I meant that I haven't helped you." She glanced out the rear window. "Have there been any, um, difficulties?"

"I would have awakened you."

"Sure. Want me to drive for a bit?"

"No."

"You could rest while I drive."

"No. Alton is less than thirty minutes away. We'll stop there."

"Okay." Miranda stared out the window. A sun-bleached farmhouse grew larger as they approached and smaller as they left it behind. She had questions she wanted to ask. The words grew too large for her throat. "Aunt—?"

"Miranda—"

Miranda wasn't certain which of them spoke first. "Sorry. Go ahead."

"No, you first."

"Okay." A breath in and out steadied her. "Why were you sent to Redemption?"

"Sedition."

"What?" She gaped at her aunt's profile. *How could she say that like she was reporting the weather?* There wasn't enough air in the car. "Why?"

"Ethan and I created SABR."

"What?" A billion questions churned. "How—when—why?"

"We had to stop the Fellowship Council."

"The whole Council?"

"The Council was a bunch of evil, ruthless men who believed they got to decide who lives and who dies. They still are. We couldn't let them destroy this country."

"They aren't all evil. The Council advises the government—"

"Don't quote Fellowship bullshit. Use your brain. Didn't you notice that only those who disagreed with the Council were Taken?"

Miranda tried not to remember Sarah. "But protests aren't sedition."

"We did a lot more than protest. We were guilty. We planned

to kidnap the Prophet. That's when everything went wrong. They were waiting for us. People died. Your Uncle Ethan and Anna were killed." Beryl cleared her throat. "They captured me. The Council declared I was guilty of sedition, among other things. "

Miranda's chest hollowed out. Memories and facts she thought she knew tangled with new memories and information. She didn't have any reason to doubt what Beryl said, but she had never had a reason to doubt her parents before either. "They gave you life in prison."

"A commuted death sentence."

Something deeper and darker than nausea filled Miranda. *Not only Daddy, but the whole Council was evil. How could they fool so many people?*

They passed a Welcome to Alton, Illinois sign. Cars filled the streets. People crowded the sidewalks, going about their business in the late afternoon sun as if nothing extraordinary had happened. Gullible fools. But Miranda wasn't fooled anymore. She'd find proof, and she'd stop her father, and all the other evil men, even if they charged her with sedition.

"Living on the run isn't easy." Beryl tossed her head, indicating the Pan Am bag she'd thrown into the back hours earlier. "Get that for me."

The vinyl seat squeaked. Miranda retrieved the bag and settled back into her seat.

"Open it."

Roadmaps, toiletries, a man's cable knit sweater, a straight razor, several rolls of dollar bills, and a stun stick filled the bag.

Beryl reached inside, her eyes still on the road. "Tell them you escaped. They'll treat you like a hero." She pushed a roll of money into Miranda's hand.

"There isn't enough money in the world—" She dropped the roll of bills into the open bag.

"Go home."

"No." Miranda tucked her cold hands under her arms.

"Why? And don't tell me it's because your parents are making you marry some rich guy."

Miranda pressed her lips together and faced the window. Why should she explain anything? Why couldn't people let her make her own decisions?

Beryl pulled the car into the parking lot of an L-shaped shopping center. A grocery store sat at one end, followed by a string of small shops. A large Lazarus department store stood in the corner. A half-dozen shops with a Rexall Drugstore at the end created the vertical arm of the L.

"Take this." Beryl placed the roll of dollar bills in Miranda's hand and wrapped her fingers around Miranda's. "There's a bus stop at the Rexall. The bus goes to the depot downtown. Choose your destination."

Miranda clapped her free hand over Beryl's. "You'll get caught if you continue north to Terre Haute," Miranda said. "The Council built an inspiration garden there in memory of Prophet Samuel. So many Fellowship leaders go there on pilgrimages that the Second Sphere patrols the whole town."

A tiny twitch in Beryl's face shot a bolt of hope through Miranda. "You teach me to be a rebel," she said. "I'll bring you up-to-date. I'll join SABR and tell the public the truth. People will believe a councilor's daughter."

Beryl didn't look convinced.

"I worked at the Fellowship Center as a teen guide. I know the councilors. I can help you."

"If they catch you, they'll send you back to Redemption. Or kill you."

Miranda's heart thumped loud and hard. She raised her chin. "Then I'd better not let them catch me."

"There are three rules. One, no contact with anyone from your past. Two, don't call me Aunt Beryl. I'm Beryl or the name I'm using at the time. And three, from now on, follow my instructions no matter what I ask you to do. Everything I ask will be for a purpose. Learn from it or don't, but the minute you squawk like a princess, I'm done. You're on your own."

"I'll learn."

"Buy two changes of work clothes, work gloves, rain gear, a heavy sweater or a jacket, a rucksack. Put on something you bought. Throw away the clothes you're wearing. Pack the rest. Be in front of the drugstore in thirty minutes."

Miranda hurried to the Lazarus store and followed Beryl's shopping instructions to the last detail. She exited the store, uncomfortable in stiff, scratchy jeans. Out of place, a stranger to herself. She'd never worn jeans before.

The clock above the sign for the shopping center said she'd finished in less than twenty minutes. Her stomach rumbled. If she hurried—

Inside the grocery store, a bank of phone booths stood to her right. She passed the phone booths and got a sandwich and drink at the deli counter. She sat at a table and stuffed food into her mouth.

She couldn't keep her eyes off the wooden phone booths. One call to one of her siblings might prove everything. *No. Beryl said no contact.* She took another bite. The sandwich turned to cardboard in her mouth. *What if Irene or David knew what had happened to her? That would be proof I'm not crazy. If Aunt Beryl knew why, she'd let me make the call.* She glanced at her half-eaten sandwich, her appetite gone.

She dug into her pocket. She had five dimes and a nickel. *Fifty-five cents should be enough.* She had three minutes. She'd have to call David. Irene would talk too long. Miranda pushed the phone booth's folding door closed. She wrinkled her nose at the smell of stale sweat. The sign on the phone read local calls ten cents, long distance fifty cents for the first three minutes. She dropped her dimes into the slot. The coins clinked into place, and she spun the rotary dial.

"Hello?"

"David? It's me, Miranda."

"Hello, stranger. How's life at the spa? Are you coming home?"

Who supplied that lie? Daddy? Her grip tightened on the black Bakelite receiver. "Not yet. I called because—I'm trying to recall something. Do you remember your childhood?"

"You mean things like going to school, playing games, holidays, and stuff? Sure. Why do you ask?"

"So your memories are good ones?"

"Mostly. When Dad wasn't being Dad."

She sucked in a breath. The stale phone booth air triggered a dry cough.

"He was either so mad he'd throw things or depressed and sitting in that stupid chair."

Miranda remembered. "He'd say, 'I'm nothing—'"

"—nobody. I'll never amount to anything.'"

Her chest hurt, and her eyes burned. "Those were bad days."

"Yeah, but him being angry was worse."

A foul lump wedged in her throat. "Did he hurt you?"

"I think he would have." He didn't speak for a long moment. She feared he wouldn't say more. "I spilled dry cereal at the breakfast table. Mom yelled at me, and I got mad. I knew if I stayed in the kitchen while I was mad, I'd get in trouble for "pouting." So I went to my room and flopped facedown on my bed. Dad came running after me." He spoke soft enough she had to put a finger in her other ear to hear. "He broke down my door and jumped onto my bed screaming how bad I was. He kept screaming and jumping up and down and up and down, closer and closer to my head. I knew I was going to die."

She ached at the pain and confusion in his voice.

He cleared his throat. "Mom came and pulled him off me, or he *would* have killed me."

"I'm sorry, David. I didn't know."

"No one did. I mean, who would have believed me?"

"I would."

"Did he hurt you?"

A woman passed the phone booth pushing a squeaky shopping cart. Miranda faced the back of the phone booth. "I've had the same nightmare over and over. Then I remembered—he——" It took several tries before she could continue. "Did *it* to me." Her throat closed.

"Did what?"

Her voice shook. "You know. *It.*"

The phone line hummed. Waves of nausea and dizziness swept over her.

"He's one sick…" David's voice cracked.

"You believe me?" The dizziness intensified.

"Yes."

She forced herself to ask, "Did you—see—anything?"

"No, I didn't. I just—know—he *could* have."

"Oh." The word escaped her like a popped balloon. *Not proof.*

"Do you want to talk about it?"

"I can't."

The phone line clicked, and an operator said, "That will be fifty cents for the next three minutes."

"David," Miranda shouted over the operator's voice. "I don't have enough change. I'll call you——" The phone clicked again, and the buzz of a vacant line droned in her ear. "Later." She replaced the receiver, but couldn't let go of it. She leaned forward, rested her head against the cold Bakelite, and tried to breathe.

Daddy had hurt David too. How many more family members had he hurt? Irene? Sandra? There must be others. One of them would surely remember everything. Maybe Beryl—The time! Miranda grabbed her rucksack, bolted out of the phone booth and out of the store.

Chapter Twenty-Seven

Kara sat on her dark blue sofa, her face frozen in a false smile. She had dreamed of this day for years, but this was a nightmare. John and James, the two Second Sphere agents she'd met at the airport, sat across from her. They sat in her green armchairs on the other side of her walnut coffee table, stiff, out-of-place twins with one rather dull brain. Her "protectors" in case Miranda's kidnapper showed up here. Kara had argued that it was far more likely she'd get a ransom call. Weldon had insisted that the two men and their recording gadgets stay. She checked her watch again. *Six hours? Donald's interview with the Assembly should have been over long ago.* She needed to move around, pace, do something.

This was the first time she regretted the L-shaped, open plan of her home. The living room and the dining room were one large room. From the dining room, one could see into the breakfast nook. A short wall hid the kitchen that ran between the breakfast nook and the front hall. She didn't dare go down the hall to her bedroom. The twins might follow.

Thanks to Miranda, I am a prisoner in my own home. She stifled a sigh. Miranda always managed to upstage her. *Kidnapped on the steps of Redemption on the single most important day in my, in Donald's, life.* Kara's need to move grew. *This is intolerable.* She stood.

The agents leaped to their feet.

She forced her jaw to unclench and smiled her most cordial smile. "Sit, gentlemen. I'm just going to the kitchen to make coffee. Would you like some?"

"That would be nice, ma'am," John said. Or was it James?

She filled the electric percolator and set it on the pink countertop. After placing the percolator's basket on the counter, she lined it with filter paper and then poured in a scoop of fragrant ground coffee.

Irene never causes trouble. Even David didn't much, though boys were always a bit naughty. She put the lid on the percolator and then spotted the basket, still on the counter.

Kara allowed herself a huge, impatient sigh. *It's too much.* She put the coffee into the pot and plugged it into the outlet. *How does one act to show grief for the Prophet, support for her husband, and fear for her daughter all at once?* Arranging her silver coffee service and best china on her silver-serving tray soothed her. The aroma of fresh coffee filled the kitchen.

A few minutes later, the agents drank coffee and munched cookies.

She sat on the sofa again and sipped her coffee. The usually bright and pleasant taste turned to acid in her stomach. She set her cup down. The sound of the front door opening robbed her of breath and spurred her pulse. She stood. "Donald?"

"No, sis, it's me." Her brother edged into the room looking sheepish. "Sorry."

Her heart slowed from thunderous to a drum roll. "Have you found Miranda?"

Weldon shook his head. "It's as if Miranda and her kidnapper vanished." He locked onto her, slid his eyes to the left.

She picked up the serving tray. "Come, help me in the kitchen. These gentlemen need seconds, and you need coffee."

Kara went straight to the sink and turned the water on, full force. If she and Weldon kept their voices down, the brothers wouldn't understand a word. She faced Weldon. "Tell me."

"It's Beryl."

She steadied herself with a hand on the cool counter. *Of all the possibilities…Beryl?* "*She* kidnapped Miranda?"

Weldon put a finger to his lips.

"Who put Miranda in the same facility as that—that —murderer?"

Weldon's cheek twitched.

"You knew, didn't you?" She spoke through teeth clenched so tight her face hurt.

"Not until this morning."

"Before or after you told me about Miranda?"

He had the grace to look remorseful. "I gave my man a list of a dozen petitioners pardoned by the Prophet on his death-bed. Miranda would be one of many."

She refilled the percolator. "What went wrong?" The constant sound of running water annoyed her.

He rubbed his chin. "Who knew that no one else would have a morning flight? She got on the bus alone."

Kara leaned back against the counter and tipped her head up to look into her brother's eyes. "How did Beryl get on Miranda's bus?"

He searched her face, touched her arm. "There are hundreds of petitioners. I didn't go through the whole list. How was I to know she was there?"

She would forgive him. She always did, but not now. "Go on."

"She killed her guardians. Disguised herself as one of them."

Kara used every ounce of her self-control to maintain a whisper. "They let her get close enough to kill them?"

Weldon knuckled his beard stubble. A nervous habit she knew too well. "There's something else, isn't there?" She steeled herself.

"Miranda made a phone call."

"She's alive? Who did she call? When?"

"David."

"David? Why didn't she call me or the police?"

He shrugged.

"What did she say?"

"Don't know. The call wasn't recorded, just traced."

She pursed her lips and tried to figure out how to contain and control the situation. Then the enormity of their problem hit her. She put a hand on Weldon's arm. "You're sure it was Beryl?"

His pale blue eyes were grave. "Positive."

"That's why you insisted those two stay here?" She tilted her head toward the living room.

He gave her a rueful smile.

She shivered. "She'll come after you again, won't she?"

"Definitely."

Kara leaned into him, her head against his chest, and breathed in the smoky leather scent of his favorite aftershave. He smoothed her hair with a light, familiar touch, caressed her cheek. Her eyes closed, and her lips parted. A chair creaked in the living room. She pulled away from him and plugged in the coffee. "Beryl will try to find Ethan and his apostates."

Weldon nodded. "I've alerted watchers along likely routes to Lynchburg, Baltimore, and Pittsburgh."

"Why would she kidnap Miranda?" She glanced at the wall clock. *Eight-fifty. Where is Donald?*

"For leverage or for ransom."

Kara gazed out the window across the patio to the manicured lawn and listened to the running water. "Or to try to manipulate Donald." She poured coffee for Weldon, handed him the cup and saucer. "We cannot let this become public. It's too—volatile." She stared pointedly at Weldon. "There's only one way to stop Beryl."

It took a couple of seconds for him come to the obvious conclusion. He mouthed the word "Azrael."

She gave him a grim smile.

Weldon bent his head toward her. "What about Miranda?"

"Doing it without Miranda present would be best, of course."

"And if Miranda is there when it happens?"

Perhaps that would make her more content with her life. "A few Second Sphere agents should be nearby, to rescue her. When Beryl is Taken, Miranda will be grateful she was spared." *And she'll be a testament against the apostates for the rest of her days.* Kara shut off the water and picked up the tray. The tightness in her chest eased, and her vision of the future sharpened again. She walked into the living room. "Gentlemen, I'm sorry that took so long..."

Chapter Twenty-Eight

After Miranda climbed into the car, Beryl handed her the worn, soft paper that was her new identity paper. Beryl hated that she had to ask, but she asked anyway. "Will this work?"

Miranda studied the paper. "How did they make the paper look and feel old?"

Beryl didn't answer.

"It's a temporary ID," Miranda said. "It's only good for four weeks."

She knew that. It also didn't need a photograph.

"Where did you get it?"

"Doesn't matter." The shopping center in Alton held a small surplus store where not everything for sale was on the shelves. She'd planned on getting a fake driver's license there. Thanks to Miranda, she'd known to ask for the ID papers. The clerk took her request, and twenty minutes later she had papers. Now she needed to get a lot of miles between them and Alton.

She drove east out of Alton as fast as she dared, grateful the sun had risen high enough she didn't have to squint. The route wove through dozens of small country towns where the speed limit dropped to a crawl. For the first two hours, Miranda had tried chitchat. Thank God, she'd finally shut up. After years in solitude, nattering voices made Beryl want to break teeth. *What am I doing? I should have left Miranda in Kansas City, Alton at the latest.* She'd told herself she could use her niece as a hostage. Instead she'd bought a fake ID and weighed herself down with a passenger.

Beryl turned onto a long stretch of road lined with farms and small groves of trees. She shifted into third gear, and the engine's throaty purr filled the car.

The afternoon wore on, and the sun's early June rays heated the air so that, even with the windows down, the car grew warm. Beryl stole glances at her niece. Miranda leaned toward her open car window as if she were too warm. Beryl had spent too many years dreaming of the sun's warmth to attempt to escape it now. She'd spent those years dreaming and planning her escape too. Never in those years had she imagined she'd have a passenger. She glanced at Miranda again, wondering *anchor or lodestone?* The girl was too open, too guileless to be a spy. Why else would a councilor's daughter be in Redemption? Why would Donald allow his daughter to be sent to Redemption? "Miranda, what was your sentence?"

Miranda started. "My sentence?"

"Why were you sent to Redemption?"

Miranda blinked at her. "I didn't think you wanted to talk."

"Answer the question." *Solitude may have rusted my conversational skills.*

Miranda blew out a noisy breath. "I told you, I found a dead body." She crossed her arms over her chest.

"Tell me exactly what you were doing and what you saw —please."

"One of the offices I was going to clean had the sign burned into the door."

"The shield?"

Miranda nodded.

Beryl stiffened, struck by cold certainty and the icy fire that had burned inside her for the past ten years. *Handiwork of the Azrael for sanctioned hits.*

Miranda cleared her throat. "I thought it was a joke and went inside and he was—on the floor—dead." She took a shaky breath. "I screamed. Sarah came. She said we had to run. We did, but there were men outside. Someone grabbed me from behind, put something over my mouth and nose. I don't remember anything after that." Her chin quivered.

Cleaners. "The men, were they wearing hazard suits or business suits? Did they have the shield on their left breast pocket? What were they driving? A van or a car?"

"I don't know. I don't remember. I thought I was going to die." She ran her hands up and down her arms. "I woke up in Redemption. I haven't seen Sarah since."

Wind and tires droned on and on. *Miranda's story makes sense. The Council can't leave witnesses to demystify the Taken.*

Miranda's story could be one of Weldon's lies. But the raw emotion radiating off her now? Not fake. She's a strange mix. Sometimes smooth and sophisticated, often as naive as a two-year-old.

Anna was like that once. Until she was manipulated to believe lies. Beryl gripped the steering wheel tighter. *I failed Anna. I will not fail Miranda too.*

"You can drive—A mile a minute—" Miranda read the Burma-Shave road signs. "But there is—no future in it." Miranda released a long breath and, looking straight ahead, asked, "Do we have a future?"

"We'll make one." The lie silenced Miranda, and they passed the next set of Burma-Shave signs without comment.

Beryl had to show her ID when she stopped at a country store for more gas after sunset. She bought ham sandwiches, and they ate in the car, speeding down the road.

She couldn't count on the element of surprise lasting much longer. Stopping in Alton had been based on an assumption that she could drive faster than Redemption could react. By now,

Weldon and the Second Sphere had mobilized. She avoided major highways when she could.

The Hudson's headlights revealed flashes of fields and pastures that lined the asphalt highway. Once in a while they passed a streak of lights, distant farmhouses or small towns. A sign read Louisville, Kentucky, 50 miles.

"So, Aunt—I mean, Beryl—"

Miranda's voice startled her. She'd thought the girl had fallen asleep again.

"How did you figure out the Council was corrupt?"

"Good people started dying." Never-forgotten faces ghosted through her memory.

"You found proof, and people joined SABR?"

She stole a glance at her niece. The dashboard lights created stark highlights and shadows across Miranda's face. "Proof?"

"Of wrongdoing."

"By the Fellowship? For believers, there's never proof enough to convince them."

"How did you get anyone to join SABR?"

"Some people live the truth, even when it's hard. Some people want to believe in something so badly they stop thinking. Some people choose the easy way and let other people decide what they should believe." *Weldon and his army of Second Sphere agents are masters at twisting the truth, creating deniability. He'd found the bus and its dead driver hours ago. More than enough time to start hunting for me.*

"They wouldn't deny real, tangible proof, would they?"

Old pain pricked deep inside. She pushed it away. "Doubters doubt. That's what they do."

"Oh." Miranda's voice sounded small, strained.

She shot another look at her niece. Miranda looked as if she was about to receive the worst news of her life. "Are we talking about the Fellowship, Miranda?"

"Of course." Miranda stared out the passenger window.

Beryl wasn't fooled, but she gave up for the moment. The glow of lights from Louisville on the horizon grew close. She eased off the gas pedal. Weldon knew a handful of places that he'd guess might be her final destination. He'd station watchers along likely routes. Places where routes funneled down to bridges or tunnels or mountain roadways. Places where the danger was the highest. Places where she would die before she let them recapture her.

They rounded a curve, and in front of them, a bridge stretched over the Ohio River. She slowed from forty-five to thirty-five and tugged the bill of her ball cap low on her forehead. With her hair tucked up inside the cap, she hoped it provided a less suspicious profile to watchers.

A pair of headlights pulled onto the bridge behind her. Her heart rate kicked into hyperalert mode. "Miranda, slide down onto the floor. Slow and easy."

Miranda's eyes widened, but she sank to the floor. "Is someone following us?"

"Yes."

Her hands grew damp on the steering wheel during the two minutes it took to cross the mile-long bridge. But the vehicle behind her made no attempt to overtake them.

On the other side of the bridge, they followed U.S. 31 through the east side of town. Behind them, the vehicle drove in and out of pools of light cast by streetlamps. The dark sedan, a Ford, followed the same turns she did.

There were too many stoplights for Beryl's peace of mind, and highway signs were hard to spot. The Ford followed. The traffic light ahead changed from green to yellow. She lifted her foot off the gas, and the Hudson's V8 engine throttled down to a pulsating purr. The Ford slowed too. The light changed to red. She pressed the accelerator. The Hudson slid through the intersection. The Ford stopped. A good sign, but not a sure thing.

Down the block, a light-colored, four-door Chrysler pulled out in front of her. Her inner alarms pinged, cranked her pulse up. *Weldon wouldn't waste a second team on a guess. How did he know?* She maintained a safe distance behind the vehicle. She had memorized the routes she needed. Now she took note of every cross street and alley they passed as potential escape routes. The car in front of her passed under a streetlight. The flash of light illuminated the driver and passenger. She couldn't see enough to be certain. She scanned the road behind them. No sign of the Ford.

"Is it the Second Sphere?" Miranda asked.

"Who else?"

They passed the last of the brick business buildings and entered an area of small shops and scattered residences. The Chrysler slowed for another traffic light. She tapped the brake, checked the rearview mirror. The dark Ford crept up behind her. The three vehicles paraded down the street. At the next intersection, she turned left and circled the block.

For a moment, it looked as if they were in the clear. Then the Ford appeared in front of them. The Chrysler pulled out of an alleyway, kept close in the left-hand lane. The headlights of a third car showed in the rearview. She sucked in a breath. *They plan to box us in. That's what I'd do.* But she wasn't as prepared to die as she'd thought. Not yet. Her pulse sang to the call of adrenaline.

She yanked the wheel and pressed the accelerator to the floor. The Hudson shot around the dark-colored Ford, through the red light, and down the street.

The Ford and Chrysler sprang after her.

A hard right at the next corner sent them down a bumpy alleyway. Tires squealed. Miranda bounced against the underside of the dashboard. Dust billowed out from under the Hudson. She wrenched the car into a hard left at the first paved street. The Hudson fishtailed, then straightened.

"Get in the seat and hang on."

Miranda climbed back into her seat.

They rocketed down a residential street crisscrossed with narrow, dimly lit streets and dark alleyways. The shadow-filled street behind them was empty. She slowed but checked the rearview compulsively. Crossing a T-intersection, a pair of headlights barreled toward them.

"Look out!" Miranda cried.

She stomped on the accelerator. The Hudson shot down the street. Behind them, a *boom-boom*. The Chrysler smashed into a parked car. The third vehicle plowed into the Chrysler. Screeching, metal-on-metal sounds ripped through the night.

The Ford pulled out of a cross street in front and drove straight at them in a game of chicken. Beryl jerked the wheel. They skidded into an alley. The right rear tapped a cluster of galvanized trash cans. The cans fell like noisy bowling pins, spewing their contents across the dusty alley.

She switched through alleys and cross streets. The Ford had fallen behind but still followed. She hadn't seen the Chrysler or the third vehicle since the two had crashed. She twisted the wheel, slid into a right turn. She mashed the accelerator to the floor. The Hudson leaped forward. The rearview mirror showed an empty road. She didn't lift her foot until the night swallowed the last glimmer of Louisville.

Chapter Twenty-Nine

M iranda squirmed, relieved a little of the pressure on her bottom side. She had never sat in a car for so long in her life. The pale ribbon of lavender above the Blue Ridge Mountains in the east hinted at the hours that had passed.

Beryl drove a slow loop around Rocky Gap, a sleepy Virginia town bisected by Route 52. She returned to the steel diner that sat on the corner, one of a dozen commercial buildings on a short main street. A bright red Open sign shone from the diner's window.

"Are you sure it's safe?" Miranda asked.

"They have to take breaks too."

Beryl parked the car in the shadows on the west side of the building.

Miranda pushed the diner's door open. A bell clanged overhead. The greasy countertops, sticky floors, and duct-tape-mended vinyl benches were vacant. Not a single person visible anywhere, not even a waitress. "Hello?"

"Y'all sit where ya like. Be with you in a minute." The woman's drawl came from behind a pass-through window to the kitchen.

Miranda stared at the clock hung on the transom above the pass-through window. Only twenty-two hours since she'd left Redemption?

Miranda followed Beryl down a hallway labeled Ladies Room. Beryl bypassed the bathroom. At the end of the hall stood a heavy, steel door. Beryl opened it and peered into the dark. She closed the door and went to the ladies' room.

Curious, Miranda opened the door too. Across a dark side street stood a brick wall with the words Phil's Hardware painted on it. An emergency exit door interrupted the brick at about the middle the store. Judging from the corner window visible at one end, the store faced the adjacent street. Miranda shrugged and followed Beryl into the ladies' room.

She rejoined Beryl at a table near the hallway. Beryl sat with her back to the wall, peering over a menu toward the windows into the parking lot.

The kitchen's cafe doors squeaked. A sway-backed woman with mousy brown hair tied in a sloppy bun crossed over to their table. "Cook just cleaned our ol' flat top. Ain't up to heat yet. Can y'all wait 'bout five extra minutes?"

Beryl gave a curt nod.

The waitress took their orders and brought them water.

After the waitress left, Beryl folded her arms on the tabletop and leaned toward Miranda. "How do you figure the Second Sphere found us in Louisville?"

"I don't know. Do you?" Miranda stared at the chrome edge of the table. She rubbed the cool metal with her thumb. *Beryl doesn't know about my phone call to David. Besides, that phone call had been long before we reached Louisville. One had nothing to do with the other.*

"Someone must have tipped them off."

Miranda glared at her aunt. "Are you implying I talked to the Second Sphere?" She stuck her chin out and tried to outstare Beryl. Beryl didn't blink. Miranda balled her fists. "Why would I tip them off? You think I liked Redemption? You were there ten years. Maybe you let one or two things slip. Maybe you lied. Maybe you weren't in Redemption that long."

Beryl pushed away from the table and stood. "I need some air. Wait for our order." She left the diner.

Miranda scowled after her aunt. *I didn't call the Second Sphere. And David would never—oh.* She buried her face in her arms. They had traced David's calls. Had they taped his calls too? Acid churned in her stomach. *I owe Beryl an apology.* She took two steps toward the door. *If I tell Beryl how stupid I've been, she'll send me away.*

"Everything all right there, hon?" The waitress held a half-dried glass and stared.

Miranda forced a smile. "Fine. Everything's fine." She moved around the table and sat where Beryl had sat as if that had been her plan all along.

She rearranged their water glasses and took a long drink. *The Second Sphere could have guessed where we are, or someone at one of the gas stops could have called in a tip. I'll apologize for what I said, but I don't need to mention the phone call.* She vowed she'd never make another one.

Outside, the parking lot was dark, shrouded in shadows much like Miranda's thoughts.

"Be another minute or two on your egg sandwiches," the waitress called across the room.

"I'll let my friend know." She strolled out the door. The parking lot was vacant. *The car's gone!* Her mouth went dry. *Maybe Beryl went to get fuel.*

Miranda hurried across the gravel parking lot to the edge of the road. No vehicle stood under the lights of the gas station. No vehicle drove up or down the street either.

She left me. She didn't even give me a chance to explain. A damp breeze swept through. She shivered and wrapped her arms around herself.

"Hey, miss," the waitress called from the door. She held a small brown sack. "You gonna pay for these?"

"Huh?" Miranda struggled to control her racing heart. "Yes, of course." She walked back to the diner.

The waitress held the door open for her and then scurried behind the counter. "Thought y'all were gonna stiff me."

"How much?"

"Two dollars and forty-nine cents."

My rucksack— She glanced toward the door, whipped her head back. She hoped the waitress hadn't noticed. She dug around in her pockets and handed the waitress three ones.

The waitress gave Miranda her change and a knowing look. "Best bet is the bus. It don't come till 'bout nine-thirty. It'll take you to Wytheville and points east. Roanoke's taxi don't take long-distance pickups. Next closest taxi cab is in Winston-Salem two and a half hours away." She tipped her head to the telephone that sat on the other side of the register. "Number's taped to the counter."

"No, thanks. My friend will be back in a minute." She picked up the sack of sandwiches and returned to the table.

The aroma of hot eggs made her mouth water. She unwrapped one and took a bite. Her stomach churned. She wrapped the sandwich back up and put it back in the bag.

A battered and dusty pickup truck rattled its way into the parking lot. Its driver, a grizzled old man in faded overalls, climbed out of the truck and entered the diner. "Hey, Linda. How are you this morning?" He sat at the counter and ordered his "usual."

A family of four wearing their Sunday best came in and greeted the waitress. *Beryl isn't coming back.* Miranda waited until the waitress returned to the kitchen, then crossed the room to the telephone. She picked up the receiver. *Where can I go?* She wished she could go home, sleep in her own bed. *I could ask for a pardon.* She'd have to ask the First Apostle—*my father?* The ticking of the clock above the pass-through to the kitchen and the drone of the phone line grew impossibly loud.

Ask—him—for forgiveness? She slammed the receiver down and pushed away from the counter. *I'll wait. For Beryl or the bus, whichever comes first.* The father of the family watched her until she'd settled back into her seat.

Other locals filtered in. Each time a car door slammed, Miranda started and stared.

Outside, dawn's fingers reached across the sky. Another car engine choked and sputtered and died.

Miranda told herself that she would not look this time, but did anyway. The vehicle that had parked near the front door was a dark Ford. *Clunk.* Three men in hats and overcoats piled out of the car and headed toward the diner's front door.

She didn't wait to see the Fellowship shield on their left breast pocket. She slipped into the hall, hid in the shadows, and listened.

The waitress greeted the newcomers.

"We're looking for someone." The nasal tenor voice faded to indistinct mumbles.

The waitress muttered a response. Chatter from the tables stopped. The few customers opposite the hallway looked down at their plates, not talking and not eating either.

"Was she about yea-high, long brown hair, name of Miranda?" The tenor spoke as if he were in charge.

"Was there another, older woman with her?" Another man asked.

"How'd y'all know that?"

Miranda's chest tightened. *Be calm. Think like Beryl.* She tiptoed down the hall. The back door opened without a sound.

She darted across the narrow street to the hardware store's side door. She pushed the door's lever handle down and pulled. Metal creaked against metal. The top of the door opened, but the bottom stuck. She braced her foot against the wall and pulled harder. After a second's hesitation, the door popped open. She slipped inside.

The darkened store had one row of fluorescent lights on. The nearby shelves held gardening tools. She spun around. The door had a push bar on this side. If she blocked the bar, the door wouldn't open. She grabbed a handful of rakes, slid their handles between the door and the push bar, then pushed on the bar. The rakes kept the bar from disengaging the latch. *That should slow them down.* She ran to the back of the store.

The first door opened on an office. The second one led up some stairs. A bang and muffled curses came from outside. The third door opened onto an office overlooking the dock. She dashed through the room and out onto the loading dock. She flew down the steps and ran.

Chapter Thirty

Beryl climbed into the Hudson, shifted into neutral, and let it roll. Downhill, she started the engine and followed Route 52 out of town. *She had to leave, for the mission. Miranda had violated the rules. No doubt she'd thought it harmless.* Thirty minutes outside of Rocky Gap, Beryl pulled over to the side of the road. *Damn.* She couldn't do it. Miranda was too inexperienced. The Second Sphere would catch her in no time.

Back in Rocky Gap, she cruised the back streets. Worn but well-tended clapboard houses circled the town. *We need a new ride.* But small towns held too few possible car thieves. *So I'll give the Hudson a new identity.* She parked in an alley two blocks north of the five-and-dime. Some of the homes that backed onto the alley showed signs of a family starting their day. Behind a dark, one-story cottage stood a Woody. She gave it the Hudson's license plates. With any luck, the owners of the Woody wouldn't notice their license plate was gone for weeks.

Now to collect Miranda. Beryl squeezed through the barely wide-enough space between the five-and-dime and the pharmacy. Out of habit, she hesitated before stepping out into the morning light.

Across the street, the diner was busier than when she'd left.

Trucks and older model vehicles dotted the diner's parking. Local license plates. *They'll be curious if a stranger walks in without a car.* She pulled back into the shadows to consider her options. A dark green Ford Tudor coupe pulled into the diner's parking lot. Three men in hats and overcoats piled out. Two went inside. The third one stationed himself at the corner of the diner. He watched up and down the street. She could smell the taint of the Second Sphere from here. *Shit.* She sidled back toward the alley. The buildings on this side of the street had shared walls. She'd have to go to the end of the block, cross the street, and sneak in the back door of the diner to grab Miranda.

A door banged. A male voice shouted. Beryl caught a glimpse of Miranda forcing her way into the hardware store. One of the overcoats raced after her. The other one came running out the front. He and the street man ran toward the street. Beryl flattened against the rough brick wall.

The man in the alley edged along the hardware store wall, closing in on Miranda. Using his shoulder like a battering ram, he slammed into the door. Metal rang but didn't yield.

Beryl bit back a laugh. *Miranda might be trainable after all.*

She slid along the wall to the alley, sprinted to the Hudson. She flung herself into the car and hit the accelerator. The Hudson roared. She spun it around in a cloud of gravel and dust.

At the corner she took a fast left, crossed the highway, cut right. She sped up the residential street behind the diner and strained for a glimpse of Miranda.

There. End of the block. Running hard, with agents gaining on her.

Beryl shot past her, skidded to a stop. She stretched across the vinyl bench seat and hit the door lever. "Move it!"

Miranda dove in.

Beryl hit the gas.

Chapter Thirty-One

M iranda glanced out the rear window of the Hudson. The sun-dappled road snaked up forest-covered mountains behind them until it disappeared from view. No pursuers. Not for more than an hour. She huffed out a breath, tried to calm down. Beryl had left her, and she'd almost been caught. Not that Beryl cared. She hadn't given Miranda one word of explanation. No "I was unavoidably detained." No "The only open gas station was a mile away." No "I'm sorry you almost got caught because I wasn't there." She glared at her aunt, looked away when Beryl noticed.

A sharp right turn forced her to grab the hand strap. For a moment, it seemed that Beryl had lost control and would crash into the forest that grew up to the road's shoulder. But they didn't crash. They turned onto the rough, overgrown track of an abandoned fire road. Miranda bounced with every bump, banged her head and arm against the car. The road narrowed. The tips of overhanging branches scraped the roof with fingernails-on-chalkboard sounds. They missed tree trunks by mere inches. The car stopped, and the engine died.

Beryl faced her, one arm draped over the steering wheel, the other on the back of the seat. "Out with it."

"Out with what?" Miranda didn't bother to rein in her attitude.

"You have been huffing and puffing for miles. What is it that you're dying to say?"

Miranda's hands curled into fists. "You left me."

Beryl got out of the car and slammed her door shut.

"Oh no, you don't—" Miranda flung open her door, sprang out of the car, slammed her door harder. "You owe me an explanation."

Beryl came around the car, fast. She stopped toe-to-toe with Miranda, glowered, and asked, "What about the explanation you owe *me?*"

Miranda's fingernails dug into her palms. "They were looking for *me.*"

"I should have left you."

"Why did you come back?"

Beryl's scowl deepened. "I take my responsibilities and promises seriously."

"I take mine seriously too."

"And what responsibility took priority over keeping our location a secret?"

"I didn't tell anyone where we were. Not even David." Miranda clamped her lips together. She hadn't meant to say that.

"Your brother David?"

"He wouldn't have told a soul, even if he knew, but he didn't. He didn't know 'cause I didn't tell him." She returned Beryl's glare.

"When did you call him?"

"Yesterday, when we bought our clothes."

"So you broke your promise minutes after making it?"

Her stomach knotted. "I did what I had to." *She's going to send me away.*

"You called him to turn me in?"

Startled, Miranda drew back. "No. I called him to see what he knew."

"About me? About my 'death?'"

"It wasn't about you. It was…" Her pulse stuttered.

Beryl stared down her nose at Miranda. "Tell me."

Indignation robbed Miranda's breath. "You don't have to tell me anything. But I have to tell you everything? You leave me, let the Second Sphere chase me, save me at the last minute, and you think that's okay?"

"I tell you what you need to do, but you think you know better. Why did you call your brother?"

Miranda forced her words through clenched teeth. "That's private."

"Take your private conversation and go find someone else to string along." Beryl jerked her head toward the road they'd left behind them.

Miranda's vision narrowed, targeted on her aunt. "You evil—" She launched herself and drove her fists toward Beryl's chest. "Old. Biddy!"

Beryl stood her ground, caught Miranda by the wrists.

Miranda wrestled and tried to land a hit until she couldn't fight anymore.

Beryl released her. "We don't have time for this. Tell me or leave. It's that simple."

She didn't want to leave. She tucked her hands under her arms, focused on the ground. "I had to ask if David knew—that —Daddy—violated me." Heaviness spread from the top of her head to her toes. She couldn't speak, couldn't blink, couldn't even feel her own heart beating. She waited for a blistering denial from Beryl. Birds chirped. Leaves rustled in the light breeze.

Miranda forced herself to look at her aunt.

Beryl stood as still as stone.

Miranda couldn't tell what she was thinking. "Say something."

"To be clear, when you say, 'violated,' you mean intercourse, don't you?"

Miranda nodded.

Beryl ran a hand through her hair. "I thought nothing I learned about Donald would ever shock me again. Damn."

Miranda gasped. "You—believe—me?"

"Why would you lie about something like this?"

"You believe me." Miranda gulped air again and again. Her chest filled and filled until she feared she'd pass out. She bent and put her hands on her thighs. She blew out long, noisy breaths, struggling for normal. Why couldn't she wear one of her masks now?

Beryl steadied her, guided her backward. "Sit."

Miranda sat on the bumper. The heat of the engine warmed her, slowly melted the crushing weight off her. "David believed me. And you believe me. Maybe there is no proof like you said, but there have to be other people he hurt." She stood up. "We need to find them."

"Sit back down."

"But they'll help us stop him."

Beryl grabbed her shoulders and shook her. "Do you *want* to get caught? You cannot act without thinking. Not while you're on the run. Your life—*our* lives—depend on you using your head—on following my instructions." Beryl released her and ran a hand through her hair. "You should've told me. You should've followed the rules."

"If I'd told you, would you have let me make the call?"

Beryl shook her head. "Not until we were safe."

Miranda's throat thickened. *How could I be so stupid? We almost got caught. I almost got caught. We still might be caught.* She squared her shoulders. *I can't be dumb-and-blind Miranda anymore.* She took a deep breath and faced Beryl. "I was wrong. Stopping the Fellowship is bigger than anything that was done to me." She looked her aunt in the eye. "Give me another chance?"

Beryl stared at her for a long moment and then blew out a big breath. "Listen up. I will only say this once. I will always put the mission first. Brave souls have fought and died for this. To honor them, myself, and my country, I will demand discipline. You will be physically and mentally toughened. You will earn loyalty and respect and a place in this fight. Do you understand?"

Miranda's breath and pulse caught. "Yes, ma'am," she said and bit her lower lip to silence the reassurances she wanted to give.

A car passed in the distance.

Beryl raised her head and stared toward the road. "We need to move."

Miranda looked toward the road. "They're coming, aren't they?"

Beryl circled the Hudson. The trunk popped open. She dug around in her things and tossed Miranda a pair of thick, wool socks. "Put those on." When Miranda had complied, Beryl thrust a rolled sleeping bag into Miranda's arms. "We're on foot from now on."

"They'll catch us."

"Your next lesson involves tree branches and sweeping. You know how to sweep, don't you?"

Chapter Thirty-Two

Anna mopped her sweaty forehead with the back of her hand and glanced at the dark clouds rolling in. She bent and pulled another weed out of the bed of tiger lilies she'd planted outside her barracks. This morning, the pastor had reminded her of the tiger lilies when he'd said that sinners were like weeds. Sinners wanted to strangle the goodness out of people. He'd called the Annas God's gardeners. She tilted her head and considered the flowerbed. Tiger lilies were a lot like her. They grew fast and burst into spectacular, toxic blossoms. The weeds continually tried to choke out the flowers. She pulled another weed out with the same precision she used in Taking sinners. She was a good gardener.

The *click-clack* of hard shoes on concrete warned her. A Second Sphere cadet appeared at the corner of the barracks, headed toward her. *A summons on the Sabbath?* The mere hope of an assignment caused a tiny stirring in her chest. The cadet looked young, she estimated sixteen years old. *A fun age.* She ran her tongue over her lips and adjusted her sweat-soaked T-shirt to show more cleavage. She reached for a weed, pretending she didn't hear his approach.

"Anna Zero-five-seven?"

She stayed on her hands and knees and lifted her head so he could look down her shirt. "Yes?"

His eyes strayed to her chest. His mouth opened, but no words came out.

She stood and with slow, sensual strokes, brushed imaginary dirt off her chest. "What do you need of me, Cadet Captain?"

He flushed a bright red and stammered, "I'm not a captain, ma'am. I'm a corporal."

She fluttered her eyelashes at him. "Would you like to play in the dirt with me, Cadet First Lieutenant?"

He swallowed hard. "I'm not—um, I have a message—orders for you." He took a step back. "The commander wants you in his office, in full gear, at thirteen-hundred hours." He ran back to safety. She laughed out loud. She never tired of testing the young ones. And he'd brought a summons.

Her pulse quickened. Full gear meant an assignment, a chance to finish her transformation, to become the Angel of Death. It did not sadden her that Anna would be no more after the transformation. She lived for the glory of serving the Father, and she craved the power of Azrael that stirred within her.

After a quick shower, she pulled on her bulletproof undergarment and laid out her armor. The fire that was Azrael burned inside Anna. She threw on her ballistics vest and shoulder plates. Their combined weight threatened to tear her hair out by the roots. She pulled her braid out from under the gear and relieved the strain on her scalp. Then she snapped the quick-connect electronic interlink between her suit and cuirass and snugged the cuirass around her neck. Azrael's fire coursed through every nerve, every muscle, every cell. She picked up her helmet and gloves and strode toward her destiny.

When she crossed the parade grounds, Anna was careful to avoid eye contact with the young Azrael tied to the shaming pole. The stench of rotten tomatoes wasn't too terrible yet. Anna considered searching for a tomato to toss at the girl, but she couldn't keep Uncle waiting. She hurried on past.

A two-story red brick building on the south end of campus held Uncle's office. His secretary's desk was vacant, but his office door stood open. She stopped in the doorway and waited. Uncle sat behind his desk and frowned at an open file before him. He looked over his reading glasses at her. "Come in."

She closed the door behind her and stood exactly one meter in front of his desk. "Oh-five-seven reporting for duty, Uncle."

"This is your assignment." He rotated the file toward her.

The photo stapled to the flap stole her breath away. The woman in the photo stared up at her with unsmiling violet eyes. Anna suppressed a glorious shudder. It would be a powerful death.

He leaned forward, watching her. "Do you have a problem with this?"

She normalized her breathing and beamed confidence at Uncle. "My covenant with God supersedes any human relationship."

"The target's current location is unknown." He took a map from the folder, spread it open on his desk, and pointed to Kansas City circled in red. "She obtained a rental car here. Two-door Hudson Commodore. Red. We think she drove this route." His finger traced a line on the map to another red circle. He tapped his finger on Alton, Illinois. "Around twenty-one-thirty last night, they spotted the Hudson in Louisville. Early this morning, they picked her up again here." He jabbed a finger at a small town in the Blue Ridge Mountains. "Somehow, she managed to evade my top operatives."

Anna peered at the map. Red lines spider webbed from Rocky Gap, Virginia, to destinations on the Eastern Seaboard, including her home, Quantico.

"We believe she'll make a stop here." His finger stabbed the map.

"Lynchburg?"

"She may have a hostage." He picked up another folder,

opened it. The photograph was of a young woman everyone in America had seen with her famous father at one time or another.

Adrenaline rushed up the back of Anna's neck, warmed her ears. Two sanctioned hits in one assignment? And they were such powerful targets that Anna was certain she would complete the final transformation. Not a muscle of her face twitched, but Azrael seared her insides with a white-hot desire to kill. "His will be done."

Uncle pocketed his glasses and walked around his desk. "Quantico, more specifically here—our workplace and home—is likely her final destination. Her goal is to destroy all this." His pointer finger circled the air, then he leveled a penetrating look at her. "All of *us*."

He sat on the corner of the desk and hooked his thumbs in his vest pockets. "There will be watchers in Lynchburg and on all routes here. Avoid the watchers at all costs. Find the target. Determine if she has the hostage. Notify me."

Azrael did not like that, but Anna nodded her acceptance of this restriction.

"Do not harm the hostage. Your orders are to *follow* the target."

A single blink was the only sign she allowed of her surprise. "Our Father does not wish Judgment visited upon the sinner?" She controlled her voice to ask for clarification and nothing more.

He locked eyes with her. "Follow. Do not make contact. This is the will of our Father."

"Yes, sir." *Follow? This isn't an assignment. It's babysitting.* Inside, Azrael roared her displeasure, sucking the air out of Anna's chest. Anna hid her discomfort and resisted the urge to clap a protective hand over her heart. She glanced at the photo sitting on his desk. Uncle and his sister smiled at the camera. As a youngster, Anna had once told Uncle that she recognized his lady friend as his sister. Anna had spent a week in the hole for that. A wicked thought crossed her mind. *Yes*, hissed Azrael, *the innocent eyes of a child often see the truth.*

He handed her a piece of paper. "This authorizes you for an autogiro and anything else you need. Dismissed." He sat behind his desk, folded the map, and closed the folders.

She pocketed her orders and left Uncle's office. Azrael's hunger rippled through her. *I am God's gardener.*

Chapter Thirty-Three

Beryl led the way up the wooded mountain, jaw and fists clenched. *How could I not have seen that Donald was the worst kind of sewer sludge?* After all he'd done to her, she'd still put him, her brother, in a different category than the other bastards. Now? She wanted to put him in a deep, dark cage. *No, that was too good for him. Castration? That was too good for him too. Torture? Probably. Crucifixion? Definitely.*

A loud creak made her freeze. Adrenaline pumped up her heart, her chest, her legs. Miranda took another noisy footstep. Beryl held her hand up. Miranda stopped.

Beryl made a slow three-sixty and looked for what was out of place. Wind whispered through the trees. She'd forgotten how that sounded. Birds warbled, and vermin scurried through leaves and underbrush. She'd forgotten that too. Squirrels chittered at one another on a nearby tree branch. They leaped in turn to another branch that creaked under their weight. *Damn. Squirrels.* She'd forgotten about them too. Had she forgotten too much?

Get out of your head, or you'll get yourself and Miranda killed.

She signaled "down" to Miranda. Crouching low, she listened to the sounds and smelled the sharp scent of pine, the sweet aroma of wet earth and decaying leaves. She dredged up memories she'd locked away. *Zee-zee-zoo-zeet.* A warbler, the black-throated one? The faint rustle-stop-rustle-stop was a rodent. Another warbler answered the first. Adrenaline seeped away, left that momentary washed-out weakness. She hadn't forgotten, but opening up to old memories was hard. She stood and motioned for Miranda to follow.

Miranda trudged behind her, breathing hard, not talking. The girl needed to get in shape. Gert could help with that, but she needed training too. She needed skills that took years to master. They didn't have years or months, maybe not weeks.

Thud. Oof.

Beryl whirled. Miranda lay sprawled on the ground.

"I'm okay." Pale and sweaty, Miranda scrambled to her feet, dusted her hands off, and gave Beryl an I'm-ready look.

Beryl walked onward. Did Miranda have the strength to rise above the damage done to her? Beryl couldn't guess.

Beryl found a narrow path, a deer trail, and followed it. She showed Miranda animal signs, scat and footprints, and more of the basic hand signals. She demonstrated how to step on the bare spots, the rocks, the roots, and shift her weight from heel to toe. Miranda's walk quieted but also slowed. Beryl wasn't certain which was worse.

Between the trees, the sun rested low on the horizon. Shadows lengthened, hiding roots and vines. Ominous clouds rolled in from the west. The air temperature dropped. She increased their walking speed.

All too soon, clouds darkened the sky, and thunder echoed from mountain to mountain. She paused long enough for them to don their rain ponchos. *We should have reached the barn by now. Is Miranda slowing me down that much?* She drove a faster and faster pace.

"Maybe we should put up a tent," Miranda said.

"Don't have one."

"You have a tarp. We could string it between two trees."

"It's not much farther."

"To?"

"A safe place." She remembered the place, knew the man and woman only by their code names. Boomer and his wife weren't fighters, but they'd said they couldn't watch the goings-on and do nothing. Beryl and Gert had hidden in their barn more than once.

The walking, the vigilance, wore on her. Miranda trailed, head down, shoulders slumped, but she didn't complain. *Maybe not a princess after all.*

Finally, the mountain leveled off, the trees thinned. She peered ahead. The meadow. She hadn't forgotten everything. A raindrop plopped to the ground. Another found its way under her collar and slithered down her back, but it wasn't the rain that raised gooseflesh. Where the barn had been was a pile of charred and broken boards and beams. A blackened fireplace stood silent testament to where the cabin had been. She scanned the edges of the meadow. There were no signs of recent activity.

She unholstered her flashlight, turned to Miranda, and whispered, "Remember the signal?"

"Three blinks, come quickly," Miranda whispered back. "One blink, run away fast."

She gave her niece a long look. The girl had been a quick study of the hand signals and trail skills Beryl had taught her so far. Far harder and more dangerous tests waited for her, for them both. Beryl drew her knife from its sheath and darted across the clearing. She crouched in front of the soot-stained fireplace. The floor of the cabin, once wood, was now a patch of barren, rain-pocked dirt. *No wood smoke smell.* She ran her fingers over the cool, damp earth. *No ashes.* She couldn't tell how long ago the fire had taken place. She dashed across the clearing to the pile of burnt wood that had been the barn.

She bent close to the blackened wood and got a whiff of old smoke. The fire had taken place at least a week or two ago. She scanned the tree line. No burnt trees and none that looked singed. *Revise that estimate—four or more weeks ago.* The cabin and barn had burned but hadn't started a forest fire. No chance the volunteer fire department had arrived in time to stop the spread. Someone had put the fire out. The family, she hoped. But her internal alarms suggested the Soldiers of the Second Sphere had been here.

She straightened and blinked the flashlight three times.

Miranda joined her. "Was this where your friends lived? Did they die in the fire? Is it safe to be here?"

"Safe? If you wanted to be safe, you should have gone home."

Miranda pinched her lips together.

Beryl sighed. "They weren't friends. Not the way you mean." Fellow warriors held a whole different place in your heart. She ignored the way her insides twisted and gave the ruins a final glance. "We only knew this place as Galilee. Get used to it. The less you know about people, the better. Turn your flashlight off. Better if your eyes are accustomed to the dark."

"Shouldn't we put up the tarp now?"

"Not here." They'd stayed in the open too long already. More than a drizzle now, the rain fell in a gentle, steady rhythm. Judging from the thunder that grew louder and louder, the storm would get worse. "Come." She led a quick pace northeast.

Thunder crashed, and lightning strobed, and cold rain pummeled the earth.

In no time, rain soaked her jeans. Water-heavy denim clung to her legs. She slogged through treacherous mud and wet leaves. The dark punctuated by flashes of lightning made her doubt her ability to find her secondary shelter. She almost missed the small clearing in front of the erosion cavern. An enormous slab of rock leaned against a rocky outcropping as if one end of the slab had fallen off its support and buried itself in the earth.

No time for decent recon. She pulled out her flashlight and turned to Miranda. "Wait for my signal."

Miranda nodded.

Knife in hand, Beryl stole from tree to tree, then into the cavern.

Nothing stirred. The air smelled of wet rock and damp earth. The flashlight revealed a smaller-than-she-remembered space. At the high end, she could stand upright, but three paces inside she had to stoop, and three more paces she had to duck-walk. A fine gray dust covered the floor. The dust held plenty of animal prints, but not a single shoe print. She returned to the mouth of the cave and blinked the flashlight three times.

Miranda came running, stumbled, and slid into the cave on her hands and knees.

Chapter Thirty-Four

M iranda watched dawn creep across the meadow, making the fog slither to the shadows. Puddles from the night's rain glistened. Birds chirped morning songs, and a light breeze stirred water-laden leaves, adding a chorus of *plink, plink, plop.* This, Miranda's second two-hour watch, seemed twice as long as the first. *This was going to be a long day.* Across the clearing, smoky-blue fog hung in the valley, and a ribbon of pale, rose-colored light topped the mountains. A much more peaceful view than the cabin burnt to the ground. A sight that had haunted her almost as much as Beryl's lack of reaction to it.

What had happened to Beryl to make her so cold? After ten years in Redemption? More horrors than Miranda wanted to know about. She rubbed grit from her eyes. Soon, it would be time to wake Beryl. Miranda glanced at her aunt's shadowy form in her sleeping bag far back in the angle of the cavern. Beryl tossed and turned. *A nightmare?* Miranda silently promised not to disappoint her aunt today.

A low-pitched whinny that ended in a honking bray came from somewhere to the east. Miranda scrambled to her feet, scanned the area outside the cave. *Beryl's friend?*

Tuneless crooning confirmed a human accompanied the animal.

Miranda turned to wake Beryl and nearly bumped noses with her aunt. She clamped her lips tight on a strangled yelp.

"Remember, quiet and slow." Beryl's whisper tickled Miranda's ear.

The crooning stopped. Miranda refocused on the clearing. Loud rustling noises came from her right.

A scrawny old woman in a baggy, orange and green plaid shirt and red and black checkered pants rode a mule out of the shadows. Her long, gray braids swayed with the stout, black mule's movements. The mule slowed, lowered his head, and nibbled the grass.

"Git up, Frank, git up." The old woman prodded the mule's sides with muddy work boots. "Got some nice oats fer you at home." The mule snorted but didn't move.

Beryl whistled three high-pitched notes. The noise startled Miranda, though she'd expected the signal.

Quick and smooth, the old woman drew a red fireman's axe from a holster at her waist. She held it poised to strike and swept the clearing with a wary gaze.

Beryl whistled the three notes again.

The old woman lowered her axe, rested the weight of it on her shoulder, and leaned across the mule's neck. "Didja hear that, Frank? Ain't heard that bird for a long spell." She sat upright on the mule's back and whistled a two-note phrase, twice.

Beryl answered, only this time she repeated the three tones three times in rapid succession.

The old woman chuckled. "Don't that beat all, Frank? Be it a trap? Or a haint?" She slid off the mule and kept her back to it. She stood in a fighter's stance with her axe perched on her shoulder.

Beryl signaled Miranda to stay put, then walked out of the cavern. She halted a few yards away from the old woman.

The old woman sniffed the wind, stepped closer, and sniffed

the wind again. Frank stomped his foot, slapped his tail from side to side. The old woman stared at Beryl, cocked her head one way, then the other. The old woman broke into a big, snaggletooth grin. "Lawd, Beryl. I reckoned you was dead."

"Not dead yet, Gert."

Gert's face darkened, and she peered up at Beryl. "You sure you ain't a haint?"

Beryl had warned Miranda that the old woman was a little odd. *A little?*

Gert took one cautious step after another. She stopped out of arm's reach, extended the blunt head of the axe, and poked Beryl's midsection. She lowered the axe and let it hang at her side. "Lawd be praised, you is flesh and blood."

"We need shelter."

That was her cue. Miranda rushed out of the cave, eager to follow Beryl's instructions. She stopped at her aunt's side.

Gert stepped back and raised her axe, ready to strike.

Miranda gasped and flinched.

Beryl blocked Gert's poised axe handle with her forearm. Beryl and Gert glared at one another without moving, statues frozen in an eternal battle.

The old woman did not lower her axe or take a single step backward.

"She's a friend," Beryl said. Little by little, Beryl's arm and the axe moved until, at last, Gert returned the axe to its holster.

Miranda released the breath she'd been holding. "I'm sorry. I didn't mean to scare you." She glanced sidelong at Beryl. *Beryl had said move slowly.*

"I ain't a-feared of you." Gert stepped up to Miranda, sniffed the air, and exhaled a breath sweetened with apples. "Just don't like no surprises." She looked Miranda up and down. "Do I know you? You one of the Lamberts from over yonder?"

Beryl's glower made Miranda wince, but she answered the old woman, "I'm Miranda." She stuck out her hand.

"Don't shake hands with no Jasper. Where you from?"

175

Miranda dropped her hand to her side. *What is wrong with me?* Beryl had warned her about the handshake too.

Beryl's mouth twitched. "She's an ignorant city girl, Gert." Beryl gave her a brief, searing glance. "One that can't follow simple directions."

Miranda's cheeks blistered.

"We need a place to stay for a while. And someone to teach this one." Beryl jerked her head in Miranda's direction. "Will you help?"

Chapter Thirty-Five

The trail grew wide enough that Miranda no longer had to push through the bushes and low-hanging branches. Thick, slippery mud beneath their feet still made the trail treacherous. Beryl and Gert's conversation had stunned her. It contradicted so much of what she knew. *Correction.* So much of what she had been told.

A light breeze stirred and sent a chill rippling across her skin. She tucked her hands under her arms. *How could I have believed such lies? Why hadn't I asked more questions? How many more lies did I believe?* She kicked a stone. Mud flew off her shoe. The stone rolled over and sank back into the slime that last night's rain had left behind. Her shoulders tightened. *No more believing everything I'm told.*

Frank whinny-brayed and broke into a trot.

The sun cast long shadows into a small glade, filled to over-flowing. Clusters of boxes and a variety of discarded furniture formed a labyrinth. Its walls were three feet wide and shoulder high. Jagged bits and pieces of broken glass, barbed wire, and sharpened stakes jutted out of the top.

Gert reined the mule to a stop at the entrance to the labyrinth. Miranda and Beryl stopped beside Gert.

"You feel it, don't you?" Gert's dark eyes searched her homestead. Inside the labyrinth sat a house and several outbuildings. The house was a lopsided rectangle of worn wood patched with tarpaper and blue tarps. The tarps billowed and popped in the breeze like a living, breathing thing. "The gov'ment men set haints against me. Weren't fer my hexes, they'd a got me."

A rusted, commercial dryer sat on the porch and watched the yard with its round Cyclopean eye. Miranda scanned the homestead. She was pretty certain that even during the depression her mother had never lived like this.

"How many traps are in there?" Beryl nodded at the labyrinth.

"Can't say fer sure." A sly smile lit Gert's face.

Miranda glanced at the old woman, then stared at the maze before her. *Maybe Gert isn't as crazy as she seems.*

"We'll follow you," Beryl said.

Gert dismounted and led them through the maze. She paused now and then to clear a snare and reset it after they'd passed through. Miranda recognized some traps as noisemakers. Others were trip wires, but there was a third kind. Gert handled those with extra care, and that was warning enough.

After Gert released the mule into the corral, she climbed the rickety front porch steps of her home. At the threshold, she paused and muttered something under her breath. She turned around three times and, without pause or explanation, entered her home.

Miranda gave Beryl a puzzled look. Beryl shrugged. She entered Gert's home without the spin and without waiting on Miranda.

Miranda followed. Inside, odors of old smoke, old grease, and sweet apples hung in the still air. She blinked, adjusting to the dim light. A white tile counter that topped a single row of battered white metal cabinets stood on her right. The porcelain sink sat on top of the counter, unplumbed.

They circled a chrome dinette table stacked high with empty

bottles and assorted pots and pans. On the other side of the table sat a cold, cast iron stove. Past the stove, they entered a narrow aisle formed by boxes and crates filled with bottles. The stuffy and dim aisle set off claustrophobic prickles at the base of Miranda's neck. They passed an opening in the wall to a bedroom.

Gert's voice came from somewhere to Miranda's left. "Check it wunst and check it twice. Cain't miss not one of my tells."

Miranda rounded another corner. Dappled sunlight shining through a lace-curtained window hit her face, made her squint. Next to the window, a stone fireplace filled the rest of the wall and reached to the rafters. Across from the fireplace stood a tiny living room. Walled by more boxes, it held a pair of worn armchairs. Spindle-legged tables holding kerosene lamps bookended the chairs. A pair of reading glasses and a gilded, leather-bound copy of *Tragedies* by William Shakespeare sat on one of the tables.

Beryl dropped her duffle bag near one of the chairs.

Gert came into view. She touched this box and that as if assuring herself they were still there. "And check it thrice to be certain." She disappeared behind a stack of crates until only her soft muttering hinted of her presence.

"Toss your stuff over there." Beryl nodded at the pile she'd made at the end of the sofa.

Miranda dropped her rucksack and bedroll and crossed to the other chair.

"Don't sit. Grab your gloves," Beryl said. "We've chores to do."

She stopped mid-sit. They were Gert's unexpected guests. She ignored her aching legs, dredged up her last ounce of strength, and returned to the kitchen with Beryl.

In the kitchen, Beryl picked up a pair of five-gallon white plastic buckets. She led Miranda outside, past a stack of firewood, and up a foot-worn path. Halfway to the chicken coop and the pole barn stood a red, cast-iron hand pump. Beryl placed one of the buckets under the spigot of the pump.

"Stand to the side, like this. Grab the handle and pump."

Beryl pumped the handle up and down. On the third pump, it gurgled and squealed, and then water spurted from the spigot. "Fill both buckets and take them back to the kitchen."

It looks easy enough. Miranda grabbed the pump handle and pushed it down.

"Find me when you're done." Beryl walked away.

"Wait. Find you where?"

"Follow your ears."

The water had stopped. Miranda pumped the handle. It only looked easy.

After she carried the sloshing water buckets to the kitchen, she went back outside. A rhythmic *thunk thunk thunk* rang in the air. She followed the sound. Beryl raised a large axe and brought it down, splitting a big log in two. Her face glistened with a fine sheen of sweat. She tossed the split pieces on top of a waist-high stack, swiveled, and took a log from a jumbled pile on her other side.

"Good, you're here," Beryl said. "Just in time to cut the starter wood." Beryl showed her how. But no matter how Miranda tried, she couldn't chop anything with fewer than four or five swings. Not even the smallest branches.

When she had a small pile of ragged firewood and aching, burning muscles, she carried the wood inside. After that, there was gardening, more water hauling, and more chopping of firewood. She brought in a small armload of kindling to the stove where Gert had a steady fire heating a hearty stew. After dinner, Miranda spread her bedroll on the floor in front of the fireplace and slept.

Her first morning visit to the outhouse was an exercise in agony. Every muscle in her body protested her slightest movement. Her feet were swollen and tender. She limped back to the house and paused for a brief moment of recovery before tackling the porch steps.

Beryl came out of the door, her rucksack on her back.

"I didn't know we were going somewhere this early." Miranda didn't know how long she could walk.

Beryl grunted and strode past her.

"Wait. It won't take me a minute to get dressed."

Beryl paused. "What did Gert wear yesterday?"

Miranda blinked. "Um, a shirt and pants. Colorful." *Ugly.*

"You'll stay here today. Gert knows what to do." She entered the labyrinth.

Miranda mouthed a silent "thank goodness," then pinned her arms against her stomach. "Where are you going?"

"Keep your eyes open and do what Gert tells you." Beryl navigated the labyrinth. "We'll talk when I get back."

"When will you be back?"

"Suppertime."

Beryl disappeared into the forest.

Miranda took a deep breath. *I'll work hard. You'll see.* She pulled herself up the steps.

Gert stood in the doorway, hands on her hips. "Whilst you was slug-a-bed, I done watered the livestock, let the hens and goats out, gathered the eggs, stoked the fire, and cooked breakfast."

"I'm sorry," Miranda said. "I'm new to this." The aroma of eggs and sausage and biscuits made her mouth water. She swallowed and tried to ignore her hunger. "Tell me what I need to do."

"Eat. Gonna need a full belly today."

After breakfast, Gert gave her a bottle of something she called liquid fire but was labeled horse liniment. After using it, Miranda knew why Gert called it liquid fire. But rubbing it into her skin eased her muscle pain.

In the garden, Miranda learned the difference between lettuce leaves, bean plants, and weeds. Later, she fed the chickens and spot-cleaned the coop and Frank's stall. Gert showed her how to milk the goats. She tried. The goats didn't like it. She pumped more water, chopped more firewood, and fell asleep before supper.

Chapter Thirty-Six

B eryl waited for Gert's answer.
The old woman bounced a measuring look from Beryl to Miranda and back. "You a-hidin' from them gov'ment men again?"

Beryl nodded, her throat too tight for speech. Ten years ago she'd awakened in Gert's home, wracked with a rib-bruising cough, a soul-sucking guilt, and a wish for a visit from the Angel of Death. She drew in a deep breath and slammed the mental door shut on her memories. Indulging in emotion would get her killed.

Gert walked back to her black mule and muttered, "She come with a city girl. 'Spects me to take 'em home, to pertect 'em." She grabbed a handful of mane and hopped on. The mule snorted a mild protest and shuffled his feet, a striking thing because of his one white leg. "Ain't the same as last time. No, sir," Gert continued. "Half the damn mountain be covered with gov'ment sniffing about."

Damn. She'd hoped— She closed the distance between her and Gert. Miranda trailed after her. "How long have the government men been here, Gert?"

"They been creepy-crawling 'round for nigh on a month now. But now they on my mountain."

It was a blow, but Beryl had anticipated something like this. "I understand. Miranda and I will move on." Richmond was closer but riskier. She'd have to head to Salem.

"Now don't go a-gettin' all nettlesome. My hexes will ward 'em off, or my name ain't Gertrude Elizabeth Howerton." She tapped her mojo bag, hanging from her belt, and swept the forest with a wary, searching look. "Hexes be strongest a-home. We best get going."

Miranda's face creased with worry. "They've been here a month? They can't be hunting us, can they?"

"Doesn't matter," Beryl said. She headed toward the cavern.

"They been a-huntin' Monkshood," Gert said.

Beryl stopped. *What? The Fellowship is hunting Monkshood?* She whirled around. "They're hunting a dead man?"

Gert looked down on her like she'd eaten the wrong mushrooms. "He ain't dead."

Beryl searched Gert's sharp brown eyes. "How do you know?"

"I seen him, didn't I?"

The world zoomed out from Beryl. She seemed far away from Gert, Miranda, and the earth. All oxygen vanished. She couldn't breathe. Years of numbing herself to the pain cracked. She battled to rebuild her mental walls. She wouldn't—couldn't —give in.

"Who is Monkshead?" Miranda's voice pulled her back to the here and now.

"Ethan." *Alive.* She sucked in air and blinked until her vision and her thoughts cleared. Miranda's hand gripped her elbow. Beryl shook it off and focused on Gert. "Where is he?"

Gert clicked her tongue. "Now how would I know'd that?"

"I have to find him, see him." Her fingernails dug into her palms. "When did you see him? Where?"

"We best talk whilst we walk," Gert said.

Beryl gave a sharp nod. "Grab your things, Miranda."

Beryl picked up the duffle bag and Miranda grabbed the Pan Am bag. They each shrugged rucksacks and sleeping bags onto their backs and followed Gert up a trail only Gert and her mule could see.

Beryl waited until the cave was out of sight, then trotted forward, and put a hand on the mule's bristly neck. "Tell me about him."

"Ain't much to tell. Seems whilst you was recovering, he were too. Don't know where. Don't know hows or whys neither. One day, 'bout eight year ago, I gets a message to meet with someone. 'Twas Monkshood."

"How was he? How'd he look? Was he—okay?"

"He looked like he looked on the television. 'Cept he was skinny. Like he hadn't et a good meal for a spell."

"Did he mention—me?"

"Child, we thought you was dead."

Of course, they did. Donald held my funeral. She clenched her fists and forced herself to focus. "What did Ethan want?"

"He had a job for me." One of her neighbors, his wife, and oldest son had been Taken. Their eighteen-year-old son, Ian, had hid three younger siblings in the woods for months. He raided farms and homes for food and clothing. One night a local SABR cell member came near to blow Ian's head off for stealing a hen afore he recognized the boy. The SABR member took the children to Ethan. Ethan brought the children to Gert. She said they were safe and strong now, and she said it with pride.

Ethan would insist on doing that himself. He'd always had a soft spot for children. Gert rode her mule across a swinging bridge suspended over a rain-swollen creek. Beryl followed, concentrating on her footing. *Wait.* "Gert, did you know Ethan before? When I was sick?"

"Do you think I'd-a kept that from you?" Gert snorted. "I never seen the man before or since."

"But he knew about you?"

Gert frowned down at her. "Reckon he could-a learned 'bout

me from any Hill person or even from some in Lynchburg. Ain't like I been a recluse."

Beryl knew Gert was right. Ethan had all the resources of SABR. She wondered what he would think when he saw her. And with that thought, she realized she was going to find him before she took care of Weldon and his Angels of Death. She had to.

They headed up the mountain, weaving between tall pines. The pines shivered in the intermittent breeze, showering them with chilly, leftover rainwater. An occasional bird chirped the only sound that interrupted the *squish-squish* of their footsteps and the sucking sounds of Frank's hooves in the mud. From time-to-time, Beryl doubled back, checked for signs they'd been discovered. She found no telltale signs, but her sense that danger followed kept her uneasy.

"Why was that barn burnt?" Miranda asked.

"She's asking about Galilee, Gert."

Gert tsked. Frank raised his head and twitched an ear back toward her. "Happened in the middle o' the night about two months ago. Could smell the smoke fer days. I feared it were the young Hobarts' cabin. Ian Henry tol' me 'twas Galilee."

"Boomer and his wife?" Beryl asked, though she assumed they were dead.

"'Cording to the investigation, they *accidentally* locked they-selves in the barn and perished."

Miranda sucked in a breath. "How horrible."

"I'd like to see them investigators *accidentally* locked up some-wheres toasty," Gert muttered.

I'll see to that. Beryl added two more deaths to the accounting she intended to shower down on Weldon and the Council.

Over time, the sun and the breeze dried up the leftover rain-water and the cotton shirt Beryl wore. Finally, Beryl asked about the Lynchburg SABR cell.

"I hear tell that they still meet up these here days."

"I have to make contact. I have to talk to Ethan."

"*We* have to make contact," Miranda said.

A mischievous smile lit Gert's face. "I'm a-thinking that you two might have to do a 'Saturday wash-up' afore you visit any city fellas."

Beryl gave her a black look. "Then get us to your place so we can do that and I can go to Lynchburg."

Gert's smile grew wider. "My place ain't but over that ridge."

Beryl glowered at Gert. "You could have said that first."

Gert chuckled. "You be as prickly as ever."

"And you're a crazy, cantankerous old woman." They both laughed. It was a strange sensation. Beryl hadn't had a genuine laugh in years. Hers sounded dry, raspy, unused. Her gut twisted, and her laughter died. Unused because laughter was a luxury she couldn't afford.

She couldn't help tossing a look over her shoulder. No one there but Miranda.

Miranda scowled at her mud-caked shoes.

Chapter Thirty-Seven

Refreshed by her shower, Kara spritzed on some Miss Dior. Its flowery scent lingered in the air. The Detroit Ladies Library Association had been appreciative of her speech, and the trip had given her and Weldon a break from the hectic pre-inauguration schedule. She snugged the ties of her rose-colored silk dressing gown, sat at the polished waterfall-style vanity, and brushed her hair. One hundred strokes with her silver-plated hairbrush morning and night kept her hair lustrous. She counted each stroke and watched Weldon's reflection in the mirror. He lay against the headboard with his hands behind his head. His face was lit with post-coital rapture, and the sheet lay indecently low over his hips.

"I love to watch you do that."

She gave him a small, seductive smile and continued brushing. Watching him get aroused entertained her.

"Won't you come back to bed?" He patted the mattress beside him.

She toyed with the idea of another round of sex, but she'd just gotten cleaned up. She didn't relish getting sweaty again. "Darling, you know I would, but I have a busy day ahead of me. And we have business to discuss." She laid her brush down on the vanity and swung around on the bench. "You saw Dr. Locke's new laboratory?"

"Yes." He lifted the sheet. "Come on. It's still warm in here."

She tsked at him. "And the hundred Azrael?"

He sighed. "His laboratory looks like a laboratory. It's all shiny and new, and he has a thousand—what's its—parthenotes. He has a thousand parthenotes growing into a thousand cute little bundles of assassins. And the expansion is almost done. Don't worry. There will be more. We'll deliver the order and have plenty to spare." He swung his feet out from under the sheets and sat on the edge of the bed. "Since you insist on talking business—" He took a deep breath. "I'm going to increase the security detail for you and Donald."

"Again? You just did."

"That was because the public expects the First Apostle-elect to have more."

"So why—" A chill shot through her. Her muscles clenched from her jaw to her toes. Her heart thrashed in her chest. "You said Beryl was in the mountains, that your men would have her in a day or two."

His eyes met hers, strong, steady, somber. "We need to be prepared. She has a surprising amount of resourcefulness for someone who has been out of touch for so long."

She gripped the edge of the bench. Sharp metal edges dug into her fingers. "Your men have no idea where she's at, do they?"

"Trying to find someone in the Appalachians is like trying to find a pebble in the rocky bottom of a creek. We will find her. But —she's not the only threat."

"Oh?" Her muscles cranked another notch tighter.

"My agents are seeing signs that the apostates are preparing for some major activity. Their sources say something big will happen on inauguration day."

Her breath caught, and a wave of dizziness washed over her.

How could this be happening? It was as if someone had set a tenth plague against her. Her blood grew hotter, filled her chest, and rushed through her veins. She forced out a huff of breath. She had worked too hard, for too long, to allow anyone to spoil that day. "We have to stop them."

He knelt before her, stroked her arms. "Trying to stop the apostates is like stomping on ants at a picnic. They keep coming."

"You mean you can't or you won't." She turned away from him, straightened the silky fringe hanging from the lampshade of the vanity table lamp.

He pulled her gently to face him. "You know I'd die for you. Tell me what you want me to do."

"It's time for stage two." She watched him through her lashes.

His brow crease deepened. "Stage two?"

"Your agents will enhance the apostates' little raids on registrars' offices and newspapers. Show them for the criminals that they are."

His face smoothed, and a wily smile broke through. "Why only enhance their raids? A rise in apostate-led attacks will turn supporters into informers."

She chuckled fondly. They made a great team. But now, she needed to finish getting ready for her next engagement. "When do you meet with your men?"

He glanced at the silver and walnut mantle clock perched on the highboy dresser across the room. "Not for thirty minutes." He held his arms out to her.

She smiled and waggled a finger at him. "You can't be late. Nor can I. The Women's Auxiliary of Detroit has paid to hear about the woman's role in the Fellowship."

He laughed. "I know how excited you are to have rubber eggs for breakfast."

She kissed him deeply. "That should hold you awhile."

He strolled through the connecting door into his room, humming, "Onward Christian Soldiers."

A few seconds later, his shower started running.

She closed and locked the connecting door and then pulled her braided suit out of the closet.

Chapter Thirty-Eight

Miranda dragged herself out of her warm sleeping bag into the chilly dawn air and met Beryl at the opening of the labyrinth.

Beryl asked her how many chickens Gert had.

"Twenty?"

Beryl sent her back to do chores.

Miranda watered Frank and put him in his corral. Then she watered the goats and released them to their pen. Four goats, three kids, and a billy. She let the six hens, one rooster, and four pullets out and gathered eggs, a dozen. Next she chopped wood, weeded the garden, hauled water, and harvested vegetables. She failed to catch the chicken Gert wanted, then cleaned and snapped beans for dinner.

After a dinner of country hash and green beans, Beryl asked how many goats Gert owned.

Miranda answered, "Four goats, three kids, and a billy."

"Good. What else did you observe about the goats today?"

Miranda smiled. She'd ace this. "The goats have a double-fenced pen because they're so agile and to protect them from predators. They are very curious and social. They recognize each other's voices. And—" She paused to be certain she had Beryl's attention. "They have rectangular pupils."

Beryl nodded. "Good. Work with Gert again tomorrow."

Miranda slapped her palms on the table. "How can counting chickens and chopping wood help me be a rebel?"

Beryl leaned back in her chair and gave Miranda a look that took her measure and found a disappointing lack. "Being a rebel isn't swooping in like the hero of some romance novel to save the day. The danger that you fantasize about, that's only a few seconds here and there. Mostly, it's hard work. Lots of hard work. No one will coddle you here."

Miranda stared at the chipped, green Formica of the tabletop. "I'm not asking for special treatment."

"Good. Be up at five a.m. tomorrow. Square away your things and get your personal hygiene done. Bring in the water and firewood, stoke the fire, and start the teakettle. Then help Gert with the livestock. After breakfast, you'll do whatever she asks and stay alert."

Miranda clenched her teeth and glared at Beryl. "I can help SABR."

"We'll see."

Over the next two weeks, Miranda's hands went from reddened and tender to blistered to tougher. Her nightly ritual of bathing in Gert's liquid fire grew less frequent. But Beryl's nightly questions about insane details remained impossible.

Chapter Thirty-Nine

S itting in the best tailor's shop in town, Kara nodded. She had
waited years while Donald moved up the ranks, had waited
eight hours while the Assembly grilled Donald, and had waited
days for the Assembly to make a choice. All the waiting would
soon be worth it. She gave her man an appraising look.

The tailor sat on his haunches, pincushion in one hand, the
other hand gesturing at the man in the gray flannel suit. Donald
stood on a small, raised dais in front of a row of mirrors.

She twirled her finger in the air. Donald did a slow turn. She
eyed the suit. It had to be perfect. Millions would be watching.
She sighed. The *V* of the wide padded shoulders, wide lapel, and
fitted waist made her heart flutter. Donald was a beautiful man,
and in that suit he was stunning. "George, you've done an impec-
cable job." Donald finished his turn and smiled his shy, little boy
smile. She wet her lips and smiled back. *Too bad today's schedule is so
full.* She let her face settle into a public, congenial smile and
turned to the tailor. "The royal blue tie and pocket-square are the
perfect touches for the inauguration. Well done."

"Thank you, Lady Clarke."

She hid the little prick of pleasure that spread through her at the formal address. *"Lady Clarke" had such a nice ring to it.* She gave herself a mental shake. *No time to dally.* "Donald, darling, what are you waiting for? Change your clothes. We're due at the church for the rehearsal in a half hour." Donald and the tailor scurried to the dressing room.

Kara sat in the little chair with its pincushion-styled seat and pulled the agenda from her purse. She knew it by heart, but everything felt so unreal and it was tangible proof that her dream had come true. The front door buzzed, sending alarm racing through her blood. Their bodyguards stationed outside should have prevented any intrusions. She reached into her purse and found the cool, smooth handle of her steel letter opener. She disengaged it from its mother-of-pearl sheath.

"Lady Clarke?" A bodyguard filled the doorway.

She released her breath and withdrew her empty hand from her purse.

He held a sealed, manila envelope. "This came by courier. It's marked Urgent."

"Thank you." She took it from him. "You may return to your post." He left. She didn't sit until after the door buzzed again. Then she pulled out her letter opener and opened the envelope. She slid out the only piece of paper inside, a newspaper clipping from the *Philadelphia Inquirer.* The headline read "Four Dead, Dozen Injured in Attack by Apostates." In the paper's top margin was a Roman numeral two in blue ink. The article screamed outrage at the increase in attacks by apostates in the past two weeks. She folded the piece of paper and tucked it into her purse. Now she knew which one of the two speeches she'd written would be the inaugural address. She folded her hands primly over her purse and waited for Donald.

Chapter Forty

Beryl eased the "borrowed" car into a parking spot and curbed the wheels. A few hundred feet away, Ninth Street dead-ended onto a terraced hill. A wide granite and limestone stairway called Monument Terrace climbed up the hill. Lynchburg had built the monument to honor locals who fought and died for their country. Plaques and statues remembered the Civil War, the Spanish-American War, and World War I on thirteen landings.

In her old woman persona, Beryl fussed with her hair. She picked up her oversized, black purse. *Last stop. If there's no message here, I'll give up on Lynchburg. Give up on reaching Ethan. Go to Salem.*

The bronze *Statue of a Doughboy* stood at the bottom of Monument Terrace. She leaned against the statue and pretended to search her purse. *There.* Blue chalk marks on the terrace wall behind the statue, a star between parallel lines. The warmth of adrenaline kicked her pulse up a notch. *The church drop.* A slow scan of the terrace and nearby buildings revealed no visible threats. Traffic noises, people noises, nothing close enough to alarm her. But she assumed nothing.

She climbed the steps, paused, and scanned for spotters or

tails. At the top of the Terrace, the *Statue of a Confederate Infantryman* provided a bit of cool shade for her next rest. The terrace sat between a two-story brick building on her left and a three-story clapboard building on her right. Across the street stood the court-house, a windowless, four-columned Greek revival building. Next to it was the church. A glint flickered in a second-floor window of the brick building on her left. *Binoculars? Second Sphere? SABR?* She fanned herself and waited. The second-floor window remained dark and lifeless. Whether the flicker was imaginary or real, she had to get into the church.

The limestone of the old church had darkened with age, smudged watermarks, and grime. A triple-vaulted arcade stretched between steeple towers on each end of the building. Midway between the towers and above the arcade was a beautiful old rose window.

Inside, cool air bathed her in silence and the scent of fresh blossoms. Her eyes adjusted to the gloom of the clerestory light-ing, and she moved forward. The lobby and the coatroom were empty. A steady murmur came from inside the sanctuary. She peered through the arched window of the interior door and slipped inside.

Rows of empty pews stretched between her and the pulpit. Kneeling at the balustrade in front of the altar, a middle-aged woman muttered prayers. Beryl waited in a shadow-veiled corner. Not another living thing stirred.

The woman finished her prayer and left. Beryl entered the steeple tower and climbed the familiar spiral, wrought iron stairs. The little room at the top of the stairs was dark and had the cloying air of abandonment. She went to the east corner, knelt, and ran her fingers along the rough edges of the stones. The crack, hidden in the shadows, was still there. She pulled out a rolled piece of paper and straightened it.

W.P. Obits out. Kemper Street Station. SE Platform 2 p.m. TMSAFR.
Q—N and A. A—no, W.P.
Q—newsstand. A—few minutes.

Wait. Today is Friday. She glanced at her watch. *Two-fifty. Too late.* That meant she had to wait until Thursday. She paced back and forth in the tiny room. *Almost a week? Did they not understand the need for urgency?* She didn't have time. She stopped. *It had taken ten years to get here. Six days? No time at all. Being ready mattered.* She'd use the time. She'd be ready. Hell, maybe she'd train Miranda. The girl was ready now or she never would be. She tore the message into tiny bits and dropped the bits in her pocketbook.

She crossed the street to Monument Terrace. A lone businessman with a briefcase loitered near the statue. He followed her down the steps. She paused her old lady shuffle. He stopped to read a plaque. She continued. He passed her when she stopped a second time. She slowed her descent even more. The businessman disappeared into the bank.

At the bottom of the Terrace, she hesitated. She could go another direction. *I need to know.* She passed the bank. The businessman exited the building and stayed behind her no matter how slow her pace. *Sloppy.*

She shuffled up Church Street. He hung back about a hundred feet. She turned the first corner, did a quick U-turn, and walked back the way she came. The man with the briefcase didn't flinch or stop, but his eyes widened.

She ducked in and out of shops, ditched her hat one place, the purse another. She stole a sweater and another hat and did several double-backs to be sure she lost him. If Briefcase belonged to the Second Sphere, he hadn't recognized her or she'd be dead. He could have, knowing he'd been made, signaled a more discreet partner. *Nah. He was too sloppy for the SS.* More likely he was SABR watching the drop, a new enough member he didn't recognize her. He'd report her description and when and where she'd visited the drop. *Still, just to be sure...*

She walked her old woman's walk into Beverly's Dress Shop. She fished some of the scraps of the message out of her purse and dropped them in a trash can by the checkout. She left the store and wandered into Monument Café. She told the hostess that she was in desperate need of relief. She was shown the ladies' room right away. Inside, she did a quick stall check and flushed the rest of the shredded paper. She locked the stall door behind her and loosened her hair. Shucking off the old woman dress in the narrow space, she banged her elbows on the metal stall walls. She tugged down the hem of the A-line skirt she wore underneath the dress. Retrieving her gun from the purse, she stuck it under her blouse and into her waistband. A pink scarf tied around her neck and a large pair of dark sunglasses finished off her disguise. She emptied a trashcan onto the floor, stuffed her former disguise into it. Then she scooped up the trash and dumped it on top of the clothes. She strode out into the bright but cloudy day.

She rounded the corner to the side street where she'd parked the car. A blue and white had stopped alongside the car she'd borrowed. She sucked in a curse. The police officer opened his driver's door and walked to the front of the parked car. He peered through the front window, then the passenger window.

She ignored the staccato of her pulse and kept her pace casual and steady. She drew even with the cars. The officer returned to his car and opened the door. She gave him a big, friendly smile. "Good afternoon, officer."

He smiled and nodded. "Good day, ma'am."

She kept walking. He keyed his radio. "Adam Six to dispatch."

"Dispatch. Go ahead, Adam Six."

"Confirm a match for that stolen vehicle. Looks like a kid took it for a joy ride. Break."

She rounded the corner and took a deep relieved breath. Unrecognized twice. It was nice to know her skill at disguising herself had stayed strong.

Chapter Forty-One

After lunch, Miranda dodged piles of junk chasing one of Gert's fattest chickens. Her foot slipped on something slick, and she face-planted into the dirt. Chickens squawked and scattered, found new places to scratch and peck. She jumped up, spat dust, and wiped her mouth. She frowned at the chicken poop on her jeans.

"Almost got that one," Gert called from the porch. On the table next to her sat young spinach and mustard leaves piled on a clean flour sack towel. Leaves Miranda had picked that morning. Gert swished the greens in a bucket of water Miranda had filled. "Can't trim spurs lessen you catch them."

Miranda clenched her fists. *What does she think I've been trying to do?* A black and white hen ventured near. Miranda crept toward it, slid one foot forward and then the other, inching closer. She grabbed at the chicken. The hen flapped her wings in panic and took off. Miranda straightened and wiped sweat from her brows with her wrist. *How the heck does anyone catch the darn birds?*

"No more a-chasing hens today," Gert called. "Else we'll have no eggs in the morning." Gert said the same thing every day. Yet the next morning there were always plenty of eggs.

"That's it." Miranda planted her fists on her hips and glared at Gert. "I've more than earned some training."

Gert chuckled. She disappeared into the cabin with her bowl of greens. When she reappeared, she wore a wide-brimmed straw hat. She carried the two water pails by the handle in one hand. In the other hand, she held a second straw hat. She plopped the hat on Miranda's head, handed her a bucket, and kept on walking. "It's strawberry pickin' time."

Miranda dropped the bucket and gaped after Gert. "You heard me, you old crazy woman. I'm not picking strawberries. If you and Beryl won't train me, I'll find someone who will."

Gert faced her. "You struck a deal, didn't you?"

"Yes." She made the word hiss through her teeth.

"Chores for food and learnin'. Right?"

"I didn't agree to be a slave." She pressed her lips together.

Gert laughed out loud. "I told Beryl it takes a special kinda city girl to work hard. Ain't their fault. City life makes 'em soft. They forget discipline and honor and how to think for theyselves." She entered the labyrinth.

Miranda stared icicles through Gert's back. The old woman didn't notice. She straightened from working on a trap. She stood tall with a straight back. It struck Miranda that Gert normally did all the chores on her own. And while Miranda had worked, Gert had worked too. Gert had offered Beryl shelter not once but twice. And the old woman did this despite the threat of the Second Sphere and certain death if she were caught. Miranda grabbed the bucket by its handle and marched after Gert. "I'll show you a special kind of city girl," she muttered.

Gert didn't say a word, but Miranda could've sworn the old woman slowed down to allow her to catch up.

After a twenty-minute hike, they reached a sun-warmed valley. Lush red berries dotted its floor. Gert got straight to work. She plucked berries a handful at a time and dropped them into the bucket. She didn't even look Miranda's way. "Pick an' choose,

Miranda. Green ones'll make you sick. But you gotta be careful o' the real ripe ones. Mayhap they be rotten inside."

"Not too green and not too ripe," Miranda repeated. She sat back on her heels and gave Gert a quizzical look. "Are we talking about strawberries or me?" Gert didn't answer. Miranda picked more berries. *I'm not rotten. I'm angry. Beryl doesn't believe me. Not about hating the Fellowship. Not about fighting—* She breathed a deflated sigh. She couldn't blame Beryl. She still vacillated. One minute, her father was a monster, and the next minute, she was. How could anyone believe he'd violated her and she'd forgotten it? "I don't know how to prove it."

"Prove what?" Gert asked.

Miranda started. She hadn't realized she'd spoken aloud. "Never mind. I shouldn't have said anything." She plucked a berry from the center of a patch of green thick with ripe, red berries.

"Ahhh. Your secrets be soul-eaters," Gert muttered.

Miranda turned a puzzled look on Gert. "What?"

Gert paused in her berry picking. "Sometimes we keep secrets to pertect others. Some o'those secrets are good, but if the secret be putrefied, it can et you up."

Yeah, she had a putrefied secret, but— "When the secret is horrible and you can't prove it, it's better not to talk about it."

Pfft. "Girl, you gotta make a choice. Believe it or don't."

"It's not that simple."

"It's always that simple. There's always a choice. It's the choices you make that reveal who you are. That's proof enough."

A chill rippled. Miranda rubbed her arms.

"Truth lives in a body. Here and here." Gert pointed at her head and her heart. "Don't matter iffen it happened long ago or if no one else saw or felt it. Don't matter if not one other soul believes you. Truth can be hurtful, but dark secrets and lies be worse. Peace follows truth. Trust this and this." She pointed at her head and heart again. "Live in truth, and there ain't nobody can tell you it ain't so."

"I'll try." Miranda didn't know what else to say. She picked berries and tried to think, to believe, that *she* was the proof. She picked up her bucket of berries and moved to another spot. Her half-full bucket swung back and forth with a lightness she hadn't experienced in a long, long time. If this was how a new way of thinking made her feel, she needed to re-think a lot of things.

She re-examined the questions Beryl had asked over the past couple of days. *What was it that Beryl wants me to see?* Miranda scanned her surroundings. She moved to a different patch of strawberries to change her perspective. "Gert, what kind of tree is that one?" She nodded toward a small clump of deciduous trees on the downward slope.

"Chestnut."

Miranda studied the tree, memorizing its shape and leaves. She changed places again and noticed a pile of rocks near the tree line. It wasn't a natural pile. It made a crude arrow that pointed east. She asked more questions and moved about the valley picking more berries. A thick stick poked out of some underbrush, parallel to the ground. Through Beryl's eyes, it could be a rifle barrel. She asked Gert about the local plants and about Gert's livestock and home. Then she had one more question. "Beryl's gone all day and disappears again for most the night. Where does she go?"

"Can't say."

"Look, I…I want to get to know my aunt better. May I ask you some questions while we're picking berries?"

"Don't know much." Gert bent over a clump of bright berries.

"How did she find you the first time?"

"She didn't. I found her," Gert said. "She were in an awful way. Lung fever, scarce could breathe, couldn't walk two steps without falling into the snow. I helped her up on Frank, took her home."

"That was when she was running from the government men, wasn't it?" Miranda guessed.

Gert grunted. "They stank up my mountain till the weather turned so cold they figured she were dead. A miracle she weren't."

Gert dropped a handful of berries into her nearly full pail. "My poultices pulled the infection out of her wounds. But no poultice could fix her soul-eating secret. Killing her Anna like-ta killed her."

Something sharp caught in Miranda's ribs, made it hard to breathe. *Beryl killed her own daughter?*

"I kept a-telling her, you cain't die. Not till justice be done." Gert shook her head. "No justice in dyin'. She didn't know it were her baby-girl a-trying to kill her man."

A cold, hard knot formed in Miranda's stomach. She bit her lip and balled her hands into fists. Berry juice oozed between her fingers. She stared at the dark red juice and shivered. She wiped her hands on the grass, but the stains were still there.

"I guess Beryl still had some fight in her," Gert said. "She got better. Never seen nobody work so hard. Made herself strong enough to leave ever day then, like she do today." Gert put a hand on her low back and stood.

"Did she go to the same place then as she does now?"

"Don't know where she went, 'cept she promised she'd make them pay. Pay for a-turnin' Anna into an Azrael who tried to kill her own pa. And pay for a-killin' my Billy Ray and little Mary. Almost made me feel sorry for that Mr. Lancaster that she said were responsible."

Miranda's thoughts skittered around like water in hot grease. Beryl killed her own daughter. Anna was an Azrael? Uncle Weldon? "Weldon Lancaster was responsible for the Azrael?" she asked. "You mean he was their boss?"

"That's what she said."

Beryl had said she was in Redemption for treason. *Maybe Mama was right. Apostates, rebels, were traitors.* Then Miranda remembered Beryl's funeral. She remembered her cousin Anna, laughing, playing. Images of the dead G-man, Sarah's limp body, and the Prayer Room flashed through her memory. The sound of her own breath rasped in her ears. Her temples pulsed.

Gert stretched. "Sun's gonna set in a couple hours. Best we get home."

Miranda straightened, and the muscles in her back protested. Her aching hands competed with her back, her neck, and her legs. But all her aches and pains were ghosts to the burning need that grew inside her. A fearsome need that made her want to hit something. Instead, she walked faster and faster until she ran ahead of Gert and quenched the need, at least for a while.

She pumped more water so they could wash the berries. Gert showed her how to sort the berries into good-for-canning, good-for-eating-now, and only-fit-for-the-goat. After they had a big pot of berries simmering, Gert led her out to the chicken coop.

At the door to the coop, Gert held a finger to her lips and motioned for Miranda to follow.

The warm and dusty air inside the coop smelled faintly of ammonia. Six hens sat on nests and purred. Gert purred too. Then she put her hands on each wing of one of the birds and picked it up. She held it for a few moments, then replaced it in the nest. She nodded a you-try at Miranda.

Miranda made the silly purring sound. She placed a hand on each wing of the nearest bird and picked it up. The bird squirmed a bit, but she tightened her hold and the hen calmed. After a few moments, she put the hen back. Gert gave her an approving nod.

"That works for when they're in here, asleep," Miranda whispered. "What about when they're out there?"

Gert gave a mischievous grin and pulled a tool from the wall. It looked like a miniature shepherd's hook. "Jest hook a leg and hoist her up real quick."

Miranda followed her out of the coop. "Why were you making me chase those darn birds?"

"You got quick, didn't you?"

MOUTHWATERING AROMAS OF FRIED BACON AND WARM CORNBREAD

filled the kitchen. But Miranda barely tasted her dinner. *Ask your questions, Beryl.*

Beryl mopped her last bite of fresh baby lettuce in hot, bacon grease dressing. She followed that with a bite of skillet cornbread. Finally, she sat back. Her chair creaked. "What was the shape of the field where you picked strawberries today, Miranda?"

Miranda put her final bite of cornbread down on her plate and locked eyes with Beryl. "It's a rounded rectangle approximately the size of a football field. Fir, maple, and chestnut trees surround it. At the north edge, there were rocks in the shape of an arrow that pointed east. On the southwest end, a stick in the bushes could have been a rifle barrel."

Beryl gave her an appraising look.

Miranda rested her forearms on each side of her plate and leaned toward Beryl. "Gert has six hens, four pullets, and a rooster. Her mule Frank is all black except for a white stocking on his left rear leg. His favorite treat is apples. This house faces south. The east side, the side with the blue tarp, has the fewest windows. Gert has dark brown eyes and a scar on her right arm. Yesterday, she wore the same orange plaid shirt and red-checkered pants that she wore the day I met her." She lifted her chin but kept her triumphant smile private.

"Be ready tomorrow." Beryl pushed away from the table and disappeared into the maze of boxes.

Miranda savored the warm, buttery flavor of Gert's cornbread. It was the best thing she'd eaten in weeks.

Chapter Forty-Two

Kara waited in the large anteroom of the reception hall next to Donald. She smoothed the silky skirt of her soft peach evening gown. This was her destiny. In moments, the doorman would throw open the massive, carved oak doors. She and Donald would pass through the archway and into history. The First Apostle and his wife. She beamed at Donald. He wore a white robe trimmed in gold, with a royal purple chasuble and a gold stole. "Ready, dear?"

He looked down at her, terror whitening his eyes. "I didn't know I'd feel so nervous."

She turned up the wattage of her smile and whispered, "Only natural, darling." She didn't want the doorman to hear. "But you won't let a little stage fright get to you, will you?"

His jaw muscles twitched.

"The Prophet is dead. The people need leadership now. They need *you*."

His chin went up, and his shoulders straightened. He offered her his arm.

She pulled in a deep breath, put her gloved hand on his arm, and nodded at the doorman.

The doors swung open. They stood a dozen steps above a sea of people. A cacophony of voices and the aromas of coffee and flowery perfumes mingled with the faint scent of floor wax.

The doorman announced their arrival with a large, handheld silver bell. The crowd hushed. Those who weren't standing stood. All eyes were on them, on Donald, on her. She smiled a humble smile, but inside? Inside, she was the Queen of Sheba, Cleopatra, and Queen Victoria all rolled into one.

Donald paused a moment, then gave a royal nod to his people. Second Sphere Soldiers in their black suits parted the crowd. She and Donald crossed the room and stood in their reception line.

She'd done her homework and gave each Fellowship member a word of personal encouragement. She played the role of the compassionate queen. She shook hands—dry and strong ones, weak and damp ones, smooth ones, rough ones. She nodded and reassured the plebeians. Yes, she would pass their concerns on to the First Apostle. And she filed juicy tidbits with potential in her memory for later use.

The steward appeared at Donald's elbow. "Dinner will be served soon, sir. May I escort you to the table?"

She and Donald took their places behind their chairs at the head table. The pure peals of the silver bell quieted conversation. People scurried about until everyone stood behind a chair. Donald said grace. A thousand voices echoed his amen. Donald sat then, and the steward held Kara's chair so she could sit. A great deal of shuffling and scraping followed. Finally, conversation resumed. The waitstaff served the consommé amid the musical sounds of crystal, china, and silver.

An attractive young assistant councilor sat on Kara's left. He'd had aspirations for a Senate seat, but the old guard of the Council had refused to endorse his candidacy. She had other plans.

She ate one bite of her cold and tangy shrimp cocktail, then turned to him. "Brother Franklin, I hear we are going to see you on the Senate floor."

He dipped his shrimp into his cocktail sauce. "If it's the will of our Father."

"You must know, everyone speaks of you as a brilliant scholar. Of both the scriptures and the law."

"Not everyone, I'm certain. And not so brilliant as some." His tone was modest, but a slight flush colored his cheeks and his lips curved.

"You would be quite successful as a senator. Smart, charming, and good-looking go a long way with both Fellowship and non-Fellowship constituents."

He looked startled, but not averse to the direction the conversation had taken. "You are very kind, but the next election is four years away."

Making people say what she wanted filled her with a floating, dancing sensation. "You mean you haven't heard? Senator Vanbibber will announce his retirement next month."

"He's resigning?" Brother Franklin met her look. "I knew he'd been ill, but not that ill."

He hadn't been. Not until Kara had convinced his wife that he'd be healthier if they left the District. *Permanently*. Kara took a delicate sip of ice water and dried her fingers on the smooth linen of her napkin.

Brother Franklin shook his head. "It is a moot thing, even if I had campaign funds. The Council rejected my request for an endorsement."

"Oh, I didn't know," she lied. She lowered her voice, only whispered loud enough he could hear. "Apostle Clarke often agrees more with the younger members than he does with the established councilors. He wants the Fellowship to take a more active role in government."

Brother Franklin sat back in his seat, never taking his eyes off of her. "Apostle Clarke is a wise man," he said. "Wise enough to deserve a major government role, wouldn't you agree?"

She gave him a genuine smile. "Perhaps. One day. With the

right friends there to support him." The tang of the cocktail sauce on her shrimp brightened in her mouth.

He looked thoughtful.

That was as far as she dared go with him tonight. She gave him a last smile and turned to speak to Donald.

Hours later, the event began to wind down. Kara had grown hoarse so she had taken a freshening break in the ladies' room. Outside the ladies' room, she heard a *pssst* from her right. Weldon leaned out from behind the corner, an expectant look on his face.

A quick glance confirmed she was alone. She hurried down the corridor and around the corner. "You couldn't wait?" she said and gave him a flirtatious smile.

His didn't return her smile.

Her pulse quickened. "You have news?" She'd told the blessed few who had asked after her eldest daughter that Miranda had the flu. "Did you find her?"

With a tip of his head, he signaled for her to follow.

She trotted after him into a storage room filled with stacks of folding chairs and tables. She closed the door, then whirled on Weldon. "What happened?"

"They are closing in on her."

"What does that mean?"

"They chased her through a small mountain town in Virginia but—"

"They lost her again?" Kara's hoarseness transformed her screech into more air than sound. "Have you no one but imbeciles working the Second Sphere? How can they keep losing Miranda?"

"She has expert help." His dry look cooled her anger.

She closed her eyes and pinched the bridge of her nose.

"They're on foot in the mountains thirty miles from Lynchburg."

She opened her eyes, wide. "Lynchburg?" Her throat and chest tightened.

"That's why I had to tell you tonight. You must cancel your trip."

Of all the places. She would never have guessed. "I can't cancel."

"The Second Sphere is flooding the area even as we speak."

That could be awkward. "It's my first official duty."

"If Beryl is in Lynchburg, there will be a confrontation. Do you really want to be there?"

"If I cancel, the press will say that I am wishy-washy about better babies." She fingered his fine wool lapels and looked up at him. "Do you *want* me to cancel?"

A shadow of doubt flickered in his eyes before a lecherous grin lit his face. "I wouldn't want it said that the wife of the First Apostle is wishy-washy." He cupped her cheek in his hand.

She luxuriated in his touch for a half second. "What am I to do? I can't keep making excuses for Miranda. We have to devise a plan, a story that will make this mess all right."

"Perhaps it's time to take the search to the next level."

She shook her head. "The daughter of the First Apostle cannot be Taken. There has to be something else we can do."

"She's with a rebel, isn't she?"

"The daughter of the First—"

He smiled at her in the way that said he was a step ahead of her.

"So—what? Miranda gets caught in an uprising?" The tightness in her chest lessened.

His smile grew.

She turned away, sorting out various scenarios. "The apostates kidnapped Miranda? What if she were wounded? Or killed? Public outrage would skyrocket. What if she does something and is a hero?" She circled a stack of chairs then faced Weldon again. "I could work with that. Miranda turns on her kidnapper. Beryl dies doing something evil. The headlines would be, 'The First Apostle's daughter saves the day.'"

Weldon looked pained. "And how do I make that believable?"

She crossed over to him, wrapped his arms around her, and pressed her body to his. "We'll come up with something."

Chapter Forty-Three

The next morning, Beryl didn't disappear after breakfast. She handed Miranda her rucksack.

"Where are we going?"

"For a walk."

Miranda pressed her lips together. *I know that.* She hadn't quite dared to ask, *are you* finally *going to train me?* She shrugged on her rucksack and stifled a grunt. The rucksack was heavier than what she'd carried before. She hurried after Beryl, who had already headed into the labyrinth.

They walked north through the forest, along creeks and waterfalls, more uphill than down. Squirrels scolded, and birds called warnings, startled, and flapped their wings. Miranda surprised herself by keeping up with Beryl despite the extra weight in her rucksack. Beryl taught her more hand signals.

The uphill trek grew more and more difficult. The weight of her rucksack dug into her shoulders. Miranda feared she'd have to beg for a stop, but Beryl held her bent her arm up with her fingers splayed, then made a fist.

Miranda froze mid-step.

Beryl stared across the valley. "At ease."

They were on a bald ridge. Across the valley, the haze turned the southern mountains into blue silhouettes. Beryl tilted her head, indicating the open plateau, and handed Gert's rifle to Miranda. "You said you could shoot. Start with the milk jugs."

About ten yards out, five glass milk jugs sat on a fallen tree trunk. *Stationary targets? At fifteen feet? At that distance, I can hit every clay pigeon in a skeet shoot. This has got to be easier.* She checked the rifle's action, chambered a round, and took her stance. Clean sight picture. Gentle squeeze of the trigger. *Bang!* The first jug shattered. She worked the action, centered the sights on the next bottle, and shattered it. The other two were just as easy.

"Now the targets."

Fifteen yards downslope, pieces of cardboard were tacked to trees. The outline of a male or female head and torso was stamped on each piece of cardboard. Black and white concentric rings centered on the bullseyes, the heart of each outline.

Miranda shouldered the rifle and acquired the heart of a target in her sights. The barrel wavered. She held her breath, fired, and missed. *Missed?* She wriggled tension out of her shoulders and repositioned herself. She hit all the remaining targets, but few of her shots hit inside the rings and none hit the heart. *What is wrong with me?*

"Don't think about the targets being people," Beryl said in a quiet, firm voice. "Second Sphere agents are warriors. They aren't going to stand still and wait for you to shoot. They will strike when you least expect it. Their attack will be fast, treacherous, close quarters, and violent. You have to anticipate violence. You have to kill them before they kill you."

"But only if they try to kill you, right?"

Beryl's grim expression darkened. "Kill or be killed."

"That's exactly what my father—what Donald—said the apostates did." She thrust the rifle into Beryl's hands. "I won't be a murderer."

"It's hard to overcome all the years of being a daughter of the Fellowship." Beryl didn't gloat but said it as a statement of fact.

"But being part of the Fellowship already made you a murderer. How many people have been Taken in your lifetime? How many didn't go home from Redemption?"

Sarah. That poor, frightened petitioner. The Prayer Room. Blood pounded in her temples. *How many had suffered in the name of the Fellowship?* Miranda grabbed the rifle and imagined her father instead of a cardboard target. She raised the rifle to her shoulder, lined up the far sight of the rifle with her father's heart, and fired. "Killed" him eight times, reloaded, and fired on the last eight targets. She lowered her weapon. She'd hit every target in the kill zone. Miranda cocked her chin toward Beryl, proud and terrified at the same time.

"What did you do that was different?" Beryl asked.

"I was focused."

Beryl's look said she wanted more.

Miranda swallowed hard and looked away. The truth weighed so heavy she couldn't speak.

Beryl gave a short nod. "Whatever you did, remember it. Use it." She held out a pistol. "This is a 1911."

The rest of the day Beryl quizzed Miranda about bullet dynamics and gun mechanics. Miranda shot the pistol until she could taste burnt gunpowder and her wrist couldn't hold the gun's weight any longer.

The next day Beryl taught her situational awareness and tactical evasion. See your attacker before the first blow. Evade if possible but never shrink from an attack. Victims shrink from attacks. Winners land the first blow and keep attacking until the opponent cannot get up.

Miranda learned the signs of imminent violence. She learned the human body's points of vulnerability. She learned to incapacitate her attacker. Beryl had her repeat each move hundreds of times. And practice went on past sundown.

On the third training day, Beryl had Miranda run up and down the mountain in shooting drills. The cardboard targets with red bullseyes were innocents to be saved. The ones with yellow bullseyes were targets to be shot dead. After a run-through, they patched the cardboard with masking tape for the next run. By lunchtime, Miranda had "killed" more than five hundred yellow bullseyes.

After lunch, Beryl drilled her on everything she'd learned. After failing a brutal exercise on how to knife an attacker, Beryl gave her a water break.

Miranda sat in the grass, holding the canteen. She studied Beryl. As a trainer, Beryl was firm, confident, and more patient than Miranda had expected. She gave Miranda tips and tricks of the trade, making Miranda more and more successful. But one thing bugged Miranda. "What if I don't know if one of the people in a group situation is an attacker or not?"

Beryl leveled a million-mile stare across the mountains. "You don't have time to make distinctions. Kill them all. Let God sort it out."

Chapter Forty-Four

Beryl leaned against the pole at the southeast end of Lynchburg's Kemper Street Station platform. As instructed, she held the newspaper folded so the obituary page showed. The growl of thunder and the sticky, pre-storm air sent people under the covered part of the platform.

Men, women, and children seethed between platform pillars. Some carried luggage, some held flowers, and others stood empty-handed. All waited for the train's arrival. She didn't recognize any of them, and none of them approached her with the code words. She didn't expect Ethan to come to such a public place. Some flunky would show up and give her directions to his hiding spot.

The crowd shifted. She glimpsed a familiar face at the other end of the platform. Hector Antares in a workman's overalls strolled her direction, straw hat in hand. She had to bite back a smile. *If Hector is here, Ethan can't be far.*

Hector looked older, a lot older, than she remembered. His dark curls were streaked with silver, his face weathered and wrinkled. But he walked with the same Latin cockiness she remembered. One of Ethan's best, he didn't show a flicker of recognition. He walked three steps past her, stopped, and faced the train tracks. He peered down the track as if looking for the train. Then he nodded at her and her newspaper. "Is that today's *News and Advance?*"

"No. *Washington Post.*"

"Today's edition is at the newsstand already?"

"Just bought it a couple of minutes ago."

He nodded, took two steps forward, and peered down the tracks. "Why would he meet with you?"

His words were an unexpected sucker-punch. Her stomach clenched, and her fist tightened on the newspaper. "We loved each other once."

"The woman he loved died ten years ago."

"Ten years in a cell, one sometimes longs for death. It didn't come."

Hector rotated, scanning the crowd as if looking for someone, until he faced her. He scrutinized her. His eyes widened, his mouth dropped open, then he swept her with a suspicious look. "*Puta madre.*" He turned back to face the tracks.

Hector hadn't recognized her. She'd anticipated this delayed recognition. She was older, grayer. She hadn't anticipated being so disappointed that he'd given up on her.

People on the platform were getting restless. The train was late.

He glanced at his watch. "Fifteen minutes. Inside table. Crystal Café." He walked away.

Beryl stayed motionless, even when the train finally arrived. Passengers disembarked. New passengers climbed aboard.

Hector had believed she was dead. Just as she'd believed Ethan was dead. Ten years. She couldn't recall a mental picture of Ethan anymore, but she would recognize him. Wouldn't she?

The whistle blew. She straightened, looked up and down the platform as if disappointed, then wandered down the length of the platform, past the building, and onto the sidewalk.

It took her less than five minutes to find the Crystal Café and get a table near the back hallway. Fans whirred and clicked overhead. Red-checkered tablecloths adorned the tables. Young couples held hands. Businessmen negotiated deals. And singles seemed endlessly fascinated with the contents of their plates. Faint kitchen noises came from the hallway to her right. Aromas of fried chicken and burgers mingled with other, impossible to identify, aromas. Her stomach rumbled and rolled, caught between hunger and nausea.

Hector came in, chatted with the hostess, and sat at the table next to Beryl, his back to her.

After the waitress took her order, then Hector's, he cleared his throat. "They held a funeral."

"Where is he?"

"Not here."

"I must talk to him."

"Ten years is plenty of time to make a double agent."

Her jaw tightened. She put her hands in her lap, dug her nails into her palms, knuckles straining. She forced her hands to relax. "I am not a turncoat."

He didn't say anything.

The waitress appeared with coffee and pie for him, black coffee for Beryl. She took a sip. The coffee was strong and hot. She blew over the dark liquid and said softly, "He'll know when he sees me. When he hears what I know."

"Tell me," Hector said. "I'll make sure Ethan gets your message." He slurped his drink.

"I will tell Ethan, no one else."

A fork scraped a plate. Hector made appreciative noises as he chewed pie.

She was not going to play along with his loyalty test. "I've spent the past ten years being loyal. Keeping my mouth shut. I can wait." She slapped a dollar down on the table and stood. "Tell Ethan I'll be in touch."

Chapter Forty-Five

Miranda gripped Gert's big black umbrella with its one broken rib and thick wooden handle tighter. The heavy, gray clouds overhead rumbled long and low. Fat drops of luke-warm rain had dripped all day, but now that Miranda was on foot, the rain came faster, the drops smaller. She bent into the wind. Despite the late afternoon hour, it was midnight dark. Splashes of light from Lynchburg's streetlamps, weary apartment buildings, and shabby shop windows did little to ease the gloom. People dashed toward their destinations without a smile or even a side-long glance. She was alone for the first time in—she didn't know how long. Her umbrella fluttered and popped in the wind-driven rain. She shivered.

Three days ago, Beryl had stopped training her and started disappearing again. She'd left before dawn and returned long after dark, stinking of liquor. Today, Beryl had returned before noon and announced they were leaving, for Gert's safety. She'd said that if Miranda wanted to join SABR, she had to do it now and she had to do it alone. She, Beryl, was *persona non grata* to SABR. She wouldn't explain. She gave Miranda detailed instructions, dropped her off in Lynchburg, and left.

Miranda had expected better from her aunt. At least she knew where she was because of Beryl's insistence that she memorize the map of Lynchburg.

Miranda approached a vacant, covered bus stop for Fellowship members. Unprotected from the rain, a couple of non-Fellowship members stood behind the yellow Other line painted on the sidewalk. A tall skinny man with very dark skin hunched his shoulders and looked at his feet. A young, white woman stood behind him, trying to shelter an infant and a toddler under her worn-out raincoat.

"You need this more than I do." Miranda offered the woman Gert's umbrella. Cool rainwater trickled down Miranda's neck.

The woman ignored her.

"For the children," Miranda said, holding the umbrella over the woman and her children.

The woman didn't respond, didn't take the umbrella, didn't even make eye contact.

Miranda closed the umbrella, put it on the ground in front of the woman, then left. *Poor woman. She probably thought I was Fellowship or law enforcement trying to trick her. I hope she'll pick it up after I'm gone.* Miranda's shoulders sagged. *What am I doing? These people won't accept me as a rebel.* She hated to admit it, but she had never had to wait in the rain or even ride a bus before. *I was a princess.*

A sign in the corner of a store window caught her eye. "Join the Celebration" it said in bold letters. It featured a picture of her father in regal Fellowship robes holding Sandra in his arms, kissing her on the head. Sandra had her head turned away and her eyes squeezed shut.

Miranda couldn't see the rest. Her vision blurred. A giant, invisible fist squeezed the air out of her. She pushed away uncertain memories and nightmares and forced her feet to move.

Determined, she sped down the sidewalk, ignoring her wet hair and wet feet and the shivers that shook her. She pulled up short when she recognized the name of the next shop, the Sweet

Spoons Soda Shop. According to Beryl, this was the place. Miranda opened the door. A bell jingled overhead.

Inside, the shop was bright and cheery and empty of customers. Behind an aqua-colored counter, a grandmotherly waitress stopped rolling utensils in napkins. Next to her, a gray-haired soda jerk held a sudsy sundae glass in midair. They exchanged looks. *Are they my contacts?* Beryl hadn't known, or wouldn't say. Miranda shook off some of the rain that covered her and started toward the back tables.

"Hey and welcome to Sweet Spoons, ma'am," the waitress burbled. She hurried around the cutout in the counter and toward Miranda. "May I offer you our best seat, over here by the front window?"

"No, thank you," Miranda said. "I'll sit over there." She crossed to the wrought iron ice cream table against the back wall, near the Staff Only door. She sat with her back to the wall. A chill rippled across her damp shoulders.

The waitress trotted after her and gave her a menu. Miranda ordered a root beer ice cream soda. She needed something that she could nurse for a long time.

"Will this be a takeaway?" the waitress asked.

What a queer question for a soda shop. Miranda smiled and settled back in her chair. "No. I'd like to rest my feet and dry off a bit before I head back out there."

"Yes, ma'am. I reckon so." The waitress scurried back to the counter. The fizz of soda was loud in the unnaturally quiet shop.

Prickles danced across the back of Miranda's neck. Soda shops in the District were busy at all hours of the day in all kinds of weather. Lynchburg was big enough that they should have some customers, even now. Miranda laid her borrowed pocket-book on the tabletop. She pulled out her borrowed handkerchief and positioned it. One corner of the lacy handkerchief pointed at the front door. It would signal SABR that she wanted to meet.

The waitress brought her soda and placed it on the table. "It shore is a gully-washer out there, isn't it?" She stared at the front door and wrung her hands.

That wasn't the coded phrase Beryl had told her to expect, so the waitress wasn't her contact. Miranda answered, "Uh-huh," and sipped her soda through the straw.

"Well, if you need anything else, I'll be right over there." The waitress returned to her spot behind the counter and whispered to the soda jerk.

Miranda sipped her soda slowly. She toyed with the edges of the handkerchief. Once, when she looked up, she caught the soda jerk staring at her. *Is he my contact? Does he see the signal and notify the contact? Or does he recognize me?* She squirmed, untucked her tea-darkened her hair from behind her ear. *No, his expression isn't recognition, it's more—troubled.* Uneasy, she ate the last spoonful of creamy vanilla ice cream crusted with root beer foam.

She stirred the remnants of her root beer with her straw, then sat back. This was going to take longer than she'd thought. She waved the waitress over.

The bell over the door jingled. The waitress clamped a hand over her mouth mid-squeal. Two men in business suits bustled through the door, shaking rain off their hats and umbrellas.

The waitress laughed nervously and crossed the last few feet to Miranda. "Don't know why I'm so jumpy." She spoke to Miranda, but her eyes were on the businessmen.

The red, winged shield divided by a white cross blazed from their breast pockets. *Second Sphere!* The two men crossed to the counter and stood in front of the soda jerk.

Miranda grabbed the waitress by the arm. "Do you have a ladies' room?" she whispered.

"Not a public one," the waitress said, staring at the soda jerk.

"I'm desperate for a ladies' room."

The waitress focused on her. "We only have one for employees."

"That'll do." Miranda scooped up her handkerchief and

pocketbook with one hand and pulled the waitress toward the Staff Only door.

"Why is your shop empty?" one of the men asked. "Don't you care if you sell ice cream?"

Miranda pushed through the door into a kitchenette prep and storage area. A large walk-in freezer stood to her right. At the back of the room were shelves of dishes and supplies and an exit. She hurried to the exit. Sweet Spoons sat in the middle of a long block. They'd be caught before they could disappear. She left the door ajar and whirled around. The waitress stared through the porthole window into the shop. On the back of the door hung two heavy sweaters. "Does the freezer door lock?" Miranda asked.

The waitress gave her a puzzled look. "Freezers don't lock. Don't want anybody to get locked in."

Miranda snatched the sweaters off their hooks. A glance through the door's porthole window revealed a glimpse of the soda jerk's face bloodied by a fist. Miranda dashed inside the freezer. She pulled five-gallon cardboard drums of ice cream to a corner, threw the sweaters behind it. All it had to do was fool the agents for a few seconds. She pulled the waitress's apron off, tossed it across the freezer threshold, and closed the door on it.

"What are you—?" The sound of something hard hitting flesh tore the waitress's attention back to the door. "No—" Her voice was a strangled whisper. She took a step toward the shop.

Miranda held her back. "You're getting hurt won't help him. We'll get help." She pushed the waitress across the room and out the door. "Run!" The waitress sprinted down the alley. Miranda eased the door closed behind her, then took off after the waitress.

The rain pelted Miranda only slightly faster than her pulse. Rainwater stung her eyes and blurred her vision. Ahead, a glimmer of light shone from a propped-open door.

She darted past the waitress, waved her inside, and pulled the door shut behind them. They were in a dark, storage room filled with clothing hanging on racks.

The waitress peered around the room. Her eyes widened.

"This is Beverly's shop," the waitress whispered. "Beverly's a friend. She'll help us." The waitress reached for the interior door. Miranda put a hand on the door, holding it closed. She pressed her ear to the door and heard voices. They didn't seem angry or upset.

Miranda put a finger to her lips, then tiptoed across to the exterior door and pressed her ear to it. Outside, the sounds of the rain damped everything else. *Are the Second Sphere agents out there or not?* She shivered and brushed away the wet hair plastered to her face.

The waitress's teeth chattered.

Miranda motioned for the waitress to follow her to the back corner of the storage room. "I'm sorry," she whispered. "I put you in danger."

The waitress shook her head. "The SS and the Fellowship put us in danger, not you." Her whisper was barely audible. She flashed an apologetic smile. "They have been watching us. Drove all our regulars away. I thought you were one of them. George insisted—" A rapid *pop-pop*, *pop-pop-pop* interrupted. She made an inarticulate, wounded animal sound.

Miranda held her hand.

They waited in silence, in the dark. Seconds ticked into a ten-minute eternity. Miranda listened at each of the doors. She heard no voices and no sirens. "It's clear," Miranda whispered.

"Come with me," the waitress said, her voice raspy and tight.

"If we hurry, we can meet my friend. She can help your soda jerk." Beryl had said she'd be at the Farmer's Market at ten, two, and seven for the next three days. *Bet she didn't expect to see me on the first day.*

The waitress swallowed, and her eyes glimmered with unshed tears. "If he's still alive, they'll take him away—" She took a shuddering breath. "I promised him…" She touched Miranda and locked eyes with hers. "That's a lovely handkerchief. Is the lace handmade?"

Miranda gaped at her. "You?" She shook her head and gave

the response Beryl had made her memorize. "Yes, my grand-mother tats all her own lace."

"So few people tat anymore. More people should learn the old skills."

"Yes, they should." Miranda's chill wasn't from being cold and wet. "I want to help destroy the Second Sphere and the Fellowship."

The waitress led the way out of the storage room. Miranda squinted against the bright lights of a dress shop. They sped down the main aisle to the front door.

"Arlene," a woman's voice called. "Did I hear shots? Wait!"

The waitress hesitated, her hand on the doorknob.

A tall, skinny woman trotted toward them with scarves and rain slickers. "You'll catch your—" The woman's hand flew to her mouth. "I'm sorry, Arlene, I didn't mean—"

"Thank you," Arlene said in a husky voice. She had the slicker half on when she dashed out the door. Miranda followed, her yellow slicker flapping in the rain.

Chapter Forty-Six

An organ and voices of various pitch rose into a passionate chorus of "Rock of Ages." Miranda froze. *How could I let Arlene drag me into a Fellowship church?*

Arlene tugged on her hand. "It's all right. You'll see." She hurried down the hall and down a staircase. At the bottom of the stairs, a large, boy-faced man blocked a door.

"Open the door, Manny." Arlene stepped forward, but Manny didn't move aside.

He put a hand on the grip of his holstered pistol.

"What are you going to do, shoot me?" She pushed past the man and through the door.

They entered a bright room that reeked of pungent ink. Five people looked up. It was an odd group of young and old, male and female. A short, skinny man in an argyle vest and round glasses looked up from the mimeograph machine he ran. "Arlene?"

Another male voice cried, "Miranda?"

"Hector?" Miranda stared at the lean Hispanic man who had been her boss. "How did you get here?" she asked, his voice echoing her words.

Hector looked as if he hadn't slept or eaten since she'd last seen him. His forehead glistened with sweat, and two nickel-plated pistols hung from his holster.

"You know him?" Arlene asked.

Miranda nodded.

"You're alive," he whispered. He put a stack of papers down, circled the table, and wrapped his arms around her. He squeezed until her ribs hurt. She grunted, and he released her. He peered down the hall behind her. "Where's Sarah?"

"I was going to ask you the same thing," Miranda said.

His shoulders sagged.

"They took me to Redemption a long way from here," Miranda said in a small voice. "Maybe they took Sarah someplace different?"

He shook his head. "I kept hoping, but… Her family disappeared too. The sign was on their door."

Bold, fierce Sarah was dead. It hurt to breathe, but Miranda had to know. "She was stealing carbons for SABR, for you, wasn't she?"

Hector's face clouded. "I had three crews working that night. The other two crews didn't even know you were gone. No one even questioned us—ever. I don't understand." He searched her face. "Why you and Sarah?"

Guilt lanced through Miranda. *Because I was stupid. I thought the sign of the Azrael was a joke.*

"Enough reminiscing," the man with the large round glasses whispered. "Who is this, and what's she doing here?"

"Calm down, Underwood," Hector said. "This is Miranda Clarke."

"The Miranda Clarke?" Underwood squinted at her.

Hector smiled and gave a soft snort. "No, as she said to me when she applied for the job, what would the real Miranda Clarke be doing hiring on as a cleaning lady?"

Underwood looked her up and down. "Okay."

She lowered her head, uncomfortable with the lie. How could

he not recognize her? Underwood turned to Arlene. "Why did you— What's wrong?"

Arlene's face was pale, drawn. "George. There were shots. I'm afraid—" Her voice cracked, but she didn't cry.

"Shots? At Sweet Spoons?" Underwood asked.

In halting words, Arlene told them what had happened. She described Miranda's actions with glowing admiration.

"Oh, Arlene." A middle-aged woman in a gingham dress rushed to her, wrapped her in a hug.

"I was so nervous," Arlene said. "Those two agents who've been watching us threatened that something would happen soon. When Miranda came into the shop, I thought she was one of them. Then she put the lace handkerchief down. George and I argued. He made me promise to help her, but she ended up helping me."

"Bless you, Miranda," the woman in the gingham dress said.

A quiet chorus of "Thank you," "Good job," and "Welcome" followed. Miranda blushed.

"Ian," Underwood said.

A pock-faced, young man quit folding papers and stood. "Yes, sir?"

"Run over and check out what's going on at Sweet Spoons."

"Yes, sir." The young man dashed to the door, took a New York Yankees cap from a nearby hook, and tugged the cap over his sandy hair.

"Only a peek, Ian. Be back here in fifteen minutes."

The young man was out the door before Underwood had finished.

"Now," Hector said. "We must hurry. We've only another hour here." He smiled at Miranda. "You want to fight? Well, you are in the right place." He gestured toward the table. "Today we fight with words."

Was it really this easy? "You mean I'm in? I'm a rebel?"

"Recruits aren't easy to come by." Underwood stuck out his hand. "Welcome. You can call me Ted." After they shook, he gestured at the table. "The young man with the hair falling in his eyes is Dayton. Next to him is Eric and Leslie." He pointed to a dark-haired man sitting at a table in the corner, wearing earphones and listening to a ham radio. "That's Mike." Ted nodded at the woman sitting with Arlene. "And that's Ruth." Introductions done, he walked to the table and started folding papers with the others.

Miranda looked around, uncertain.

"You were expecting a test or something?" Hector gave her a grim smile. "Look around you. We're not military. We're regular people fighting injustice the best way we know how."

He handed Miranda a flyer that still smelled of ink. Titled *Against Tyranny*, it reported the latest laws restricting non-Fellowship members, whom the Second Sphere had harassed, and listed items that needed "redistribution."

The man next to Hector took the paper from Miranda. "She can help Leslie." He was taller than Hector and had a squarish face with a short trim beard and mustache. He looked familiar.

Hector took the paper from him and gave it back to Miranda. "You need another set of hands, Nick." He spoke in a low voice and nodded at Arlene who sat in a chair, watching the door, and chewing a thumbnail.

"She's a stranger. She'll stick out," Nick said. "After the ruckus at Sweet Spoons, distribution is going to be twice as dangerous as usual."

"I didn't know what good a violinist could do when I first met you," Hector said, "but I trusted you."

A violinist. Now she remembered. The red scar from his cheekbone to chin had confused her.

Hector grinned. "She's been through Redemption and helped Arlene escape the SS, Nick. I think she can handle shuffling paper." Hector patted Nick's shoulder. "Show her the ropes. Between tonight and tomorrow night, you should get a good idea of how she'll work out."

"There goes my survival rate," Nick muttered.

Hector returned to the table. He cranked the mimeograph machine back to life. The machine's rhythmic *click-swish, click-swish* signaled the others who resumed quiet conversations.

Miranda held out her hand. "Nicholas Rose, it's a pleasure to meet you. I had tickets for your 'Back Home in America' performance at Carnegie—"

His eyes didn't leave her face, but a muscle in his jaw twitched, made his scar jump.

She clamped her mouth shut and dropped her hand to her side. She'd forgotten. A flush whooshed up her neck to the top of her head. His performance had been canceled amid a scandal. A newspaper had reported that Nicholas Rose was born Nicholas Rosenthal. Jewish name. Didn't matter if he was or wasn't a practicing Jew after that. He wouldn't join the Fellowship. Carnegie Hall and all his other appearances were canceled. "I'm sorry," she said.

He shrugged. "That was a lifetime ago. Besides, it gave me a cause." He glanced at the people seated around the table. "And friends." He smiled, and his whole appearance sparked with life. He looked back at her, and the smile vanished. "Are you the cleaning lady or the daughter of the First Apostle?"

She bit her lower lip. Miranda, the cleaning woman, wouldn't be able to afford those tickets. She gave him her best daughter-of-the-councilor smile. "Can't I be both?"

He shrugged. "Okay. Doesn't matter."

She blinked, stunned. How could they not recognize her? Her face had been plastered in all the society pages. She glanced down and saw her once smooth, aristocratic hands now reddened, rough, and calloused. Scabbed over scratches dotted the backs of her hands and her ragged fingernails were dirty. She hid her hands in the folds of her soft, worn-thin skirt and saw the poor-fitting, borrowed clothes she wore. She didn't look as if she belonged on the society page. *Didn't matter anymore. Not as long as they let her fight.*

He had her sit beside him at a plastic folding table at the end of the room. "Listen up. We don't have much time, and you have to know a lot of things before tomorrow night." He reached inside his jacket and set a 1911 automatic pistol on the table in front of her. "This is an automatic pistol. It fires—"

"A 9mm bullet." She pulled the Luger out of her waistband at the small of her back. "Which is smaller than the .45 caliber in this gun."

"Can you shoot it?"

She aimed it at the wall over his left shoulder. "Where do you want the bullet to go?"

"No need for that kind of stuff." Nicholas pushed the muzzle aside and down.

Did he even notice my finger wasn't on the trigger?

"So you can shoot, and you're a quick thinker who kept Arlene out of trouble. If you can follow directions, you'll do okay."

It wasn't praise, but it would have to do.

"Tonight you and I will pretend to be a dating couple, strolling through town. Tomorrow we'll be part of a larger operation. If you don't do exactly what I say in either of these things, you will get us arrested or killed."

"Tell me what you need me to do."

"Do you know where the National Guard Armory is?"

She searched her memory. "On Constitution Lane?"

"Yes." Nicholas got up and went to the mimeo machine. He returned with a blank piece of paper. He told her that the Lynchburg National Guardsmen had left yesterday for their annual maneuvers. The Armory would be unoccupied all week. He sketched a rough layout of streets and buildings and a wooded lot. "We will rob the armory tomorrow night." He explained the whole plan.

She asked few questions, concentrating on memorizing every planned step.

"Do you need me to repeat anything?"

She shook her head. "I've got it."

"Right." He didn't hide his skepticism on his face either.

"At eight o'clock Ian will shoot out the security light on the back of the Armory." She recited the rest from memory with only two corrections from Nick.

He cocked his head to the side and studied her for several long moments. "Okay." He went to the mimeograph again. This time he returned with two stacks of *Against Tyranny.* "Now you get to show how well you follow directions."

Ian came through the door, subdued. He locked eyes with Hector and shook his head. Arlene sobbed quietly into her hands.

Nick bowed his head a moment, then turned back to Miranda. He handed her one stack of folded flyers. He stuck folders from the second stack inside special pockets lining his shirt and pants and inside his socks. He looked up at her. "If the SS sees you with those…"

She turned away, unbuttoned her shirt, and stuffed papers inside. "Where are we going?"

"We're delivering papers, SABR-style."

Chapter Forty-Seven

M iranda climbed the tree-lined grand staircase called Monument Terrace alongside Nick. He'd demonstrated a few techniques and had given her tips on how to distribute the papers without being seen. After the first few fumbling attempts, she found she had a knack for doing this.

"Darling," Nick said. "Let's sit for a moment." He guided her to the curved wall opposite the Fellowship side. The concrete wall and bench labeled Others.

She poked a few flyers into the bushes beside her and a couple on the damp bench to sit upon. Here, in the shade, everything was damp.

Nick draped his arm over her shoulders.

She stiffened.

"Relax," he whispered. He chuckled. "Smell the roses and pretend you like me."

The roses from the garden surrounding the terrace filled the air with their delicate perfume. She turned on the fake charms of a councilor's daughter.

"That's better," he said.

He has no idea how good I am at pretending.

"Now, without drawing attention to yourself, slip some of those papers onto the bench."

She beamed at him. "Already done, sweetheart." She smoothed her skirt, revealing the corner of the flyers.

He leaned close and whispered in her ear, "Have you done this before?"

Her smile grew wider, more genuine. "Never."

"I love the smell of the air after a rain, don't you?"

Wait. Was that all? No "good job" or "you're a natural?" She forced herself to sit and nod as if he'd said something brilliant.

After a few minutes, they descended the stairs and wandered around downtown, dropping flyers at bus stops and public restrooms. Posters featuring her father were everywhere. She wanted to rip them down, shred them, and stomp on the shreds. But the number of policemen on patrol had increased. It was almost curfew time for "Others." People scurried about finishing their errands and hustled home.

They strolled down Main Street behind a young family. The mother carried a little boy who slept on her shoulder. The father had one arm wrapped around a bag of groceries and held the hand of his young daughter.

"Daddy. Daddy. Daddy. Look it," the girl cried and pulled on her father's hand. She pointed to a store window filled with toys. "It's a Baby Sleepy Eyes. I wanna see."

The father scooped his daughter up in his free arm and lifted her eye level with the cherished doll.

"Daddy, if I'm very, very good, will Santa bring me a Baby Sleepy Eyes this year?"

The father gave his daughter a tender kiss on the cheek. "Princess, you are always a very good girl. I'll put in a good word to Santa."

"Thank you, Daddy." The little girl threw her arms around her father's neck and squeezed.

An ache surged to Miranda's throat and filled her eyes. She whirled away and led Nick across the street.

"Are you all right?" he asked.

"Why wouldn't I be?" She left his side for a moment and stood in the door alcove of a ladies' dress shop. Pretending to admire the dress in the window, she blinked and swallowed and placed the last of her flyers on the ledge. She rejoined Nick. "I'm out. Do you have any?"

He smiled at her, but his eyes were clouded. "I've been out for half an hour."

"What's next?" she asked with a fake joyful anticipation that sounded fake.

"We're done. Time to go home."

"With you?"

He laughed. "I'm not that bad, am I?"

"No. I didn't mean— I only—" She sighed. "Never mind. I'll be okay."

"You don't have a place to sleep tonight."

She shrugged. "I guess I thought that being part of SABR meant something like a big family campout or something." *Why did I say that?* "Pretty lame, huh? Don't worry, I'll figure something out. See you tomorrow at eight-thirty sharp." She hurried away, figuring she'd try the cheap hotel down the street, afraid she'd spend the night on a park bench.

"Miranda—wait." Nick caught her by the elbow. "It won't be a family campout, but Oscar and Ruth will put you up for a few nights until we figure out a more permanent arrangement."

She hesitated.

"We take care of each other," Nick said. "In that, we are like family. And you are one of the family now."

She smiled, hoping it didn't look as awkward as it felt.

"I'll take you there. After all, Ruth might have some leftover pot roast for dinner." He tucked her hand in his elbow, and they strolled out of town.

Chapter Forty-Eight

The dark, overcrowded cellar room of the old warehouse reeked of alcohol and sour sweat. They called it a speakeasy. Beryl called it a hellhole.

She sat at a corner table as far from the makeshift bar as space allowed. The round pedestal table rocked on the uneven floor. The same unstable table she'd sat at for the past three nights. With the same police officer, one of Lynchburg's finest. She'd supplied him with drinks for the past three evenings in a row. He liked to throw back a few beers after going off-duty. And when he drank, he hinted he knew things about the leader of SABR, about Ethan.

"Come on, baby," he mumbled.

She leaned close to hear him over the boisterous crowd.

"Drink up, you're falling behind." His eyes roamed from the pink scarf tied around her neck to the shadow of her scant cleavage.

She allowed him to drape one arm over her shoulder but kept her back pressed against the chair. She wouldn't let him slide his arm down and feel the gun tucked into her waistband. Beryl gave him a fake, flirty smile. "Don't worry about me." She spoke in his ear, hating the coo she had to put in her voice. "What made you so thirsty tonight?"

He plunked his glass down, sloshing beer over the side. "Gotta get my courage up for tomorrow." The fingers of the hand over her shoulder drew indecent circles on her exposed skin.

His touch disgusted her, but ten years of Redemption allowed her to hide it. "Are you going to shoot someone?" She couldn't bring herself to bat her eyes.

He giggled. "Nope"

"Do you want to?"

He wagged a finger in her face. "It is my duty to do my duty even when said duty gives me the creeps."

"Let me make you feel better." She pulled his head down into her cleavage.

He mumbled something.

She pulled his head up.

He beamed a sloppy smile. "Gift of courage right there."

She put his head in a more polite-society place on her shoulder. "If you found it creepy, I wouldn't want to go—where did you say you're going?"

"The Colony."

He meant the place across the river. "Ooh. All those loonies would give anyone the creeps. Here, have some more liquid courage." She slid her lukewarm, watered-down highball to him.

He gulped it down.

Someone turned on a radio. Blaring jazz added several decibels of noise to the booze-fed jocularity around them. Beryl had to raise her voice too. "What's the creepiest thing about that place?"

"The obstacle course."

She must have misheard him. "What kind of obstacle course do they have for a bunch of crazies?"

He yawned. "Full military-style." He snuggled against her.

"For their security force?" She forgot to make her voice flirty.

"Nope." He yawned again. "Only one night watchman."

Beryl's neck warmed. *There could only be one reason for an obstacle course in such an unexpected location.* "One night watchman? Then why do you have to work there tomorrow?"

"Tomorrow's special."

"What makes a loony bin special?"

"Special guest, a real VIP."

"And you get to escort this VIP around?"

He shook his head. "Not escort, protect. Whole squad."

"This VIP needs a lot of protection? From what?"

"From…apostates…an'…reporters." He let loose a long, low, sour-smelling belch. His head drooped. She eased him forward until his head rested on the tabletop.

"Why reporters?" she asked in his ear.

Half open, his eyes had that unfocused glaze that meant he was about to pass out. She repeated her question, louder.

"First 'postle's big news." His eyelids drooped further.

Electricity fired through her, tightened her muscles. "You're going to protect the First Apostle?"

"Nope." He cradled his head in his arms.

Not the First Apostle? "Then who?"

"Next…best…thing…"

Did he mean Kara was coming to Lynchburg? "What time?"

His mumble devolved into a soft snore.

If Kara was coming to Lynchburg, Weldon was too. Beryl considered shaking her policeman awake, making him answer her last question. But she couldn't afford for him to remember this conversation. Better to let the alcohol take him than to risk her mission. She excused herself from the table and the speakeasy.

Outside, she drew in big breaths of the rain-cleansed air and plunged down the road, avoiding the big puddles in the gutters.

He'd meant Kara. He had to. Kara had used the feebleminded in contrast to her "better babies" in the past. She'd do it again. It was a five-hour drive from DC to Lynchburg. Would they drive in tomorrow? They might fly here. Kara might insist on that. Either way, they'd stay overnight at one of Lynch-

burg's finest hotels with her bodyguards. Kara is First Lady now. She probably has more bodyguards.

Beryl grinned. Didn't matter how fine the hotel, how many, or how trained the bodyguards, she would find them. The idea of killing Weldon in his sleep *and* finding the Azrael made her lightheaded.

An obstacle course at a home for the imperfect? It had to be Azrael training grounds. *How many recruits has Weldon hidden there? Six? Twelve? Doesn't matter.* She knew better than to engage them on her own, but with Ethan and his SABRs at her side... She shivered. After ten long years, tomorrow promised to be the day. Savage joy surged through her blood, overwhelmed her. She curled her fingers and her toes until her muscles strained. Slowly she uncurled her fingers and toes and breathed calm back into her body. Her thoughts cleared. *Full security won't be at the hotel or the Colony until tomorrow.* She had a lot of recon to do tonight. She'd find the hotel first. After all, finding the hotel shouldn't take too long.

How many fancy hotels could there be in this town?

Chapter Forty-Nine

The hot, still air, filled with the stench of human sweat and urine and excrement, made Kara want to gag. She fought the urge. This "inspection tour" of the Virginia Colony for the Epileptic and Feebleminded was her first public duty as the First Lady of the Fellowship. She would not disgrace herself. Still, she made a mental note to never again agree to an inspection right before dinner.

She stepped daintily between the rows of mattresses that lined the floor. Weak, natural light came from narrow, nailed-shut windows that looked over the three other women's dormitories on the campus. The only other light came from a single row of bare lightbulbs hung from the center beam of the ceiling. The bulbs illuminated a path through to the other side of the room. It also revealed that the mattresses on each side of her were dark with stains of unknown origins. That was enough for Kara. She didn't care to see the stains in greater detail.

At the head of each row of mattresses stood a woman in a dingy housedress with her head bowed, eyes down.

"Are these residents the caretakers, Dr. Locke?" one of the Virginia Board of Eugenics members asked.

"Yes, they are of stable demeanor and capable of menial chores."

One of the women rocked forward and back, making the floorboards creak. Kara grit her teeth and narrowly avoided screaming for the woman to stop.

"Where are the rest of the patients?" another board member asked.

Dr. Locke pushed his horn-rimmed glasses back to the bridge of his nose. "The residents are at their after-supper exercise period." Weldon had insisted they be removed for "security reasons."

"I've heard you delouse every patient," one of the reporters said. "Is that true?"

"One of our nurses examines every new admission. She assigns anyone with lice to the delousing ward where they have daily exams and treatment until the problem is eradicated. Lice-free patients live in a ward such as this one."

Lice? Kara suppressed a shudder. "I'd like to see the dining area and the kitchen now."

"Of course." Dr. Locke led the way down a dark, narrow staircase.

She followed, steadying herself with a gloved hand on the worn, wooden railing. The Virginia Board of Eugenics representatives followed her. Her retinue of Weldon, her bodyguards, and the reporters and the photographers trailed after them. After Donald's inauguration, the number of reporters and photographers and sycophants that dogged her had grown from less than a handful to fifty-odd people. It had forced her, Donald, and Weldon to become resourceful at securing private conversations.

Chapter Fifty

Beryl slipped through a gap in the Colony's perimeter guard at the back of the cemetery. She crept from gravestone to gravestone. Her jeans were cold, wet, and caked with mud leftover from yesterday's rain.

Wires stretched between wooden posts marked the end of the cemetery. On the other side of the fence, clumps of bushes hid the rest of the Colony. Beryl ignored the adrenaline buzz that urged her to rush forward. She breathed slowly, moved slowly, stayed hyperalert. She wormed across to the fence, took cover behind a tall, fragrant white hydrangea, and peered through the branches. Her policeman hadn't lied. Across the way stood hurdles, a wire belly-crawl, and an inclined wall. A military-style obstacle course. *Weldon, you crafty son of a bitch. Who would expect Azrael at a home for the rejects of Fellowship society? Hell, he could hide hundreds of Azrael here.* That was a sobering thought.

According to the overworked and underpaid maid at the Virginian Hotel, Kara had reserved the penthouse suite for this evening. Beryl had given the maid a paid night off and made a sketch of the unguarded room's layout. Now all she needed was proof the Azrael lived here and confirmation that Weldon was in town.

A paved road ran between the cemetery and the obstacle course. No one was on the road, nor around the nearby building labeled Infirmary. *Of course. Weldon would want to keep the prying eyes of Kara's entourage as far from the training grounds as possible.*

She vaulted the fence and flattened herself behind a bushy magnolia. She scanned again. Still no movement. Inching through thick weeds and grass added to her collection of scratches and bug bites that itched and burned. She didn't care. There had to be a barracks somewhere. If there were as many Azrael here as she suspected, she'd get a message to Ethan. That would bring him to Lynchburg.

She rolled into the ditch beside the road. Cool mud oozed into her shirtsleeves and shoes. A dozen barracks-like buildings stood half a football field away. She assumed they held Colony residents. The Azrael would be in a building or buildings isolated from the others. Like the one over there, set back from the road, glimpsed in a gap between tall hibiscus shrubs. She smiled a grim, gotcha smile.

She hunkered down in the ditch and squirmed about one hundred meters. Raising up, she peered over the edge of the ditch and studied the building straight across from her. Crumbling concrete steps led up to a pillared porch. On the porch, a white, wooden rocker had only one armrest. The screen door stood ajar, held open by a rusted, gallon-sized can labeled Tomatoes. The interior front door stood open too. The hallway beyond looked dark and empty. She darted to the side of the building. No sounds of occupancy. And still no light. She hugged the brick wall and headed to the back of the building.

The mud path leading to the back door held many layers of deep footprints. Muddy footprints led through the open door into a kitchen. Beryl followed them. Open cupboard doors revealed bare shelves. An old six-burner range with oven stood at one end of the railroad-style kitchen. Beryl sniffed. Nothing but a faint burnt smell.

She entered the dingy hallway. The floor creaked. She shifted her weight from one foot to the other and reduced the volume of the creaking. The dining rooms, the living room, and all the upstairs rooms were vacant. A saggy mattress here, a broken dresser there hinted at previous occupants. Then she spied an abandoned rag doll.

Beryl stooped and picked up the rag doll. It looked like the one she'd made for Anna. She brushed her mud-smeared hand over the brown yarn hair, the embroidered face, the dress made from an old sweater and a worn cotton apron. Deep inside her chest, an old ache blossomed and grew, gnawing at her, weakening her.

Chapter Fifty-One

The smell of kerosene in Oscar's stuffy garage made Miranda lightheaded. She leaned against the workbench. She'd spent the morning memorizing code words and maps and safe places until she was certain her poor brain would split like an over-ripe tomato. She hoped there would be no more memorization at this meeting. Oscar's 1931 Duesenberg sat behind them, leaving plenty of room for the seven of them at the workbench.

Jack stood at the end of the workbench, a sheen of sweat glistening on his dark face. Strewn along the top of the workbench was an odd collection of empty bottles, rags torn in strips, wooden rods, corks, and bottle caps.

"What we have here is an assembly line," Jack said. "Leslie and Miranda will take an empty bottle, a rag, and a dowel. Wrap the rag around the dowel, like this." He demonstrated, twisting a little of the fabric around the wooden rod. "Stick it in the bottle and unwind it." He withdrew the rod. Part of the rag lay in the bottom of the bottle with the tail of the rag hanging outside the bottle. "Leave three inches of rag outside; less than that, and the fuse is too short."

Miranda tamped down the eagerness that bubbled inside her.

She couldn't wait to strike a blow against her father's beloved Fellowship.

Jack nodded at Oscar, Ian, and Nick. "You'll fill the bottles with kerosene. Be careful. Don't spill anything and don't disturb the fuse."

"Hector and I will cap the bottles. Any questions?" No one spoke up. "Let's get to work."

Miranda discovered that pulling the stick out of a soda bottle without the rag was trickier than it looked.

Chapter Fifty-Two

K ara hurried Dr. Locke and the others through the kitchen. She was weary of this everlasting tour. *Two hours? Once you've seen one elderly six-burner gas range with oven and a pair of older model Frigidares, there isn't anything else to see.*

The dining room held three rows of long wooden tables spanning the width of the building. Here, the windows were open on both sides of the building. Fans whirred overhead. A cool breeze, filled with the scent of wet earth and summer flowers, flowed through the room. Kara drew in a cleansing breath and sighed. She glanced at Weldon.

He stood beside the hallway entrance to the room, hands behind his back. Every inch of him exuded official Second Sphere business. He touched his earpiece, listened a moment, mumbled a response, then looked up at her. With his eyes locked on hers, he brushed his hair back from his face. That was the signal. Soon, somewhere on the Colony grounds, chaos would erupt. Kidnappers would snatch her daughter. After that, the Fellowship would declare war. She ran the tip of her tongue over her lips.

"Lady Clarke?"

She turned toward the reporter who spoke. "I'm sorry. Would you repeat your question?"

"There are some who object to the compulsory sterilizations done here. Is it possible that some of them aren't necessary?"

"I'm the mother of three beautiful children grown into wonderful adults," Kara said. She directed her mostly genuine smile at the reporters and the representatives of the Virginia Board of Eugenics. "It would have devastated me if any of my children were born with defects like the residents here. But if I had a feebleminded child, or if I knew I carried genes for epilepsy, I would have demanded that I be sterilized for the good of our nation. And I would thank God that I was born in a nation devoted to having strong, healthy—"

All the bones in her body trembled. Glass rattled. An invisible hand knocked her to her knees and sent showers of plaster dust down on her. The *boom* of the explosion knifed through her ears.

Chapter Fifty-Three

B eryl blew out a breath, dropped the doll, and tried to dispel the tingle that traveled up her legs. The tingle escalated and shook the windows. *Boom.* A wall of air slammed her to the floor. A thousand needles pierced her eardrums. Her bones vibrated like a tuning fork struck with a sledgehammer. Buzzing filled her ears. She lay still and fought the disorientation. *An explosion. Nearby.* She lurched to her feet. Glass crunched underfoot. She peered out the now-broken window. *The obstacle course? Who would blow it up? Why? SABR? Doesn't seem likely.*

Three Fellowship vehicles came roaring up the road and squealed to an emergency stop near the devastation that was once the obstacle course. She drew back. She hadn't heard anything but the buzzing in her ears. She peered around the open curtain. A dozen armed men poured out of the vehicles. *They got here awfully fast, too fast to be part of the perimeter guard.* The sound of gunfire penetrated the buzzing that filled Beryl's head. Four agents were shooting at one of the three vehicles they'd just exited.

This reeked of an underhanded Weldon trick. At a hand signal from one of the four shooters, the shooting stopped. The leader pointed at the building Beryl was hiding in. *Shit!* She spun toward the kitchen. She was on a tilt-a-whirl ride. She reached for the wall. Missed. Her knees hit the floor. The spinning in her head continued. She crawled to the wall, used it to steady herself, and climbed to her feet. Deep breaths and slow blinks. The twirling in her head lessened, but the room still swayed with each step. One hand on the wall, she moved toward the kitchen as quickly as possible.

The perimeter guard, plus these twelve, the guards posted around the building Kara was in, plus personal bodyguards meant a force of at least thirty agents. And given the game Weldon had just played, they'd have to increase personal protection for Kara. *Damn. No chance of getting close enough tonight. Must warn Miranda and Gert. Get out of Lynchburg. Find Ethan.* She careened out of the building toward the cemetery.

Chapter Fifty-Four

Kara didn't have to fake her increased pulse rate or breathlessness. Her ears rang, and there was a fine coating of grit and dust on her skin and clothes. Weldon and her bodyguards rushed to her side. Using their bodies to shield her, they escorted her to the "secure" room in the basement. Her hand shook when she raised it to wipe dust from her mouth. *Why hadn't Weldon warned her? That had been close. Too close.* "What's happening? Where's Miranda?" she asked, keeping to the script they'd devised.

"I'm trying to find out," Weldon said, his voice sounded distant and tinny. His look of concern was perfect.

"Your daughter was here?" Dr. Locke had not been in on the plan.

"She planned to be here for the tour," Kara answered. "Her car had a flat. I pray she's still a safe distance away."

"Excuse me?" Weldon said, pressing his earpiece into his ear. He listened for a moment, then his long face, grayed by plaster dust, went pale. He glanced at her and then glanced away.

The board members and press members crowding the small room hushed. Flashbulbs popped.

"Kara," Weldon said in a strangled voice. He cleared his throat. "Lady Clarke, I'm afraid I have bad news."

She swallowed the pretend lump in her throat. "About Miranda?" She stood a little straighter. "Tell me."

"The explosion took out a section of the road just outside this building. Miranda's driver got the car stopped in time, but a gang of apostates attacked. Your daughter, Miranda, has been kidnapped."

She sucked in air as if she'd been punched in the stomach. Flashbulbs *pop-pop-popped*. *Good*. They helped her look surprised, scared, maybe even shocked. "You have to find her, Weldon. Save my daughter."

Chapter Fifty-Five

M iranda poked the fabric-wound stick into the milk bottle, rotated the stick, and the fabric unwound like it was supposed to. She withdrew the stick and slid the bottle across the workbench toward Nick.

"While you're working, let's do a final run-through." Hector flipped and caught a bottle cap over and over in one hand.

"At seven p.m. I shoot out the bulb in the security light for the backyard," Ian said. "I disappear in the woods behind the armory."

Nick put a funnel in the mouth of one of the rag-stuffed bottles. "At eight, I walk past the armory, round the corner, and hide in the shrubbery." He poured kerosene into the bottle.

The oily smell freshened, and Miranda's head swam.

Nick nudged Miranda.

"Oh." She looked up from the strip of plaid fabric she wound on the stick. "I come from the south side of the wooded lot at eight-fifteen and join Nick."

Ian didn't even look up from the soda bottle before him. "I bring my guitar case with the old man's bolt cutters inside to Nick at eight-twenty."

"And at eight-twenty, Hector and I light the incendiary bottles in the abandoned building at the back of the Colony," Jack said.

Leslie handed Ian a quart milk bottle with a blue rag hanging out of it. "At the same time, I stop for Oscar at the corner of 16th and Wise."

Hector nodded. "At eight-twenty-five, I call the fire department. And from the little trash fire last week, we know the police and fire department will arrive ten to fifteen minutes later. As soon as we hear the sirens, Jack and I start for the armory."

"At eight-forty, I cut the chain-link fence," Nick said. "I hold the fence open while the others crawl through. I crawl through last and reposition the fence so it looks closed."

The kerosene fumes made Miranda's eyes burn. It must have bothered Oscar too. He opened a window and the side door a crack.

"I tape the kitchen window and break it," Ian said. The kerosene can he picked up made a metallic pop. "I crawl through the window and open the back door by eight-fifty."

"Nick boosts me up into the ceiling," Ian said. "I crawl across and cut through the ceiling into the locker. By eight-fifty-five I'm inside the locker and open it."

Nick slid the can of kerosene toward Hector. "We haul guns and ammo out to the dock."

"Where I'm waiting with the truck," Leslie said and poked a plaid strip of cloth into another bottle.

Something thumped the wall and rattled the tools on the wall and the bottles on the worktable. Rattled Miranda's chest long enough to alarm her. "What was that?"

"An explosion," Nick and Jack answered.

"How far away?" Hector asked.

"Less than five miles," Jack answered. "East."

Hector turned to Ian. "Go. Find out what you can. Report back here in ten minutes."

Ian grabbed his cap and bolted out the door.

"Should we bug out?" Nick asked.

Hector thought a minute. "Not yet. Better wait for Ian, so we know what's going on." His glance included them all. "Finish what you're doing." He turned to Jack. "Come with me a moment." They went to the garage door and had an urgent, whispered conversation.

Silent and grim, Miranda and the others continued turning milk and soda bottles into incendiary devices. Ten minutes ground past. Hector paced in front of the side door. Finally, Ian banged the door open.

"The—explosion—was—at the Colony." He gasped for breath between words. "Can't say how close, but near our building."

"No." Hector looked stunned.

"The police and firemen are there."

"Was it a bad furnace?" Oscar asked

"They said *we* blew it up. And they say we kidnapped Miranda Clarke, the First Apostle's daughter."

"That's not true." Miranda stepped forward. "No one kidnapped me."

"Well, doesn't that beat all?" Jack rubbed a hand through his thick black hair.

"This doesn't change the big picture," Hector said. "You and I will still start a fire in the abandoned house. They'll figure it's a secondary fire due to the explosion."

"That place will be under investigation or under guard for days," Nick said.

Hector gave him a steady look. "Jack and I will use all our evasion skills. Stick to the plan." He made eye contact with each of the others. "Bug out. Two-minute intervals. Go to your safe places. We hit the armory tonight as planned."

Miranda grabbed Nicholas by the elbow. "I wasn't kidnapped. My parents know I wasn't. What do I do?"

"Now is not the time to play games." Nicholas picked up a box. "We stick to the plan." He hurried out of the garage.

They left one by one at two-minute intervals.

Miranda watched them all leave. She, a small pile of rags, and the smell of kerosene were the only signs that something had happened here. The explosion and the claim that she'd been kidnapped nagged her. *My parents know I left Redemption, and by now they know Beryl did too. Why pretend it happened today?* Miranda caught her breath. *It's a trap.* She didn't know how they were going to use this against Beryl, but they were. She had to warn Beryl. A glance at her watch told her she'd have to find Beryl in a hurry. She dashed out of the garage.

Chapter Fifty-Six

Nearing Main Street, Beryl grew more and more uneasy. It had taken her too long to change out of her muddy clothes. Townspeople clogged the sidewalks. Their chatter and movements made her twitchy. Finding Gert would be easy. Miranda would either be at the meeting place or not.

The clock tower of the Farmer's Market showed she had two minutes. She wouldn't make it. She had picked up a tail. *Damn. Do these guys know all the regular townspeople on sight?* She surged forward, jaywalked across the street. She stopped. She feigned oohing over the dresses in J.C. Penney's front window and studied the reflections of the street. *Sure enough.* Tall, dark, and ugly stopped and turned toward the street as if looking for someone. She stifled a snort. *Get a load of his sunglasses.* He looked at his watch.

A man in a gray fedora walked past the tail, talking to himself. Sunglasses answered back.

She hurried inside the Penney's store, to the ladies' department in the back. She paused at a dress rack, pretending to look for her size but watching the front door.

In came Sunglasses. Fedora Man came in a moment later.

She grabbed a dress and hurried through the curtained

entrance to the ladies' dressing room. Inside, she thrust the dress at the dressing room attendant. "I got the wrong size, get me a four."

The attendant's smile froze. "Of course, dear." She left.

Beryl trotted down the aisle of curtained dressing rooms. At the end of the aisle stood a door with large red letters, Emergency Exit Only. On the wall beside it was a large, red fire alarm pull.

"Excuse me," the attendant at the entrance to the dressing rooms shouted. "You can't go in there."

Beryl pulled her gun out, yanked the fire alarm, and darted out the door and down the alley.

Fire bells rang, loud and shrill.

The Penney's back door banged open. Male voices cursed fluently.

Beryl spotted the back door of the S. S. Kresge store. She ran at the door full tilt. The press bar didn't give an inch. She staggered backward.

She whirled and faced her opponents, who were only a few running steps behind her.

"Oh no, you ain't!"

Gert? No! The axe arced downward. *Thwack.* Sunglasses crumpled to the ground. Gert yanked at the axe embedded in the dead man's spine. His partner swung, gun in hand, toward Gert. The sound of the agent's gun and her own split the air. He dropped facedown.

Beryl bent, grabbed his gun, and stuffed it in her pocket. She frisked the body. "Grab that one's wallet, weapon, and anything else we can use." Slipping Fedora Man's wallet into her other pocket, she spun toward Gert. "We don't have time to—"

Gert lay sprawled on her stomach across her victim.

Beryl's heart and lungs seized. Her vision narrowed. All she could see, all she could hear was Gert. *No. No. No. Not again.* She knelt beside the old woman, rolled her over, cradled her. Gert was pale and covered in blood, impossible to tell whose. "Gert?" She searched for a wound.

257

Gert's left hand pressed her stomach. Blood bubbled between her fingers.

Beryl lifted Gert's hand. More blood poured out. She pulled her neck scarf off and pressed it to the wound. "It's not that bad, Gert," she lied. "Open your eyes, old woman." Gert's blood saturated the scarf and pooled around her hands. "You'll be all right." She wished it were true.

Gert's eyes fluttered open. She smiled up at Beryl. "Damn gov'ment man got me." Her breath gurgled.

"You saved me." Beryl tried to smile. "Again." She shook her head and held Gert close. "I was too slow. Too goddamned slow."

Gert laid a hand on hers, light as paper.

"I be fine." Gert took a couple of shuddering breaths. "I'm gonna see my Mary." Her eyes fluttered closed.

Beryl put an ear to Gert's chest. No whisper of breath, not even a faint *lub-dub*. She hugged her friend, then smoothed Gert's soft, thick braids into place. "I can't stay," she whispered.

She laid Gert on the pavement, caressed the old woman's face, then stood. She stared at her bloody hands, her torn and bloody blouse. She ripped it off, wiped her hands as clean as she could, bent, and yanked Fedora Man's shirt off. She slipped on the man's shirt and tucked it in. She frisked Sunglasses and pocketed his wallet. *Did he really not carry a gun?*

She stuffed her bloody hands into her pockets and exited the alley. Full sound came rushing back. The Penney's alarm clanged. A woman screamed, and in the distance, sirens wailed. She strode away, uphill.

Chapter Fifty-Seven

Miranda strained to glimpse Beryl or Gert among shoppers and tables of fresh produce, crafts, and assorted concessions near the southeastern entrance to the Lynchburg Farmer's Market.

The clock with its oversized Roman numerals rose from a large flower box filled with purple bearded irises in the center of the market. *Two minutes before seven. I made it.* She whirled and scanned faces. *No Gert or Beryl.* She wiped the sweat beaded on her upper lip with the back of her hand. A teenaged girl wearing a soft yellow cardigan over a white blouse and a full, plaid skirt walked toward her.

The teenager stopped and turned an earnest look up at her. "Is that the right time?"

Miranda looked up at the time. Seven o'clock. *Beryl, where are you?* She forced a smile. "I hope so."

"Oh." The girl seemed taken aback. "I'm sorry to have disturbed you." She walked away.

Teenagers. Miranda scanned the market. Many tables were empty. The vendors had already packed and gone. *Maybe Beryl has been and gone.*

The unmistakable sound of a blaring fire bell brought a momentary hush to the market. Someone yelled, "Fire! Penney's is on fire!" People shouted, pushed, and shoved. The crowd surged across the street and down the block, toward the store.

Miranda moved too, swept forward by the crowd.

The *whoop-whoop* of approaching sirens pierced the crowd noises.

Someone screamed and screamed and screamed. It was unnerving.

The crowd ran. So did Miranda.

In front of the store, the market crowd slowed to a stop, mingled with the people who'd fled the J.C. Penney store. People asked one another, "Where's the fire?" "Did you smell smoke?" "Who pulled the alarm?"

Miranda worked her way toward the storefront. *So many people.* A fire truck arrived. The firemen jumped off and ran into the store before the truck came to a complete stop. A police car screeched to a halt behind it.

She ducked into the alley. It was crowded too. And loud. A police whistle sounded two short blasts. She pushed against the crowd but couldn't force her way any farther than about halfway down the alley. She glanced over her shoulder. A policeman inched his way through the crowd. She faced front and got a glimpse of a clear spot in the alley where a couple of firemen knelt on the ground. Someone lay on the pavement between them. One of the firemen shook his head and then stood. The second fireman stood, and they walked away.

A bloodied body lay on the pavement. The body wore Gert's dress. Sounds and sights faded. All Miranda could see was the body in the dress. Impossibly still. Impossibly pale. Dove-gray braids neatly draped on top of each shoulder. *No. It can't be Gert.* As if to mock her, Gert's lifeless face filled her vision. Miranda couldn't catch her breath. Waves of dizziness threatened to topple her. Her vision blurred. She put a fist to her mouth. The press of the crowd kept her upright. Two policemen reached the scene. One hunched over a pair of legs in men's trousers—

Her stomach clenched, then eased. *No, not Beryl.* Beryl had worn one of Gert's "finds," a skirt and blouse. Miranda forced herself to look. *Blood. So much blood.* Three bodies. Two men. And Gert. One of the men had Gert's axe in his back.

"Why bring an axe to a gunfight?" one officer asked.

"Better question," said the other officer. "Where are the guns? Had to be two."

Beryl had to have been here—with Gert. If the men were Second Sphere and they tried to grab Beryl, Beryl would have fought back. Gert too. Gert's dead. Beryl's gone. She could be hurt. Miranda let people jostle past her and move forward, forcing her toward the street.

She reached the street and turned back toward the Farmer's Market. Rounding a corner, her vision blurred, and her knees weakened. She leaned a shoulder into a rough brick wall.

"Are you all right?"

She glanced up into a stranger's face, nodded wordlessly, and straightened. *Can't stay. Got to move. Find Beryl.* She started uphill. From time to time, she had to rub her eyes to clear them or touch a brick wall to steady herself. *They. Killed. Gert.*

Her heart slammed against her ribs. She walked faster. She gasped fast, shallow breaths. *Use your head, Miranda.* She stopped and turned, looking for Beryl. But Beryl was in her head. *Situational awareness. Never lose it.*

She paused at a display window, forced herself to take deep, calming breaths. She focused not on the perfect living room on display but on the street mirrored in the window. She didn't see anyone following her.

Her focus changed. Inside the perfect living room, the words CBS News Bulletin flickered in black and white on the television screen. The words resolved to the black and white images of two news commentators behind a desk. She couldn't hear what they were saying. The next image on the screen was of the devastation left by the explosion at the Colony. Then there was another shot of the Colony and—her mother. *Mama is here?* Covered in dust, a visible tear track ran down her mother's face. *Mama never cries.* Mama always said you have to show the public emotion but never let them see your real feelings.

Then Miranda's own face stared back at her from the television. It was one of the public photos of the family. Following her photo were mug shots of Hector and Beryl. The caption said they were "suspected kidnappers."

Miranda glared at the screen. Doubts about letting God sort it out vanished. She strode toward Constitution Lane.

Chapter Fifty-Eight

The skin of Beryl's hands pulled and itched with drying blood. Gert's blood. Deep in her right pocket, her fingers tightened on the grip of Fedora Man's gun. She clutched his wallet in the other pocket. A matron hurried past, carrying a furled umbrella and a large shopping bag. Beryl glared at her. *Are you one of them?* The woman gave her a startled look. Beryl crossed to the other side of the street. She slowed her pace and drifted past hat shops and dress shops and jewelry stores.

A black sedan cruised slowly toward her. *Second Sphere?* The car drove past. A temporary reprieve. She ducked into an alley. Midway down the alley, a stinking oversized garbage bin screened her from the street.

Fedora Man's wallet held forty dollars in small bills, a Second Sphere shield, and a New Jersey driver's license. Sunglasses' wallet revealed he, too, was from New Jersey. *From Weldon's elite team. Sent here—for me.* She took out the IDs, pocketed the cash, and crammed the wallets deep into the trashcan. The shield went into her pocket to be dumped later. She took a second look at the driver's licenses, but she couldn't focus on the cards. All she saw was her bloody hands. Hands that shook as if she were palsied.

Gert. Dear God, why Gert? Her knees folded, and she slid down the wall and sat in the dirt. She buried half-born sobs in her knees.

She took deep shuddering breaths until she had control again. She forced thoughts of Gert, pain, and grief into a dark mental crevasse filled with suppressed memories. *Focus. How much time had she lost?* The sky, once a silver-gray, had darkened to a deeper gray.

She thrust her hands deep into her pockets again and sauntered out of the alley. She used the "look both ways" routine to scan cars and faces. She crossed the street and strolled uphill to the Esso Station.

The two pumps out front were vacant. The garage doors were closed. The lights were off. A sign on the corner of the building pointed to the ladies' room.

She plunged her hands into the water before it had a chance to warm. The blood sluiced off. She scrubbed her hands. With each drop of Gert's blood that slipped down the drain, her anger rose.

It took every ounce of restraint to dry her hands on the rough cotton towel from the roll-a-towel dispenser without ripping it from the wall. She opened the door forcefully but caught it before it banged the wall. *Control your anger. Direct it. Let anger hone the steel that is your resolve.* She stepped out into the muggy night air filled with enough resolve to extinguish Kara, Weldon, the Fellowship, and the Azrael.

Behind the gas station stood an open barrel of oil-smelling sludge. She dropped the two agents' IDs and shields into it. She walked down the street fast, but not fast enough to draw attention. Every instinct she had screamed against her going back into town, but she couldn't leave yet. She'd lost Gert today, but she sure as hell wasn't going to lose Miranda too.

Beryl turned onto the block where the soda store was. Police crime tape crisscrossed the door to the Sweet Spoons shop. Inside, the store was dark and featureless.

Worst-case scenario, Miranda is dead or on her way back to Redemption, which is as good as dead. Best-case scenario, Miranda has joined the rebels and is with them. Either way, there was nothing more Beryl could do for her. Another soul for whom Beryl owed vengeance. It was time she began paying her debts. Her pace quickened.

Neon signs glowed above dark store windows. A rare vehicle cruised past, headlights off. The blue Ford four-door didn't look official, but she turned off Main Street and circled the block before heading south again. Part of her wanted to turn back, to kill Weldon in his sleep tonight. But security and media would surround Weldon and Kara. *Never should've considered taking Weldon out first.* First, she'd take care of the Azrael, then Weldon.

Beryl ignored the temptation to steal a car. That would be foolhardy. She'd have to walk or hitchhike three, maybe four, hours to Sweet Briar, a college town. College kids were reckless with the car daddy bought them. She shortened her stride, pacing herself.

She passed a bus stop sign. Stuck to the lower right corner of the sign was a piece of blue tape. The bus stop dead drop had a message. Beryl slowed and scanned her surroundings with extra care. In the dark, many watchers would likely be spotted, but a single, skilled watcher would never be seen. She hoped there was one. She needed to exact a tiny bit of vengeance.

Beryl pretended to stumble, gave an exaggerated sigh, and hobbled to the bus stop bench. Propping her foot on the seat of the bench, she bent to re-tie her shoe and faked fumbling the shoelace. She slipped her fingers under the seat and found a small metal box taped there. Jerking the tape loose, she palmed the little box, tied her shoe, and walked away.

She walked a zigzag up one block, across, and down the next block. After four blocks, she figured she would have spotted a tail by now. She finally allowed herself to look at the little box. It smelled like the peppermint-flavored lounges for stomach ailments. A folded piece of paper lay inside.

Remember where it started? Monkshood waits.

Her stomach tightened. She remembered. The little cabin in the woods had been a lovely treat one weekend. *Was it a safe house now?* Ripping the message into tiny pieces, she dropped some into a large puddle pooled in the gutter. She walked with renewed energy and scattered the rest of the pieces here and there. She tossed the little box into a bunch of bushes. Beryl settled into a loping stride to conserve her energy. She had a long walk before she could steal a car and drive to the little cabin.

Chapter Fifty-Nine

Anna sat at the table in the over-warm kitchen of a small farmhouse and let the cat rub against her leg. The pattern of calico on its back reminded her of a cat she'd had when she was younger. She'd used the farmhouse as her base, striking out in her autogiro daily to hunt for signs of the target. Uncle's information was vague. The target was in the Shenandoah Forest. She'd head for Lynchburg or Charlottesville or Richmond. Too big an area to search and be successful.

But she didn't hunt alone. The thing inside her had led her to souls when it hungered.

Today was a recovery day, so she'd stayed at the house. She'd spent hours running through the routines she used to keep her skills sharp. The open frequency of her radio scanner provided a background noise of low static. There were occasional bits of local police chatter but nothing interesting.

She broke down her rifle, a Mauser MP60 caseless assault rifle, cleaned it, and put it back together. She rechecked every aspect of its action. A click from her radio scanner caught her attention.

"Sack to Rope: Splice. Smoke or Fire?"

She listened to all the Second Sphere's observation reports. A little edge she'd found helpful from time to time.

"Snare to Rope: No Sparks."

Nothing in Norfolk.

"Springe to Rope: No Sparks."

Nor in Richmond, Petersburg, or Danville. She sighed. *Perhaps today is not the day.*

"Noose to Rope: Smoke."

She sat forward. *Lynchburg? Her hometown? The target is smarter than that. Isn't she?*

"Rope to Noose: Commit Smoke."

Yes, Lynchburg, tell us about your suspect. She packed her rifle into its carry-case.

"Sunburn Socket free in empire."

Disguised female on foot, in downtown Lynchburg? Has she gone senile in her old age?

"Knot loose. Alpha maneuvering for zero-zero."

She frowned. *The surveillance team lost the target? Maybe age wasn't a factor.*

SHH. Her scanner picked up the two keystrokes on her private frequency. *Would she go to Lynchburg?* She smiled and toggled her mike switch. *Acknowledged.* SHH. *Requesting a cleanup crew.* SHHHH. SHH. SHH. SHHHH.

The farmer and his wife had contributed little to assuage Azrael's hunger. She shivered. Azrael yearned for the target's soul as it had for no other.

She pulled the map out of the front flap-pocket of her pants. It was roughly one hundred thirty miles to Lynchburg.

Hefting her go bag, she hurried out the back door. She stowed her bag in her bullet-shaped autogiro, a twin-seated Buhl AZ-187-C, and climbed into the cockpit. The engine coughed and whined and set the double, contra-rotating pusher props into motion.

The autogiro rolled down the farmer's drive. It picked up speed. The overhead rotor began to turn. Soon, it whirled with its familiar eggbeater sound. The autogiro lifted. She was airborne. A slow smile lit her face. She'd be in Lynchburg in less than an hour.

Chapter Sixty

At twenty-one after eight, Miranda bounced on her toes, unable to do anything but wait at this stage of the robbery. Their intel was right. A floor-to-ceiling, heavy-duty, chain-link fence enclosed the weapons locker at the National Guard Armory. A padlock secured the door, or was it a gate?

Ian's bolt cutters *snicked*. The lock clattered to the floor. The sound scraped across Miranda's bones and whisked a shiver across her skin. *Surely someone outside could hear that.*

"Calm down, Miranda," Nick whispered. "No one can hear us."

She nodded and quieted her body. Her insides remained jumping-bean jittery.

Ian opened the door to the locker. Finally, she could do something.

"Can you carry this?" Nick handed her a narrow, rectangular box. It was heavy for its size, but no heavier than one of Gert's water buckets. She guessed that the white gibberish lettered on the sides of the olive drab box indicated which type of ammunition filled the box.

"I can take two," she said.

Nick handed her another. She grabbed the handle and silently thanked Beryl and Gert for making her carry the water. Nick took one end of a long box, and Ian took the other. She followed them through a gymnasium-like room into a storage and dock area. They left their loads and hurried back to the locker.

When they returned to the dock, Leslie was parked outside. Nick raised the door, then he and Ian moved the boxes into the truck bed. Miranda returned to the weapons locker for more ammo.

She and the others made two more trips back and forth.

On her way back for a final load, a poster caught her attention. Her father—again. "Wouldn't you like to know what your daughter's doing right now?" she whispered. She whirled away from the image and banged her right hip into a desk corner, sending several small items clattering to the floor. A grunt of surprise and pain escaped her. She crouched low, flicked on her flashlight, and searched for the items.

"What are you doing?" Nick asked. He carried four ammo boxes.

"I knocked a couple of pens off the desk," she had to admit.

"Nothing else?"

"Only pens." She held up three felt tips.

"Finish picking up and get to the dock. We're done." Nick hurried toward the dock.

She stood and put the pens on the desk. She had hoped to prove how valuable she could be to SABR. Instead, she'd proven she was a klutz. She could feel her father's disapproving stare. She glared at the image. A devilish thought blossomed. She drew a cartoon speech bubble from her father's mouth. Inside the bubble, she wrote, "I rape little girls." She stepped back. A sense of power filled her, her lungs swelled, and her shoulders squared. "Let's see you talk your way out of that," she whispered and left.

Nick waited, alone. He tilted his head in a "follow me" motion and disappeared around the corner of the building. Miranda almost ran back inside to tear down the poster, but its absence would be noticeable. And she didn't want to tear it down. It was her personal stroke of rebellion. If she were lucky, they wouldn't spot the alteration for days and then blame one of their own for it. She hurried after Nick, toward her new life as a rebel.

Chapter Sixty-One

Moonlit fog gave the tops of the tall pines an unearthly glow. The light barely penetrated to the rough ground Miranda walked. There was a sense of safety in the shadow of the pines whose needles quieted their footsteps. No one could have followed their serpentine path north and deep into the George Washington National Forest. She followed close behind Nick, for fear of getting lost. Sweat gathered in a pool between her aching shoulders, trapped by the weight of her rucksack. Despite the late hour, she was energized, eager, exhilarated. She, Miranda Clarke, was a rebel. She'd done dangerous, illegal things, all for the cause. Now she was going to meet the leader of SABR, her uncle. Soon Beryl would come, and they would fight her father and the Fellowship side by side.

She collided with Nick's rucksack. He'd stopped. She murmured an apology for not paying attention, stepped to his side, and swallowed a gasp. Nick had said they were going to a hunter's cabin. She'd imagined a hunting lodge with high log rafters, ferocious animal trophies, and a swarm of rebels. A rough-hewn shack with a single, boarded up window stood in a small clearing scarcely larger than the shack. No more than ten feet wide and twelve feet long and surrounded by tall pines, it made Gert's home look palatial. No sign of life showed, not even the tiniest glimmer of light around the door.

"Where is everyone?" The night was so quiet she couldn't help but whisper.

"Inside." He didn't whisper.

Not a swarm. "How many?"

"Monkshood and two or three of his men." He cocked his head. "Did you expect more?"

"Not really." She hadn't thought it through. Of course, it was safer for Uncle Ethan to travel alone or with a small group.

Nick took a step toward the cabin.

She touched his arm. "Wait."

He turned to face her again.

"Does Uncle Ethan, I mean, Monkshood, know I'm coming?"

"We told him." Before she could open her mouth again, he added, "And we told him you said you were *the* Miranda Clarke."

She blew out a shaky breath. *If only Beryl were here. If only...* After so many years she wasn't certain what to wish or expect. Still, she was here. It was time. "Okay. I'm ready."

Nick rapped on the door. It opened.

Uncle Ethan's once robust frame was skeletal. His face had the hollows and shadows of a much older man. He ran his hand through his hair, still thick and dark, though streaked with gray. The gesture swept his hair back, except for the stubborn piece that always fell into his face. He studied Miranda. "Come into the light." His voice was low and melodic and familiar.

Nick shut the door behind them.

Hector and two other men stood behind a table. The light was a single, sputtering kerosene lantern set on a wooden table. Hector bent to fiddle with the lantern. The light steadied and grew, adding the smoky tang of kerosene to the hot, stale air.

Miranda put on a smile and stuck out her hand. "Hello, Uncle Ethan."

Recognition blossomed. "Miranda. It is you, isn't it?" He wrapped her, rucksack and all, in a joyous bear hug.

She couldn't move or speak or breathe. *This is Uncle Ethan. Family. Why can't I hug him back? I should hug him.* A wooden pat his on his back was the best she could do. Then the need to move away overwhelmed her. She pushed against his chest, breaking his hold.

"I can't believe you're here." He looked her up and down. "My goodness, you've grown into quite the young lady."

"It's her? You're sure?" Hands on his hips, Hector's look was flat out unfriendly.

Miranda gave him an "I tried to tell you" glare, then refocused on Ethan. "They told me you and Aunt Beryl were dead." There was so much she should say; so much she wanted to say.

"I'm here. You're here. That's all that matters."

"Even Beryl thought—"

He gripped her arms so tight she grimaced. "You've seen Beryl? How is she? Where is she?" He peered at the door behind Miranda.

"She's not here."

The spark in his eyes dulled.

Miranda couldn't stand how disappointed he looked. "She's coming soon." Because the only reason Beryl wouldn't come was unbearable.

His stiff smile didn't look reassured.

"I couldn't believe it when I found out she was alive," Miranda said. "Then we were both shocked to hear that you were alive. I mean, we had your funerals and everything."

"Your parents 'buried' me? And Beryl?"

She nodded. "I won't ever forgive them."

"Yeah, I have a few things on my list of 'won't ever forgive' too." He gave her a sidelong glance. "I can't get used to your dark hair." He reached out, brushed her hair back from her face.

She recoiled. "I'm too sweaty." It sounded like the lame excuse it was.

His puzzlement was quickly smoothed away. "Have you eaten?"

"Yes."

He gestured toward the table. "Come on in. You know Hector? This is Pete and Conrad."

The tall, skinny man, Pete, nodded. So did Conrad, but he was built like a linebacker.

"Let's sit and talk," Uncle Ethan said.

Chairs scraped the wooden floor as they each settled around the table. They stared at her. She was a child again, under the measuring scrutiny of her mother. She didn't squirm, but she looked away, surveyed the cabin.

A potbellied stove and a couple of shelves hung on the wall opposite the table. Two pairs of bunk beds lined the walls at the back of the cabin.

"Why are you here, Miranda?" Uncle Ethan's question startled her. Not that he asked, but that he asked so abruptly. "Your parents say we kidnapped you."

"I know. I've been thinking about that." She leaned forward. "I know a journalist or two I can call and tell them the truth."

"The same journalists your parents know?" His finger tapped a folded newspaper. "The ones who think we are criminals?"

She opened the paper. The above-the-fold picture of her was from a lifetime ago, a lifetime of designer dresses, a lifetime of meaningless social obligations. The headline screamed "Miranda Clarke Kidnapped." "Colony of misfits attacked" captioned a photo of a building's blackened rubble. "Chauffeur and guards murdered" claimed the caption below another photograph. The battered and perforated limousine looked real.

The article included her father's plea for Miranda's safe return. He vowed to destroy SABR so no one else would have to fear for their daughter. The audacity of the lies, the rhetoric, and the hate that spewed from a supposed leader of the Fellowship fed a fire inside her. An unquenchable heat roared in her ears. *He has to pay for what he's done.* She slapped the paper down on the table. "This is why I'm here."

"Spare me the party line. I invented it. Tell me why you're really here."

"*I'm at war.* With the Fellowship." She tried a defiant glare. He didn't react. She crossed her arms over her chest. "You know I can shoot."

"Have you ever shot a person? Actually killed someone? Have you ever seen a dead body?"

The memory of Gert lying in a sea of blood roughened her voice. "I'm not a child who needs your protection, Uncle Ethan." She beamed her determination at him. "I don't need your permission either. I want to fight because I don't want to live in a world that forces me—" Her breath caught in her throat. Frozen, locked solid, she couldn't speak. Deep inside her, far below the pit of her stomach, her nightmares were a gaping black hole sucking her into a soul-eating void. She gripped the edge of the table, fought the darkness. "—a world—that forces—anyone—to do anything." The next breath was easier. "I won't go back—not to Redemption, and not to being the councilor's daughter." *Especially not that.* The darkness inside receded. She locked on Ethan. "I'm fighting for those inalienable rights you used to tell me about. I'll fight with or without SABR. So tell me"—she squared her shoulders—"with or without?"

He didn't look away, and he didn't speak for several long moments. "I can't promise you anything until I after I talk with my captains." He indicated Nick and the others with his chin.

She blinked, more hurt than surprised. "You don't trust me."

"Miranda," he said, his voice soft and kind, "as your uncle, I trust you. As the leader of SABR with a price on his head, I can't be suspicious enough." He dismissed her with a wave of his hand, all softness gone. "Take one of the bunks on the right. There's a curtain for privacy. We'll talk again in the morning."

The curtain was a rough, wool blanket hung over a rope strung between the bunks. She lay on top of a worn quilt and stared at the rope "springs" that formed the bottom of the top bunk. The men mumbled, but the tone and tension in their voices revealed that they argued—over her. She couldn't believe Uncle Ethan would kick her out, not until now. If worse came to worst, she would leave first thing in the morning and walk due east, out of the forest. Exhaustion sapped her ability to plan further. Sleep overtook her long before the argument ended.

Chapter Sixty-Two

Beryl walked ahead, Hector's gun pressing a .45 caliber circle into her back. Walking past the former resort cabins, she tried to prepare herself. They rounded the bend and the sight of the honeymoon cabin triggered memories of the sexual awakening and the melding of two souls. She blushed like a schoolgirl. Those memories belonged to the heartbreaking story of someone long forgotten. In the here and now, a weed-choked path led to a sagging porch. Most of the chinking between the logs was missing, the windows were curtainless and broken, and a messy bird's nest perched atop the chimney.

The cabin door creaked, and a thinner, more angular Ethan stepped into the sunlight. Her heart stuttered.

Ethan was down the steps and standing before her in an instant. He stopped close enough for her to breathe in the faint spice and leather of his favorite cologne. She locked eyes with his impossibly green ones. An ache rose and threatened to choke her. She swallowed.

"Beryl." His deep, melodic voice caressed her. His hand cupped her cheek. "It *is* you. How can that be?"

With an effort, she remembered her purpose. She put her

hand on his, gently took it from her cheek, but did not let go. "They told me you were dead."

They stared at one another for a suspended moment of time. Unspoken regret and pain and loss flowed between them and left an unbreachable gulf.

Running footsteps approached. "Beryl!" Miranda charged toward her.

"Whoa." Beryl held her hand up, braced for a blow.

Miranda pulled to a stop, short of a body slam. "I'm so glad to see you. When I saw Gert, I was afraid—"

"There's a lot of that going around," Beryl said without smiling. She turned to Ethan. "We need to talk—alone."

"Follow me." Ethan led her toward the cabin.

"Um, I'll talk to you later," Miranda said.

"Stick around," Beryl said over her shoulder, dreading going inside that cabin. "We won't be long."

"Okay."

"You can put your gun away, Hector." Ethan didn't take his eyes off Beryl. "And—"

Hector lowered his gun and answered, "Yes?"

"Wait with Miranda."

Inside the cabin, the sun cast rectangles of light through the windows. The largest rectangle stretched to a sofa with stuffing leaking out. Beryl avoided looking into the shadowed doorway of the bedroom and pretended the pain in her chest didn't exist. "Not a very secure meeting place."

A smile ghosted across his face. "My sentries stopped you."

"I *let* them stop me."

They stood inches apart, staring but not touching. There was a scar at the base of Ethan's throat, and his left arm was stiff. His recovery must have been long and difficult. Time blurred, and Ethan's body crumpled across a bleacher seat. An obscene amount of blood puddled on the concrete beneath him. A sea of grief swamped her. A touch brought her back. His eyes locked with hers. She cleared her throat and swallowed a lump of unsaid things. "How did you survive?"

"I don't remember." He shrugged. "Hector said he heard you, but by the time he reached me, you had disappeared. He took me to a doctor friend who admitted me to a local hospital under a false name. They say it was a miracle I survived those first three months." A pained expression pinched his face. "Your trial was over before I was conscious. They found you guilty of sedition and treason, gave you a death sentence." His lips twitched. "When I was well enough to leave the hospital, Hector found safe places for me to heal." He opened and closed his left hand. He looked down at his hand as if surprised by it, then stuffed it into his pants pocket. "How are you alive?" The slightest twinge of doubt edged his voice.

The doubt iced her veins. She stepped away into the shadows on the other side of the broken window. Dust stirred with her steps. "The Prophet commuted my sentence from death to life." She gave a mirthless chuckle. "I was in isolation, the living dead, for ten years. I survived for you, for Anna, for my mission."

"Mission?"

A lifetime ago he would have understood. "Vengeance."

"Against the Council?"

"The Fellowship Council, Weldon, anyone involved in the Azrael project. That project is an abomination. I will grind it into dust." Had his injury taken the steel out of Ethan?

"It can't be done."

The knot in her belly twisted and tightened. Her blood thudded against her eardrums. "You've given up?" She couldn't keep the incredulity from her tone.

"They move the trainees at random intervals. We can't even determine how many there are, much less how many work as Azrael."

Her vision narrowed, sent Ethan to the far end of a long tunnel. "How hard did you look?"

A thunderstorm flickered across Ethan's face. "I'm leading the resistance, remember?"

"In less than three weeks, I found one of their training grounds."

"Where? How many were there? How did you escape?"

Her anger deflated. "They were gone. I saw their obstacle course and a dormitory."

"Where?"

"Lynchburg. They blew it up."

His eagerness vanished. "The explosion Hector spoke of. Did you see anything else?"

"Like what?"

"How many were there? Where did they go next? Where is Weldon getting recruits?"

"Don't you remember? He recruits through church school. Only the brightest and the best." Her words even tasted bitter.

"That changed ten years ago."

She ground her teeth together. *Of course.*

Ethan sank onto the sagging sofa. Its springs squealed. "Hector thinks Weldon is recruiting from staunch Fellowship members. But not one of the elite's children have disappeared for six months or even just one month, except for Miranda." He glanced at the door.

"Are people still being Taken?"

He faced her again, his expression dark, ominous. "In record numbers."

"Then he's getting recruits from somewhere." She strode to the door, yanked it open. "Miranda. Come in here." A thin breeze puffed, rustled dry leaves, and stirred the shreds of sofa stuffing.

A moment later a pair of light footsteps and heavier ones mounted the steps to the cabin. Miranda entered first. Hector followed.

"Where would Weldon go to recruit volunteers?"

"Volunteers for what?"

"Doesn't matter. Any kind."

"I don't know."

She seized Miranda by the shoulders. "Come on, Miranda, think. There's got to be someplace he goes to over and over."

"He goes with Mama to her Better Baby talks."

Those? Kara gave those talks all over the country. "Where precisely?"

"Mother visits every women's league that sponsors a Better Baby Contest in Virginia."

Beryl wanted to smack herself in the head. "When she goes to the women's leagues, does she also visit the local home for the unfit?"

"Yes, she says that it helps remind people—"

"Damn. I was there. I saw it with my own eyes, and yet I didn't see it."

"Beryl," Ethan said softly. "You're talking riddles. What did you see?"

"They take their "volunteers" from the homes for the unfit."

Doubt and confusion puckered his face.

"Don't you see? No one misses them."

"He wouldn't take the unfit—"

She gaped at him. *Has he gone stupid too?* "You know they aren't all unfit. The Fellowship hides the unwanted, the unruly, the undesirables there too."

He crooked an eyebrow at Hector.

Hector rubbed his chin. "We weren't looking for anything like that."

Ethan gave a sharp nod and strode to a small table in the corner of the room. "We need a map of all the homes for the unfit in the state."

"I don't think such a map exists," Hector said.

"Then we'll make one." Ethan dragged the table to a patch of sunlight, pulled a state map out of his back pocket, and spread it open on the table. He looked up at Miranda.

Miranda crossed the room, her face drawn. "Weldon only visited the largest state-run homes with Mother. There were five…" She peered at the map. "There's the one in Lynchburg.

One in Petersburg, and Williamsburg." She stabbed the map with her finger. "And Staunton."

"That's four," Hector said.

Miranda's fingers swept back and forth across the map, searching. "Marion."

"Did she visit any in other states?" Beryl asked. Multiple cities in Virginia were difficult. Multiple states would be near impossible.

"Yes," Miranda answered. "I don't remember…"

"Exclude the out-of-state homes, for now." Ethan looked up at Hector. "We need to investigate."

Hector crossed his arms and leaned against the wall. "All our teams are working on their assignments."

"I wasn't thinking of sending any of them."

Hector straightened and stood at parade rest.

"I'll travel faster alone," Beryl said. "I can be in Staunton in less than two hours." She traced the route with her finger, tapped twice on the dot that represented Staunton. "I'll check it out tonight. I'll make a loop from there to Marion to Petersburg, then Williamsburg. I should be back here in forty-eight hours."

"I'll go with you," Miranda said.

"No." Beryl and Ethan spoke in unison. Beryl glanced at him, surprised they'd agreed about something.

Miranda folded her arms across her chest. "Then we split up. I go east. You go south."

Ethan caught Beryl's eye and said, "This trip will be dangerous."

"And we can cover them in half the time if one of us goes south and the other goes east." Miranda's glare dared them to disagree.

Beryl hesitated. She didn't like it, but given the distances between the cities…

Ethan frowned at Miranda. "No. Not this time. I need you and Nick—elsewhere."

"Yes, sir."

Was that sarcasm? Hmm.

Ethan turned to Beryl. His wistful expression made her uneasy. "If I could talk you into staying, I would. I know I can't. Hector will go with you. The two of you will go to all four sites."

She gave Hector the stink-eye. "I don't think that's a good idea."

Ethan cleared his throat. A flood of memories, arguments with Ethan, filled Beryl. She turned to him and opened her mouth. The past ten-plus years hadn't changed his stubborn I-will-not-argue face. She almost smiled. "Why?"

"Teamwork."

She had no tolerance for bullshit. "You mean suspicion."

He didn't change expression. "I said teamwork, and that's what I meant. SABR works in small teams now."

She had half a mind to walk out and not come back.

"You came to me for a reason."

Yes, I did. She needed his resources, and she couldn't outstare him, not even now. She sighed. "This team member is leaving now." She strode toward the door. "My car is—"

"Your stolen car?" Hector said. "We'll take the Chevy. Come with me." He stomped across the floor and out the door before her.

Beryl caught the door before it slammed shut. She hesitated, glanced back at Ethan.

He smiled. "It's good to have you back."

Deep inside, her chest ached. She turned and caught up with Hector.

Chapter Sixty-Three

Azrael barred the barn door. Remote and abandoned, it was the perfect location for what she had to do. She raised her eyes to the heavens. A ray of moonlight reached through the rotted and broken roof toward her. "Thy will be done," she whispered.

She turned to look at the man and woman she'd tied to wooden chairs in the center of the room. The woman was a witness to spread fear. Azrael ignored her and focused on the young man. He glared at her through the thick round lenses of his eyeglasses and made unintelligible sounds behind his Sellotape gag. His thick, coal-black hair stood on end. It pleased her to fancy it did that because of his fear, though she knew it wasn't. But the stinking wetness on the front of his pajama bottoms—that was from fear.

She stepped closer and stood not quite directly in front of him. Faster than he could blink, she slipped in close, shot out her fist, and smashed his nose. She followed that with a one-two shot to his ribs and danced out of reach.

He moaned pitifully. His head drooped and rolled between his shoulders. His glasses fell to the floor. Blood dripped from his nose to his soiled pajama bottoms.

She grabbed his hair, raised his head, and stared into his pain-glazed eyes. "I know you're an apostate. Don't deny it again." She drove a fist into his soft belly.

He gagged, retched, and choked.

She stepped beside him. Putting a boot against the edge of the chair back, she grabbed the far corner of the tape and pushed with her foot. *R-r-r-ip!* The tape came off his mouth. The chair, with him in it, crashed to the floor. Sour-smelling vomit spewed, and he gasped for breath.

"You, or one of your cell, know this woman." She pointed to the photograph she'd nailed to the nearby pole. "You will tell me where you are hiding her." She raised her foot and stomped the back of the chair, splitting the slat in two.

He screamed in anguish when she kicked him in the left kidney. When she kicked him again, the most he could do was moan. Then, he started to cry.

Chapter Sixty-Four

Miranda wiped her sweaty palms on her skirt and watched the ladies' room attendant at the Charlottesville train station. The woman left at the same time every day for her five-minute break.

The attendant disappeared around the corner, and Miranda strode into the ladies' room. She banged each stall door open as she passed. She couldn't believe her luck. They were all empty. She hurried to the sinks and opened the third towel dispenser with the key Nick had given her. She didn't know what was in the envelope she taped to the inside of the dispenser. She didn't need to know. She was about to complete her first official assignment as a member of SABR. She hoped this would convince Uncle Ethan.

She withdrew the key from the dispenser. The door to the ladies' room squeaked. She clenched her fist, hiding the key, and twisted her hands in the cotton towel hanging from the dispenser. A middle-aged woman entered and went straight into a stall. Miranda jammed her trembling hands into her pockets and left.

The platform was crowded and noisy and steamy hot. The train wasn't due for ten minutes. If it was on time. Still, man, woman, and child peered down the tracks as if their look would

hurry time or the train. Miranda strolled to the edge of the platform and peered down the tracks too. Nick had gone to the north-
bound platform across the tracks. She couldn't see him, wasn't
supposed to. He had his own dead drop to fill. Inch by inch, she
moved toward the back of the crowd. In three minutes, they
would greet one another like old friends and go to another town
for another drop.

She followed instructions and sat on the bench at the far end
of the platform, facing the ticket window. A train whistle sounded
in the distance, and all eyes focused on the spot where the tracks
met the eastern sky. Miranda rose, intending to slip off the platform unnoticed. A trio of boys loitering on the sidewalk made her
hesitate. They nudged one another and laughed and pointed at
something or someone on the platform.

One of the boys darted past Miranda and ran headlong into
an elderly woman. The woman fell to her knees, and her purse
and luggage and flowers went flying. She reached for her purse.

"Crawl for it, unbeliever." The boy kicked her purse into the
crowd and burst into laughter when the woman crawled after it.

Emboldened, the other two boys climbed onto the platform
and kicked her suitcase back and forth between them.

The old woman cried out in dismay. Every time she bent to
pick up her suitcase, one of the boys swept it with a kick that sent
it toward one of the other boys.

Miranda glared at the backs of the people on the crowded
platform. They had to hear the boys' raucous laughter and the old
woman's pleas. Yet not one man or woman on the platform
turned to help. And no security guard or police officer was
in sight.

The kicking and sliding of the suitcase fell into a rhythm.
The boy at the far end kicked the suitcase back toward his
friend. In two strides Miranda was there, placed her foot on the
suitcase, and brought it to a halt. After a moment's shock, all
three boys moved toward her. "Where are your manners?" she
said in her best councilor's-daughter scold. They stopped.

"Didn't your fine, upstanding Fellowship parents teach you to respect your elders?"

"We don't respect no unbeliever," one of the boys said. He gave her a surly frown. A train whistle blasted. The train was near. "Come on," he said to his friends and took a step toward her. "Three against one."

"Shame on you," she said, giving them an imitation of her mother's most disapproving look. The two friends hung back, glancing from her to the third boy and back. Finally, they turned, hopped off the platform, and disappeared down the sidewalk.

The train whistle sounded again, and its brakes squealed. The third boy glanced at the approaching train, then glowered at Miranda. "You unbelievers aren't worth the trouble." He sauntered after his friends.

Miranda blew out a breath, relieved that her bluff worked. She retrieved the suitcase, found the battered bouquet of sweet-smelling flowers, and handed the old woman her things.

The old woman gave her a sad smile and clutched her bag to her chest. Behind her, the train groaned to a stop. The old woman turned toward the train. Miranda didn't wait for a thank you. She wouldn't have heard it over the train anyway.

She went straight to the corner where she found Nick, fuming.

"Let's go." He strode away. She had to trot to keep up.

Nick glared at her in a sidelong glance. "What were you thinking?"

"I'm sorry?"

"I saw you confront those boys. You call that being invisible?"

"That old woman needed help. Besides, it worked out fine. No one saw me leave." She gave a rueful smile. "No one saw me help the old woman either."

"What if one of the boys went for the police?"

"They didn't."

"The police officer would have taken you to the precinct for questioning and would have found—"

Miranda drove her fingers into her palms. "Nothing. I'd

already delivered the envelope." She stopped, fists on her hips. "Why are you assuming that I didn't look for police officers before I made my move?"

Nick didn't stop, didn't even look back.

She hurried to catch up. "I took a calculated risk to help someone. If I'd been arrested or taken in for questioning, so what? I don't know anything."

"The so-what is that SABR needs every able-bodied person we can get." Nick's patient, patronizing tone set her teeth on edge. "The so-what is that any police in the area increases my risks too. The so-what is that we both could've ended up like George, the soda shop owner."

"Chances are pretty good I'll end up like George even if I never do anything but distribute fliers." Her stomach churned. "Besides, if SABR doesn't help people, what good are we?"

"If you can't follow directions, what good are you to SABR?"

Her face heated, and she pressed her lips together.

Nick stopped at a battered, gray Studebaker and opened the passenger door. "Get in."

They would meet Uncle Ethan at his next safe house. He moved his location daily for his safety. Miranda couldn't imagine a more exhausting lifestyle.

Outside the city, they parked in the lot next to a gas station. Nick got their rucksacks out of the trunk. They walked down the road, out of sight of the gas station, and then veered into the tall weeds and bushes along the road.

"We all make mistakes in the beginning. Thing is, those mistakes can be fatal."

"Apology accepted," Miranda said.

Nick whirled on her. "Everything you do affects your team. The loss of a single team member affects the team and affects SABR."

"What good is a team if we sit back and watch jerks abuse old women? I thought SABR was about stopping abuse."

Nick sighed. "It is, but we're after the big—"

"Oh? So the old woman wasn't important enough? What if it had been an old man, a young woman, a child? Who decides who is important enough?" She stomped past him, not caring where she went. She huffed breath in and out and dug her fingernails into her palms. Her teeth and jaw ached.

A hand touched her shoulder.

She spun around, knocking Nick's hand from her shoulder. "Don't touch me."

Nick put his hands up and took a step back. "You did a good thing, helping that woman," he said softly. "But if I don't challenge how you're thinking, how you're making decisions, then I'm not teaching you how to be part of SABR, am I?"

That threw ice water on her anger and sent shivers through her. She tucked her hands under her arms so Nick couldn't see her tremors. After an exchange of sullen glances, he led the way.

It took twenty minutes of hard walking over uneven ground, through scratchy scrub brush and tree seedlings and saplings for her to be calm enough to speak. "If it had been you on that platform, rather than me, would you have helped the old woman?"

A smile flickered across Nick's face. "Probably."

She clamped her jaws tight and vowed she'd never turn her back on someone who needed help, no matter what.

They did two more message drops before meeting Ethan outside the bowling alley at dusk. The news wasn't good. SABR members were being harassed, arrested, or Taken in every city in the nation. More than two dozen SABR members had been killed in three different locations. Nick's younger brother was among the dead.

Chapter Sixty-Five

C rouched behind the reeking trash bin, Miranda trembled. Finally, she had a chance to do something real, but she felt guilty for her excitement. Nick hunkered down behind the first trash bin. Head down, he checked his weapon, his grief a palpable barrier around him.

Days ago, someone had scouted Culpeper, a quaint town in Northern Virginia. Nick had gotten their orders from Uncle Ethan last night. He put together a team of four to rob Culpeper's registration center.

At five o'clock, most of the small town businesses closed and traffic noises faded. At five minutes before six, Nick gave the signal. Miranda pulled her bandana up over her nose and followed Leslie, who followed Nick. They slipped inside. Mike brought up the rear.

Empty folding chairs on linoleum floors filled the storefront. An overweight man in a three-piece suit sat behind a desk in the back of the room. The large, double-door metal cabinet behind him held blank registration papers. Three tall filing cabinets held the records, or rather copies of the records. They sent the originals to a central office in DC two hours away.

Miranda flipped the Open sign to Closed and pulled the shade down over the glass door. Mike closed the window shades.

Nick kept his head tilted away from the one security camera near the ceiling in the corner. He had made it clear that he didn't like it, but he followed Ethan's order. The Fellowship Council was to know that SABR had upped their game.

"This is a holdup," Nick said, his voice muffled by his bandana. "Freeze."

The clerk jumped up from his desk and raised his hands. "Please." His voice and hands shook. "I got a family."

Miranda took her position next to the door, her weapon at the ready. Mike positioned himself opposite her.

Nick waved his gun, indicating the man should sit back down. He did, and Nick bound and gagged the man.

Leslie had gone straight to the metal cabinet. She opened both doors and scooped blank registration forms into the large black rucksack she carried.

Nick went to the desk and filled his sack with cash. Seconds later, Nick and Angela were out the door, followed by Mike. Miranda hesitated a moment. This was it, the moment Uncle Ethan had said he needed her to strike a personal blow at the Fellowship. She stood in full view of the security camera, pulled her bandana down, and raised her right fist. After a count of ten, she dashed out the door.

Nick waited for her, scowling. "What took you so long?" He took her hand and pulled her forward like a child.

"I did what Uncle Ethan told me to do," she said, assuming he knew. They passed several dark shops whose display windows glowed. Most folks were home, preparing for dinner.

"He told you to delay and risk us all getting arrested?"

"Of course not." *Uncle Ethan hadn't told Nick?*

She explained what she'd done and that Uncle Ethan had promised the video recording wouldn't compromise the team. He'd said no one would see the tape until long after the robbery.

But sirens sounded before they'd even reached the car. Scowling, Nick drove the speed limit out of town.

Chapter Sixty-Six

Beryl and Hector hunched behind a hedge and deliberated how they'd search the massive Southwestern State Hospital complex. Seventy-plus years of age, the main structure was three times as long as the Lynchburg Colony building and five stories tall. Seven stories, if you counted the attic and basement. There were a dozen lesser buildings, a barn, and a warehouse scattered around the property. She whispered to Hector that they should circle around to the back of the property.

Hector grumbled under his breath.

"It's big," Beryl agreed. "But I still don't think the Azrael trainees will be in the main buildings. They'll be somewhere in the back, in an isolated building."

Hector grunted. *Agreement or disagreement?* Beryl didn't care.

In a crouching run, they kept hedges or blank building walls between them and both lit and dark windows.

The back of the property was a mass of overgrown plants. Hector shot I-told-you-so looks at her. She peered over the bushes they'd sheltered behind. Around the bend stood three colonial brick buildings, each as isolated from the main building as they were from each other. Watching Hector's mouth drop open at the sight, she gave him a told-you look of her own.

"I'll take the far building," she whispered. "You take the near one. We'll meet at the back door of the middle one in fifteen."

He nodded and darted toward the rear of the nearest building.

Beryl followed the hedgerow around to her target building. Weak light in some of the windows suggested that an interior hall light was on. Those windows were open. Dark windows kept secrets. That was okay, as long as none of them held surprises. She crouched low, scurried across the lawn, and flattened against the brick wall. The musty, unpleasant odors of unwashed bodies and old urine made her catch her breath. It was all too familiar an odor. She shut thoughts of Redemption out of her mind and focused. Breathing through her mouth made the smell more endurable. She bobbed up and peered through the first window. Beds made darker rectangular shadows in the night-shrouded room. The beds had clean, empty lines.

She ducked and crept to the next window. A quick bounce up, peering inside revealed more empty beds. She moved on, pausing at each window until she reached the end of the building. Each room held ten beds. A few of the beds held lumpy shadows, the sleeping rejects of society.

She dashed around the front of the building to repeat her window inspection on the other side. *Thump. Thump. Thump.* Slow and rhythmic, she couldn't identify the sound that came from inside the building. *Mechanical? Human?* The rooms on this side were identical to those from the first side. The thumping grew louder the nearer she got to the last window. She edged to the window's frame, scraping her back against the wall. A wounded-animal yowl ripped through the air. Beryl dropped to a crouch. Adrenaline roared through her body, urged it to move. She squelched the urge, stayed where she was.

Footsteps padded, coming closer. "Every blessed night." The

beam of a flashlight shot out of the last window. Beryl made herself as small as possible.

"Why do you insist on hurting yourself, number forty-one?" A screech of wood against wood split the air. "There. Like to see you hit the wall from there."

Something moaned and panted.

"The doctor says since you can't walk, you are harmless." *Harrumph.* "If the doctor had to sleep here with y'all, he'd sure enough order a stronger sleep powder. But there's more than one way to skin that hare. Here, take a nip. Now, now, don't waste it. Drink. There you go. That ought to give us both a good night's sleep." The flashlight danced across the window and shot out above Beryl's head. Then the light was gone, and the footsteps padded away.

The further the footsteps, the louder the moaning grew. Another voice joined the moaning, then another and another. Five voices, if Beryl had counted correctly. She waited beneath the window until she could no longer hear the footsteps. Eventually, the moaning quieted. Her first peek into the room revealed a pale rectangle of light around the door. The next peek, she saw shadowy occupied-bed shapes. She peered around the lower edge of the frame with one eye. Five of the ten beds were occupied. The shapes were small. *Children?*

One of the occupants rose up on an elbow. Light cast from the hallway illuminated her face, her wizened, old lady face. She looked like a grotesque version of Beryl's dear, departed grandmother. The girl gave three soft grunts. Soundlessly, the other four children stirred and partially rose. One by one, the girls turned to face Beryl. Beryl stifled a gasp. They were identical. The first girl rocked back and forth and gave Beryl a big, toothless smile. Another girl stared, open-mouthed, spittle dripping from her chin to a rag doll she clutched to her chest.

Something clogged Beryl's throat. She couldn't breathe. She dropped to her knees. Memories flooded her. Memories of six-year-old Anna kissing the fuzzy yarn-hair of her doll, Winifred.

Memories that insisted the doll held by that misfit was identical to Winifred. Beryl dug her fingernails into the flesh of her palms. She reminded herself that all little girls loved dolls, that many rag dolls had fuzzy hair. She cursed herself for being a sentimental fool, for wasting time.

She shuddered. She'd seen a lot of lunatics during this scouting trip, but this girl, these five girls... She'd never seen anything like it. She shuddered again and reminded herself she was looking for Azrael. She darted across the lawn to the hedgerow. Hector was waiting.

Chapter Sixty-Seven

B eryl hated being the passenger, hated the disapproving silence that emanated from Hector, and hated that not one of the homes for the unfit had any sign the Azrael had been there.

No sloppy work to blame. She'd watched Hector's thorough search of the first place. To avoid the whole trip being a waste of time, she had persuaded Hector to avoid big towns on their way back. If she had calculated the mileage right, they would pass a certain cemetery soon. At the sight of the first row of gravestones outside of Locust Grove, she was filled with relief. *I remembered.*

Now to get Hector to stop. "If you don't want me to pee in your car, you'll pull into the next drive."

"It's a graveyard." Hector looked at her like she was crazy. "You can't wait? It's less than an hour—"

She did a little dance in the fabric-covered seat to illustrate her need.

He pulled into the cemetery drive and parked.

She turned on her flashlight. "I'll have to find a bush or a tree. Back in a minute." She slammed the car door and trotted down the row of monuments scented with dying flowers. At the gravestone with the sleeping child carved atop, she turned left. An ancient oak with a massive trunk stood at the end of the row. She hurried forward. Hector would get impatient soon.

She swept her flashlight back and forth across the earth between the last row of graves and the fence. She searched for the small, ancient gravestone that marked the eternal resting place of a long dead Jeremiah Jones. The stone was so old and eroded, the name was visible only when the light hit it at an angle. If the marker remained undisturbed for more than a century, she'd been certain it would remain so. It was. Five feet away from the stone, the fence line was still weed-choked.

She knelt at the post opposite Jeremiah's headstone and dug at the dry, hard earth with her knife. She'd used a stolen spoon ten years ago, so the package wasn't very deep. She uncovered the tin box, dug it out, and opened it with shaking hands. The parchment paper that wrapped the book was dry and intact. She sat back on her heels, savoring the fact that she had won this small victory and anticipating a bigger victory to come. Unwrapped, the book was smaller than she remembered. She wanted to open it and read under the flashlight, but Hector was waiting. She tucked it under her shirt and trotted back to the front of the cemetery.

"*Qué chingados,*" Hector said. "How long does it take to pee-pee?"

"I had to find a big enough tree to go behind." She climbed into the car. Hector slid behind the wheel, muttering in Spanish under his breath. She didn't care.

Chapter Sixty-Eight

The things Kara had to do to have a modicum of privacy were seriously annoying. She had bribed her bodyguards and disguised herself with this ridiculous hat and large, dark sunglasses. She held her floppy-brimmed hat and scooted onto the bench seat in the back booth of her favorite diner. Ever the gentleman, Weldon slid back into the seat opposite her. Public life had put an unexpected strain on herself and her family. She smiled at her brother. Weldon didn't look well. She peered over the tops of her glasses. He was pale and drawn as if he hadn't eaten or slept in days. His fingers tapped the table with rapid, nervous energy.

The waitress came, took their orders, and hustled away.

Weldon glanced toward every squeak of a stool and every clank of a utensil against a plate. *I may have underestimated the strain on him.* She reached across the table to still his warm hand. "We knew something like this could happen."

"It's blowing up in our faces." His breathy whisper sounded on the edge of panic.

"It's been a bigger sensation than we expected," she agreed. "But we planned for this, remember?"

Across the room, the waitress picked up dirty dishes from a

departed customer's table. The plates clattered. Weldon jumped and threw a glance over his shoulder.

Kara placed her napkin in her lap. She had to calm him down. Their plan relied on his calm leadership of the Second Sphere and the Azrael. "I forgot to factor in the First Apostle newsworthiness. But it's a two-sided coin that will help us too."

He tilted his head like a dog trying to understand a command. "How can you say that? I can't muzzle this one. Every reporter in the country would have to be Taken."

She gave him her best reassuring smile. "We don't have to stop the news, not if we guide people to the correct reaction." The waitress hustled over to their table with a hot, juicy burger for Weldon and a salad for Kara. Kara breathed in the mouthwatering aroma of the burger and resented a woman's need to keep her waistline trim.

The waitress left. Weldon pushed his burger to the side. "And how do you propose to 'guide' people's reactions?"

Did her little brother really have no appetite for what he called the best burger west of the Potomac? Now she was really worried. "We stick to our plan. You will make certain your friend at CBS will 'find' Sister Patricia and interview her on television."

"And you think she'll convince them the rebels forced Miranda to rob that registration center?"

"Of course she will."

"Did you actually look at the film clip? Miranda was holding a gun. She practically waved at the television." His voice squeaked.

"Keep your voice down." She glanced at the nearest customer, a bearded guy. He kept eating, not paying the slightest attention to Weldon or her.

Weldon ducked his head and locked her in his stare. "If she's declared an apostate, what will happen to your precious First Apostle publicity? They'll turn on you so fast—"

Kara pouted. "You don't trust me."

Weldon had the grace to look uncomfortable. "Of course I do. It's the reporters I don't trust."

"You wouldn't worry so if you had seen Patricia speak about how the rebels brainwashed her. I don't know how the guardians did it. Her performance is Oscar-worthy. Her big brown eyes brimming with tears, the tortured sound of her voice, her heart-wrenching story—the reporters and the viewers will eat it up. They'll scour the countryside looking for poor, brainwashed Miranda."

"I don't know." Weldon drummed the tabletop again. "What if the guardians' programming fails while your woman is on live television?"

"Failures don't get released from Redemption."

"Until Miranda."

She sat back. She had never known Weldon to be so disagreeable. Change jangled in the jukebox. The Carter family sang "God Gave Noah the Rainbow." "You know what we need?" She leaned forward, allowing him a sneak peek down her V-shaped neckline. "A short vacation. The yacht?"

"You know I can't get away right now."

She pushed her lower lip out and let her eyes fill with unspilled tears. "Not even for one night? It's in times of stress when I need you most."

He reached across the table and stroked her cheek. "You know I'd love to, but I can't."

She blinked. Tears fell.

"Okay, Okay." He wiped her cheek with his thumb. "I'll arrange for CBS to discover Patricia then join you there. The sea air will do you good." He pulled the burger back and took a big bite.

She speared a bit of salad with her fork. *Never underestimate the power of a woman's tears, brother dear.* Her salad had a satisfying crunch.

Chapter Sixty-Nine

B eryl worked the pick on the hardware store's lock. She hadn't lost her touch. But she'd lost her husband. Ethan wasn't Ethan anymore. She'd wanted to go back to Lynchburg, find more clues. He'd told her to forget it. *Forget it? How can he not need to obliterate Weldon and the whole Azrael Project?*

The lock clicked. She turned the doorknob, pushed the door open, and listened. No alarm. She peered inside. The store had one row of overhead fluorescents on in the back. If they were careful, they wouldn't be seen. She signaled the other three hidden across the street.

Miranda, Mike, and Nick slipped past her, through the door, and to the sporting goods section of the store. Each of them broke into a display case and packed ammo and guns into their bags. They were good little soldiers, sticking to their assigned weapons.

Beryl packed her bag with two shotguns, two hunting rifles, and plenty of ammo for them and for her pistol. She had other plans. The book she'd spent ten years rotting in Redemption for? Written in Greek. She had long since forgotten what little Greek she'd been taught. She'd thought about showing it to Ethan, but he wouldn't understand. *The Council sure thought Kara hid some powerful information in that book.* Beryl planned to hunt down a minister or professor of Greek. *With that information, I won't need Ethan and his amateur soldiers.*

She tied the bag shut, slipped an arm in each handle, and shrugged the bag onto her back. She staggered a little until she shifted the bag to distribute the weight. A quick exchange of glances confirmed Miranda and the others were ready to leave. She ignored a flicker of temptation to say goodbye to Miranda and led the way to the door.

At the door, she scanned the street. The moonless night made the street as dark as it could be. Nothing, not even a breeze stirred. She signaled for the first guy, Mike, to go. But it was too quiet. No crickets. Not a sound. She pushed Mike out of the line of fire and leaped backward.

The *pop-pop-pop* of a pistol sounded, followed by dozens of other shots. She slammed the door. Two car engines roared, came near, then shut down. "Everyone okay?" she called. Mike, Nick, and Miranda answered in the affirmative.

Nick crouched at the window. "One shooter at ten o'clock. Two police cars blocking each end of the street. Can't see the fourth shooter."

Beryl nodded. "The dock provides our best cover."

"If they are smart, they'll be back there too," Mike said.

"We'll leapfrog to the delivery truck and out from there."

"I can hotwire the truck," Mike said.

Beryl shook her head. "You'd be a bullet magnet."

"Not if we take the keys." Miranda wasn't joking.

Nick gave Miranda an approving look. "She's right. We saw keys in the office when we cleared it."

In moments they had a plan. Nick got the keys, and the four of them duck-walked below the windows of the loading dock office to the door.

"On three, two, one." Beryl stood and fired two rounds. Glass rained inside and out. Gunfire pelted the dock. She and Miranda and Nick provided cover fire. Mike dove out the door, rolled across the floor, and dropped three feet to street level. He threw open one of the truck's two panel doors and hefted his rucksack into the cargo area. Nick tossed their three, heavy rucksacks out the door and across the dock. Mike heaved the rucksacks into the truck. The gunfire from across the street increased. Bullets hit the wall behind Beryl, spewed shards of concrete that pinged against the wall. One piece nicked her hand. She returned fire. Nick and Miranda did too. Mike took a position behind the truck and began firing toward the street. Nick ran out the door, skidded to the edge of the loading dock, and jumped. A muzzle flash catty-corner across the street told Beryl a new opponent had arrived. She laid down cover fire for Nick while he climbed into the cab of the truck. Beryl pulled her second pistol and began shooting two-handed. "Now, Miranda."

Miranda dashed out the door, across the dock. Beryl followed, both guns firing. She kept firing until Miranda climbed into the passenger side of the cab. Mike signaled Beryl to come. She ran and leaped inside. She skidded on her heels, spun, and reached for Mike.

Mike grabbed the door as if to close it.

"Get in." She leaned out further, reaching for him.

He spun toward her, his mouth opened, and he stared at the red stain spreading on his shirt.

Beryl seized him by the wrist, braced her feet against the lip of the doorframe, and pulled Mike into the truck. She pounded on the metal sides of the truck and shouted, "Go!" The engine gunned, and the truck pulled away from the dock with the panel door swinging.

Chapter Seventy

M iranda was numb, past feeling fear. The police had followed them in a running shootout for an hour. After another half hour, Nick found a hidden drive to pull into, but it was too late to do Mike any good. Beryl sat, stony-faced, opposite Mike's body, her blood-soaked jacket tied around Mike's chest. Nick said the bullet probably had hit Mike's aorta or heart. He didn't have a chance.

They drove another two hours, not willing to risk leading the police or Second Sphere here, to the safe house.

Miranda slid out of the truck cab and had to grab the door handle to keep from falling. Her bones and muscles were only semi-solid.

Hector charged out of the two-story farmhouse toward them, followed by Manny. "Get inside, quickly."

Nick came around the front of the truck. "We need to take care of Mike." He sounded worn out.

"Manny will see to him."

Nick tossed Manny the keys.

"Follow me." Hector led them inside. They passed through the vestibule into the parlor.

Ethan sat on the edge of a dark green armchair leaning toward a black and white console television. On screen, Miranda's parents stood behind a podium in the small theater at the Fellowship Center. Miranda froze in the doorway, transfixed by the images.

"Our daughter, Miranda, is a kind, upstanding Fellowship member," her mother said. "Miranda has dedicated her life to volunteer service. She works here at the Center. She visits hospitalized children and does all kinds of charity work, from raising funds for animal shelters to feeding the poor. Miranda would never harm any living thing, and she would never break the law if she were in her right mind. The only explanation is that they brainwashed her. Please, we want Miranda back home where she belongs."

Her father took up the plea. "I grant amnesty to anyone who helps Miranda return to us. But the recent increase in the destruction of property, thefts, and murders by apostates is intolerable. We cannot have a return to the riots, lynchings, and depravity of the years during and after the Great Depression. We cannot allow it. After seventy-two hours, there will be a cleansing." He exchanged looks with Kara. "Even if Miranda is not with us. A reckoning will rain down on all apostates without mercy. For the safety of our people, our property, our country, they will be wiped from the earth."

Ethan turned to face them. "This is a declaration of war."

Everyone in the room turned to stare at Miranda. She shook her head no. *No, this can't be happening. No, I won't go back.* She couldn't speak. She couldn't breathe. She couldn't allow people to be killed because of her.

"This isn't Miranda's fault." Nick's voice sounded firm, kind, and distant.

"Maybe not, but if we can use her to save hundreds of thousands of lives, should we not?" Hector asked.

"She's the reason we've had an increase in volunteers over the past few weeks."

"They won't be volunteering now."

"It's time to go on the offensive."

"Send her home."

Miranda couldn't focus on who said what. The loud, passionate argument that stormed around her churned inside her too. But one thing she knew. She couldn't let her parents or the Fellowship kill everyone. "Stop." She couldn't think with all the noise. "Please, stop."

The voices fell silent, and everyone faced her, again.

She stood ramrod straight and focused on Ethan. "This war has been brewing for a long time, long before I joined you. You had to expect the Fellowship would threaten you at some point. Are you going to give in at the first threat?" She couldn't read Ethan's expression. She dared a glance at each of the others. Manny looked uncertain. Hector glowered at her, and Beryl seemed surprised. Nick gave her an encouraging smile.

She took a deep breath. "We need to let the Fellowship know that SABR isn't afraid. We aren't going to cower in the corner because they are rattling their swords."

Uncle Ethan folded his hands together and sat back in his chair. "What do you propose we do instead?"

"I'll be your spokesperson. We respond to the Fellowship on the television and in the newspapers." Inspiration struck. "We tell our story and demand equal rights."

"Are you *loco*?" Hector shouted.

Beryl shook her head. "Your parents will still claim you're brainwashed."

Miranda smiled, more certain of herself than she'd been in weeks. "Not if I tell stories about the abuses that are happening."

"How would you do that?" Ethan asked.

"I make it personal for the viewers. I tell them about how a mom stands in the rain with her infant tucked into her coat while a covered bus stand is empty. I tell them about a man denied access to the drug store for supplies to treat a minor infection and he dies." She turned to Hector. "Hector, you know the average

Fellowship member has blinders on. They don't know about the abuses, or they ignore them because it doesn't touch their lives. We have to make those abuses visible. Make them real."

Ethan tilted his head and squinted at Miranda.

"She's right," Nick said. "I wasn't a member of the Fellowship, and I ignored all the signs until I was a victim."

Beryl wore a funny expression on her face. "She's almost right. Ethan and I know that talking and telling stories get you nowhere, and if you give her up, you might as well get your Fellowship cards. But"—her expression hardened—"it's time to strike back, hard."

"With what?" Hector ran a hand through his hair. "They have armies. We have Suzy Homemaker and Fred the Farmer."

"Angry Suzy Homemaker and Fred the Farmer make formidable enemies." Ethan held up a hand, halting all comments. "It's late. I'm not going to make a decision tonight. We'll talk in the morning. Manny, show everyone their rooms, please."

"Yes, sir."

They followed Manny upstairs without chitchat or grumbling. She and Beryl were given a bedroom to share. Beryl climbed onto the bed fully clothed and on top of the covers. She was asleep almost immediately. Miranda washed up in a basin of lukewarm water on the washstand in the room. She was grateful. They hadn't thrown her out, yet. She took off her clothes, then slipped between the sheets and stared at the ceiling. If she came up with the right scenario, Ethan would agree to her plan.

Chapter Seventy-One

Beryl's internal alarm clock woke her in the predawn dark. The flowered wallpaper, lace-curtained windows, and soft bed were not Redemption issue. She pushed away nightmares that said otherwise and recovered her pistol and Kara's book from between the mattress and box springs. Tucking the book inside her shirt and the pistol in her waistband, she gave a quick finger-comb of her hair and straightened her shirt and jeans. She tiptoed around the trundle bed where Miranda slept. *How can she sleep? Her fate will be decided today.* Beryl pressed her lips together. *Not my concern.* She pulled the door closed behind her, the latch snicked closed. *My only concern must be Weldon and his Azrael.*

After a few minutes of rummaging in the kitchen, she found what she wanted. Armed with coffee and a Danish, she eased out onto the front porch where Manny stood guard. "I'm awake. Why don't you go in and catch a few winks? I'll keep watch for a few hours."

"Monkshood didn't tell me you would keep watch."

She shrugged. "He's a little distracted by that business this evening."

"You armed?"

She patted the pistol in her waistband. "And I can shout real loud when I need to." She grinned and encouraged him inside with a tip of her head. "Go on. You'll be sharper after a couple of hours rest."

He shook his head. "You want a little privacy, that's fine. I can give you the porch, but I won't abandon my watch." He walked down the porch steps and took a parade rest position on the brick walkway.

The wide porch had white pillars and railings and wrapped around the front of the house. A pair of wooden rocking chairs flanked each side of a low table beneath the parlor's picture window. She bent and settled into the rocker at the end of the porch. A corner of the book inside her shirt poked her in the ribs. She set her coffee down and pulled the book out. Hardbound, every page was covered with a scribble she assumed was Kara's. Every damn word was Greek, a language she'd loathed in school. A language she'd forgotten as soon as she'd finished the class.

She sat and scanned the horizon. The night air was warm and dry and still as if the world held its breath waiting for dawn. A faint aroma of licorice perfumed the air. As far as the eye could see, tobacco plants nearly five feet tall stood in neat rows. *Being here is a tactical mistake.* She'd intended to leave this morning, walk into the tobacco field, and disappear. *But after last night, Ethan has to know this is war.*

She tapped the spine of the book. Should she stay and convince Ethan that stopping the Azrael should take top priority? She made up her mind and tucked the book back inside her shirt. She'd wait for Ethan's decision, then leave if she must.

The dark richness of her first taste of real coffee in ten years took her by surprise. She savored the next sip and the next. The sky lightened, and birdsong welcomed the morning sun.

Ethan forbade discussion of Miranda or the Fellowship until after breakfast. Then he asked Beryl and Hector into his temporary office.

Ethan perched on the front edge of an ancient wooden desk

marred with scratches and dings. "Shut the door and sit down. Please."

The last to enter, Beryl closed the door. She sat in the yellow and brown plaid armchair closest to the door. Hector sat in the twin of her chair with one ankle resting on his other knee.

"Miranda was right. I was expecting something like this declaration of war. I had hoped we would have a more time, but we're ready. We're going on the offensive, and we need to know if we can count on you, Beryl."

She didn't speak. He knew her mission.

"*I* need you."

His words tore at her. How many years had she wished to hear him one last time? To fight by his side one more time? She studied him. He was a shadow of what he'd been, not only physically but deep inside. Expectations, time, and fear had weighed him down, changed the way he saw things, what he felt.

"I was like you once," he said. "I wanted to rip off Weldon's head and cram every Azrael down his neck. But the rebels, our rebels, needed me. So I put my needs aside. Donald's announcement changed everything."

She searched his face. Somewhere miles beneath her toes, tiny fireflies of hope swarmed and rose inside her. "Say it."

"We must stop the Azrael before this cleansing begins."

"But I didn't find them."

He exchanged a look with Hector and then locked eyes with hers. "Hector kept a secret from you."

Adrenaline and fire exploded. She rocketed to her feet. Her chair banged into the wall. "You found them?" She blasted Hector with a glare.

Hector unscrambled his legs and stood.

Ethan rose and put a cool hand on her arm. "Not them, but information. Information that might help us find them."

She shifted her glare to Ethan and forced air through her locked-with-rage jaw. "Are you going to tell me what he found?"

"Hector tells me you made an extra stop on the way back. A

stop you haven't explained." He gave her a tight-lipped smile. "We used to trust each other with everything. I still trust you. If your cemetery visit is pertinent to fighting the Fellowship, I trust you'll share with us."

Deadly calm quieted her breathing, her voice. "Don't try to manipulate me. I've survived the best."

Ethan gave her a mildly amused look. "Sit down. Both of you."

Hector sat, a rattlesnake waiting to strike.

She crossed her arms and stayed on her feet.

"I said I trust you." Ethan gestured to her chair. "Hector will share first."

She perched on the edge of the chair.

Ethan sat back on the edge of the desk and nodded at Hector.

"The first building was clean, cleaner than what my white glove crew used to do. I figured we were chasing ghosts. By the third spotless building, I suspected you were onto something." He snorted. "Not the Azrael, mind you, but something. I searched for detritus, something that had been overlooked. Found nothing until Staunton, and only charred paper there. I wrapped the paper in my handkerchief and brought it to Ethan."

"I sent the paper to a chemist friend. He fixed it so we could read it and transcribed the information." Ethan pulled a folded paper from his left shirt pocket and handed it to her.

The paper crinkled in the expectant silence. It trembled in her hands—*inations 100, Live births 44, Mutations 24, Deaths in the first year 17, Survivors to age five years 3.*

She cocked her head and stared at Ethan. "Babies? How does this—? Oh, holy damn. You think they are using the wombs of the unfit to grow babies—to grow Azrael?"

"It's slow, but it makes sense. We proved to them that recruiting children without parental consent was—dangerous."

"No parent in her right mind would agree to that training regime." Her voice was flat, but blue flames of hate blazed inside.

Ethan swallowed. "If you can add to this information, we'd like to hear it."

She hesitated. *Hell, I have nothing, so what will it hurt?* "I found her doll."

Ethan shook his head. "I'm sorry?"

The stabbing, tearing feeling in her chest was back. "Anna's doll. The one I made. Or, an exact duplicate."

"Oh."

Hector leaned forward, his chair creaked. "That's odd."

She didn't understand.

"Don't you think it's odd? Your daughter has been dead for ten years, but you found an exact duplicate of her doll?" Hector bounced a look between Beryl and Ethan.

"She took it to the school," Beryl said, painful memories tightened her throat. "Maybe one of the other—recruits—took it or remembered it and made one like it."

Ethan studied his hands. "And the extra stop you had Hector make?"

"Remember how suspicious we were of Kara's Better Baby Contest?"

Ethan gave her his you're-going-to-tell-me-something-bad look.

"I stole a book from the safe in her office and hid it. The stop was to retrieve that book. I had hoped—" She took the book out from her shirt and tossed it to Ethan. "Can't read it."

Ethan opened the book and thumbed through the pages. "Greek?" He flipped pages and looked up at Hector.

Hector held his hands up. "Don't look at me. My school didn't teach Greek."

Beryl gaped at him. She hadn't thought of it that way. She looked at Ethan.

His grin stretched across his face. "I know what you're thinking." He opened the door and shouted, "Miranda!"

Chapter Seventy-Two

Miranda opened the slim, musty-smelling book Ethan handed her and recognized the swirls and curlicues of her mother's handwriting. She glanced up at Ethan. "What is this?"

"You know the handwriting?" Beryl asked.

"Of course I do. It's my mother's." She turned back to Ethan. "Where did you get this?"

"Took it from the filing cabinet of the Superintendent of the Better Baby Contest for the Commonwealth of Virginia," Beryl said.

"The Better Baby Contest?" Miranda repeated stupidly. She snapped the book closed. The year inscribed on the spine was 1950. Eleven years ago. Memory clicked. She gaped at her aunt. "*You* were the thief?" Miranda remembered the uproar, her mother's panic, and her father's depression. "Why would you steal bookkeeping logs from the contest?" Her words echoed her mother's. She cringed inside.

"That is not just a bookkeeping log." Something about Beryl's voice sent a cold wave of alarm through Miranda. *If this book proves Mother's wrongdoing, will it also have proof against Father?*

"Please." Ethan gestured at the desk.

Miranda settled into the wood and leather desk chair and opened the book to the first page. "January 2, 1950. Salaries. CEO one dollar, CFO one dollar—" *Charitable of mother and Uncle Weldon to work for a dollar.* She looked up at Ethan and Beryl. "Do you want every word, or are you looking for something specific?"

"Names, activities, anything out of the ordinary."

She scanned the page slowly. Slowly because reading Greek wasn't natural to her. Slowly because expenses for management, facilities, supplies, and donations were mind-numbing. Slowly because she didn't want to miss the slightest hint of wrongdoing. At the bottom of each page, she gave Ethan and Beryl a summary. "Nothing but supplies for the office and notes about contract negotiations with the Alexandria Convention Center." Her mother had worn them down and gotten everything she'd demanded.

"Wait." Miranda flipped the page back and re-read the last two entries, then turned to the next page. "This says on February 18, 1950, the Trustees approved the purchase of land in Stafford County. It's underscored."

Hector shifted his weight. He drummed his fingers on the plaid upholstery of the armchair. "Does that mean something special in Greek?"

"They didn't use underscoring in ancient Greek."

"So it meant something to Kara." Ethan settled on the arm of Hector's chair.

"How much property and where?" Beryl asked.

"It was a hundred-acre farm. There's a lot number, and it says it is on the border of Stafford and Prince William County."

"Why buy land? Were they planning to build their own fair-grounds?"

"There are no other notations."

"Continue." The way Ethan said it, it wasn't a command but an entreaty.

No one spoke or moved. The dry sigh of paper pages and Miranda's summary punctuated the silence. At the end of

February, she found a payment to an architect and a retainer fee for a contractor. After that, in addition to the usual entries, there were payments for construction. Big payments.

An hour later, she found a curious notation. "Listen. 'May 9, 1950, freezer, $6,057.'"

Beryl frowned. "For one freezer?"

Miranda nodded.

"Must be made of gold." Hector stood, then sat on the floor, his back against the wall.

"Commercial freezer?" Ethan asked. He sat in the plaid armchair.

"All it says is 'freezer.' Then there's a whole list of medical stuff, like for a hospital."

"Like at the Better Baby Contests?" Ethan asked.

"No. There's two dozen incubators, cardiopulmonary monitors, ventilators, stainless steel tables, and—" She gestured at the book and turned the pages, twice. "A *lot* of equipment."

Ethan, Beryl, and Hector exchanged looks. They knew something but weren't telling her. Her pulse kicked up a notch. The three of them looked expectantly at Miranda. She returned her attention to the book. The next thirty or forty pages were filled with black ink numbers itemizing routine expenses. The entry for December 1 made her stop. She read and read it again, and then read it aloud. "'December 1, 1949. One hundred artificial inseminations. Live births, forty-four. Twenty-four terminated for defects.'" She gave Beryl a desperate look. "Tell me this is about rabbits or dogs or cows." Beryl's expression said enough. Chills ran up and down Miranda's back and arms.

Ethan turned a sad look on Beryl. "We should tell her about Anna."

"I don't think that's necessary."

"I understand." He sounded as if he meant that. "Would you like to leave while I tell her?"

Beryl glared at him. His expression didn't change. "I'll do it." Beryl leaned forward, propped her forearms on her legs, and stared at the floor. "Anna was—a challenge to raise. Even as a toddler, she threw epic temper tantrums. We tried less discipline and more discipline. We tried Dr. Sackett's remedies. We even tried Dr. Spock. Finally, when she was ten, my brother, your father, recommended a specialist. *The doctor*—" The tightness of her voice and the heavy sarcasm of her tone tore at Miranda. "—had us send Anna to a girls' boarding school in Upstate New York. It was a working farm where the students had daily chores and one-on-one tutoring. It seemed like a good idea at the time." She laced her fingers together and pressed her thumbs against her lips. Her knuckles whitened. After a moment, she straightened but still did not meet Miranda's look. "They wouldn't let us see Anna except for once every three months for the first year. It was supposed to help her change her behavior. We don't know exactly what happened during those first three months. When we saw her again —" Beryl's voice broke. Her jaw muscles twitched.

Ethan cleared his throat. "She was a changed child, so polite and well behaved. We thought they'd saved our daughter. But, even during our short visit, we began to sense that something was wrong." He sighed. "At our next visit, she was cool, detached, remote. Beryl wanted to take her out of the school. I—" He swallowed. "I insisted we give her more time to adjust." His gaze sent waves of remorse to Beryl. "Beryl snuck back to the school a couple of weeks later."

Beryl stared over Miranda's shoulder into a dark and distant place. "I followed Anna, her teacher, and several of her classmates to the barn. When they were inside, I crept up to the side of the barn. I couldn't hear much until the screaming started. Inhuman screams." Her voice shook a little. "I took a chance and peeked through the window. The teacher stood there and watched Anna skin a piglet alive. When she killed the little pig, I thought, thank God, she has some mercy, but then she turned. I saw her face. It wasn't mercy that lit her eyes and flushed her skin."

Aghast, Miranda asked, "Why would they do such a thing?"

"I confronted the school administrator with that very question." Beryl finally made eye contact with Miranda. "Weldon told me she was the top student in her class, that she'd be a first-class Azrael."

Miranda put a hand over her mouth. She didn't know what to say. The room was dead silent for several breath-holding moments before she could speak. "My mother knew about this?"

"Yes."

The pieces fell into place. Miranda shoved the book to the center of the desk, stood, and backed away from the desk. She sucked in air, clenched and unclenched her fists. "Uncle Weldon—and my mother—are making feebleminded women pregnant and raising those babies to be Azrael?"

"Killers."

Part of her silently screamed, *oh, dear God, my own mother, my uncle* over and over and over again. Another part of her burned with the question, "How do we stop them?"

"We have to find them," Hector said quietly.

She sat back down and pulled the book toward her.

Chapter Seventy-Three

P ain and the coppery taste of blood reassured Beryl that she wasn't in Redemption dreaming of this planning session. She'd chewed her right cheek raw from biting it so many times.

In a matter of hours, Ethan's men had found the property Kara had bought near the Marine base in Quantico, Virginia. A flyover had confirmed that it was a Second Sphere training facility. Shortly after nightfall, five of Ethan's lieutenants gathered around the long farm table in the dining room of the safe house.

"Jack, how many demolitions men do you have capable of handling a big job?" Pete Foster, Ethan's tactical expert, asked. Pete's long skinny neck and jug-handle ears made him look like a gawky teenager, made it hard to take him seriously.

Jack Davidson, the demolitions expert from Lynchburg, looked him square in the eye. "Every man in my platoon is proficient at blowing stuff up."

"Hector, how many men are available if we had to deploy tonight?" Pete asked.

"We have six hundred, forty men in this district." Hector's answer came quickly as if he'd expected the question. "Two hundred can be here tonight. Four hundred will be here within twenty-four hours. The others would take another day or two."

"How many of the two hundred are sharpshooters?"

"Only fifteen, but all two hundred can hit the target at seven yards. About eighty reliably hit a bullseye at fifteen."

"How many sharpshooters total?"

"Twenty-five qualified, another nine or ten nearly qualified."

"Good." Pete eyed the redheaded Texan next. "Conrad?"

"Yes, sir?"

"Do we have weapons for four hundred, including thirty sharpshooters?"

Slumped in his seat, Conrad scratched his chin and frowned in concentration. "We've only eight BARs," he said. "But there are more than enough thirty-aught-six hunting rifles for the shooters. We've got Tommy guns. Handguns—we've confiscated a hundred .357s and more than three hundred .45s." He nodded. "Enough to give each man a handgun and plenty of ammo—for each weapon." Conrad straightened, folded his arms on the table, and fixed his gaze on Ethan. "What is this all about?"

Ethan's chair scraped against the wooden floor. He stood. "The loss of SABR lives in recent weeks has been—staggering." He scanned the faces around the table. "Last night's announcement made it clear that the Fellowship has declared war on us. We must put the Fellowship on notice, we will not go down without a fight."

"Yes." "All right." "About time." To a man, they voiced agreement with tones that reflected anger, grim determination, and firm resolve.

"Just tell us when and where," Conrad said.

"The Fellowship is trying to hit our cells one by one. They are big enough they can do that. We can't. We will strike hard and fast at targets with the most impact." Ethan nodded at Pete and sat back down.

Pete picked up a roll of butcher paper off the floor beside him.

"Our first target is a training ground for Second Sphere and —Azrael."

A sharp intake of breath was the only audible response. The butcher paper crinkled in the silence. Pete pulled a roll of masking tape from a deep pocket in his jacket and taped the corners of the butcher paper to the table. Squares and rectangles and long wiggly lines covered the center of the paper.

"Building permits were heavily redacted," Pete said. "Fortunately, one of my guys managed a flyover. There are about fifty buildings in seven distinct areas."

He circled a cluster of rectangles with a red marker. "Administration." His pen hovered across the paper to circle another group of rectangles. "The common areas—the PX, the mess, and the hospital." Five more areas circled, one at a time. "The armory, magazine, and motor pool—the airport—the marina and dock— the power plant and warehouses, and the housing areas. The plan calls for a coordinated attack with nine platoons."

Beryl had already memorized the schematic. She focused on watching the men around the table.

"How many Azrael are at this training facility?" Conrad asked.

Pete looked at Ethan, who gave him a nod. "Given the number of barracks, we estimate there will be about two thousand Second Sphere cadets and anywhere from twenty-five to a couple hundred Azrael."

Jack let out a low whistle. "I've been in a lot of fights with slim odds," he said. "But a battle with a couple hundred dark angels—"

"They are not angels, my friend." Hector stood at the foot of the table. He braced his hands on the table and leaned forward. "They are flesh and blood. Deadly, but flesh and blood just the same." He paused a moment before continuing. "We know from Baltimore that as many as half of them will be female."

"You don't say." Conrad crossed his arms and leaned back a

little. "Flesh and blood women?" A slow, lecherous grin spread across his face. "Maybe there's another way we can best them."

"What are you going to do, Conrad?" Pete asked. "Knock 'em dead with your looks?"

"There be times when one look 'tis all it takes," Conrad said, his fake Irish accent belied by his drawl. He swept his carrot-red bangs back into place. "It's our red hair, don't you know?"

"This isn't a joke." Beryl stood and glared from one to the other. "If you think of them as 'just' women, you'll be dead. Even under the best circumstances, you've almost no chance of surviving this."

Conrad sobered. "Don't you think we know that? Allow us our jokes to ease the tension."

"They aren't 'just women' to me," Jack said, his voice low and tight. "I was sixteen when my father was Taken. Conrad lost—"

"We have all had losses, thanks to the Azrael," Ethan said, "some more personal than others. None of us want an army of them loose in the world."

"Don't worry your little ol' head none," Conrad said. "When the time comes, we'll do what needs to be done."

Beryl looked from one man to the other. Each man had visible scars and hard-eyed determination. *Yes, they'll do what they have to. Will it be enough?*

"Enough small talk. We are true soldiers now, act like it." Ethan stood tall at the head of the table. Everyone focused on him. He gestured at Pete.

"They don't allow the Azrael to have weapons in their barracks," Pete said, "so our best chance is to—"

"Wait. How do you know they don't have weapons in the barracks?" Conrad asked. "In Baltimore, they had Mausers and knives and garrotes and this evil-good body armor—"

"Beryl," Ethan asked. "Please tell them about the body armor."

He asked because of Anna. Memory's knife twisted in her chest. She cemented her mental wall against the pain with fresh anger.

"A direct hit cracked their black armor, but the bullet didn't penetrate the bodysuit they wore underneath. Only a blade slipped between the pieces of their armor penetrated the bodysuit." *Killed Anna.*

"Close fighting with two hundred *lady* Azrael—" Conrad said. His expression was grim.

"That is why we catch them flat-footed," Pete said. "We blow the barracks while they're sleeping—before they can get to their weapons."

"We gather in Kopp." Pete's finger stabbed the map. "An abandoned town in the middle of a forest."

"The perimeter fence is mostly for show," Ethan said. "It's made of stone and chain-link, but it's six feet tall. And there's a security fence a hundred feet beyond that—ten feet of chain link topped with barbed wire."

"Ethan takes in a recon team. Twenty minutes later the signal will go out." Pete pointed at the map. "At the signal, Ethan's recon platoon will secure the hospital and the admin buildings. Hector's platoon will wipe out the power plant. My platoon will assume control of the airport and motor pool." His finger bounced from one place to another. "Conrad, your platoon will take or destroy the magazine and the armory, here and here. Manny's platoon will take the marina and dock, and Jack will have four platoons."

Jack bent his lanky frame over the table. "We will hit the barracks"—he circled a group of rectangles with his finger—"the officers' housing here"—he circled a nearby, smaller group of rectangles—"and here." The third circle was the smallest area.

"Each team consisting of four men: two demolitions engineers and two shooters-sappers. We put timed charges under each of the exits set for oh-one-thirty. Shaped charges under the floor at the midline supports will blow at oh-one-thirty-five. White phosphorus charges will go off at one at oh-one-forty. What doesn't blow will burn."

Murmurs and nods of approval circled the room.

"Shooters positioned along the perimeter will smoke any survivors," Jack added.

Doubt gnawed at Beryl's gut. She stared at the map, sick with the knowledge that she could not do this alone and certain that even the whole SABR army wasn't enough.

"Four doors, twenty barracks—one hundred twenty-eight phosphorus charges, sixty-four satchel charges, plus one hundred twenty-eight charges," Ethan figured aloud. He turned to Jack. "Can your resources handle that?"

"They can."

"When can they deliver?"

Jack didn't hesitate. "Three days."

"Three days?" Hector asked incredulously.

Jack grinned. "They've been stockpiling. All we need to do is move it from there to here."

"Excellent," Ethan said. He turned to Conrad. "What about the weapons? How long to bring them in?"

Conrad studied the map and rubbed his chin.

The dry rasp of his fingers against his stubble set Beryl's teeth on edge.

"Forty-eight hours if you need them fast," he answered. "Two weeks or longer, if you're going for stealth."

"So long?" Ethan asked.

Conrad shrugged. "What's most needed, speed or secrecy?"

"Both," Ethan said. "Surprise is our best weapon."

"In Baltimore, they had a communications system built into those long johns they wore," Beryl said, voicing one of her doubts. The coordination of the Azrael attack had been far superior to anything Beryl had ever seen.

"Our new radio system is up to the job."

Manny gave a toothy smile. "I've made a few tweaks. No one else has anything like it."

Ethan stood. "We don't know how many Azrael are there. Some of those barracks are for Second Sphere cadets, agents, and officers. When the recon team goes in, we'll learn more. But this is voluntary. No one will be thought less of if he decides to opt out." He glanced at each person with a solemn smile and waited a full minute. No one spoke. No one left the room. "Thank you."

"Any questions?" Pete asked.

Beryl had to ask. "What if the Azrael aren't there?"

"That's unlikely," Ethan said. "The recon team will get an estimate to Pete. He will adjust the plan as needed. We hit the facility regardless of how many are or aren't there. And we won't leave a single functioning weapon or piece of armor intact. Right?" A round of grunts, yeahs, and rights swept through the men. "Any other questions?"

"How do we get out?" Conrad asked.

"We'll commandeer vehicles from the airport and motor pool. Anything else?"

"When?" Jack wanted to know.

"What day of the week is the most difficult?" Ethan asked. "Monday," he said, answering himself. "We'll hit them in the early hours of Monday."

"This Monday?" Conrad echoed. "Three days. Fast."

"Any objections?" Hector looked at each person in the room. No one spoke. "Manny, pour us a drink."

Manny went to the side table and grabbed a bottle of bootleg Canadian whiskey and a stack of paper cups.

Beryl accepted the cup Manny offered her. He took the last one himself.

Hector raised his cup. *"Muerte ala Azrael,"* he said. "Death to the Azrael."

Beryl stood and raised her glass with the others.

"Death to the Azrael," they chorused.

Death to the Azrael, Beryl echoed silently. The whiskey burned all the way down.

Chapter Seventy-Four

Miranda woke, pulse racing, muscles tensed. Thunder rumbled in the distance. *Where am I?* She lay in a trundle bed with a light blue cover over her. Beryl slept in the bed across the room. *Oh. The safe house.* She drew a deep breath. *Another nightmare.* It had started the same as all the others—her father molesting her—but instead of feigning sleep or giving up, she'd fought back. *Was it a memory?* She sat up on the side of the bed. *It doesn't matter.* Her lungs expanded to their fullest. *I fought back.* "Ha." She clapped her hands over her mouth. She hadn't meant for that to be so loud.

Going back to sleep was out of the question. She glanced down at her jeans and wrinkled T-shirt. The mental image of her mother's horrified expression tickled her. She sailed down the stairs, humming tunelessly. Fighting back hadn't changed the outcome, but she'd fought him. She *was* a fighter.

The parlor was dark and empty. In the kitchen, someone had left a light on over the stove. The aroma of coffee filled the room. The pot sat on an unlit burner on the gas stove, but the side of the pot was still hot to the touch. She went to the sink and stared out the window.

Outside, the yard and the tobacco fields beyond lay quiet under a silky black night sky dotted with thousands of stars. *Beautiful. And so unlike the city—* Miranda stopped, surprised at herself. The first images in her head were of Lynchburg, not Falls Church or Washington, DC. How could that be? She'd grown from a gawky teen to an adult in those cities. Her mother had called DC the place of the future. *Not my future. Not anymore.* As a rebel, did she dare think of the future?

The clock on the breakfast nook wall read 2:45. She'd settled down for a nap almost twelve hours ago. She wondered what Beryl and the others had done while she'd slept. *Guess I'll find out in the morning.*

Her stomach grumbled. She scrounged around in the refrigerator. Soon she had a turkey and Swiss cheese sandwich and a tall glass of milk.

She carried her meal into the front parlor. The upholstered chair looked inviting. It sat in the corner by the big Wurlitzer radio and had a side table for her sandwich plate. Manny appeared in the doorway beside her. She started, juggled her plate and glass, and narrowly missed dumping the contents onto the floor.

"Are you all right, Miss Clarke?" he asked.

Miss Clarke. She hadn't been called that in months. *How odd it sounds now.* "Yes, I'm fine," she told him. "A little surprised to see another night prowler."

He flashed a grin. "Could call me that. But I'm only making rounds."

She tensed. "Is something wrong?"

"No, not at all," he reassured her. "Only a precaution."

"Oh."

"Shouldn't you be in bed?" he asked.

She smiled and shook her head. "I've slept all day. Couldn't sleep anymore if you gave me ten pounds of sleeping powder. Everyone else has gone to bed, haven't they?"

"Yes, ma'am."

"Please, don't call me ma'am, and don't call me Miss Clarke either. I'm Miranda."

He saluted her. "Okay. Miranda, is there something I can do for you?"

She shook her head again. "I was going to listen to some music," she said, gesturing at the radio. "Won't you join me?"

He glanced up the stairs. "I could take a short coffee break. Thanks. I'll be back in a few minutes." He padded off, melting out of sight into the darkened hallway, and after a few steps, she couldn't hear him at all.

She turned on the radio and recognized the "Waltz of the Flowers" from the *Nutcracker Suite*. Adjusting the volume so the music didn't reach much beyond the chair, she nestled back, ate her sandwich, and listened. After the waltz finished, "Für Elise" began.

She closed her eyes. Someone stroked her hair. She flinched, opened her eyes, and searched the shadows. No one was in the room. Behind her, a pair of windows looked out on the night-darkened lake. No one was outside. She sighed.

The soft strains of Vivaldi's "Concerto in D Major" soothed her a bit.

Manny returned several minutes later. The dainty china coffee cup looked ridiculous in his massive hand. "Vivaldi? A strings woman," he said and shook his head. "Not me. Give me Wagner and brassy horns any day."

"You like classical?" she asked in surprise.

Disappointment wrinkled his little boy face. "Because I'm big, I can't appreciate good music?" He settled onto the sofa opposite her.

She gave him a contrite smile. "Sorry. I didn't mean to be rude."

"I like the ballet too," he said, his tone daring her to disbelieve him.

"Oh?" she asked, trying not to laugh at the images that sprang into her head. "Which one do you like best?"

"Well, to tell the truth," he said, looking a little sheepish, "I don't like very many. I tend to prefer the ones that tell a story, like *Swan Lake* or the *Nutcracker Suite*."

"I've never seen a ballet," she told him, staring into her milk glass. "I've been to the opera. Have you?"

"I went to see *Tannhauser* once."

She realized she was being rude, talking without making eye contact. She smiled at Manny over the rim of her glass.

"It was—" His eyes widened, the veins in his temples bulged, and his face started to turn red.

She giggled. "That good?"

One hand went to his throat, the other reached over his shoulder, flailed at his back. His face purpled. He lurched up off the sofa. A black, human-sized, insect-like creature rose from behind the sofa.

Miranda screamed and leaped to her feet.

Black legs snaked around his waist. He stumbled forward, shook himself violently. Manny roared. Blood burst from his neck, spraying her.

Breathless, Miranda scrambled backward, half climbing over and half tipping over her chair.

Manny's face blanched. He crashed to his knees. The black creature on his back withdrew its black limbs. He fell forward.

A sharp, hot odor fouled the air.

The creature rose, straddling Manny's body. Its inhuman head swiveled right, then panned back left.

It had no face. It evaluated Miranda blindly.

An explosion of noise came from the hallway. Hector burst into the room, flame spitting from pistols in each hand. Beryl followed, her gun flashing.

The black thing turned. A wall of flame erupted from its center. Plaster and millwork above the door rained down. Beryl jumped back. Hector fell to his knees. The creature whirled and passed within inches of Miranda, then vaulted through the window.

Beryl leaped over Hector. She dashed past Miranda, firing her pistols again and again. She dove through the blowing drapes and vanished from sight.

Darting to a position beside the window, Hector peered out, guns high.

Miranda stared at Manny, ringing filling her ears. He was dead. And she, Miranda, had lived.

Hector left the window and helped her into the chair. A moment later he pressed a glass tumbler into her hands, then lifted it to her lips.

She gulped the amber liquid. It scorched her throat, set fire to her stomach. The ringing in her ears grew unbearably loud. He tilted the cup again. She swallowed. The ringing faded some.

"Where are you hurt?" Hector asked. "Where are you bleeding?"

She looked down at herself. Blood covered her blouse, her hands—she could even feel it on her face. "Not mine. Manny's," she said, her eyes drawn to his body.

"Where did she come from?" Hector asked, glancing at the window.

"We were talking about opera," she said, trying to remember. "I thought he was joking, but—" Her vision blurred. "He was dying."

"Miranda, it is very important." Hector locked eyes with her. "Where did she come from?"

She blinked back her tears and shook her head. "I don't know. I went to the kitchen for something to eat, then came in here. Manny came by, on his rounds. We talked—it was on his back—" She gasped. "It was hiding behind the sofa, waiting for us!"

Hector knelt at Manny's side and closed his friend's eyes. "She could have killed us all in our sleep," he muttered as if talking to Manny. "But Azrael, she had a specific target. And I don't think you were it, my friend."

Miranda gaped at Hector. "Wait a minute," she said. "That

was an Azrael?" A cold lump slid down her throat, chilled her through and through. She could've been the one on the floor.

"We've got to get out of here," Hector said. "She could come back."

Hector pulled Miranda to her feet. "Take five to shower and gather your possessions. Be down here in fifteen minutes or less."

Miranda started upstairs, then stopped and turned to Hector. "What about Manny?"

He glanced at his dead friend. A shadow crossed his face. "There is nothing we can do for him."

"We can't leave him here."

"He will forgive us," Hector said.

The bang of a gun outside made Miranda flinch and crouch on the stairs. Bullets thwacked against the siding.

The front door burst open. Beryl sprang inside and slammed the door shut behind her. "She had company."

Chapter Seventy-Five

Beryl couldn't believe she'd allowed herself to be a sitting duck trapped in this house. She should have left when Ethan and the others had left yesterday. "Hector, cover the rear and the east side." She kept watch through one of the west-facing windows. *At least the tobacco fields are a good distance from the house. No one can get close without crossing a lot of open ground.*

The gunfire had stopped the moment she'd entered the house. She checked her weapon. *Six rounds left.* She patted her waist. *Damn.* She'd been in such a hurry when she'd heard Miranda scream that she hadn't put on her holster.

"Miranda?" She glanced at the steps where she'd last seen Miranda.

"Here." Miranda's answer came from her right. The girl had taken a position by the broken parlor window.

"Where'd you get the weapon?"

"From him." Miranda tossed her head in the direction of Manny's body.

"Good. Need ammo. Our room. Grab my holster and rucksack."

"Yes, ma'am."

Miranda crept toward the stairs.

Beryl returned her attention to the edge of the tobacco field. *How many men are out there?* The odor of gunpowder mixed with the licorice smell of the tobacco plants. The rasp of the tobacco leaves in the wind and the chittering of cicadas provided excellent cover.

Whether it was two or a battalion, the armed assailants surrounding them had to be Second Sphere. *The only reason we aren't all dead is Miranda. Kara's pleas on television made it clear she wanted the girl back in the family fold. Miranda wasn't having any of that, but perhaps we can use Miranda to escape. Whatever we do, we'd best do it before sunup.*

"Pssst. Beryl." Hector called from the other end of the hall.

She glanced that way.

He sat in the kitchen doorway, back to her, facing the porch door. "Do you see anyone?"

"No one. You?"

"No."

"Is there a secret passage out of here?"

"That would be nice, yes? But no. No secret passage. We'll have to do this the hard way."

"Yes, and no," Beryl said. "Why haven't they stormed this place?" She gave him a second.

He shrugged.

"Because they want at least one of us alive."

"One of us—oh."

"We can use her."

"I can hear you, you know." Miranda's voice came from the stairwell.

"You want to use her as a shield?" Hector asked.

"No. Her presence will make them cautious," Beryl answered. "Once we reach the tobacco field, we split up. We meet at Post Oak Cemetery now or Kopp in twenty-four hours."

"I will need more ammo."

"Miranda?"

335

"I know." Miranda crawled toward Hector.

Beryl watched tobacco plants move against the wind. She fired a double tap into the general area. "I'm paying attention, boys." The movement stopped.

By the sound of it, Miranda made at least two more trips upstairs and two into the back parlor. When she returned to the front room, she had two lumpy rucksacks and a cleaner face. She still wore a lot of Manny's blood. Beryl could hear her scratching places where the dried blood irritated her skin. "They'll hear that scratching a mile away," Beryl grumbled.

Miranda deposited a dark shirt, jeans, and a pair of shoes and socks beside Beryl. Then she returned to the front parlor.

Beryl slipped on the clothing without taking her eyes from the yard. The rasp of fingernails on skin grew unbearable. "Damn it." She glared at Miranda. The girl had scrubbed herself pink right there in the parlor with her gun close at hand. She dropped a once-white washcloth onto the floor and reached for a pile of dark clothing. Beryl grunted grudging approval and scanned the night-darkened yard again. *Nothing.* The SS were willing to wait until dawn, but Beryl didn't dare wait that long. As soon as the sounds of Miranda changing ceased, she caught Miranda's eye and gave a head jerk toward the kitchen. Miranda grabbed a rucksack and moved. Beryl slung her rucksack onto her back, cracked open the front door, fired into the tobacco, then followed Miranda.

Hector glanced at their approach but didn't move from his watchful position.

"Post Oak Cemetery in an hour," Beryl whispered. "Or the gathering."

Hector nodded.

Miranda gripped the belt at the small of Beryl's back and turned to Hector. After a moment's hesitation, she found a hold on Hector's belt.

Beryl opened the back door.

"Ladies first," Hector whispered.

She didn't argue.

Halfway across the lawn, a bullet buzzed through the air between her and Miranda. *Damn. They don't care if they hit Miranda.* "Break."

Miranda ran full-tilt toward the tobacco plants.

Beryl fired in the direction of the shooter, then charged at him. He disappeared into the tobacco field.

Behind her, Hector's guns barked.

Return fire obliterated all other sounds for several long moments. Then the gunfire stopped. The tobacco leaves rustled in the breeze. The crickets and other creatures of the night were wisely silent.

Beryl wove between plants, varied her pace, and used the wind to camouflage her passage. She walked the length of two football fields. *The edge of the tobacco field has to be close.* The crack of a not-too-distant gunshot pierced the air. *Miranda? Hector?* She paused, listened, and scanned the area around her.

The wind carried a new, irregular rustling of the tobacco leaves to her. She crouched beneath the leaves of two large plants, pointed her pistol, and held her breath. The noise drew closer, slowed, and stopped. She breathed when the wind sighed. A faint crackle warned her that he was on the move again. The sounds of his movement faded into the natural sounds of wind-stirred leaves. She counted out one hundred twenty seconds before she dared move.

She wove through a half-dozen more rows of tobacco, then there were no more leaves to hide her. Pale light from the eastern horizon revealed a fifty-yard clearing of tall grass. A small stand of trees on the other side, her next cover. She dashed to the trees, crossed the stand quickly, and struck across a neighboring field toward the abandoned town once known as Kopp.

Chapter Seventy-Six

P ain knifed through Azrael's chest with every breath. She needed a steadying hand on the autogiro for a moment while she caught her breath. *Can't delay.* She pulled out the first aid kit. Gritting her teeth, she wrapped the tape around herself. The bullet that had shattered her breastplate had bruised, maybe broken, a rib or two. Taped, her chest felt better.

God's wrath flared within her. *The ones who did this will be punished.* She looked up through the camouflage net to the star-filled heavens. "Thank you, Father, for the fullness of your grace," she prayed. "Under your watch-care, I have commended one of the unbelievers to Hell. Thank you for your blessings. But Lord, the most impenitent and impious of sinners has spurned your judgment. For this, she deserves the darkest of deaths. I pray it is your will that I, your loyal servant, shall be the one to deliver her up for your justice. Thy will be done. Amen."

She stood. *The target probably congratulated herself for having driven an Azrael away. Foolish woman.*

Azrael repacked the first aid kit and tucked it in the pouch behind the pilot's seat. *I will find you again. And, next time, the Lord's will* shall *be done.* Noticing the chronometer on the autogiro's dash, she frowned. She'd taken too long. She gathered the camouflage net into a neatly folded rectangle and stowed it in the storage bin in the back of the autogiro. She prepared the vehicle for takeoff, and herself for the ordeal to come. *Uncle will not be pleased.*

Chapter Seventy-Seven

Miranda stopped, pointed her gun, and listened. The gunfire had stopped, and now the tobacco plants around her rustled in the breeze as if nothing had happened. She refused to believe anything other than Beryl and Hector had escaped.

The stars above her winked in an ebony sky, but the eastern horizon had a bluish tinge that hinted at dawn. She moved east in a random zig-zag. She reached the last row of tobacco plants and hesitated. More than a hundred feet of open grass lay between her and her next zone of concealment, a strip of trees and shrubs.

She glanced to the right, then the left. It looked vacant and peaceful. She knew better than to believe appearances. Retreating two rows into the tobacco field, she worked her way north.

Ahead of her, the plants shivered. She ducked behind a tall tobacco plant and pointed her gun. A man stepped into view. He was young and trim and holding a gun. He swiveled toward her, raised his gun, his finger on the trigger. Miranda fired. He took two steps toward her. On the third step, his legs crumpled beneath him, his breath rattled, and a thin stream of blood bubbled from his chest. Miranda turned and ran.

She ran out of the tobacco field, across the grass, toward the trees. A gunshot cracked the air. She ran faster. A rapid exchange popped and banged behind her.

Inside the tree line, she turned north and outran the commotion. She jogged east, then back north. Her lungs burned past endurance. She leaned against a tree trunk, gasped quiet, desperate breaths. Her arms and legs shook. Her thoughts ping-ponged. Manny's bloody body. The look on the face of the man she shot. The man she had killed. She retched. She wasn't quiet. There was no way to vomit silently. Her stomach convulsed again and again. Dry heaves left her wrung out.

She sagged against the tree, relieved. Relieved no agent had heard her retching. Relieved she was alive. *Is Beryl alive? How had Beryl reacted to her first kill? Not relevant. It was kill or be killed. I am soldier Miranda now. Let God sort it out.* She loosened some earth with her knife, covered her vomit, and walked away.

She traveled for hours, grateful that she had memorized the route to Kopp. She walked parallel to the road but out of sight, in the shelter of wooded areas or scrub brush when she could, away from the road when she had to circle a fenced property.

She found a stale-smelling shell of a burned-out house that sat well back from the road. She fell into a fitful sleep. Running and blood and the crumpled body of the man she'd killed filled her dreams. She gave up on sleep and walked on. Shortly after noon on Saturday, she reached Kopp. A SABR member on watch accepted her code word and guided her to the camp. Beryl and Hector were already there. As glad as Miranda was to see them, the fact that they looked as dirty and exhausted as she gave her great satisfaction. Nick was there too. She smiled a stiff, half-hearted smile. His face brightened for a moment then clouded.

Ethan hurried toward her, arms spread.

She steeled herself.

He gave her a quick squeeze, then stood back. "Glad you made it." His hand on her arm guided her toward a tent. "Debriefing."

Beryl and Hector's stories were about hiding and running.

Miranda reported her encounter with the agent in a flat, unemotional tone. Beryl gave her a nod of approval, and this time it didn't matter.

Ethan assigned each of them to a squad. Miranda's squad leader was Nick. Her role as mule was to carry munitions, to provide cover fire, and most of all to follow orders. Their assignment was to search several office buildings at the center of the compound. Miranda breathed a little easier. She could do that.

"The next six hours, I want you all to rest," Nick said. "Sleep if you can."

Miranda trudged to the women's tent, opened the flap, and stared at the dozen or more sleeping forms inside. Beryl lay atop her sleeping bag just inside the door. She opened her eyes, gave Miranda a sleepy smile, and closed her eyes again.

Miranda closed the flap and walked to the perimeter of the camp. She chose an isolated spot, spread her sleeping bag, and sat on it, using a rough tree trunk for back support. She drew her knees to her chest and held on tight. Spent, she had no tears, but she ached inside. Ached for Sarah and Gert and George and Nick's brother, and for the agent she killed, and for all the Taken. No matter how tight she hugged her knees, the ache rolled and twisted and burned. Burned away the old Miranda until only smoldering embers remained.

Footsteps approached. *Nick.* She turned away from him.

"Miranda?" he whispered.

"Go away." Her voice was hoarse, unrecognizable.

He sat beside her, wrapped his arms around her, and, without another word, held her.

She sat stiffly in his arms.

His hold was gentle, solid, unmoving. They sat that way for a long, long time. Slowly, Miranda began to relax. She leaned into him. Still, he held her without doing or asking more. His soft, regular breathing and the steady beat of his heart eased the pain a little. She sat, listening to him and to the hushed bustle of the rebel camp preparing for war.

Chapter Seventy-Eight

The empty lockers and the bare cots lining the walls of the barracks confounded Beryl. They had searched ten barracks so far, all vacant.

Her shoes made soft *wisp-wisp* sounds against the concrete. She went to the third floor, Ethan covered the second, and Ian searched the ground floor. They met at the south staircase.

"We need to think this through." Ethan's flashlight swept across Beryl's legs and continued to the west. She went to the west side of the building.

Ian crouched by one of the south-facing windows and peered out. "They built a lot of barracks." He took off his dark cap, wiped his pockmarked forehead, and replaced the cap. "Why didn't they fill them?"

Ethan stared between the blinds of an east-facing window. "Maybe their plans were bigger than what they could do."

"Doesn't make sense," Ian continued. "Maybe they're out on some sort of maneuvers."

Beryl scanned the dimly lit west lawn and shook her head. "They don't exist."

"How do you know that?"

"The buildings are too clean," Ethan told him quietly. "They show no signs of being lived in."

"Our odds have improved," Ian whispered.

"In Baltimore, the odds were five-to-one, in your favor," she reminded him. "It didn't help."

"Yes." Ethan turned his back to the wall and sat with one leg outstretched, the other bent. "We lost a lot—of people—in Baltimore."

His voice held a tightness that sliced through Beryl. He'd never forgive her for killing their daughter. She couldn't blame him. If the situation had been reversed…

"Did you notice?" Ethan asked.

Yes, she had. "The buildings aren't filled yet," she said. "Look around. They aren't abandoned, they're ready—waiting—for thousands of women recruits." She'd thought her hatred for Weldon couldn't get stronger. When he couldn't find another Anna, he used those poor demented women as baby factories. *How many women and children's lives has he ruined?* She might not find all the children, but she could damn well find and stop Weldon. Without him, the project would fail.

"How could you know—" Ian smacked himself in the forehead. "The bathrooms."

Ethan nodded. "They are building an army of Azrael. Whether we find a dozen or a thousand, we will pay a heavy price, again." He sighed. "It is the price we must pay for not stopping them before."

Before Anna became one of them? Before Weldon joined the Second Sphere? Or before the Fellowship grew to be so influential? "I didn't come here to talk regrets." Beryl had felt enough of that in Redemption. "We've two more barracks to check out." She pushed off the cool, concrete floor.

"Wait." Ethan folded his leg beneath him, groaned, and stood.

The night air was damp, fragrant with green, growing things. She relished every breath, every odor. The next building stood dark and was vacant, like the others. She dashed to the final building and approached the door. *Wait. The flower bed. Tiger lilies.* A flood of memories welled up, stopped her in her tracks. *Eight-year-old Anna laughing at the streak of mud on Beryl's nose, clapping in delight at the first blooms, declaring herself a princess of tiger lilies.*

She signaled Ethan to stop.

He dropped to a crouch.

She pointed her flashlight at the flowers.

He blew several hard breaths in and out. He recognized them.

She hadn't thought Weldon that smart, but he'd obviously set up the doll at the Colony and the lilies here as an emotional trap for her and Ethan. *Not going to win that way, Weldon.* She tucked the memories and the hurt back deep inside. She bent low, crept forward, and plastered herself to the wall as low as she could. A quick peek through the window revealed a dark interior filled with dark shapes. The dark shapes were cots lining the walls like the previous buildings, but there was a difference. These cots had the square look of made beds. It was impossible to tell from here if they'd ever been occupied.

She pulled her pistol out of its holster and signaled Ethan. Ethan signaled Ian, who waited in the shadows of building number eleven and kept watch.

She did a slow, listening circuit. At each window, she slid up the rough brick wall, glanced inside, and moved on. The building was quiet, as quiet as the previous buildings had been. It was vacant now, but she couldn't tell more than that. She signaled Ethan to come.

Ethan, then Ian, flattened against the wall beside her.

"Beds made," she whispered. "No one home."

"Same search pattern." Ethan's voice was so low she had to strain to hear it. "Be ready." He held his pistol in the high and ready position.

Ian slid the window open, then covered her while she entered.

Beryl slipped inside and covered Ethan and Ian as they entered.

Ethan crossed about six feet and recoiled as if he'd seen a

ghost. The cot he stared at held another doll. Same curly hair, same homemade dress. Beryl breathed through the pain and swallowed hard. "It's not hers," she whispered. "Don't let it get to you."

Ethan straightened and hurried to the staircase.

The upper two floors held unmade cots. A neatly folded bundle, sheets, and a blanket sat on the foot of each cot. The immaculate bathrooms had a fresh pine scent. She met Ethan and Ian downstairs again.

Ian pointed to the lockers, then held up six fingers. *Only six? Perhaps Ethan was right. Weldon hadn't been as successful as he thought he'd be. No. That wasn't right. Beds were—waiting.*

Ian grinned like one of the Colony residents. Evidently, he thought six Azrael would be an easy takedown. Assumptions like that were likely to get him killed.

"Green light," Ethan whispered into his walkie-talkie. "Green light."

Chapter Seventy-Nine

The bright moon dared Miranda and her team to find shadows to conceal their approach. That had been easier in the tree line before they'd breached the "farm's" two fences. It was not so easy in the administration area of the complex. Four buildings circled an open parade ground. Behind the buildings, low shrubs and flowerbeds stood in the moonlight.

Nick darted between flowerbeds to the back door of the tallest building. Eric followed and picked the lock, then Nick signaled her and Dayton inside.

Their team goal was to find documentation of the Azrael project. Miranda hoped to also find proof of her father's misdeeds. Something to prove he was the kind of man who could abuse his own daughter.

Nick sent her to the top, the fifth floor. She moved through the dark, wood-paneled hallways and, in her memory, heard Sarah's cleaning cart rattle. *Wish you could see me now.*

The offices held nice desks and filing cabinets filled with requisitions for food and materials and office supplies. Nothing that hinted at the Azrael or any other transgressions.

Boom-Boom-Boom. The building shook with the first explosions.

347

Miranda crouched and braced herself with a hand on the nearest doorframe. She almost felt sorry for the Second Sphere agents who had been awakened by that.

The shaking faded. Five minutes until the next series of explosions, only ten minutes until this building would be blown. She hurried forward to the next office. A secretary's office guarded the door to a corner office. The nameplate on the door read, "Commander." *How odd. No name. Why?* The corner office had floor-to-ceiling windows on two walls. Bookshelves and photographs of standard Fellowship dignitaries lined the other two walls. The heavy, dark wood furniture had a square, masculine look. Miranda scanned the bookshelves, then stepped behind the desk and caught her breath. Her mother and Uncle Weldon smiled at her from a photograph in a silver frame. Beryl was right. Weldon was the head of the Second Sphere. She slammed the picture facedown on the desk. Glass cracked. Miranda clenched and unclenched her fists. Her parents, her uncle. Her life had been one big, fat lie. She was never the monster. They were. They'd fooled everyone. Beryl was probably right about the Azrael too.

Miranda ripped into the desk's drawers, scanning files, tossing them onto the floor. She emptied the desk and moved to the lateral file. There were hundreds of files on every sort of person, public and private. The files reported radical leanings, extramarital affairs, drug smuggling, murder, and homosexuality. There were committee reports, congressional investigation reports, and reports on the Second Sphere.

She opened each file and scanned the first, middle, and last pages. She shrugged off her rucksack. Selected financial and Second Sphere action reports went into it. Everything else went on the floor. Not one file hinted at the Azrael project or anything about her father.

A rapid exchange of gunshots sounded close. Miranda picked up her rucksack and headed for the door. Another explosion shook the building and made the desk chair roll into the bookcase. The door swung partially closed. On the wall behind the door hung a large, framed photograph of her father in First Apostle robes. She stood transfixed, glaring at the beatific pose she knew to be fake. She yanked the picture off the wall, smashed it against her knee, then threw it down and stomped on it. She didn't stop until the powdered glass shredded every recognizable feature. Glowering at the ruined photograph, she sucked in air until her pulse slowed to something like normal. Finally, she raised her gaze to the wall. Her mouth dropped open. The picture had hidden a wall safe.

She should call Nick. *No.* She was looking for more than proof of the Azrael. She had to try to open it on her own. *People use familiar numbers, Nick had said. Numbers like birthdates, identification numbers, address numbers, and the like.* She tried Weldon's birthdate. *No luck.* She tried her father's birthdate. *No. Mother's birthdate?* This time the handle moved, and the safe door opened.

It was jam-packed with stuff. Thick envelopes held stacks of hundred dollar bills. A cloth bag held gold coins. She pulled out a plastic evidence bag, heavy with a Mauser pistol. Under the pistol was a stack of file folders stamped in red "Official" and "Confidential." She fanned through them, stopped cold by the sight of her father's face. Beneath the photograph were her father's height, weight, hair, and eye color. Under traits, it read, "charismatic speaker, leader." The preferences line was blank. She flipped the page over. *Nothing? How could Uncle Weldon uncover the secrets in everyone else's lives and miss the secrets in her father's life?*

She turned the page. There were notes with dates and times of meetings. Lots of notes. *No time to read them now.* She flipped pages, stopped, and backed up. *What is a bill of lading doing in Father's file?* The ship's name was *Seabird.* Flekkefjord, Norway, *Die Föderation von Deutschland w*as its homeport. Tiny, precise, hand-written block letters listed equipment and supplies. *The same supplies Mother had listed in her bookkeeping ledger.* The port of loading was Genoa, Italy. The port of delivery was a set of coordinates. Underneath the coordinates, in even smaller block letters it read, "Hog Island." Miranda couldn't breathe. *They delivered the supplies to*

Hog Island. She remembered the creepy teenager and shivered. *Were they delivering supplies on that day too? Is that why she was there? Maybe they store the supplies there.*

Miranda flipped the bill of lading over. The back was blank, but the next page made her heart skip a beat. It was a photograph of the *Faithful Seas.* Her father was on deck escorting a young girl into the cabin. The file held a dozen photographs of her father and the same young girl on the yacht. Each photo had a different date. The last photo's date was less than five days ago.

The dock was unfamiliar, but Miranda had a nagging feeling she knew the little girl. The photographer never got more than a glimpse of girl's profile. Then, in the last, most recent photograph, Miranda noticed that the girl wore an earring. A cluster of pearls that clipped onto the ear and made a ten-year-old girl feel like a woman. A feeling Miranda remembered. A secret gift Miranda remembered. Earrings Miranda had forgotten and now remembered. Her jaw tightened. A fierce-as-fire gotcha rang through her. These pictures and her own earrings hidden at the beach house would convince everyone.

Beryl needs to see this—the list—and the photographs. Beryl would know— An explosion rattled the building, driving Miranda to her knees. The glass windows shattered. Chunks of ceiling tile, broken support beams, and clouds of dust rained down. Miranda tucked into a ball, both hands covering her head. Her nose burned, and her throat spasmed. Coughing racked her.

"Miranda?" Nick called from the doorway. "Are you in here?"

"Over here," she sputtered. A large piece of ceiling tile covered her, but she was able to shift it enough she could stand.

"Thank God." Nick grabbed her hand and pulled her the rest of the way free. "Can you walk?"

She took a couple tentative steps. Nothing hurt. She gasped. A large section of brick and twisted metal I-beams had crashed through the window and onto Uncle Weldon's desk. Broken ceiling pipes spewed water, drenching the books in one bookcase. Flames shot from another pipe, setting a bookcase on the opposite wall ablaze. Curtains flapped, feeding the fire until they were consumed.

"Let's get out of here." Nick tugged her toward the hall.

"No." She twisted and jerked. "My rucksack. The pictures." Flames raced up the ceiling tile that had covered her, that covered her rucksack and the file of photographs. Intense heat drove her back. Nick grabbed her and carried her out of the room.

He didn't put her feet down until they were outside. Miranda coughed and sputtered and faced the building. Flames leaped from the fourth floor windows. Smoke poured out of broken windows on the remaining floors. A sour taste filled her mouth, sapped the strength from her limbs. "You don't know what you've done."

"I know I saved your life," Nick said. Exasperation colored his words.

She put a hand on her hip pocket. The sole remaining photograph was there. *At least I have one.* A familiar whine zipped through the air.

She and Nick exchanged glances and dropped to their bellies behind the nearest bushes. A barrage of bullets dug into the dirt around them. "Who's shooting at us?" she whispered.

"Not our—" Another volley of gunfire obliterated Nick's answer. He signaled for her to follow him. They army-crawled until they reached the end of the bushes.

"If we head southeast, we can join Conrad's squad," Nick whispered.

Miranda shook her head. "I have to find Beryl."

Even in the shadows, Nick's body language reeked disapproval.

"I've vital information. I'm going to the hospital."

Chapter Eighty

B eryl led the way through the hospital's shattered glass sliding doors and into a brightly lit hall. The clashing odors of antiseptics and acrid gunpowder lingered in the air. "If you find Locke's notes or any strange equipment," she said to Hector. "Don't touch it. Call me. I'll deal with it."

Hector grimaced. He still didn't like her giving orders, but he didn't argue. He raced to the elevator.

She pushed through the emergency room doors and nodded a greeting to the rebel with a camouflage-greased face. He held a gun on a doctor, two nurses, and an older woman in street clothes huddled against one wall. A body lay under blood-soaked sheets on a nearby gurney. She lifted the corner of the sheet. A middle-aged male stared vacantly at the ceiling, a guard judging from his uniform. She replaced the sheet.

"Keep them here until you receive the signal," she told the rebel and banged through the door into a wide hallway. The etched plastic sign on the wall pointed to various departments. She checked Radiology first.

The SABR crew that had breached and swept the building had been thorough. The rooms were vacant of people. She looked through drawers, files, and books. None of the materials mentioned Weldon or the project.

In the laboratory, she pulled books off shelves, swept contents out of cupboards, and emptied drawers. There was nothing of interest, not even in any of the specialty labs. She took a little more time searching the administrative offices, but not much. She knew at a glance that none of it belonged to Weldon. She checked every fallen Second Sphere agent. There were fewer than she'd expected, no more than a dozen. They carried nothing but personal identity papers and personal junk. She left nothing unchecked, not even the public restrooms. Finally, she strode to the interior door marked Exit, nudged it open, and peered through the crack. *No one.* In one quick movement, she slipped through the door and crouched on the landing. Beryl aimed her gun up the stairs, then down. *Nothing.* She trotted up the stairs to the door marked Seventh Floor.

She eased the door open, peered through the crack, and recognized the team leader, Jack.

Jack had his gun aimed at the door, at her.

"It's me, Beryl," she whispered.

Jack nodded and put a finger to his lips.

She joined him in front of a pair of closed, solid doors.

He nudged one door open a toe's width and scrutinized what lay on the other side. After a moment, he threw the door open and motioned her and the others through. They entered a small waiting room or lobby. A pair of fire doors with small, square, wire-reinforced windows at eye level, stood at each end: 7 North and 7 South. Jack's next signal directed them toward the door bearing the name 7 North.

The fire doors opened with a soft click.

Rows of beds with bared mattresses lined the walls. The air held a vague medicinal smell.

"Looks like this one's empty," one man said in a hushed voice.

More emptiness? Beryl had a bad feeling.

Jack and his men trotted ahead, their shoes tapping a soft staccato down the hall. They cleared rooms along the interior wall, their tension evident in the jerky way they moved.

They followed the hall, a squared-off U-shape, back to the little waiting room. Jack checked the stairway before waving them across to the other set of fire doors, the ones labeled 7 South.

Jack peered through one of the doors' windows. "Well, I'll be —" He pushed the door open.

Twin beds lined each side of the large ward. Many of the beds were empty. Some were not.

"Children?" one of the men said, stunned.

A stout woman with dark hair in a tight bun stomped toward them. "What's the meaning of this?" she demanded in a library voice.

Jack raised his gun. "Don't come any closer, ma'am."

Here and there a child stirred, rubbed sleepy eyes, and sat up. Soon they were all sitting up, watching. Beryl scanned their faces. Her heart stuttered and thrashed in disbelief. She scanned them again. They were all little girls, all lookalikes, and they all looked like her Anna. *Eighteen of them.* A cold wave hit her, settled like a mountain on her chest.

"They can't all be twins or whatever, can they?" Jack murmured. He pointed his gun at the woman. "Who are they? What are they doing here?"

She had no answer.

"They couldn't be— Are they Azrael?" Jack asked.

Caught between memory and reality, Beryl struggled to understand. *How? Why? Anna?* She took an involuntary step toward the closest one.

"You shall not hurt us," the nearest little girl said, rising from her bed. "It is the Lord's will." She raised a wicked-sharp combat knife and leaped at Beryl.

Instinctively Beryl fired her gun. The bullet caught the little girl in the middle of her chest. She fell to the floor like a rag doll. Beryl stared transfixed by the little body.

The woman lunged at Jack. Jack fired, twice. She collapsed in a bloody heap.

Bloodcurdling, little-girl screams filled the air. They launched themselves out of bed. Knife-wielding identical girls, who couldn't be real, surrounded Beryl and the others. A knife slashed Beryl's arm. She blocked the next parry with her injured arm and fired into the little body. The men struggled with the girls. They couldn't make themselves fire their weapons and tried to fend off the girls. The girls felled two men in seconds. Beryl's training took over. She fired again and again and again.

In minutes, a dozen little bodies lay crumpled in pools of blood—murdered. Every muscle in Beryl's body strained to keep her upright. She kept her gun steady despite the fact that there wasn't enough air in the room. A wave of dizziness swept over her. She bent, braced herself on her thighs, her gun pointed at the ground. *How? Why? Did Weldon know what this would cost me? Of course he did.* The shakes hit her. She staggered to a wall, slid down, and sat with her back to the wall, unable to take her eyes off the little girls.

"Are you injured?" Jack asked.

It was a lifetime sentence, this Curse of Cain she carried. The numbness began the way it had the first time, spreading from the center of her chest to her extremities.

"Beryl? Are you hurt?"

She blinked and focused on Jack's concerned face. "I don't think so." *Did I say that?* Her voice sounded so very far away. She looked down at herself. A gash on her left arm wept blood. Otherwise, she had no injuries. "A flesh wound." Her gaze was irresistibly drawn back to the little dead bodies.

Three men's bodies lay under the children, their blood mingled with the blood of their killers, blended, indistinguishable from one another.

"They weren't children," Jack said. "They were assassins."

Is he trying to comfort me? A woman who carries the Curse of Cain cannot be comforted.

355

"You understand?" Jack peered at her. "If they had lived, we'd all be dead."

She nodded.

"We have to go," Jack said. "There may be more. We can't let any of them get away."

Beryl stood. Somehow the numbness didn't affect her movements. That was good. If there were more, their mutual destruction was her destiny.

Chapter Eighty-One

G lass crunched under Miranda's foot, the glass that used to be in the emergency room's sliding doors. She lifted her foot to step through the empty metal frames, and the doors slid open.

Gunpowder and antiseptics made an acrid, eye-burning combination. In the center of the waiting room, two rebels stood next to stacks of boxes, handing out weapons and ammunition to the rebels who streamed past. The drone of grim voices, the *snick-click* of reloading, and the rhythmic clack of marching boots filled the room.

Nick tapped Miranda's shoulder and pointed.

Beryl sat in one of the blue, plastic bucket chairs that circled the perimeter of the waiting room, her eyes fixed on something only she could see.

Miranda hurried to her. "Beryl?"

No response. SABR soldiers' shoes drummed across the tile floor. One group on their way out, the other on their way in. *She can't hear me.*

Miranda touched Beryl's shoulder. "Are you all right?"

Beryl shrugged her off. "Why does everyone keep asking me

that? I'm the same woman I was when I came here: a mother who kills her daughter."

"Wha—?" Nonplused, Miranda stood still for a moment. "What happened?"

Nick waved off Miranda's next words. "Tell her what you found."

"I was searching the offices, Uncle Weldon's office…"

Beryl looked away.

Miranda gaped at her. "Fine," she said, stunned that Beryl, of all people, would react that way. "If you don't care about where they hid the Azrael supplies, I'll find someone who does." She whirled away. *I'll find Uncle Ethan.*

Beryl seized her arm painfully, forced Miranda back around. "You know where they are?" Beryl's eyes had a feverish quality.

"I have a hunch." Miranda felt feverish too. "We need to go to my parents' beach house, get the yacht, and I can take you there."

"They're on an island? The family island?"

The intensity of Beryl's searching look fed the fire inside of Miranda. "A bill of lading says they are or were."

"Show me."

Miranda quirked her mouth. "It burned up in the fire. But I know what I read."

"Hector!" Beryl's bellow cut through the noise.

Heads turned, and Hector's name echoed across the room. The soldiers parted for Hector's passage.

"Who called me?" He scanned the room, and his gaze rested on Beryl. "I should have known. What do you want?"

Within a few minutes, Miranda had briefed them on what she'd found and suggested a plan where she and Beryl would scout the island with the yacht.

"I'll have to talk to Ethan about that," Hector said, pulling his walkie-talkie from his belt.

Beryl sat up straighter, opened, then closed her mouth.

"You object?" Hector asked.

She looked down at the floor and shook her head.

Hector moved to a quieter spot across the room. A few minutes later, he returned with two squads following him. Ethan and one of his squads would meet them at the airstrip. All they had to do was cross the compound to the airstrip.

Outside, they moved in small groups, darting from burned-out vehicle to hedgerow to charred building. Streetlights flickered, transforming the scene around them into a series of stark snapshots. Strange odors hung in the air: acrid, cloying, nauseating odors that left a foul, oily taste in Miranda's mouth.

Beryl went first, her head moving in a constant, slow scan of the area ahead.

Miranda followed, her pulse thrumming in her throat.

Nick fell in behind Miranda.

Through the shadows and thick acrid smoke, barely recognizable bodies lay on the ground at odd angles or hung out of windows. Uniformed or not, Second Sphere, SABR, or Azrael, all had a stillness that rendered them the same.

Miranda rounded the corner of another burned-out building. A final gauntlet of three and four-story warehouses lay between them and the flight tower two hundred yards dead-ahead. *Almost there.*

A scream pierced the air, followed by a salvo of gunfire. Miranda's pulse leaped.

"This way." Beryl tugged at Miranda, forcing her into a crouching run. Beryl threw herself flat onto the asphalt behind a smoldering jeep.

Miranda did the same. She gasped short, shallow breaths and peered under a fender. Muzzle flashes strobed all around her. *How can anyone tell who is SABR and who is Second Sphere or Azrael?*

A tremendous explosion ripped through a nearby building. Rubble rained onto the street. Dark shadows ran from the falling debris.

"Cover them." Beryl blasted the second-story windows on each side of the street.

Miranda raised her pistol. The deafening *rat-tat-tat* of a

Tommy gun punctuated by the *ping-ping* of bullets on metal made her duck for cover.

"Shooters on the roof." Beryl pushed Miranda around to the side of the vehicle they sheltered behind and sent a shower of bullets at the roof of the building across from them.

Miranda aimed and fired over and over. Her pistol's toggle locked open. *Empty.* She leaned against the burned-out jeep and thumbed the magazine release. She reloaded as fast as she could. In her haste, she dropped the last bullet. Something told her to look up. A few yards away stood a young girl—face streaked with soot and blood, a dark plait of hair hanging over her shoulder—heedless of the bullets and destruction around her. Her thin half-smile held no warmth. Her eyes held no fear, no tension, no excitement, only death. Staring into those eyes, Miranda sucked in a breath. She finally understood Beryl's obsession.

Beryl had her back to the girl.

A blade glinted in the girl's hand.

"We are Azrael," the girl said, her voice slicing through the din of the battle around them.

Beryl turned.

The girl raised her knife.

Miranda slammed the magazine into her gun and fired.

The girl fell back a step, grimaced, and straightened. Smiling that half-smile again, she stepped forward.

Miranda shot again.

The girl spun left and fell, dropping her knife. The blade chittered harmlessly against the asphalt.

Miranda stopped her mouth with the back of her free hand, breathing hard, unable to take her eyes from the body.

Beryl squeezed Miranda's upper arm, gave her a nod, then took off.

Miranda couldn't move. A gentle touch on her shoulder startled her.

"Come on," Nick said. He led her to an autogiro where Beryl

sat "on guard" in the passenger seat. He gave Miranda a leg up into the seat behind Beryl and then climbed into the pilot's seat.

Moments later they taxied down the runway, the autogiro's wings vibrated, the blades picked up speed, and then they were airborne.

Chapter Eighty-Two

K ara made one last walk through the banquet dining room. The breakfast caterers had finally gotten the place cards in the correct positions. She stopped at the head of the table, Donald's seat, and placed her hands lightly on the arched back of the chair. The table sparkled with gold-trimmed plates and goblets. Towers of oranges, apples, grapes, and bananas in decorative bowls dotted the tables and scented the room. The room that would soon fill with powerful people. People whose support would launch Donald's political career. She had all but a couple in her hands already. She'd reel in the few outliers this morning.

"Lady Clarke?"

One of Donald's burly aides stood in the doorway. "Yes?"

"The First Apostle says you are to come at once."

She bristled inside and considered refusing. It was five o'clock in the morning, too early for such a summons. But a refusal would cause talk among the servants. Now was not the time for rumors to circulate about the first couple. "Of course." She swept across the room and followed the aide.

He led her down the hallways to the bustling office of the First

Apostle. There were a half-dozen councilors circling and clamoring at Donald. *So early in the morning?* Donald sat behind his massive oak desk, his only protection from the press of people. He ran a hand through his hair. *Not a good sign.*

"I beg your pardon, Your Reverence, but we have to do *something now.*" Lucas's face was splotchier than normal.

"I told you, I must— Ah, my Lady." Donald stood and came to greet her. He kissed her cheek and said, "Gentlemen, you'll excuse me for five minutes." His aides, two burly young men, shooed the councilors through the floor-to-ceiling double doors to the sitting room. The latch snapped shut. "Kara, we're ruined." Donald's voice and face reflected a level of strain that alarmed her.

She patted his cold, clammy hand and led him to the settee on the other side of the room. "Darling, I'm sure we can work out whatever is wrong, but I'm in the dark. What on earth is going on?"

"They're attacking." Low and gravelly, his voice reflected his tension.

She fought her overwhelming desire to shout and managed a restrained whisper. "Who's attacking who, Donald?"

He hunched forward, rested his elbows on his knees, and rubbed the back of his neck. "The apostates, the rebels, are attacking in DC, Charlottesville, Columbus, Ohio, everywhere."

"Well, that was stupid of them. They've spread themselves too thin. Weldon's Second Sphere will stop this."

"Dozens of Second Sphere are dead all over the country. They even attacked the farm."

A chill zipped down her spine. Her chest tightened. "But Weldon got away?"

"I don't know."

"What do you mean you don't know?" She stood and strode toward his desk. "I'll call him and find out."

"You can't."

She whirled and faced Donald. "What do you mean, I can't?"

"The phone lines are down."

"What?" Her voice was too shrill. She took a deep breath. *Weldon will be okay. He knows how to take care of himself.* She kept her voice low and deliberate. "How do you know all this?"

"Weldon sent a courier." Donald pulled a paper from his inside jacket pocket and handed it to her.

"*Urgent.* Rebels overran Ohio and DC Stations, attacking the Farm. You *must* go to Hog Island *now.* Can't guarantee safety until relocated."

Kara looked up from the paper at her husband. "I don't understand. Why didn't the Azrael stop this?"

Donald stood and circled the settee. "How do I know?" He gripped the wooden curlicue of the settee's back and leaned forward. "What do we do? What do I say to Lucas and the others?"

Kara's blood buzzed. Adrenaline heightened her senses. She squeezed the front edge of the soft velour settee cushion she sat on and rubbed the fabric with her thumbs. Focusing on something real helped. *How do we use this to better position Donald? He mustn't seem weak, indecisive. Declare a civil war? No. Civil unrest. Military law.* She forced the tension out of her muscles. "This is civil unrest at its worst. You'll talk to Everett immediately. He'll have to declare a national emergency and impose martial law. All citizens must wear their identity papers around their necks in public. Nonessential personnel must stay at home today—indoors. And he'll order a strict curfew of eight p.m." She stood and faced Donald across the settee. "Everett, President Bricker, must send in the National Guard. Our people, the people of this nation, need protection from this evil."

"Weldon says we should go to the island."

She put on her best I'm-not-worried face. "We will. After you talk to President Bricker, you need to make an announcement. You will reassure the people over the Fellowship radio, and then we'll leave. The people will know you warned the president, that you took action against this threat. You will be the apostle who saved our country from civil war."

The furrow in Donald's brow smoothed, his shoulders squared, and he stood taller. "John?"

One of Donald's aides appeared in the main office doorway. "Yes, Your Reverence?"

"Call the President. Tell him to clear his schedule for an emergency meeting. I'll be there in thirty minutes. Oh—"

The aide hesitated.

"And call for my car."

"Yes, Your Reverence." The aide scurried out of the room.

Kara went to Donald's side and stood on her tiptoes.

He bent, and they kissed. Lust tickled her parts. Excitement like this always tickled her that way.

"I love a man who takes charge," she whispered in his ear. "I'll make our excuses at the banquet." She stepped back. "Matthew," she called.

Matthew showed up in the doorway.

"Prepare His Reverence for a formal meeting with President Bricker. He leaves in ten minutes." She followed the young man out of the room. What would she say to the dignitaries who would be arriving soon?

An emergency situation was accurate, but not the tone she wanted. *A trauma for our nation? Not quite... Oh, of course. It is a trauma, and there will be victims who need our help. We'll reschedule after this situation calms down. It'll be a charity fundraiser.* Kara smiled. *Everyone loves a charity drive, especially when they can feel patriotic too.*

She went to her dressing room and changed into her gown designed for this morning. Too bad she'd wear it for so short a time. Her girl fussed with her hair, setting this curl and that with a rose-scented hairspray.

"Lady Clarke," the girl said and tweaked a curl at the back of Kara's head. "I heard about those awful attacks, and I'm praying for the country as hard as I can."

"Thank you." Kara gave a Madonna-like smile. "Our country

can use all the prayer we can give right now." *And who better to pray for the nation than the First Apostle?* "This is why the First Apostle and I will be secluding ourselves for a few days of fasting and prayer." *On a certain, well-guarded island.*

Chapter Eighty-Three

The public beach was as dark and deserted as Miranda had known it would be. The familiar scent of ocean air and the tingle of salt on her tongue did nothing to calm her jitters. Ethan, Hector, Nick, and the others waited with the autogiros in the parking lot. Man-made dunes inland and the windswept but smaller dunes on the bay side sheltered the lot and kept the men hidden. Only she and Beryl would take the walk.

Visible in the moonlight, the pier stretched from the beach parking lot across the rolling grass-tufted dunes, across the sand, and far out into the water. At the end of the pier, a blue navigation light blinked against the slate-gray sky. Miranda left her shoes on the pier and walked barefoot to the water's edge. Beryl wouldn't step onto the pier until Miranda reached the end of the public portion of the beach.

Ethan and Beryl had argued about who should go and whether borrowing the yacht was better than flying the autogiros across the bay. Beryl had argued that the autogiros would draw more attention. Ethan wasn't happy, but he had agreed the yacht would be a more stealthy vehicle.

Miranda wasn't happy either. She strolled southward, at the

water's edge, stepping over barnacle-covered rocks and bits of oyster shells. Hypnotic waves lapped the shore. Reflections of the moon made a silver ribbon in the midnight blue bay waters.

She didn't have to turn to see if Beryl followed. Beryl wouldn't hear of Miranda going by herself. Miranda would have to find an excuse to go to the house before they took the yacht to the island.

Lukewarm water lapped Miranda's feet, erasing her footsteps. If her parents' bodyguards caught her, they couldn't trace her steps back to Ethan and the others.

The stars and moon faded and the eastern horizon brightened. The dark finger of a rocky jetty reached out into the water and spurred her heart rate. It marked the edge of her parents' property. Miranda bent and pretended to examine the sand like a beachcomber. From here, the beach house looked dark. She scanned inland—were her parents' bodyguards there? If so, she hoped they stayed in the gatehouse. Of course, if the guards were there, her parents would be in the house. If they were, she had her gun—and Beryl.

She drew closer to the house and wished she were alone. Slipping away from Beryl to get her pearl earrings would not be easy.

The windows of the beach house mirrored the now pewter-colored sky. *It looks empty. Do I go inside now?* She glanced back at Beryl, her figure a shadow against the sand. Miranda sighed and crossed the sand to the boathouse.

She eased the door open and entered, gun first. A faint light glowed in the windows and below the bayside doors. The dinghy and motorboat moored in their berths and bobbed in the water that lapped at the pilings. The yacht's berth was empty.

"Step aside." Beryl's irritated whisper breathed across her shoulder.

Miranda moved out of the way.

Beryl entered, closed the door behind her. "Damn. Where's the yacht?"

"How should I know?" Miranda answered, her whisper as irritated as Beryl's.

"Double damn." Beryl gestured at the dinghy and motorboat. "Those two together won't hold everyone."

"I guess we will have to take the autogiros," Miranda said. She willed Beryl to agree and start back up the beach.

"They're still too loud." Beryl seemed disinclined to leave.

"Look, Beryl, I have to find something—in the house."

Beryl shook her head. "That would be stupid. It'll be dawn soon." She studied the motorboat. "Could that carry twelve people?"

"I don't know." Miranda pulled the photograph out of her hip pocket. "Look at this. That little girl is wearing the same earrings my father gave me."

Beryl looked at the photograph, then gave Miranda a so-what look.

"My earrings are inside. When we show my earrings and this photograph to people, they'll know he's a—a molester of children."

Beryl snorted. "Earrings prove nothing. The photograph is of a man holding a girl's hand—on a yacht. Nothing in that photograph says molester."

"But I have the same—"

"Miranda." Beryl seized her shoulders. "Are you still looking for proof? Your proof is only here." She thumped Miranda's chest. "And in the people who believe you. That photograph? You're seeing things that aren't there. We have to focus. People will die if we take too long."

Miranda's chest ached where Beryl had struck it and deeper. She stared at the photograph. It was as Beryl said. Her father held the little girl's hand. *Nothing more. Proof would make it so much easier...* She swallowed a hard, painful lump, a dense, dark mass that sank inside and weighed down her arms, her legs, her soul.

"What is the maximum number of people we can have on that motorboat?" Beryl's tone demanded an answer.

"We had eight people on her once." She tried to focus. *Could we squeeze four more on board without swamping her?* The dinghy had less wiggle room. Six would push it to its limits. "I think we can fit everyone on those two. It'll be tight, no room for extras. But we can get sixteen across to the island."

Beryl studied the two vessels, nodded. "Reduce the men in each vehicle by one or two, and we can carry enough weapons and ammo." She gave Miranda an approving nod. "That'll work."

"Do you remember how to pilot the motorboat?" Miranda asked.

"Of course I—" Beryl began, stopped open-mouthed, and cocked her head. She grabbed Miranda by the arm. "Listen."

The chug and burble of a large boat motor sounded near and was coming closer.

They crouched behind the door and waited.

The soft thud of a boat hitting dock bumpers signaled that the boat was moored at the end of her parents' dock.

"It'll just take a few minutes," Donald called. His rapid foot-steps rang on the deck, then became whisper-quiet when he hit the sand.

Miranda drew her Luger. *Four bullets, if I kept count correctly. It had better be enough.* She'd put her last magazine in back at the farm. She raised up and peered through the window. Her father disappeared through the kitchen door. She returned to a crouch and duck-walked to the door.

"Where are you going?" Beryl whispered.

"I'll distract him so you can get away."

Beryl shook her head. "Better to wait it out."

Miranda glared at Beryl. "I *have* to talk to him."

"*Talk* to him?" Beryl's incredulity sharpened her voice.

Miranda didn't answer.

"You are a fool if you believe, after all these years," Beryl spoke slowly, "that he'll admit to anything."

Of course, he'd deny it. But she'd know. She put her hand on the doorknob.

"Stop!"

Miranda glared at Beryl. "The only way I'll stop is if you shoot me."

Beryl had her hand on her holstered weapon. "Someone on the boat will see you."

Miranda gave Beryl a humorless smile. "I know a trick or two."

Chapter Eighty-Four

M iranda darted across to her mother's five-foot-tall "hedgerow" of northern sea oats. The sea oats concealed a narrow path between them and the fence that lined her parent's property.

She hesitated at the front edge of the hedge. There was open sand between her and the deck stairs to the front door. She glanced at the guardhouse. It was dark. *Vacant.* She dismissed it.

She peered up at the front window. Inside, swaths of dark and darker shadows painted the living room. *Father must be upstairs.*

She took a deep breath and bolted up the steps to the front door. In moments, she'd slipped inside. She gave a self-satisfied grin, pleased she hadn't forgotten how to sneak in.

She took slow, calming breaths, the way Beryl had taught her, and scanned the room. The familiar teal and orange color scheme was barely visible in dawn's shadows. Her father clomped around in his bedroom upstairs without regard to how much noise he made. She positioned herself in the center of the foot of the stairs. *Won't you be surprised to see me?*

Her pulse trembled in her throat. *Not good. He'll see me before he even reaches the stairs.* She sat on the sofa. He couldn't see her here, but she couldn't see him either.

She stood and banged her shin on the kidney-shaped coffee table. Reaching for her shin, she hit the tape recorder that sat on the edge of the table. She caught the recorder before it fell and held her breath. *Did he hear that?* She scolded herself for not noticing the recorder earlier. *Father always leaves it on the edge of the table.* Her lungs burned, and he still hadn't come to investigate. She sucked in air and lowered the recorder silently onto the coffee table's second shelf, hesitated. *He'll say something.* She pressed record.

She tiptoed across the room and stood against the sand-colored wall, next to the staircase. *Still can't see him.* But she could hear him better.

The thud of his heavy footsteps drew nearer, came down the stairs. She swayed a little, driven by the beat of her own pulse. She didn't dare breathe. A large, yellow and brown tweed suitcase appeared.

He took another step, swung toward the kitchen, and dropped the suitcase. "Miranda?"

She looked into his washed-out hazel eyes and forced a little-girl smile. "Hi...Daddy." Calling him that name made her stomach lurch toward her throat.

"You're alive." He pulled her to him in a tight embrace. "I thought we'd lost you." His tear-choked voice glanced off her.

His cologne filled her nostrils. She choked, covered it with a fake cough, and pulled away.

"Did they hurt you?" He scanned her up and down. "How did you get away? No. Never mind. Your timing is perfect." He took her hands in his. "We'll show everyone that the apostates are losing. We're beating them. We got you back."

The front door banged open.

"No," Beryl said, deadly calm. "We've got you."

"Beryl, no," Miranda cried.

373

"What is this?" he asked.

"This is me, taking you hostage," Beryl said. "We'll see how you like being a prisoner."

Chapter Eighty-Five

I f Beryl could have crowed, she would have. She squashed the urge to bounce on her toes and held her gun steady, trained on Donald's heart. "Move over to the couch—nice and easy."

Disappointingly, he did as he was told.

Miranda sidestepped to stand between the two wicker chairs with their aqua cushions.

"Go ahead, Miranda. Ask your questions."

"What are you doing?" Miranda gaped at her. "You were supposed to stay in the boathouse, where you'd be safe." At least she'd kept her gun trained on Donald.

Beryl gave Donald an evil grin. "I am safe. He isn't." If she'd had any other prisoner, her position would be untenable. Both the kitchen and the living room door were angled shots, and to cover them she had to stand with her back to the staircase. But Donald, coward that he was, sat on the couch, his head in his hands, moaning. *He wouldn't have lasted ten minutes in Redemption, much less ten years.*

She glanced at Miranda who gave her a pathetic, stricken look. *Why isn't she asking her father all her questions?* "Speak up, Miranda." Beryl focused on Donald. "You'll answer her questions, then tell us how many Azrael are on the island and what they're protecting." Silence. "We don't have all day, Miranda."

Miranda sucked in an audible breath.

"Wrong. You don't have another minute," Weldon said.

Beryl whirled to face Weldon, and so did Miranda, but they were too late. He'd come through the kitchen and had his gun trained on Miranda's heart.

Weldon stood centered behind the two wicker chairs. He motioned at Miranda. "Give me the gun."

Miranda swallowed and glanced at Beryl.

Beryl nodded.

Weldon smirked, took Miranda's gun, and aimed it at Beryl.

Miranda gave Beryl a sidelong glance.

She's going to try a spin kick. It won't work. He's out of her reach. Beryl gave an almost imperceptible shake of her head. Every instinct she had told her to pull the trigger. But if she did, he'd kill Miranda. A tiny tremor shook her gun hand. *I can't be responsible for another Anna.*

"Put your weapon down, Beryl." Weldon showed no sign of a tremor or the slightest hesitation. He cocked his pistol, an older model Luger. The model with the extremely touchy trigger.

Ethan and the others will wait another two minutes, then they'll come looking for us. She took her finger out of the trigger guard, held the gun between the thumb and first finger of her left hand, and lowered it to the ground.

"Kick it to me," Weldon said. "And put your hands up."

She did. The gun screeched across the tile.

He bent at his knees, keeping his head up and his gun trained on Miranda. He tucked Miranda's gun in his belt, scooped up Beryl's gun, and aimed at Beryl.

Miranda blinked, a couple tears escaped, rolled down her cheeks. She blinked again, and the tears stopped.

"Donald, catch." Weldon tossed a pair of handcuffs.

Donald caught them.

"Put them on her." Weldon nodded at Beryl. "Hands behind

you, Beryl. And no tricks." He waved his cocked gun at Miranda.

"I won't try anything," Beryl said. "Un-cock your weapon." She allowed Donald to apply the cuffs, winced when he cinched them too tight.

"Donald, hold her." His gun waved at Miranda again.

Donald pinned Miranda's upper arms to her body, held her at arm's length away from himself.

Weldon laughed. "Good. Now——" He stepped toward Beryl.

Pop-pop-pop. Distant gunshots. Beryl's body didn't betray her, but her heart did flip-flops in her chest.

"My men found your friends." Weldon's fox-in-the-henhouse smile made her want to beat him senseless.

"Not my friends." Her voice sounded steady, trained by years in Redemption. *Ethan had no choice now. He'd have to save his men and get to the island without Miranda. Without me.* That was intolerable.

A radio crackled and went silent. *Sounded like…yes, Weldon has a walkie-talkie clipped to his belt.* The walkie-talkie crackled and went silent again. *A signal. Meaning what?*

"I'm going to lock Beryl up on the boat," Weldon said. "She'll meet justice on the island." He waved her forward with his gun.

She didn't like the way his smile broadened. *At least I'll get him away from Miranda.* She walked slowly across the deck, down the stairs, across the sand, and toward the dock. Weldon followed, but not close enough.

Kara stood on the dock. She clapped her hands. "You did it! Weldon, I could kiss you."

Weldon chortled. "And Donald has your daughter, inside."

"Miranda?" Kara's gaze went to the beach house. She started toward the house but blew a kiss to Weldon. "I'll reward you later."

"Don't forget," Weldon called to her. "We leave in——" He glanced at his watch. "Two minutes."

Beryl walked slower, playing the defeated woman. *I'm not going down on your terms.* The kitchen door latch opened. At the sound of it closing, she barreled toward the boathouse.

Chapter Eighty-Six

A scream bubbled inside Miranda. *He's going to kill Beryl.* She swallowed over and over until the scream retreated. Her hands tingled. *Father's grip.* He was cutting off the circulation in her hands. "Daddy," she said in a little girl voice. "You're hurting me."

"What?" He wrenched his focus from the kitchen doorway back to her. "Oh, I'm sorry." His grip loosened a little.

She stared at him, unable to understand. *How could he do that to his own sister?* "How could you, Daddy?" The question slipped out, and it wasn't about Beryl.

He blinked at her. "How could I what? Wage war against the apostates? Miranda, I am the leader of the Fellowship. It's my duty to protect my people." His grip loosened a little more.

"What about me? Who protected me?"

"Obviously, our Father did. It's a miracle you got home in time, free from the apostates at last."

She couldn't believe he was pretending not to understand. "I don't need protection from SABR, Daddy."

He looked puzzled. "We tried to save you, honey. Weldon

searched for you. We put out rewards." He shook his head. "None of that matters now. We have to leave."

Beryl was right. He'll never confess. Fine. "We can leave after Beryl is safe. You owe me." Jaw clenched, fists tight, she closed the space between them.

He moaned, low and aroused.

What? Miranda couldn't breathe. *Is he aroused? Oh, God. But—* "You can make Weldon let Beryl go. You do that, and we'll have some special Daddy-Miranda time, hmmm?" She rubbed her head on his chest, swallowed the urge to gag. She gave him her best puppy-dog eyes.

He licked his lips. "We have to leave. The President ordered me to safety."

She pouted. "But you're the First Apostle. You tell him and the Council and Uncle Weldon what to do."

"That's what I thought," he muttered. He gave himself a tiny, but visible, shake. "I'm the public face of the Council. I obey the president."

"You will obey him, Daddy—after you help Beryl." She leaned against him. "I know you love me." She tried to sound throaty, sexy, but it sounded stupid.

"I do, Miranda. I do." His hand touched the top of her head, slid down to her cheek.

She pressed hard against him and tasted bile.

He cupped her cheeks between his hands.

He's freed me. Now Beryl. "Please?"

"We have to hurry." His hands slid down to her shoulders and pulled her close. "I have to give the squadron a blessing."

She fought her rising nausea with the mental image of Beryl at gunpoint. She pinned him against the wall, slid her hands down to his buttocks and squeezed, hard.

"Miranda? Honey?" His voice trembled.

"I need you, Daddy." She made her voice purr. "Like you once needed me." She tugged his belt loose. "Make Weldon release Beryl."

His pants fell to the floor. "Miranda, what's your hurry?" He backed into the wall.

Part of her screamed in horror, the other part of her reveled at his weakness and circled it like a shark. "I missed you, Daddy. Didn't you miss me?"

"Miranda, we shouldn't be doing this."

"Why? Don't you like me anymore?" She caressed his boxers and felt his bulge. She couldn't bring herself to put her hand on his skin. Not even for Beryl. Contact with the thin fabric between her skin and his made her stomach writhe. Its sour contents burned the back of her throat.

"We have to leave." But he put his hands on her waist.

"We can. After you order Weldon to let Beryl go." *Please, God, make him give the order.*

"My ten minutes are almost up." He swallowed. "Weldon and I have to be there for muster. And I have to bless them."

"You don't like my haircut, do you?" Miranda pouted again. "You used to love stroking my hair, my body."

"We have to wait." His tone sent a new wave of nausea through her.

"You don't like me anymore. It's because I grew up, isn't it? Irene grew up too, didn't she? Is little Sandra too big now? Is that why you have to visit the little girls in Quantico?"

"Yes, no, I—I never touched Sandra. It's not what you think. Those girls need—I can't—" His hips pressed against her.

She wrapped her fingers around his boxer-covered manhood. "You said you *needed* me to help you. Remember?"

"Of course I remember, and you did help me, and I—"

"Now I need your help," she said. "Order Weldon to free Beryl."

"Sweetheart, I can't. Not right now. We can—we can—help each other—there."

Her grip tightened with every depraved word he uttered.

"Not now—I can't—I have duties." He groaned, whether

from pain or something else Miranda couldn't tell. "The decanting—I have to—be there."

"You hurt me, Daddy. You can make it up to me. Help me help Beryl." She had to make him want to help Beryl. She fluttered her eyes, leaned into him more, and gripped him more firmly.

"You ran off the stage when Ryan proposed. We were concerned about your state of mind. So I signed the Redemption papers—"

What? She'd meant— *But he*— A vile blackness rose from deep inside her. Her fingers clenched until her knuckles strained to burst through her skin.

"Miranda? You're hurting me."

"Not half as much I'm going to." Her voice rasped. Every muscle in her body tensed, ready to use those close-personal fighting techniques Beryl had taught her.

"Well, well, well. If it isn't our long-lost daughter returning to her roots."

Miranda released her father and whirled to face her mother.

Kara stood in the doorway between kitchen and living room, arms folded across her chest. She gave a pointed glance up and down Donald, then gave Miranda a terrible, knowing smile. "I always knew you had Clarke-Lancaster blood in you. I was right, wasn't I?"

Chapter Eighty-Seven

Miranda stood cold—stone—still, more frozen-in-place than a statue.

"You thought you needed to find love." Kara tsk-tsked. "You had it all along, didn't you?"

Buzzing filled Miranda's ears. The floor swayed.

Kara shrugged. "Ryan will get used to it. In time." She glanced at Donald. "Pull up your pants, dear. We've business to discuss." She gestured toward the chocolate-brown couch. "Shall we?"

Donald dressed hastily and sidled past Miranda to sit in one of the wicker armchairs. He held one of the tangerine and aqua throw pillows in his lap.

Miranda couldn't move.

"Miranda, what's wrong— Oh. You want a welcome home?" Kara strode to Miranda's side and gave her a perfunctory hug. "Darling, of course we're glad to see you, that you escaped those horrible apostates without harm." She wrapped an arm around Miranda's shoulders and forced her forward to sit on the sofa next to her. Kara kept her arm locked around Miranda. "The doctor said your experience would traumatize you and you would need to talk about it in your own time. But darling, we don't have the luxury of time. People are dying."

Gunshots in the distance punctuated her statement. Miranda flashed on the image of Sarah's limp body, of Gert lying in the street, of the carnage at Quantico. *Nick and Hector and—* Her heart stuttered with every gunshot. She closed her eyes and pushed away her fear and the continuous sounds of gunfire. Opening her eyes again, she noticed her mother's too-smooth expression. She doubted if her mother had ever known anyone who had actually been killed.

A gunshot sounded close, really close. Miranda glanced involuntarily toward the kitchen.

"Looking for Beryl, dear?" Kara squeezed Miranda's shoulders. "Don't worry, she's in Weldon's capable hands. We're worried about you. The doctor says finding out we had lied about your aunt's death confused you. Darling, we did that to protect you. You were a little girl. You didn't need to know that your aunt was a murderer and a traitor to our country. And it wasn't going to be a lie. They gave her the death penalty. The Prophet was too —took mercy on her and commuted the sentence. A sin Weldon will rectify."

"Life in Redemption isn't much better than death," Miranda muttered.

"If that—woman—hadn't kidnapped you, you would've been preparing for a wedding next week."

A date was set?

"Instead, we have to—take a sabbatical. Don't worry." She patted Miranda's hand. "It's only temporary." She looked at Donald. "Darling, did you get the suitcase from beneath our bed?"

"Right here." He crossed the room and picked up the large, striped tweed suitcase.

Bang! This time she was certain. The gunshot came from the direction of the boathouse. Miranda tried to stand.

Kara's arm around her shoulders tightened.

Another shot split the air. In the moment between heartbeats, silence stretched far longer than minutes or hours. The boathouse door banged shut. The sound crushed the air out of Miranda's lungs. Beryl would never cause that much noise.

The kitchen screen door banged open and shut. Maybe Beryl was trying misdirection?

Weldon appeared in the doorway, his face flushed. "She tried to get away, but I *got* her."

His boast made Miranda weak. Her mother released her. Miranda sagged into the sofa's cushions. She hung her head, unable to bear looking at Weldon.

"You killed Beryl?" Kara rushed to Weldon's side. Her joy and relief shredded Miranda.

"I did." Smug, self-satisfaction filled his voice. "She's growing cold on the deck of the yacht's berth."

"I want to see." Kara pulled Weldon into the kitchen. The door slammed behind them.

The slam rang in silence. *Silence. The gun battle is over too.*

Miranda swallowed a sob—it sounded like a hiccough. *Beryl's dead. Who else? Hector? Nick?* She wrapped her arms around herself, not seeing and not hearing, rocking back and forth.

Slowly her gaze focused again on the lower shelf of the coffee table, to the recorder, still running. She glanced at her father through her lashes. *Where is he?* He stood in the kitchen doorway, looking toward the boathouse. She placed her elbows on her knees and covered her face with one hand. She watched him as she reached for the tape recorder and eased the stop button down.

Donald turned at the sound of the tiny click.

She covered her face with both hands, peeked through her fingers.

He scanned the living room, shrugged, and turned his back on her, craning his neck, peering at the boathouse.

She popped the tape out of the player and dashed out the front door.

"Miranda!" Donald cried.

She ran up the beach, toward the now-silent gunfight.

Chapter Eighty-Eight

M iranda flew across the sand that sparkled in the growing
sunlight. The pier was a dark line in the sand. She
scanned the beach for signs of the SABR team. Not a man,
woman, or rebel was in sight.

Her feet threw clods of wet sand behind her.

She drew nearer and nearer. The pier stood vacant.

She prayed desperate prayers for Nick's safety, for everyone to
be safe. She dashed under the pier into deep shadow and stumbled over something large and soft yet firm. Landed flat on her
face. Rising up to her hands and knees, she wiped sand from her
mouth and nose. Then the stench hit her: gunpowder, rotting
seaweed, and—sewage? The mixture made her eyes water. She
pinched her nose shut, turned, and gasped.

The man's face-in-the-sand body was only visible in contrast
with the somewhat lighter beach beyond. "Oh, no. Please, no."
She scrambled forward, crab-like.

Reaching for the body, she hesitated. Whose face would she
see? She touched him. No pulse, no breath animated his body.

She pushed and prodded. He rolled over.

She sucked in great shuddering gasps. *Not Nick. Not Ethan.*

Thank— A flush swept over her. How dare she be thankful? This man died because of her. She should at least recognize him. But she didn't. She searched his pockets and found nothing. He'd followed instructions not to carry any identifying papers on a SABR mission.

She closed his eyes, folded his hands on his chest, and searched the shadows. Her eyes had grown accustomed to the dark. Three men lay like rags piled on the churned-up sand, a sight made surreal by large blotches of black-as-blood sand.

One she didn't know but she recognized young Dayton from Lynchburg. Her eyes burned.

The third body lay facing away from her. It had a familiar shape. Her throat tightened. She crawled toward him. The closer she got, the deeper her hands and knees sank into the sand. Her breath seared her lungs. She knelt beside the body, a hand hovering over his shoulder. Teeth clenched on her lower lip, she touched him. The man's skin was cold, waxy. She pulled him toward her.

Hector's eyes were clouded.

A soundless cry ripped Miranda's throat. *Oh, God, what have I done?* She slumped forward, her chin on her chest, and rocked back and forth. *I'm sorry. I'm so sorry.* Her breath came in great, shuddering sobs. *Hector dead. Beryl dead. I should have stayed in the boathouse. It's all my fault.*

She pulled the cassette tape from her pocket and stared at it, aghast. Aghast at what she'd done, how she'd behaved, how utterly useless it had been. She threw the cassette. It flew up through the rafters high above her head and wedged itself into the crux between a brace and a crossbeam. *I can't even throw it away right.*

Shouts startled her. Fifty yards away, a group of men in suits hesitated on a rise dotted with beach grass. Miranda hid behind one of the pier's support beams. After a moment, she peered around the support. One man waved several other men inland. The remaining men moved in search-line formation, toward the pier.

She faced the beach north of the pier and froze. Another search-line moved toward her from that direction. She glanced back at the first group. Neither group had seen her yet. She flattened against the sand and army-crawled until the water lapped at her chin. She dove under and swam.

Chapter Eighty-Nine

Miranda surfaced, gasping for breath, choking on salt water. She flutter-kicked and rotated until she could glimpse the shoreline. About two pool lengths away, men came out from under both sides of the pier. One man pointed at the water. She dove and swam. She didn't bother to look at the shore the second time she broke the surface. After several quick breaths, she dove again. She fought the push of the incoming tide.

She didn't stop until she estimated that she was more than five hundred feet from shore. Treading water about a quarter mile north of the pier, she scanned the shoreline again. No sign of Nick or Ethan or the others. *Had they taken off in the autogiros?* She hoped so. No Second Sphere agents in sight either. She swam in a large circle and watched the beach. The shameful scene with her father replayed in her head. Her mother's words blazed through her.

Was mother right? Am I so much like them? A shudder racked her.

If only she could talk to— But Beryl was dead. Hector was dead. And if Uncle Ethan survived, he would never forgive her. She was alone, utterly alone. She lost her rhythm of stroke and breath and took in a big, salty gulp of water. Coughing and sputtering, she flutter-kicked in place until she'd cleared her throat. She rolled over to float on her back.

Father had said something about decanting wine and blessing the squad. What had he meant? She couldn't figure it out. *It meant nothing. Hector and Beryl died for nothing.*

Miranda took a couple of ragged breaths and tried again but it was as useless as—chasing chickens. *"You got quick, didn't you?"* Gert's voice sounded clear in Miranda's head. She stopped floating and tread water. *There's another way to look at this. The squad needed a blessing because—they were leaving on a dangerous mission?* Made sense. But why would the First Apostle decant, not bless, wine? *Maybe he's not decanting wine. But if not wine, what?* She had no idea. *"Pick and choose, Miranda."*

She watched the rising sun wash out dawn's vivid rose, purple and gold clouds. What if the incubators were never at the farm? What if Hog Island was more than a port? What if it was the final destination? What if decanting had something to do with the pregnant women or the babies they wanted to grow into Azrael? She raised her head, gasping for air. *What if her father had to decant the incubators?* She had to tell Beryl— Miranda bit her lower lip. Not Beryl. *I'm not going to be soft and silly about this. I'll be a soldier Beryl would be proud of.* Miranda stroked toward shore, determined to find whoever was left of SABR and lead a mission to the island.

Chapter Ninety

Exhausted, Miranda let the gentle swells drive her toward the shore. At the top of every swell, she studied the beach. *It's summer. People are always at the beach. Were they scared away by the gunfire? Or are there agents hiding, waiting for me?* Second Sphere Agents or not, she'd have to go to shore soon.

A man came out of one of the public restrooms at the north end of the beach. The glare of the early morning sun on the water made him unidentifiable. She couldn't even swear that he was a he. He paused at the water's edge and scanned the water.

Best not to take chances. She dove under the water and swam until her lungs burned and she had to resurface.

"Miranda? Are you out here?"

She spat out a mouthful of briny water. "Nick?"

"Yeah."

She tread water, bobbing on the swells until he reached her side. "You're alive! Are the others—?"

"Been watching you. And the Second Sphere. Couldn't get to you sooner. Follow me." He took a few strokes back toward the far end of the public beach.

Questions swamped her almost as surely as the salt water

around her. *Does he know about Hector? About Beryl?* She sure as heck didn't want to be the one to tell him.

When she caught up with him, he put a finger to his lips. He led her close enough to shore that her feet could touch bottom. Sand oozed between her toes.

He stayed crouched in the water for long moments, then motioned for her to follow. He stood. He was wearing briefs. She closed her eyes for a half a moment. *Now is not the time to shrink back with modesty.* She opened her eyes, focused on his upper body, and followed him.

Nick led her across the beach and disappeared into the public men's room. She hesitated at the doorway, decided to wait. His arm shot out, grabbed her, and pulled her inside.

"Oh." Fishy, stale urine odors made her breathe through her mouth. One porcelain sink and three urinals hung from the concrete-block wall she faced. She averted her eyes and pulled up short at the sight of Jack and Nick and Ethan and two others crowding near. "You're all here." *Dumb thing to say.* "I was looking for you. I need to tell you—" *There is no easy way.* "Hector and—"

"We know," Ethan said.

Miranda blinked, surprised. "You know about Beryl?"

"What about Beryl?" Jack cocked an eyebrow.

"She's dead."

"I am not." Beryl stepped out of a stall, buttoning the top button of her shirt, a man's shirt.

Miranda gaped at her. "Uncle Weldon said he killed you."

"Weldon is a liar." She rolled her left shoulder and winced. "And a bad shot."

"He took Mother to see your body."

"I played dead until he left, then rolled over into the yacht's berth and swam away." Her penetrating look would have made Miranda squirm in the past. "You said you had news. My death wasn't all, was it?"

"No." Miranda took a deep breath. "I know how to defeat my —the Fellowship."

Beryl searched her face. "Your parents told you something?"

"Sort of." Miranda glanced at Nick who finished tugging on his jeans. *What will he think of me?*

"Miranda, we don't have time—" Beryl began.

Ethan gave Beryl a searing look. "Let's hear her out."

Miranda took a deep breath and started talking, afraid that if she stopped she'd stop for good. "The yacht wasn't in the boathouse. It arrived while Beryl and I were inside, deciding what to do." She glanced at Beryl, who pruned her lips but didn't disagree. "My father went into the beach house. I followed him."

"And you allowed this?" Ethan's question of Beryl was more heated than Miranda had ever heard him sound.

"Beryl couldn't stop me," Miranda told him. "I wanted to—" Her ribs hurt from the knocking of her heart. "Confront him. In Redemption, I—"

"Cut to the chase, Miranda." Beryl's tone wasn't as hard as before.

The room swayed with her heartbeat. She focused on Ethan's third shirt button. It was baby blue. "He abused me. Sexually." She waited for reactions. No one said anything. The silence was complete as if everyone held their breath. She peeked up at Ethan.

His frown was drawn and dark, but he didn't say anything.

Jack studied his shoes or the sand on the concrete floor.

She braved a glance at Nick. Nick's expression of sympathy was almost more than she could bear. She looked away, refocused on Ethan.

"He'd just come downstairs when Beryl came in. Then Uncle Weldon came and took Beryl away." Miranda's voice shook. "He was going to kill her. I had to—convince my father to order Weldon to free her—" Chills rippled across her wet skin even though the room was unbearably warm. "I was desperate. I—" She took a shaky, shallow breath. "I—accosted him. Mother caught us before— But he admitted that he abused me, and other little girls. We can use that. Play it on the radio. Show people, Fellowship members, that the Fellowship leadership is corrupt."

Ethan shook his head. "It'd be your word against his."

She gave him a level look. "I recorded it, stole the cassette tape. It's under the pier."

"That's what you threw into the pier supports?" Nick asked. "That cassette tape?"

"Yes." She faced Nick, chewed her lower lip.

Concern etched a line on Nick's forehead. "This tape, you're okay with it being made public?"

She couldn't face any of them, so she stared at the crack in the concrete floor. "No, I'm not okay. I wish it could be—private. I wish—" She took a breath then met his look straight on. "It doesn't matter what I wish. What happens to me, what people think of me, isn't important. Too many people have died. We have to destroy the Fellowship."

"You're certain?" Ethan asked, peering at her.

Miranda locked eyes with him. "Yes."

Ethan turned to one of the young men. "Get that cassette tape. Take it to our friends at WRVA in Richmond. Talk to Barry. Tell him, 'The daisies are blooming.' Those exact words. Tell him this needs to air immediately and as often as possible. Go now."

The young man nodded and took off.

Nick opened his mouth to say something.

She held up her hand. "Let me finish." She lifted her chin. "My father said he was needed on the island for a blessing and a decanting."

Miranda glanced at the men and Beryl. It was plain that they didn't understand. "I think that was his delicate way of saying a birthing."

Beryl's expression hardened.

Ethan drew back, a strange expression on his face.

"Don't you see?" Miranda asked. "All those incubators were delivered to the island *and* are waiting for a hundred babies. They must have figured out how to make a hundred pregnant women give birth at the same time. It's going to happen any minute now. Father, Mother, and Uncle Weldon are probably on the island already."

"Oh God," Beryl said in a breathy voice.

Jack was pale. "One hundred different women giving birth to identical girls at the same time? That's not possible, is it?"

"I wouldn't have thought so before today." Beryl nodded at Ethan. "We need the autogiros. Now."

"Identical?" Miranda bounced a look between Jack, Beryl, and Ethan.

"I'll explain on the way," Beryl answered, already moving toward the door.

Ethan reached for the walkie-talkie clipped to his belt and whispered into it. "Ready for immediate pickup." He clipped the walkie-talkie back to his belt. "Everyone out to the parking lot. Get aboard and get airborne as fast as possible."

"What about the noise," Pete said.

"If we travel into the wind," Miranda said, "the ocean breezes will mute the noise to anyone on the island."

Jack objected, "They'll see us coming almost before we lift off."

"Let them see us," Miranda said. "The autogiros have no insignia. We'll head south, toward Cobb Island, until the last minute. Once we're over the ocean, we'll circle back to Hog Island."

"Has to work," Ethan said. He looked as grim and determined as Beryl did.

Four autogiros swooped across the sky and landed.

"I barely remember the island," Ethan said. "You?"

Beryl shook her head. "Miranda knows it well."

Miranda squared her shoulders. "I'll need a gun." Nick reached behind his back and gave her a pistol. Her fingers lingered a moment on his hand.

Ethan opened the door and nodded at her. "We follow your lead, Miranda."

THE WHINE AND CHOP-CHOP OF THE ROTORS WERE TOO LOUD FOR conversation.

They flew toward Cobb Island, then climbed to nine hundred feet and turned north. High above Hog Island, they spotted a water tower and generator shack on a hillock, the highest ground on the island. Her parents' yacht was moored in the bay, unable to navigate the salt marsh that lined the island's western shore.

Miranda pointed at the yacht's launch beached a dozen yards from a handful of the crumbling shells of abandoned buildings. Two of the buildings had a fresh coat of paint, and a huge, new Quonset hut nestled between the two restored houses. Clumps of scrub trees might have hidden small buildings or a group of men, but not many.

Miranda directed Jack to land on the spit at the south end of the island. Mostly saltwater marsh, the sandbar was barely long enough to land all four autogiros. No guards came to challenge them.

They gathered in the shelter of three scrub oaks and made their plan. Ethan led his team of four toward the power plant and water tower. Miranda led Beryl, Nick, and Jack toward the houses and Quonset hut.

Chapter Ninety-One

Kara winced each time Donald came close to bowling over the Chippendale piecrust side table with its Victorian-era porcelain lamp. It pained her that he could be so careless. She would never use any of these things in her own home, but they triggered sweet memories of her childhood. Weldon had done an amazing job of restoring and furnishing this island house. There were even sprigs of fresh lavender in a vase like her mother used to place every morning. The scent soothed her.

"We have to leave the country before it's too late." Donald paced away from the Chippendale.

"It's barely breakfast time," she said in her most calming voice. "The Second Sphere are on their way. Besides"—she waved her hand indicating the area around them—"we're safe. No one knows where we are, and we're surrounded by water, a highly defensible position."

"According to Weldon." The scorn in Donald's voice pricked her. "So far your brother has been ineffective at taking care of this problem."

She stood up. "Under the extreme secrecy with which he must

work, Weldon has done the best he can. You should not have stopped Beryl's execution ten years ago."

"And how would that look? Yes, folks, the First Apostle condemned his own sister to death."

He dropped into a chair, a cloud of dust puffed around him. "We'd be safer in South America." He put his head in his hands.

She blew out an exasperated breath. "We've got Azrael we must deliver, or we won't be safe anywhere."

"I don't know why I let you and Weldon make that deal."

The front door banged open.

"What the hell did you think you were doing?" Weldon made a beeline for Donald, grabbed him by the shirt collar, and pulled him to a stand.

"Weldon?" Kara rushed forward, put a hand on each man's chest, and tried to separate them. "What are you doing?"

"Did you hear what he said?" Weldon shouted, his face mottled and ugly.

"Just now?"

"No." Weldon gave her a crazed look. "To Miranda." He let go of Donald with a shove that sat him back down, releasing another cloud of dust. In two strides, Weldon reached and turned on the Cathedral radio that sat on the console table. Static filled the air, then Miranda's voice—

"You used to love stroking my hair, my body."

"We have to wait." Clearly Donald's voice.

"You don't like me anymore. It's because I grew up, isn't it? Irene grew up too, didn't she? Is little Sandra too big now? Is that why you have to visit the little girls in Quantico?"

"Yes, no, I—I never touched Sandra. It's not what you —"

The voices on the radio grew distorted. Kara swayed, dizzy.

Weldon sprang to her side, helped her to the sofa. She sat on the rough horsehair covering and didn't even complain.

The blasted radio kept playing the recording. She heard her own voice.

"You thought you needed to find love." Over the radio, the tsk sounded harsh. *"You had it all along, didn't you?—"*

"Ryan will get used to it. In time." Kara couldn't breathe. *"Pull up your pants, dear. We've business to discuss."*

The radio personality called for Donald's resignation, then asked for his listeners' opinions. *"Castration's too good for him—" "How dare she call herself a mother, much less a Fellowship member—"*

Kara clapped her hands over her ears. "Turn it off." She couldn't believe how wicked Miranda had been.

Weldon shut off the radio and faced her with the most defeated expression she'd ever seen on him.

Donald moaned and wept into his hands.

Outside, the early morning breeze rattled the shutters and brown pelicans squawked and cried.

Kara clenched her jaw and crossed her arms. *No one defeats Kara Lancaster Clarke. No one. Not even a daughter who has chosen not to be a daughter.* She took in Donald's state, then Weldon's. *Obviously, it's up to me to save this family.* She lifted her chin. "We'll need a strategic withdrawal. We'll go to Argentina. Our friends there will help us rebuild. It will take time, but with the right people backing us, we'll get the American people to forgive us our sins and beg us to return." She stood. "Have you found David?"

Weldon gave her a look she knew far too well.

Has the whole family gone crazy? What on earth could David be up to? "How long until Irene and her family arrive?"

Weldon glanced at his watch. "Last I heard, they planned to be here in about fifteen minutes."

Thank goodness. She closed her eyes a moment.

"What do we do about Miranda?" Weldon asked.

Kara gave Weldon an incredulous look. "Miranda has chosen her side. Her fate has nothing to do with this family." She paced to the window and stared out at dawn's pale rose and yellow that ribboned the bay waters. "Tell Doctor Locke he's moving. He can bring only the essentials." She faced her men. "Donald—" He didn't seem to hear her. "Donald! Quit your sniveling." She'd made this family what it was, she'd do it again.

Donald took a shuddering breath and raised his head.

"Tell the captain to chart a course to Argentina. We leave in—"

"Doctor Locke will want a couple of hours or more." Weldon's tone almost rose to his old sarcastic self.

"We'll leave in half an hour."

"Without David?" Donald asked in a strained voice.

She stood straighter. "If we must." She faced Weldon. "Tell the doctor and the captain they've got thirty minutes. Not one second more."

Weldon charged for the door.

"Weldon."

Hand on the door, Weldon stopped and faced her.

"Miranda is a traitor. Kill all the traitors. Especially Miranda."

Chapter Ninety-Two

Miranda peered through the beach grass. As they'd thought, two of the seven buildings were habitable. One of the houses was a long, flat-roofed, single-story building. The three-story Tudor, not more than three hundred feet away, was where Miranda figured her mother would stay. From a distance, it looked weathered and old, but close-up the painted illusion showed. Its brick-raised foundation pillars were intact. The shutters hung properly, and the railing of the widow's walk around the cupola was unbroken.

She glanced at her watch. With every passing second, their chances of detection grew. But they'd agreed to give Ethan and his team ten minutes to position themselves at the generator shed and the water reclamation plant and tower. Only two minutes to go. *How does Beryl stay so calm? Nick and Jack too.* Miranda couldn't swallow, her mouth was so dry.

Her parents wouldn't be alone. Weldon was here, somewhere, and at least some of the pregnant women had to be inside. Bodyguards, Second Sphere agents, and Azrael had to be here too. All Miranda and the others had going for them was the element of surprise.

She glanced at her watch again and signaled "go." She darted for the front door. Nick followed. Beryl and Jack took the back.

The door wasn't locked. Its well-oiled hinges sighed. She sidled along the half-open pocket doors to the front parlor and took a quick peek into the antiques-filled room. Vacant. She walked through to be certain. Nick checked the dining room on the right side of the stairwell. She met Nick in the modern-looking kitchen.

"Clear," he whispered.

Footsteps clacked on wooden stairs. Miranda and Nick exchanged glances and hurried toward the front of the house.

Coming down the stairs was none other than her parents shepherded at gunpoint by Beryl. Jack followed Beryl.

"Look who I found," Beryl said. "I was going to shoot them, but I decided you might want that honor."

Miranda's pulse drummed in her throat. She backed up, her gun surprisingly steady.

"Thank goodness you're here, Miranda." Kara glided down the stairs and advanced toward Miranda. She held her head up, but there was dried blood in the corner of her mouth and she had a puffy lower lip.

Donald held a bloody kerchief to his forehead and had a purpling and swollen-shut eye.

"What happened to them?" Miranda asked without taking her eyes off them. She backed up, leading them into the front parlor.

Nick slid the pocket doors all the way open and entered the parlor first. He positioned himself near the velvet-curtained window and trained his gun on Kara and Donald.

"They needed a little persuasion to tell me what I needed to know." Beryl didn't sound the least bit repentant.

"You couldn't wait until we searched the other buildings?" Miranda hadn't intended to speak aloud.

"No, Miranda. In case you've forgotten, we have a mission." Beryl glared at her.

"Beryl has been locked up so long she doesn't know who we

are," Kara said. Her swollen lip exaggerated her pout and made her typically precise enunciation mush-mouthed. "Tell her."

Miranda exhaled a sharp breath. "Tell her what, Mama? That you lied to the entire country about the purpose of the Better Baby Contest?"

"Miranda, whatever are you going on about? I never lied about the Better Baby Contest. The contest helped thousands of parents raise better babies, healthier babies."

Miranda waved her parents to the camelback sofa. "The parents of children you put in the Azrael project might say differently."

"We helped those poor parents." Kara sat, her back ramrod straight, and smoothed her skirt. "Their children weren't normal, they were never going to be normal. We found a greater purpose for them." She raised her head and aimed a defiant look at Miranda. "There is no shame in serving our Lord."

Beryl snorted. She and Jack stood, blocking the doorway.

Dumbfounded, Miranda had to take several deep breaths before she could speak. "You don't get it, do you? You set those children up for abuse. You made them murderers."

"The Lord's work is a burden and a joy."

Miranda's blood roared. She squeezed the grip of her pistol. Her trigger finger twitched. "Was it a burden or a joy to watch Father abuse me?"

"Miranda? How dare you talk to me that way?"

Miranda pushed her gun hand out and took two slow steps toward her mother. "You didn't even try to protect me, did you?"

Kara averted her face.

Miranda froze, surprised. *Mama's afraid.* A chill scuttled down Miranda's spine. She wasn't sure she liked it. She gave her mother a tight smile. "I don't need you to protect me anymore, Mama. And no one—*No. One.* Will ever hurt me like that again."

Kara opened her mouth.

Miranda shot her mother a you-dare-you-die glare.

Kara sighed and pressed her lips closed.

403

"Are you going to shoot them or talk them to death?" Beryl asked.

An edgy twitchiness filled Miranda. *Watch it, I'll shoot you.* She bit her lip and huffed until she could control herself.

"You aren't going to shoot them, are you?" Beryl's incredulous look made Miranda's stomach tighten tighter than a stopper knot.

"Whether I do or don't is *my* decision," Miranda said, meeting Beryl's gaze without flinching.

"If you don't have the stomach for it—" Beryl shot a hate-filled look over Miranda's right shoulder and took a step forward.

Miranda blocked Beryl's approach. "Did they tell you where the pregnant women are?"

Beryl didn't take her eyes off Miranda's parents.

"Focus, Beryl," Miranda said in her most Kara-like command. "You have one job to do. Where are the pregnant women?"

Beryl blinked at her, made a visible effort to re-focus. "There are no women."

"What?" Miranda gaped at her.

"We're in the wrong place, again?" Nick asked.

"Right place." Beryl nodded toward Kara and Donald. "They say they grow them in containers."

Miranda couldn't tell if Beryl believed that or not. "Jack?"

"I'll believe it when I see it."

"Then go." She glanced at Nick. "All three of you. Do what we came here to do. I'll take care of them."

"I'm staying." Nick planted his feet shoulder-width apart. "You need backup."

Beryl strode to the door, but a moment before she touched the knob, the door opened.

"What the hell?" Weldon exclaimed.

Bam! Beryl's bullet hit him center chest. He jerked.

Air whooshed out of Miranda as if she'd taken a punch in the stomach.

Kara screamed and lurched toward the door. Donald held her back.

Beryl fired again and again.

Weldon's face went slack, then his body. He fell half in and half out the door.

Kara kept screaming.

Guns still in hand, expressions neutral, Jack and Nick hadn't moved.

Beryl spun and aimed her gun at Kara.

Kara gasped and fell silent.

Miranda stepped between Beryl and Kara. "I said I'd take care of this."

Beryl slowly changed her focus from Kara to Miranda to Weldon. She kicked Weldon's body savagely. "That's for Ethan." She kicked him again. "And Gert." She kicked him twice. "And that's for my Anna." Then she walked away.

Chapter Ninety-Three

Anna searched for Uncle first. She picked her way through the twists of blistered metal and smoldering puddles. Scorched earth was all that remained of her flower garden. *They invaded our home.* The thought pricked like a thorn.

Across the compound, she'd found every building touched by ruin. At first glance, some appeared to have been spared. When she looked closer, she saw the broken windows and ransacked offices. Flames in other buildings still licked the sky. Death's foul, cloying odors assaulted her, burned her nose. Heavy gray smoke hung over everything, muddying the morning sky as if even the sun choked on the thick air.

Anna searched until she was satisfied that Uncle wasn't one of the stinking bodies. Azrael's hot, rage-filled breath seared her throat. All those souls destroyed—all that power wasted. Now she had to know if the little ones had survived.

The hospital was as ruined as the other buildings. The stench of death etched her resolve for revenge even deeper. She pointed her tactical flashlight at the floor and stepped over bodies of nurses and doctors she had known since birth. Debris and more bodies littered the stairs.

She paused outside the doors to the little sisters' ward. No living sounds came from within. The roaring and ripping inside her chest warned her of what she would find inside. The broken bodies of the little sisters filled Azrael with a ravenous need for vengeance. A scream rose from deep in her chest, shot through her throat, and blasted from her mouth.

Anna raced downstairs with a speed she didn't know she had. Azrael's determination and desire drove her faster. She reached the autogiro field and fell to her knees. Rubble and broken auto-giros littered the concrete runways. Oily smoke tinged with kerosene added new injury to her nose and lungs. Azrael nudged her forward, searching until she spied the partially collapsed hanger building at the farthest end of the airport.

Riddled with small and large holes, the metal siding leaned. The building resembled the shape Aunt Allison called a parallelo-gram. The doors wouldn't slide open. She rammed the left door with her shoulder. The metal rang and shook. The doors remained closed but not unmoved. A gap had opened at the bottom center of the door. She'd been told that her upper body strength was remarkable, but it wasn't enough to force the door open. She needed a tool, a pry bar. She found a four-foot section of metal pipe about fifty feet away.

She wedged the pipe in the opening and moved the door a little more. Repositioning the pipe, she tried again. The doors sprang open. She landed on her butt. The metal building rumbled. She scooted backward and waited. The rumbling faded away. The building remained erect at its crazy angle. Shining her flashlight inside, she spotted an older model autogiro with a spare rotor through the windshield. Azrael urged her inside.

The windshield was the only visible damage. She cleared debris from the path to the doors and pushed the autogiro outside. Outside, she did a more thorough inspection. Azrael crowed with delight when the engine coughed once, then roared. All Anna had to do now was clear enough runway for takeoff.

Chapter Ninety-Four

Miranda stared at Weldon's dead body. Something heavy sat in the pit of her stomach, but it wasn't grief or hatred or anything she could identify. *Shouldn't I feel something?* Her mother's grief streamed down her face.

Kara pulled away from Donald. She perched on the edge of the sofa, not bothering to wipe her tears. Donald patted her shoulder ineffectually.

Miranda watched as if she weren't related to them, as if they were total strangers, as if they weren't real at all. Her finger rested lightly on the trigger of her pistol. *I could end them right now.*

Her father fixed on the barrel of Miranda's gun. Her mother glared in her best disappointed-in-you face. Miranda didn't waiver.

"What did we do to make you treat us this way?" Kara demanded.

Miranda's vision clouded. Already taut, adrenaline-fueled muscles knotted tighter, turned her hands to stone. She wanted to pull the trigger. Wanted to riddle her parents with fear and hurt and anger. Wanted bullets to rip through her mother's body. Wanted to kill her father piece by piece. "You—" She couldn't unclench her jaw. Her breath huffed through her teeth. The haze that fogged her vision robbed her of speech, obliterated clear thoughts.

Nick stepped close. "Are you all right?" he whispered.

She inhaled a sharp, short breath. His words, his concern, shook something loose inside. Her vision cleared. She wiped her dry lips with the back of her free hand, then aimed a brief smile at Nick. "I need to be alone with my parents."

Nick didn't say anything for a moment.

Is he going to argue?

"I'll be on the other side of the door." He managed to make it sound like a threat and a promise.

The pocket doors behind her thrummed, then clicked shut.

"If I killed you both, no one would blame me," Miranda said. *Would I?*

Kara squared her shoulders and lifted her chin. "Then get it over with."

When did Mama's tears stop? "Did you recognize when you stood at the point of no return?" *Did I say that out loud?*

"You have no idea what I went through." Kara raised chin a little higher. "I had no choice."

A tremor swept through Miranda. *I said something like that. Does that make me like Mama?* She suppressed a shudder. That was an absurd question. *How can I not be like Mama?* She'd rather be like Beryl. Her memory replayed Beryl kicking Weldon's body. *Is that who I want to be?* "No," she said aloud.

"There's always a choice. It's the choices you make that reveal who you are." Gert was right. For once, Miranda saw past her anger and confusion. She remembered family birthdays and Christmases, unreasonable rules and punishments, and never wanting for food or shelter or clothes, and she knew what she'd do. "Stand up."

Her parents exchanged glances. Donald stood, took Kara's hand, and "helped" her stand. Holding hands, they raised their chins and faced her.

She waved the muzzle of her gun. "Outside."

"Where are we going?" Kara asked.

"Move."

Still holding hands, they walked slowly past her.

Miranda kept her gun trained on them and followed them. "Open the door," she ordered.

Her father slid the doors open. Nick blocked the doorway, a puzzled look on his face.

"I'm not Beryl, and I won't be my mother."

Nick smiled broadly. "What are we doing with them?"

"Exile."

"What?" Kara whipped her head around and gaped at Miranda.

"Eyes forward and keep moving," Miranda told her.

Kara opened her mouth, closed it, and moved forward. After a few unsteady steps in the sand, she bent and carried her high heels the rest of the way.

"Nick, I need you to go ahead and secure the yacht."

He grinned and saluted her before dashing ahead of them.

By the time they reached the marsh, a crew member waited in the launch. The rest of the crew, Irene, and Felix stood at the brass railing under Nick's watchful eye and unwavering gun.

"Mama? Daddy? Miranda?" Irene shouted, surprised at first, then outraged. "I don't understand. What is going on?"

Miranda didn't reply until the launch crossed to the yacht and she'd followed her parents aboard. "You have a choice, Irene. Exile, never to return to America, or surrender as a prisoner of war."

"War?" Irene took a step toward their parents.

"Stay where you are," Nick warned.

She stopped but cast frantic glances from Kara to Donald, to the muzzle of Miranda's gun, and the muzzle of Nick's gun. "Do you want us to surrender, Mama? Daddy?"

Donald drew himself up. "The First Apostle doesn't surrender."

Kara patted his hand. "Of course not."

Miranda scanned the faces. "Where's David?"

"Probably a prisoner or dead," Kara said. She glared at Miranda as if Miranda were personally responsible.

"Anyone who wants to stay, move to the shore now, or join my parents in exile,'" Miranda said.

Several members of the crew hurriedly crossed the boarding ramp and stood on the shore.

Kara gripped the brass railing and looked the other way.

Miranda motioned the closest deckhand to the gangplank. "Prepare to get underway." She waved her gun at another deckhand. "Hoist the tender."

The deck hands looked to their captain.

The captain nodded.

The deckhands went about the business of preparing the ship for a voyage. At Miranda's order, Nick took her parents, her sister and family, and the interior crewmembers into the dining salon and secured them there.

"Let's chart a course." She motioned for the captain to climb up to the pilothouse first.

The teak and burled wood command center held the captain's chair, the ship's wheel, and an array of technology to help the captain pilot the boat. They mapped a course two hundred miles due east.

"Once you're out of US territorial seas, you can go whatever direction they want you to go," Miranda said. "Except back home."

The captain gave her a measuring look.

"We've got control of the Coast Guard," she lied with a straight face. "They will sink this ship on sight if you cross back into any of our territorial waters. Understand?" *It will be a miracle if he believes me.*

He looked out the window toward the mainland.

She flushed. She hadn't thought about the crew being exiled too. But she couldn't let them return to the mainland. She softened her tone. "You and your crew can radio family to meet you in the Bahamas or a *foreign* port of your choice."

"I understand," he said.

"Time to get underway," she said.

"Getting underway." The captain took the helm, and the yacht's motor burbled to life.

At the yacht's top speed, 45 knots, it would take four and a half hours to travel the two hundred miles. Miranda didn't have time to travel the distance with them.

After ten minutes, Miranda stood. "Captain?"

He looked up from his navigation board. "Yes, ma'am?"

"Can I trust you to stick to the charted course?"

"Don't worry, ma'am. I have no desire to become a prisoner of war nor visit Davy Jones' Locker."

"Have the tender prepared," she told him and left the bridge.

Less than five minutes later, she and Nick took off in the small motorboat that was the yacht's tender. She wasn't worried about the passengers on the yacht. They had rubber lifeboats if needed.

She piloted the boat a short distance toward the inlet to the bay, then let it drift. She watched the yacht hold its course out to sea without regret. She wasn't Beryl. And, thank God, she wasn't her mother. She'd done the only thing she could.

"That took a lot of courage." Nick watched the yacht too.

"No. It took fear. I'm terrified of what I'll become if I keep killing people." Immediately she wished she hadn't spoken. "I'm sorry, I didn't mean—you aren't—" She bit her lower lip.

He faced her with a sad smile. "I know who I am."

She took his hand and met his eyes. "It's a terrible weight, but you are a good man. Brave and loyal. The best man I know."

His smile broadened. "You don't know many men, do you?"

She couldn't help it. She smiled too. *Perhaps we'll have time to get to know each other better. If we both survive this war.* She pushed the throttle lever, and the boat surged back toward the beach house.

Chapter Ninety-Five

Crouching, Beryl ran across the beach grass. She flattened herself against the Quonset hut wall to the right of the window.

Tremors shook her. She gasped for breath. She couldn't believe it. She'd done it. She had killed Weldon. *Where's my victorious adrenaline rush?* She had fantasized killing him so many different times, so many different slow and painful ways. She'd never imagined not soaring with vindication.

Jack darted across the beach grass to the opposite side of the door.

A dull noise from inside reminded her that she wasn't finished. She rose and peered through the window. Two men in white lab coats sat at a small square table, concentrating on a chess game. A third man sat at a console in the middle of a collection of blinking lights, whirling tape drives, and large dials. From the depths of the bunker, a bell rang.

Beryl pressed back against the wall and held up three fingers.

Jack nodded.

The men inside laughed loud and hard. Wood scraped against wood.

She leaned toward the window again and caught a glimpse of the three men. They shrugged on environment suits, complete with battery packs. They moved to a large stainless steel door in the center of the back wall. One of them turned a wheel attached to the middle of the door. When he opened the door, a small cloud of vapor appeared and vanished.

The three men ducked through the opening. The door closed behind them. Beryl signaled Jack and unslung her HK automatic rifle from her shoulder.

In one fluid movement, she opened the front door, stepped inside the building, and swept the HK's muzzle in an arc covering the room. Not a soul in sight. Jack eased the door shut behind him. She waited until his rifle covered the left half of the room, then descended the six steps to the anteroom. Jack followed.

Buzzing, humming equipment and the odor of hot electronics filled the cramped room. Metal lockers labeled Environment Suits lined the north wall to the east corner. The computer and console filled half the room. A parka hung on a door in the northwest corner. The table and four chairs occupied the center of the room. Under the window rested an unmade cot. A coat rack with more parkas took up the southwest corner. The south wall, like the east one, was stainless steel and held a door that looked like it belonged to a walk-in freezer.

She glanced at Jack. He secured another piece of tape over the satchel charge he'd placed under the console.

She crossed the room to the door the men had passed through. It had a small window, and frost had formed on the inside. She squinted. The frost didn't quite obscure her view of the interior.

On an endless catwalk suspended from the ceiling of the bunker, one man checked small consoles at outcroppings along the catwalk. The other two men studied rows of stainless steel cylinders hanging on opposite sides of the catwalk. Below were at least one more catwalk and more cylinders. The three men, intent on their tasks, moved away from the anteroom.

Jack crawled out from under the console and stood. She caught his eye, nodded at the freezer door on the south wall, and got an answering nod. He headed to the door at the end of the console. He had to find and rig the power feed.

She put on a parka and entered the freezer, her gun held high. The medicinal smell was her first clue. In the center of the room stood a stainless steel table. The contours of the sheet spread over it suggested a recent death. A morgue. A countertop with upper and lower cabinets, also stainless steel, lined one side of the morgue. The opposite end of the room held another door with an interior latch handle that had to open into the bunker.

The dull *phfut* of a broken seal alerted her that the three men were returning to the anteroom. She eased the freezer door closed, flattened against the wall next to the door, and waited for them to sound an alarm. They didn't. *Jack must have found a good hiding spot.* She shivered and figured the three men had resumed their chess match.

She considered her choices. Her muscles stiffened more with each minute she spent in the cold. The size of the freezer door meant at least one of the men would be out of her sight for a few seconds no matter how wide she threw it open. During those seconds, someone would sound an alarm or pull a gun. Even if she were lucky enough that Jack appeared in time to give her backup, her chances were slim. That left the one way out. Her quick glimpse of the interior wasn't long enough but—

She sidled past the table with its burden. Something tugged at her parka. She whirled. The sheet covering the body swirled to the floor. On the table lay the bloodless body of an Azrael, chest and belly splayed, autopsy-style. A long, ugly scar wormed down the inside of the right lower leg. Beryl froze. *It can't be.* A tingle rippled across her skin. She reached across the body, lifted the corpse's left hand. The scar across the palm, the one Anna had gotten when she was nine, was there. Beryl dropped the hand and stepped backward into the wall of cabinets. Breath-robbing pain stabbed her with every heartbeat. She gripped the parka at her chest and rubbed.

It's Anna, the real Anna. My Anna.

Tiny holes riddled every inch of Anna's skin. "What have they done to you?" Beryl whispered. The pain in her chest abated enough that she could breathe again. She stepped up to the table and smoothed Anna's lifeless hair into place. "I was such a fool," she murmured. Her breath fogged in the cold air. "I didn't trust my instincts. I didn't take you out of that damn farm." She caressed the cold, waxen cheek. "Look at us now."

Beryl took a deep breath, steadied herself. She put down her HK and slipped off the parka and the rucksack underneath.

"It's my fault," she whispered. Pulling out a satchel charge, she taped it under the table. Then she taped one inside the cabinet doors and returned to the table where Anna lay. "All my fault," she said softly. She forced a phosphorus charge into Anna's abdominal cavity. "Mama will fix it." Beryl glanced at her watch and grimaced. *Time is passing.* She stroked Anna's hair one last time. Then she set the timer for fifteen minutes, flung the sheet back over Anna's body, grabbed her gear, and left.

The warehouse section of the Quonset hut stood open to the steel ribs holding the structure up. It was a tiny bit warmer here than in the morgue. A sea of undulating hoses and wires stretched from the ceiling to stainless steel cylinders as far as she could see. She estimated the building to be three hundred feet long. There could be five thousand of those cylinders in this place.

The platform she stood on was part of a catwalk system that ran down the middle and each side of the bunker. It stretched the length of the building, stopping in front of a large hangar-type door at the end of the building. On her left, stairs led down. She slipped the parka back on and sidled over to the door to the anteroom. A quick glance through the window revealed no one was around the chess table. Part of the console was beyond her scope of vision, but it appeared empty as well. The wheel in the center of the door moved. She leaped to the side of the door, flattened against the wall, cocked and aimed her weapon.

Jack's head and gun appeared around the edge of the open door. He grinned. He "walked" two fingers off his other palm and spread his hands indicating the men had left the building. He flashed ten fingers at her followed by another three fingers. *Thirteen minutes to detonation.* He focused on the interior. His eyes widened. He held up six fingers. She held up three fingers and pointed down. Within moments, she walked on the lowest of the three catwalks. Jack's footsteps overhead moved down the catwalk.

She eased through the wires and hoses that dotted the first cylinder like pins in a pincushion. There was a porthole. She rubbed her sweaty palms across the parka, then stepped in close.

A murky liquid made for low visibility. Beryl leaned in closer. The body of a child, curled into a fetal position, floated in the fluid. It stretched and straightened a bit. Beryl gasped. Expecting this was one thing. Seeing was another. The stabbing chest pain returned, but Beryl wouldn't let it stop her. She darted to the next cylinder and the next. Each held an Anna, a child. *Grown from what? A piece of my Anna? A piece of me?* She forced herself to examine the closest Anna.

She guessed the Anna's height to be about thirty-six to forty inches, as tall as the little girls in the hospital. If they had been recently decanted, they had an inborn desire to kill. *Like my Anna?* She glared at the unnatural child. *They aren't growing better babies. They're growing killers—like me.* "No more," she whispered. "No more."

She glanced at her watch, reached into her rucksack, and taped a charge to the first cylinder. Its timer would go off when the one in the freezer did. She taped charges to random cylinders, rigging the place for maximum destruction. It took six and a half minutes to reach the end of the row of cylinders.

At the end of the cylinders stood a large loading bay with a crane suspended from a grid of tracks on the ceiling. The man-sized door next to the hangar door looked tiny in comparison.

Four forklifts stood in a tidy row near the man-sized door. At the end of each row of cylinders, a large freight elevator stretched from floor to ceiling. Heavy power cables snaked from the ceiling to junction boxes on the concrete walls of a room next to the first elevator.

Beryl hurried to the power room. The sign on the heavy steel door read Danger—High Voltage. Inside she wrinkled her nose against the acrid odor of ozone. The static charge raised the hairs on her arms. The enormous breakers in the room had electric motors to operate them. Each had a satchel charge taped to it. *Jack, where are you?*

She stepped out of the power room and spied him at the opposite end of the loading bay. He crouched near a large stainless steel tank labeled **LOX**. *Less than five minutes to go.* She jogged to his side. "We don't have enough stuff left to blow a hole in that, do we?"

"Nope." He taped several satchel charges to the housing of a large gearbox attached to the valve of the **LOX** tank.

"Then what are you doing?"

Jack grinned. "Fixing a necklace for this baby." He picked up a long rectangular piece of metal: a fork from one of the forklifts. Grunting, he placed it against the charges. "Hold that."

"Is this necessary?"

"The explosions in the power room and on the waste tank will start a fire. The temperature discrepancy would rupture this baby if it got hot enough." He picked up a heavy chain next to him and wrapped it around the gearbox, fork, and charges. Driving a locking pin through a couple of the links, he secured it in place. "But when these charges go off, it'll blow the fork away from the gearbox. This little necklace will rip off the gearbox." Jack rattled the chain. "Then all that lovely liquid oxygen under pressure will rush out and mix with all the ammonia and other chemicals. When the mix reaches the right proportions—it won't leave anything bigger than a dust speck."

Jack picked up a timer, attached it to the charges on the gearbox, and set it. He picked up his gear. "In two minutes, first bang. In five minutes, we'll be flying with or without a vehicle."

Two steps away from the man-door, the piercing shriek of a warning Klaxon split the air. The building lights came up to full.

Beryl banged the door open and entered a brightly lit concrete culvert with steep sides—the loading ramp. Klaxons screamed.

"Run!" Jack yelled as he dashed past her.

Flinging off her parka, she ran. At the top of the ramp, the roadway leveled off and running was easier. She caught up with Jack and stole a backward glance. Four slender figures, dressed in black, came running around the corner of the bunker.

"Here they come," she warned and doubled her efforts.

She barreled toward the island's only stand of trees, hoping to reach it before the Azrael got within firing distance. A small group of men burst through the trees, coming at them.

"Get out of my way," an irritable baritone cried. A short, slender man with oversized glasses pushed to the head of the group, his dark bathrobe flapping behind him: Arnold Locke. "Save the cells first," he cried. "The cells—" Then he saw her.

She fired. The shot cracked through the air. Locke fell face-down and didn't move. The other men stopped, stunned.

Eric came running from the north, his gun blazing.

Behind her, shots rang out, whined past, kicked up sand around her.

Jack whirled, fired off a couple of rounds, and ran for the trees. "Don't stop."

The Azrael fired rapid bursts as they ran. Ahead of her, Eric stumbled and spun, firing a three-round burst past her. He squeezed off another burst into the sand as he fell.

She kept running.

A thunderclap roared.

She opened her eyes and stared at the cloudless blue sky. Ringing filled her ears. The air smelled of ozone and smoke. Jack's face appeared over her. He pulled her upright. Over his shoulder, a couple of Azrael struggled to their feet. They shook their helmeted heads and swayed or fell. Smoke and fire billowed out of the Quonset hut into the culvert. She lurched to her feet, stumbled. Jack tugged at her. Half crawling, half falling, she ran.

Ethan stood beside the only intact autogiro on the island's airfield. Jack waved his arm in circles above his head. Ethan hopped into the autogiro. Its engine whined. The front propeller spun.

"In you go." Jack grabbed Beryl by the shirt and tossed her into the tiny jump seat behind the pilot. He wedged himself between the seat back and the canopy. The autogiro rolled down the runway.

"We're too heavy," Beryl shouted.

Ethan shook his head, gave the engine full power, and kept the autogiro's nose pointed west. The overhead rotors turned slowly, then faster. They bounced off the airstrip, then rolled onto and down the dock. Seconds before they reached the end of the dock, he yanked back on the jump yoke. Thumping, clattering, growling, the autogiro clawed its way airborne.

Blinding white light enveloped them.

Chapter Ninety-Six

All Beryl could see was Ethan's head and the shrapnel-fractured canopy overhead. The autogiro rattled and clattered and shook with bone-bruising vibrations. She licked her lips and tasted something acrid and metallic. She swiped the back of her hand across her mouth and stared at her hand covered with blood. Hers?

Someone shouted something unintelligible. Beryl shook her head, opened her mouth, and hot stabbing pain lanced her ears.

"Keep the nose up," Jack shouted above the sputtering engine. "Hold that jump yoke."

Ethan strained to hold the lever back. Blood made his shirt wet and sticky. *His?*

The autogiro lurched and fell. Her stomach surged upward. She closed her eyes and braced for the crash. It didn't come. The little craft shuddered and climbed.

How close are we to shore?

The vibrations worsened. They twitched and bounced convulsively. She didn't know how Ethan managed to hang onto the wheel. Shoreward winds caught them. They soared forward, wobbling.

The autogiro jerked, then dropped.

"Up, you piece of—" Ethan said through his teeth.

The autogiro's nose rose. They leveled off. The engine sputtered and coughed, then died.

"We're going down!" Jack cried.

Her stomach rose to her throat. Her head felt light, snapped forward and back. The smack of a giant belly flop and the screech of ripping metal filled her. They bounced and hit the water again. Her head slammed against the pilot's seat. Pain blotted out everything.

Chapter Ninety-Seven

Miranda grinned. Sinking the tender in her parents' boathouse had been satisfying, in a perverse way. Nick was mad. He strode through the sand a few feet ahead of her. She quirked her mouth and shrugged. *He'll get over it.*

They walked inland around the pier. An explosion echoed across the bay.

Miranda clapped a hand to her chest, startled even though she'd expected it. She searched the horizon. White smoke billowed and covered the tops of the island's trees. *Where are Beryl and the others?* Nicholas pointed.

An autogiro rose from the island. The island flashed a brilliant white. *Boom!* Miranda's bones vibrated. She stumbled backward. The sensation passed almost as quickly as it came. She searched the sky for the autogiro. It skimmed the waves. It rose upward, then dipped low again. Miranda's muscles strained as if she could somehow help hold it aloft.

The autogiro dropped into the water with a giant splash.

Nick kicked his shoes off and ran into the water. Miranda pulled her shoes off, then hit the water running. Waves broke against her legs. The tide was coming in. That meant it would bash the autogiro against the shore. And Miranda had to fight the current every step of the way.

After the awful sounds of the crash, all had grown quiet. Even the ocean's steady murmur had muted. The briny wind carried sharp odors of hot metal, pungent fuel, and acrid ozone. When the water reached Miranda's waist, she dove in and stroked as fast as she could. She concentrated on the crumpled autogiro's dark outline. She watched for the tiniest movement, a sign of life, but saw none. Iridescent rainbows of spilled fuel gleamed on the waves.

A man-sized shadow rose out of the broken cockpit and pulled at another body. The shadow faltered and fell into the ocean, dragging the other with him. Miranda surged toward them. She reached the wreckage. The man had one arm draped over the side of the autogiro. His grip loosened, and he slipped into the water. Miranda plunged after him. Grabbed him by the shirt. *Ethan.* He had hold of Beryl by the neck of her shirt. Waterlogged, the two of them were too heavy.

"Nick, help!" She struggled to keep Ethan's face above the waves.

Nick appeared at her side. "Got him." He slipped an arm around Ethan's chest.

Miranda locked her arms under Beryl's and around Beryl's chest and frog-kicked toward shore.

Nick swam a little faster than she did.

With the tide's help, she reached shallow water quickly. She stood to pull Beryl ashore. The waves pulled the sand out from under her heels and pushed Beryl's limp body into Miranda. She stumbled.

"Ethan keeps asking for Jack," Nicholas shouted. "Have you seen him?"

"No," Miranda answered, huffing for breath.

A wave splashed Beryl's face. She coughed feebly.

"Beryl? Can you hear me? It's me, Miranda."

She coughed again, and then went quiet and still.

"Don't quit on me." Miranda clenched her teeth and pulled. Her muscles burned.

She dragged Beryl past the water line. Miranda sank to her knees, drinking in air, trying to catch her breath. Watery blood covered Beryl's face and streamed from a long gash down her left arm.

Nick had gotten only a few feet further than Miranda had. He stood bent over, hands on his knees and gasping for breath. Ethan lay at his feet.

Ethan roused and rose up. "Beryl? Jack?" Blood streamed from his face. He struggled to stand. "Got—to—find—" He saw Beryl. "She—alive?"

"Yes," Miranda said.

"You're hurt," Nick said. "Stay down."

"Where's Jack?" Ethan stood, took a couple of faltering steps. His left arm bent at a strange angle, and he dragged his left foot. His eyes closed, and his good knee buckled. Nicholas caught him and eased him to the sand.

"Do we have a first aid kit?" Miranda asked.

Nick nodded, waved his arm inland. "In the—autogiro," he said between gasps. "I'll—get it." He jogged up the beach.

Miranda checked Beryl's injuries: a nasty purple lump on her forehead. A pulpy place on the back of her head that seeped blood. A deep slice on her arm. Her wet skin was pale and cool, her pulse—rapid and thready.

Nick handed her the first aid box. "How bad is she?"

"Bad. We need to get her to a doctor, quick. How's he?" She nodded at Ethan, who lay on the sand with his uninjured arm draped across his face.

"He'll live," Nick said. "Fractured arm, leg, a broken rib or two—God knows how many cuts and bruises."

Miranda cleaned the cut on Beryl's arm and wrapped it with gauze.

Nick shielded his eyes and scanned the shoreline. "I'll walk the beach," he said. "If Jack—"

She gave him a wan smile.

He trotted along the water's edge, scanning the water.

She cleaned and bandaged the wounds of her two patients as well as she could with their meager supplies. Driftwood made clumsy splints for Ethan's arm and leg. She tied the last roll of gauze around the lower part of his leg splint. Ethan moaned. Beryl never made a sound. That worried Miranda.

Not long after she'd finished, Nick returned, alone. They didn't speak of Jack.

"Beryl can't wait any longer," Miranda told him. "We've got to get her to a hospital. Norfolk's the closest."

"No," Nick said. "Norfolk's too dangerous. We've got a hospital in Richmond."

"In Richmond? But that's—" *It doesn't matter. I trust Nick.* "How fast can the autogiro get her there?"

"In about an hour. But—" he protested. "It won't carry all four of us."

"Will it carry three?" she asked.

"Third one has to stand more than sit."

"Okay." Miranda nodded. "You take Beryl. She needs attention the soonest."

"I can't leave you and Ethan here. Someone might have seen the crash—"

"We don't have any other choice," she reminded him. "Even if we had another autogiro, I can't pilot one. I'll have to—" She flushed, remembering the boat she'd sunk. "Borrow a boat."

"I don't—" he began. He gave her a look that said he'd forgiven her for the sunken boat.

"I know this area. I'll find a boat and meet you in Richmond in four—" *Do I dare try to take Ryan's speedboat? Not a good idea.* "Up to five hours depending on the boat." *Three and a half if it's a speedboat.*

He hesitated, then nodded. "Make it to Richmond, you hear me?"

She looked him in the eyes. "I will. Let's get Beryl in the autogiro."

Nick rolled the autogiro to the edge of the parking lot, as close to Beryl as he could get.

Several long, sweaty minutes later, they had loaded Beryl. Nick climbed into the cockpit and reached for the door. "I don't like this," he said.

"We'll be all right."

"Here." He shoved his rucksack at her. "The radio is in this. When you get to Newport News, turn it on channel nineteen, and call for Teacher. You're Pupil."

"I'll call. I promise."

He stared at her, his expression unhappy, torn.

"Get out of here." She pushed the door closed and stepped back. She thought he'd refuse again. Instead, he lifted one hand, gave her a small salute, and revved the engine.

She watched as they rolled out of the parking lot. The autogiro's motor whined, moving it faster and faster down the road. The rotors *chop-chopped*, and the autogiro soared into the air.

Miranda returned to where Ethan lay. He had roused again. She coaxed him to stand. One of Ryan's old speedboat competitors lived two doors down from her parents' beach house. Ethan didn't look like he could walk that far. The Smiths' house next door was nearer.

She staggered under Ethan's weight. He was getting weaker. "Look, you can see the boat from here." The Smiths' fishing boat wouldn't get them to Richmond as fast, but it would do.

Ethan moaned, slipped out of her grasp, and collapsed into the sand. She glanced at the neighbors' house. It looked empty, but the owners or a random swimmer could show up any moment. Miranda knelt beside Ethan and whispered, "Let's try this again."

His eyes fluttered but didn't stay open.

Wiping her forehead on her sleeve, she calculated the distance: ten or fifteen feet of sand and about thirty feet of dock. She pulled his good arm over her shoulder and tried to pull him upright. "Come on, Uncle Ethan," she whispered.

"We've only a little farther to go, half a football field. You can do it."

He nodded.

Struggle as she might, she could not lift him to his feet. Finally, she eased him back to the sand. "We can do this." She bent at Ethan's head, locked her arms around his chest, and pulled. His arms slipped up over his head, out of her grasp. She sighed, grabbed his good arm, and pulled. Sometimes he could bend and push with his good leg. Slowly, they moved across the sand to the pier.

The pier was both easier and harder. His splinted leg and arm thumped and bumped across the boards. She winced at every noise, hoping she wasn't further injuring him.

Finally, she reached the *Sea Queen*, a twenty-two-foot utility boat with pilot and co-pilot chairs forward and a wraparound bench seat in the stern. She laid Ethan on the dock and tightened the *Sea Queen*'s stern and bow ropes until her fenders rubbed the dock. Miranda pulled and pushed Ethan to a sitting position against the boat. His eyes remained shut, his body limp. She climbed into the boat and tugged on his good arm again. Pulled until his head and arms dangled over the grab rail. She reached under his shoulders and pulled—he hung up on his belt. Miranda climbed out of the boat again and whispered, "Sorry." She grabbed him by the belt and seat of his pants, pushing him farther and farther until his own weight pulled him aboard with a thud. Hopping back into the boat, she straightened him out, cast off the lines, and pulled in the fenders. She went forward to the pilot's seat and lifted the cushion. *No key. Not under the seat either.* Miranda groped blindly under the dash. *Found it.*

She backed the boat away from the dock, reversed, and cranked the wheel hard. They sped seaward at full throttle.

The sun sat on the horizon. Gulls wheeled in the sky. She followed the channel buoys that marked the way safely between the islands. Worried, she cast occasional glances at Ethan's still form when she could. *I'm doing the only thing I can do for him right now.* She hoped it was enough.

Miranda ran the boat hard down Hog Island Bay and out into the Atlantic. Bow pointed south, she locked the wheel and checked Ethan.

He was still breathing, thank God, but his clothes were damp with salt spray and his forehead feverish. She took the stern bench cushion and put it beneath his head. Then she searched for and found a tarp in the storage beneath the seat. She spread it over him.

His eyes fluttered open.

She sank to her knees beside him. "Glad you're still with me."

He smiled weakly. "Where am I?"

"On a boat," Miranda said, "on the way to the hospital in Richmond."

"Beryl? Jack?"

"Nick took Beryl in the autogiro. We'll meet them at the hospital." She put her hand on his shoulder. *He's so thin.* "I'm sorry, we—didn't find Jack."

Ethan closed his eyes.

"Stay right here," she said and retrieved Nick's rucksack from the mate's chair. She took the canteen of fresh water out and gave Ethan a sip. He raised his head, swallowed, and then lay back down. He sighed and went limp. Miranda sucked in a breath and put her ear to his chest. *Still breathing.* She released her breath and rubbed the grit of salt spray from her face. *Four hours is too long.*

She returned to the pilot's seat and pushed the throttle past the red, maximum speed line. It took an hour to round Fisherman Island, an hour to cross Chesapeake Bay to the mouth of the James River, and another two hours to cruise up the James to Richmond. At full throttle, it ought to shave an hour off that time. If the engine would hold full-throttle that long.

The boat bounced along the waves. Salt wind whipped her hair. She checked Ethan every few minutes. He would open his eyes occasionally, wince when the boat bounced, and once asked for more water. Close to Fisherman's Island, she realized what she'd been missing. There were no fishing boats and no pleasure boats on the water. Her uneasiness grew. They had no *camouflage*. She sped the boat up, leaving Fisherman's Island far behind.

She piloted a direct course and pushed the engine past its safety margin. They made it to Richmond in a little less than three hours.

Nick responded to her radio call with directions to a certain boat ramp where he, an ambulance, and a medical team waited. Ethan was loaded into the ambulance, and it took off. Miranda finally had a chance to ask, "How's Beryl?"

"The doctors say she'll live, thanks to us. But she's got some serious injuries. Healing will take time." He smiled at her. "You're pretty good at this rescuing stuff."

She didn't know what to say. *Rescuing felt a whole lot better than fighting.*

"Maybe that's what you're supposed to do."
Maybe.

Chapter Ninety-Eight

K ara breathed in the rich aroma of her *café Americano* and surveyed the patrons of Café La Biela. It had surprised her that so many English-speaking Europeans lived in Buenos Aires. That meant she didn't have to learn the Rioplatense Spanish spoken by the Argentineans. And a recent military coup had tipped the scales in favor of a new Fellowship here. The people were colorful and hospitable and loud, and in need of saving.

A gust of damp, chilly air swept through the door accompanied by Irene's infectious laugh. She and Felix surrendered their wet raincoats and umbrella to Rodrigo, the *maître d'*.

Rodrigo escorted the couple across the restaurant. Irene exchanged greetings, and sometimes hugs, with acquaintances along the way. Irene and her family had acclimated to life in Buenos Aires quite well. Kara found that very useful.

Irene gave Kara a kiss on each cheek, then sat in the chair held by Rodrigo. "Brrrr. I'll never get used to winter in July," she declared.

"Good afternoon to you too." Kara allowed a slight curve of her lips to show she wasn't entirely put out. Irene and Felix fussed about discussing the menu and placed their orders. After Rodrigo left, Kara put down her coffee cup and asked Felix, "What did the governor say?"

Felix leaned back in his chair. "There's too much unrest still."

That's what I get for sending a henpecked husband for information. "It's been a year," she said, her voice more controlled than her knotting stomach. "What the Fellowship Council needs is strong leadership. Our leadership—"

"I'm sure you meant to say the First Apostle's leadership," Felix's voice was mild. He leaned back in his chair and crossed his legs.

"Of course that's what I meant." *Surely even Felix knows Donald always follows my counsel.*

"A year is nothing. The governor assures me he will endorse the Fellowship soon."

"Thank you for trying, Felix. I guess we must continue being patient." *I'll handle things from now on despite the confounded "Argentinian way."*

The waiter brought Irene's *café cortado* and those crisp croissants Argentineans loved. Felix got his usual, *un café*, black coffee.

"Mama—" Irene stirred her coffee. "Can't we settle down? Be happy, here in Buenos Aires?"

"Of course we can be happy here. But we can't settle here. Our calling is in the United States." *Oh my goodness, the South Americans are getting to me. Now I'm calling America the United States. We have to find a way home before Irene and her family go completely native.*

Across the table, Donald caught Kara's attention and rolled his eyes to his right. She glanced casually in that direction. Herr Wolfram Lutz approached their table. Wolf was shorter and slimmer than Donald, but his erect bearing and thick, dark hair made him taller in Kara's eyes. She smiled into her *café Americano.* Wolf had been reticent, a six-month project, but she'd found him a satisfactory substitute for poor, dear Weldon.

Donald stood, shook hands. "*Buenos días*, Herr Lutz."

"*Guten abden*, Herr Clarke und Herr Earnshaw." Wolf could speak Spanish like a Buenos Aires native but always greeted

Donald in German. He shook hands with each man. "*Señora* Earnshaw, you look *espléndido*." He bent and pecked Irene on the cheek.

Kara offered him her cheek and a coquettish smile.

His kiss was tender, his whisper breathless. "*Liebling*."

"Donald, darling, won't you offer Herr Lutz a chair?"

A few moments later, Wolf had placed his order, and the usual pleasantries ensued. After the waiter brought Kara her second cup of *café Americano*, Donald said, "How are things going at the construction site?"

"My crew works hard," Wolf said. "But we wait for plumbers and electricians to finish before we put up the interior walls."

"It will get done in accordance with God's plan." Donald was much happier now that the seeds of the Fellowship had grown enough followers to build his own church.

"Are the stained glass windows in yet, Father?" Irene asked.

Donald arched an eyebrow at Wolf.

Wolf gave a curt nod. "They have arrived. We install them when weather permits. Today"—he indicated the rain-streaked window beside them—"weather does not permit. It is a good day to curl up beside the fireplace?"

"Ooh, that would be wonderful," Irene said. "Our apartment doesn't have a fireplace." She gave Felix a knowing smile. "We'll have to find other ways to keep warm."

Kara swirled the last of her *café Americano* in her cup. "I hope you enjoy your evening, Herr Lutz. It's work for Donald and me this evening. He has faithful to visit in the hospital, and I have an order to pick up at *la verdulería*."

Donald rose and held her chair.

Wolfram and Felix, gentlemen that they were, stood.

Kara gave Wolf her hand. His lips brushed the back of her hand like velvet, making it tingle.

He raised his gaze to hers.

She ran her tongue over her lip. A couple of hours in Wolf's company before she went shopping would help the time pass.

Chapter Ninety-Nine

Azrael waited in the near-dark of the living room with her back against the wall, between the two eight-foot-tall French doors hidden by heavy blue drapes. The doors opened onto a balcony that sat at treetop level above Avenida del Libertador. The formal dining room on her right and the bedrooms down the hall to her left stood vacant.

She had borne the weight of her bulletproof jumpsuit and body armor for more than an hour. The tick-tock of the grandfather clock in the living room and the erratic electricity's muted hum were the only the sounds in the opulent home.

Unaided, she could discern the deeper shadows of the two overstuffed sofas, ornate antique chairs, and tables. Pressing a button on her wrist pad would light the visor of her helmet with the eerie green glow of night vision. She relied on her own powers. Her powers—every muscle, every nerve—hummed like a tuning fork, alive with purpose and anticipation.

Driven by a new purpose, the surviving Azrael had hunted the target for more than a year, but she'd found him. The False One. She'd studied him in his new habitat. Every morning, he had sweet rolls and coffee. Then he'd go to his desk. His woman visited the *verdulería* and bought fresh fruits and vegetables. On sunny days, their cook served them lunch on the balcony. After lunch, they recruited board members, donors, and new congregants. Every day at five p.m., they met their daughter and her family at the café, La Biela, for *merienda*, a light meal before returning home.

He would be home soon. And she would enter her final transformation and lead the Azrael to greater glory.

Chapter One Hundred

Kara's mouth tasted funny. Her eyes wouldn't open. She struggled to wake up. Finally, she forced her eyes open. It took a few seconds for the images she saw to penetrate. Faint moonlight from the room's one small barred window cast a pale rectangle on the room's only door. She sat bolt upright. Her head spun, her stomach rebelled, and she spewed her last meal all over the floor.

After she recovered, her cheeks burned. No one should see her like this. But the room had no sink or washcloths or towels. The only amenity was a stainless steel toilet bowl mounted against one wall. She went to the door. *Where is the doorknob?* She pushed on it. It didn't move. She pushed harder. It still didn't budge.

"Hello?" she called. "I've been ill. I need to go to the bathroom."

She waited. Unable to tolerate the filth that had splattered her any longer, she wetted a corner of the room's one blanket in toilet water and dabbed at the ruin. When she finished, she dropped the blanket over the unsightly mess on the floor near the cot. She looked around the room again. Where on earth was she? She rubbed her face, trying to remember what had happened. The last thing she'd remembered was lying next to Wolf. Had she gotten ill? Was she brought here until she'd recovered?

Another glance at the room, a shudder, and she decided that it didn't matter how she'd gotten here. She'd had enough. She marched over to face the door, hands on her hips. "Let me out of here," she said in a loud, firm voice.

"Calm yourself, sinner," said a disembodied voice over a tinny intercom.

"Don't call me that. I am not a sinner."

"The terrible wrath of God rains upon all the faithless and immoral."

Someone had made a terrible mistake. "When the First Apostle finds out what kind of mistake you've made, you will be sorry for the rest of your life." She smiled, anticipating the other's horror when she realized how much trouble she was in.

"The Lord guides us."

"Quit your babbling and get me out of here."

"Repent and believe in God."

Kara snorted. "I don't need to repent. I'm the wife of the First Apostle Donald Clarke, and Herr Wolfram Lutz is a good friend." She wasn't certain why she mentioned Wolf.

"First Apostle who?"

"Donald Clarke," she said impatiently. "My husband."

"Now, sinner, you know the First Apostle is Elijah Baker." The voice oozed patience and condescension.

"Don't try any of your tricks with me," Kara said, hiding the fear that had crept into her. "I demand to speak to my husband, First Apostle Clarke."

"Who?"

"Donald Clarke."

"There is no Donald Clarke. Let us pray—Holy Father, unto whom all hearts are open, all desires known—"

Kara gaped. That was the Sinner's Prayer. She wasn't in a holding cell. She was in Redemption. *Keep calm. You can talk your way out of this.*

"Cleanse the thoughts from our hearts—" the voice continued.

"Oh, sister," Kara said in her most winning voice. "I'm sorry, I'm afraid my recent illness made me forget myself. But I'm better now. I remember, First Apostle Baker, of course."

"Blessed be the Prophet—" continued the chant.

"Herr Wolfram Lutz knows me," Kara said. "Call him. He'll tell you it's all been a horrible mistake."

"Blessed be the counselors. May they guide our leaders in the paths of righteousness—"

"You're right. Herr Lutz is much too busy to be bothered with my small problems," Kara said, trying to think. "Director Lucas Matthews. Oh my, he'll be most distressed. You'd better call him right away—"

"Blessed be the seminarians—"

"You aren't listening to me," Kara shouted, panic rising in her chest.

"Blessed be the holy angels, Azrael. May they pass over us this night—"

"*Get me out of here!*"

Chapter One Hundred One

Miranda guided the *Lady Angelfish* through the blue-black water. Now and then, light flashed behind heavy clouds and thunder rumbled in the distance. The squall had passed quickly. Soon the clouds and thunder would move on as well.

The cabin door squeaked. Beryl worked her way to the stern. Her hair was white now, and she had a limp. It was a miracle she'd survived the autogiro wreck. The doctors had sworn she would never walk again. But Beryl wouldn't hear the word "can't." If the doctors said ten repetitions were good, she did twenty. She never gave up.

Beryl settled into her modified fishing chair. She lowered her night goggles into place and raised her HK, rested its barrel on the grab rail. Her head and the gun barrel swept the shoreline.

Miranda throttled back the engine. The *Lady Angelfish* did not move forward without Beryl's approval.

Moments later, Beryl gave Miranda a thumbs-up and the half-smile her partially paralyzed facial muscles would allow.

Something had happened to Beryl on that island. She smiled more these days. Of course, something had happened to Miranda too. She'd spent a year working odd jobs so she could restore the old cabin cruiser she'd bought. It had taken most of that year to talk Beryl into signing on as captain's mate. Now only two months into the season, Miranda's Safe Harbor idea had grown into a network. Dozens of boats and land vehicles had rescued and relocated hundreds of refugees.

The fishy smell of shallow water hit her, and the shadowy outline of the fishing pier grew more distinct. Miranda scanned the vacant gravel boat ramp and road. A light flashed in the tree line surrounding the parking lot. A long flash followed, then another quick one.

Miranda returned the signal with a five-cell flashlight.

The light in the trees flashed on and off. Once.

Beryl finished her scan of the area and gave Miranda another thumbs-up.

Before Miranda had maneuvered the *Lady* up to kiss the pier, dark figures darted out of the trees. Six.

She set the throttle at idle and went below. She jumped the gunwale and secured the stern line to the pier's end post. One line meant the *Angelfish* rocked forward and back with the waves, but it also meant only one line to cut for a fast getaway.

Miranda caught her breath at the sight of Ethan and Nick leading the refugees up the pier.

Ethan gave her a quick and powerful hug. "It's good to see you." He spoke in a low, hushed tone.

She grinned at him. "You look better than the last time I saw you."

He chuckled. "And you are as beautiful as I remember." He gestured at the *Lady*. "May we?"

"Permission to board," Miranda said.

He hopped over the gunwale and helped the refugees aboard.

Nick stepped forward, and his slow smile grew, almost erased the deep lines of fatigue in his face. "Looks like life at sea suits you."

"You should try it sometime." She flushed. She hadn't meant that the way it sounded.

"I will, someday."

She couldn't help but smile back at him. *Someday—when the war was over?* "The only thing I don't like about my life is that I can never stay in any one place very long." She peered around him at the stragglers. "Hurry," she called in a hushed voice.

∾

Beryl propped a foot up on the grab rail and kept a watchful eye on the shore. Footsteps approached. She didn't bother turning—she'd always know Ethan's footsteps.

"I wanted to have a word with you, if that's all right?" Ethan's melodic voice still gave her heart palpitations.

"I'm on watch." That sounded too harsh. "But you can talk."

"I understand." He didn't sound harsh. "Last month, they found a half-dozen Azrael, dead."

Beryl gave him a quick, sharp look. "Dead? How?"

"Old age."

She blinked at him. "What?"

"The autopsy showed some defect that makes them grow old years ahead of their time."

She sat very still. She remembered the five "old" children she'd seen at Southwestern State Hospital. Her heart beat hard and fast. "Could all the Ann—Azrael have the same defect?"

He shrugged. "These three had the exact same brain defect."

The memory of her Anna's mutilated body dried Beryl's mouth. *They would have died eventually.* She cleared her throat. "Does that mean they're all dead or will die soon?"

"No one can say for sure." An uncomfortable silence fell between them.

It's never totally silent on a boat. The engine idles, the waves lap, wind flaps ropes and flags. She liked this kind of silence. She scanned the shoreline. Ethan's presence made her skin tingle, but it wasn't unpleasant.

He broke the silence first. "I don't blame you. I never did."

Her chest tightened. She couldn't move, couldn't speak.

"Well, I thought you should know," Ethan said and left.

She heard him disembark and watched him walk to the shore. All the Azrael were a piece of her Anna. If her Anna had the same defect... Beryl's vision blurred, and warm tears trickled down her cheeks. "Thank you," she whispered.

Chapter One Hundred Two

Miranda had the feeling Nick wanted to talk to her. She waited for the four refugees to enter the cabin. "News of David?"

"Still in the New England area. Working for the good guys," Nick answered. He sighed. "There's no easy way to say this." He looked uncomfortable. "Your parents were Taken."

"My parents?" *My parents are dead.* She probed at her feelings. Nothing.

"I'm sorry. I should have broken the news more gently."

I should feel something. She tried again. *My mother is dead.* Nothing. *My father is dead.* No tears. No anger. No fear. Not even a sense of vindication.

Ethan walked past. "See you soon," he said and hopped over the gunwale. He walked to the shore, turned, and waited.

Nick peered down at Miranda. "I'm sorry for your loss."

"Don't be." She gave him a rueful smile. "They weren't the parents they should have been."

"Are you relieved?"

Am I? "No...I—pity them." *They never knew how sick and twisted they were.* Nick wore a concerned expression. She smiled. "I'm okay. No, I'm better than okay."

He searched her face and then shook his head. "You are one strong woman, Miranda."

"Don't forget that next time you come to ask a favor." She smiled broadly, fondly at him.

He leaned forward, placed a chaste kiss on her lips, and whispered, "Until next time." He vaulted over the gunwale, landed on the pier, and tossed the stern line to her.

Miranda caught the line, the soft touch of his lips still warm on hers. She climbed into the cockpit and backed the *Lady Angelfish* away from the pier. Once the Lady was clear, she saluted Nick and Ethan, then wheeled the boat toward the bay's inlet.

Miranda guided her vessel out of the bay and into the ocean. She held the wheel lightly, letting the boat find the water's rhythm, keeping her on a course for open water. Nick's words had stirred a lot of memories. She probed at them: her time in Redemption, escaping with Beryl, the terror of her nightmares—her desperate need for proof.

Thank God that's over.

It was over. The voice of guilt and shame didn't rule her anymore. Even the hate and anger were ghostly remnants of what they had been. She could even revisit the old feelings without the fear and pain she'd once felt. She could stay connected to the here and now—

And I like it.

She took a deep breath of ocean air. It had the warm, tangy smell of hope.

THE END

Thank You For Reading

Did you enjoy My Soul to Keep? Here's what you can do next.

Write an honest review. Reviews help books get noticed.

All reviews are gratefully received.

It Doesn't Stop Here!

Miranda and Beryl's adventure **CONTINUES** in Book Two of the My Soul to Keep series. *If I Should Die* follows Miranda, Beryl, and the others as the war with the Fellowship heats up.

Please sign up for Lynette's newsletter, "The Point of View," for the latest information on new stories, deals, and special offers at:

https://mailchi.mp/bb6911c8db67/signupforlynettemburrows

About the Author

Lynette M Burrows is the co-author (with Rob Chilson) of two novellas, "The White Hope" and "The White Box," published in *Analog Science Fiction and Fact* magazine. She has had short stories for children published in regional and national magazines. *My Soul to Keep*, is the first in the My Soul to Keep series. It tells the story of Miranda, a woman, struggling to survive in an American theocracy, who must come to terms with past, present, and future violence in her life.

Lynette enjoys real cream in her coffee, the pleasure of real books, and the crack of a nine millimeter, not necessarily all at the same time…but they all appear in her stories!

She pens her stories of empowerment and survival at Burrows Hollow, the ~~space station~~ earth-bound home to Lynette, her artist husband, and their three Yorkshire Terriers.

To connect with Lynette, email her at: lynette@lynettemburrows.com or you can find out more about her and her work at her website: https://lynettemburrows.com and follow her on Social Media:

facebook.com/LynetteMBurrowsAuthor

twitter.com/LynetteMBurrows

Made in the USA
Las Vegas, NV
14 July 2021